The Time Custodian: Inheritance

C.R. Stalley

First published in 2026

Paperback ISBN: 978-1-9194497-0-8

Printed in the United Kingdom

Dedications

For my family,
in the darkest chapters, you were my light.
Your unwavering love carried me through the storm.

And for the wanderers,
for those who walk through life feeling misplaced,
who stumble more than they stride.
May you find, in these pages, the courage to keep going.

PROLOGUE.
The Woman Who Didn't Belong.

Whitechapel, London, 1888.

The gas lamps flickered like dying stars while London waited for its next scream.

Thomas Donovan pushed open the heavy wooden door of *The Fox and Hound* tavern. The familiar scents of aged wood, spilled ale, and roasted meat mingled in the air. It was a chilly Wednesday evening in 1888 and the tavern was alive with the sound of raucous laughter and animated chatter, a welcome distraction from the dark streets of London.

Thomas made his way to a familiar corner booth, easing himself into the worn wooden seat. The conversations around him carried an undercurrent of tension. He didn't need to strain to hear the snippets of grim talk floating through the smoky air.

"Another girl's been found," a burly man with a bushy beard declared loudly, his pint slamming down onto the table for emphasis. The men gathered around him quieted, their expressions dark. "This one… this one was bad. They're saying her throat was cut from ear to ear."

A sharp intake of breath swept through the group. One of the younger men, his face pale and drawn, leaned closer. "I heard it's not just her throat. They're saying her… insides. Taken out. Like he's some kind of butcher!"

"A butcher? He's worse than that," another man growled, his voice low and trembling with anger. "A butcher kills for meat, for purpose. What he does, it's… it's evil. No one's safe. I've got a wife, a little girl barely ten years old. You think I'll let them out of my sight after sundown?" He shook his head violently. "Not a chance."

Thomas's stomach turned as he listened, the weight of their fear seeping into his own chest. *Jack the Ripper*. The name hung over London like a dark cloud, blotting out the stars. Some monsters lived in stories. *This one walked Whitechapel*. Every week brought new rumours, new horrors. And every night, the streets seemed quieter.

The bearded man took another swig of his ale before leaning into the group, his voice a harsh whisper. "They're saying he's too clever for the police. Knows exactly where to strike, exactly when. Like he's got the devil himself guiding his hand."

Thomas clenched his fists under the table, his mind wandering to his daughter. Mary was thirteen, with dark curls and a mischievous smile. She was the light of his life, and the thought of her walking *these streets*, even in daylight, sent a cold dread through him.

"I don't know what we can do," the younger man admitted, his shoulders sagging. "How do you protect them? It's not just the working girls anymore. It could be anyone."

"We keep them close," Thomas said aloud, surprising himself with the force of his own voice. The group turned to him, their faces grim but nodding in agreement. "We keep them close, and we stay vigilant. That's all we can do."

He didn't stay much longer. The oppressive weight of the tavern's conversation was too much to bear. Promising himself he'd return to share a drink another time, he excused himself and stepped out into the night air. The streets were eerily quiet, the lamps casting faint pools of light onto the cobblestones. He wrapped his coat tighter around him, the chill biting through the fabric as he made his way towards home.

As he passed an empty stretch of street, his eyes caught a figure standing alone under the glow of light. At first, he thought it was a young woman heading home late, but something about her appearance stopped him in his tracks. Her clothing. It was like nothing he had ever seen before.

She wore trousers made of a strange, tightly woven blue fabric that clung to her shape. They weren't the heavy work trousers men wore but something thinner, more casual. On her feet were peculiar shoes—soft-looking things with no laces. A bright red garment covered her torso, the hood hanging loosely down her back, and over it, she wore some kind of shiny, padded coat that gleamed faintly in the lamplight. The combination was both vibrant and bewildering, like *nothing* that belonged in his world.

"Miss!" Thomas called, his voice echoing through the empty street. The woman turned toward him, her face illuminated in the dim light.

"You shouldn't be out here!" he said, quickening his pace. "It's not safe!"

She tilted her head slightly, as if considering his words, but didn't respond. Instead, she turned and began walking away, her movements unhurried, almost purposeful.

"Wait!" Thomas called again, breaking into a jog as she turned a corner ahead of him. His boots clattered loudly on the uneven paving, the sound harsh against the eerie silence of the night.

When he rounded the corner, he let out a shaken gasp. The alley was a dead end, hemmed in by tall brick walls. There was no sign of the woman, no sound of retreating footsteps, no doors she could have slipped through. She was simply… *gone.*

The air felt wrong here, heavy and charged with an unnatural stillness that pressed against his chest. He glanced around, his eyes scanning the shadows for any trace of her, but there was nothing. Not even a footprint in the thin layer of dust covering the cobblestones.

"Miss?" he called out again, his voice quieter now, tinged with unease. The hair on the back of his neck prickled as a faint chill rolled over him, colder than the night air. He couldn't explain it, but something had changed in this place.

Thomas stepped further into the alley, his boots scuffing. The sense of unease deepened. He turned in a slow circle, his breath visible in the chill. The walls seemed to loom closer, the silence pressing down on him like a physical weight.

And then, just as suddenly as it had come, the strange feeling dissipated, leaving him standing alone in the quiet alley. He ran a hand over his face, trying to shake off the lingering sense of unreality. Had he imagined it? The woman, her strange clothing and disappearance. None of it made sense.

He turned and made his way back to the main street, casting one last glance over his shoulder. The alley remained empty, silent, and unremarkable. But Thomas couldn't shake the feeling that he had glimpsed something extraordinary, something beyond his understanding.

The city continued, oblivious to the mysteries hidden within its darkened streets. Somewhere, the woman he had seen now existed far beyond his reach, leaving behind only questions.

CHAPTER 1
A World Aflame

Lucy Calder hunched over her laptop, the dim screen casting a pale glow over her tired face. Her faded green jumper hung off one shoulder, sleeves fraying at the cuffs, and her tangled light brown hair was shoved behind her ears, more out of habit than style. Her eyes—hazel, rimmed with fatigue, flicked across the screen as if the words might shift into something worth reading if she stared long enough. The walls were scuffed, the wallpaper peeling in places, and the tiny kitchen carried the faint, stubborn smell of burnt toast no matter how much she scrubbed.

The flat was silent apart from the sound of traffic on Brixton High Street below. Her one-bedroom home, crammed into an ageing block just off the main road, felt less like a sanctuary and more like a holding pen.

She shifted in her chair. Her long legs curled awkwardly beneath her and stretched her stiff back with a wince. Her build was slight, not quite athletic, not quite frail either.

This wasn't what she imagined for herself at twenty-six. Fresh out of university, she'd been the rising star of her History with Creative Writing degree. Her writing had been sharp, her curiosity boundless. People believed in her. She believed in herself.

Now, though, the future she once dreamed of felt like a cruel joke. The thoughtful essays she'd once imagined writing had given way to churning out articles and bite-sized blurbs for *PastTense Media*, a history start-up that only paid attention if the content included a meme or a trending sound. Her deadlines blurred together under titles like *"Five Shocking Plague Cures That Actually Existed"* or *"What Your Favourite Historical Empire Says About Your Attachment Style."* The stories she cared about didn't drive traffic and traffic paid the rent. Barely. Even that fragile existence felt like it was slipping through her fingers.

She let out a long breath and leaned back in her chair, her eyes wandering to a small, framed photo perched on the shelf above her desk. It was one of the few personal touches in the flat. The photo showed her as a child, no older than eight or nine, sitting between her parents, Evelyn and Edward Calder.

Whilst her memories of them both together were hazy at best, her mother, Evelyn, stood apart from Edward in ways that had only deepened Lucy's admiration. Where he had been warm and steady, Evelyn was fierce, focused, and utterly relentless in her pursuit of the past. She wasn't just respected in her field; she was a revered and acclaimed historian. Colleagues spoke of Evelyn Calder with awe, calling her research transformative. Her ability to reconstruct history, to breathe life into long-forgotten events and make them feel immediate, was unmatched. People often said that reading her work was like stepping into a time machine.

Evelyn had been a striking woman with a quiet authority that made people stop and listen. Her dark hair, often tied back, was streaked with silver, and her green eyes lit up whenever she spoke about history. She had a calm, fair complexion and a warmth that drew people in—part brilliance, part something softer.

She dressed with effortless elegance; smart blouses, tailored trousers, earthy tones that echoed the places she studied. There was always purpose in the way she carried herself. Focused, unshakeable, but never cold. To Lucy, her mother had been a force of nature: fierce in her work, fiercely loving when she let herself slow down. Even now, Lucy could almost hear her laugh, bright and familiar, like a voice from the next room.

For most of Lucy's childhood, Evelyn's career had been her constant companion. There were always manuscripts sprawled across the dining table, annotated maps pinned to the walls, and dusty bookshelves stacked with obscure tomes. Evelyn would spend hours lost in her work, her focus so intense it was like the world around her ceased to exist. Her projects often took her far from home, to ruins and libraries and remote villages in search of lost stories.

After Edward's sudden disappearance when Lucy was a child, Evelyn's work took on a new edge. A kind of desperate crusade. She seemed to bury herself in her research, as if trying to outrun the pain. And then, four years ago, she too was gone.

Evelyn had vanished while on a research trip to Nanjing. She'd been following a lead on the Taiping Rebellion, a radical political movement disguised as a religious awakening that had been brutally suppressed in the mid-19th century. Something about Evelyn's behaviour in those final weeks had unsettled Lucy. She'd been unusually secretive, locking her notes away and working late into the night.

When Evelyn failed to return, the local police conducted a search, but their efforts yielded nothing. The official report listed her as presumed dead, but Lucy had never truly accepted it. Her mother wasn't the kind of person who simply disappeared. Evelyn Calder didn't get lost—she thrived in the unknown, piecing together fragments of history with meticulous precision.

Lucy had never forgiven herself for the distance between them in those final years. They'd argued often. Evelyn, frustrated by what she saw as Lucy's aimlessness, and Lucy resentful of her mother's constant absences. Their last conversation, a brief and bitter phone call, still rang in her ears. She'd shouted something about not wanting to be "second place to a dusty pile of old relics." She hadn't known it would be the last thing she ever said to her mother.

The guilt of it lingered like a dull ache, one she carried with her every day. Losing a father at Thirteen and a mother at Twenty-Two does that to a person.

Her phone buzzed across the desk, breaking her train of thought. Lucy sighed when she saw the name.

"Hi, Jade," she said, trying to sound more awake than she felt.

"Afternoon." Jade's voice crackled through the speaker—brisk, businesslike but not unkind. She had that clipped, semi-irritated tone of someone who'd sat through too many editorial brainstorms with whiteboards and beanbags. She certainly wasn't the type of editor Lucy imagined working for.

"Just finished your Tudor dating piece."

Lucy winced. *How to Flirt Like a Tudor.* A headline she hadn't written, just inherited, along with a pile of reference links and a stock image.

"Right. Was it… okay?"

"It's fine," Jade said, drawing the word out like she was trying to make it stretch. "But fine doesn't drive clicks. We need something punchier. The intro's a bit slow, and the plague breath joke?" A pause. "Funny, but maybe not first-date shareable, you know?"

"I can rework it," Lucy said quickly. "Punch it up a bit. I was aiming for tone, but—"

"Yeah. Just… try leaning into the weird a bit more." Jade didn't wait for a response. "You've got a good voice… when you let it out. Right now, it's reading a little formal. Again."

Lucy's jaw tensed. "Right. Less lecture, more TikTok."

Jade gave a short laugh. "Exactly. If you can get it back to me by Friday, that'd be great. Shouldn't take much. Cool?"

"Cool," Lucy replied.

"Perfect, speak soon," Ending the call before Lucy could respond.

Lucy stared at her phone for a moment before setting it down on the desk. The silence came back fast and heavy, like the flat had been holding its breath. She glanced at the blinking cursor on her half-finished document, then shut the laptop without saving. The Tudor dating piece could wait. Her brain wasn't in it. Not today.

Her phone buzzed again. Not a call this time, a message.

Natasha: *Still good for tomorrow? 6ish at Côte, Southbank. Let me know if anything comes up. x*

Lucy didn't open it. Just watched the preview fade from the lock screen.

Natasha was the kind of friend who showed up once or twice a year like a dentist appointment. Necessary, mildly painful, and always followed by the sense that you'd been judged. They'd known each other since uni, back when Lucy had a proper circle. There were group chats, late-night takeaways, drunken debates over lectures and dreams and dissertations. She'd felt like someone then— connected, sharp, held. But people drifted. Some moved away, some got married, some just… stopped keeping in touch. There wasn't a fallout. Just silence. Life got in the way. And now there was only Natasha.

Even that felt more like obligation than friendship— Natasha, with her perfect job and curated life and barely concealed pity. Lucy could already hear the fake-concern in her voice.

Lucy left the message unopened while trying to calculate how much time she left to reasonably postpone and what the reason was.

"Fuck it," she said with a defeated sigh. If she wasn't going to drink wine or spiral, she could at least make herself a proper dinner. Or more fittingly, attempt to.

* * *

Lucy stood in her tiny kitchen, the hiss of vegetables in the pan filling the room with warmth and spice. She moved with mechanical intent, chopping, stirring, flipping—trying to cook herself out of a mood. It wasn't working.

With one hand, she reached for her laptop on the counter, flipping it open to her mother's archive. The screen flickered to life, a row of familiar titles lining the page. After a moment's hesitation, she clicked on *The Inferno of 1666: A World Aflame.*

It had been years since she'd read Evelyn's work. The words hit like a voice from another life—measured, vivid, alive. The flames began in Pudding Lane, her mother wrote, but it was the wind that made them monstrous. Lucy read on, spoon hanging in her hand, forgotten.

The kitchen seemed to grow quieter, as if the world were holding its breath.

Evelyn's prose was hypnotic. The rush of footsteps on cobblestones, the desperate calls for water, the sting of smoke in your throat, it was all there. Lucy could feel it creeping in at the edges of her senses. A phantom heat. A distant roar. The image of London burning unfurled before her, more real than anything outside her window.

In her rush to keep up with the article, she turned the heat up higher, completely oblivious to the disaster unfolding in front of her. The oil began to splatter, and she could hear the sound of it hissing, but her focus was still glued to her mother's words. Suddenly, a burst of flames leapt from the pan, catching the edge of a nearby kitchen towel. Lucy's heart raced as she finally looked up, panic flooding through her veins.

"Shit!" she shouted, grabbing the towel and tossing it aside. The fire crackled, the heat licking at her skin, and she felt an overwhelming sense of urgency. She had to put it out. She instinctively reached for the nearest empty mug and filled it with water before hurling it towards the fire. The water splashed everywhere, only making the flames grow larger. Lucy knew you shouldn't do this. She knew better, but panic made her reckless.

The heat from the pan flared, startling but containable. Lucy backed away, eyes flicking to the damp towel now singed at one corner. But something about the air shifted—subtly at first. The kitchen, once filled with the comforting scent of garlic and soy, began to smell… wrong. Smoke, yes, but not the kind that belonged in a flat. This was thicker, older—like burned timber, pitch, and something metallic laced through the air.

She reached for the fire blanket, but her hand faltered mid-air.

The space around her pulsed, like a ripple had passed through it, like reality had briefly flexed and then forgotten how to settle. A low pitched but very present hum began to replace the sounds of the stir fry. The colours of the kitchen dimmed, edges softening as if viewed through heat haze. The fridge behind her groaned, but not with its usual electrical sound. It sounded like wood splintering under pressure.

Lucy froze and the world around her became distorted and obscure.

The air grew denser. Not hotter, but *heavier*. It pressed against her chest, as if history itself was leaning in to watch. Her skin prickled. Her balance shifted.

Beneath her feet, the laminate floor rippled, *not visibly, but in sensation*—and when she took a reflexive step back, her heel didn't land on smooth plastic. It landed on something uneven. Solid. Cold.

Cobbles.

She looked down. The floor was no longer her kitchen. It was rough-hewn stone, slick with soot and grime, and glowing faintly beneath the light of fire.

Lucy's pulse thundered in her ears as the obscurity cleared.

The cabinets were gone. The walls stretched, twisted, dissolved. The white tiles above her hob melted into charred timber, then into smoke.

Sound changed. It deepened. The sharp hiss of cooking oil became the roar of a distant blaze. Shouts emerged. Real ones, panicked and raw. Sounds bouncing off narrow alley walls. Colours flickered orange and gold, not from her overhead kitchen light, but from fire. Raging, alive, somewhere just beyond her line of sight.

It was like time itself seemed to hold its breath, and in the space between blinks, her kitchen ceased to exist.

She turned, and the world was on fire. It was like stepping into hell on Earth.

Panic began to creep in as she found herself standing in the middle of a street, surrounded by buildings that were crumbling and engulfed in flames. "What the fuck?" she breathed, disbelief washing over her. The sky was dark with smoke, and the cries of people boomed all around her. The sound was a cacophony of fear, anger, and desperation, and she felt the weight of it pressing down on her.

As she stumbled backward, trying to understand how she had gotten here, she caught sight of the buildings. Their architecture was old, completely different from the modernity of Brixton. Then it hit her, as she recognised the distinct shapes of the structures that her mother had described in her research. The intricately designed façades, the narrow streets—this was London, but not as she knew it. The realisation sent a chill through her. She was *in* the Great Fire of London.

The heat of the flames seemed to surround her, the sights and sounds swirled around her in a dizzying blur. People rushed past her, their faces streaked with soot, eyes wide with terror as they cried out for help. "Water! We need water!" someone shouted, desperation lacing their voice. Another voice joined in, "There are people trapped inside! We have to save them!"

Smoke began to gather in Lucy's throat as she absorbed the horror unfolding around her. The air was thick with dense, dark smoke which was filled with the scent of burning wood and the unmistakable odour of destruction. She could hear the crackle of the fire and feel the heat radiating off the nearby buildings, overwhelming her senses. The ground shook as part of a structure collapsed nearby, sending debris flying through the air. Lucy felt the heat on her skin, more intense than anything she had ever experienced, and instinctively took another step back.

"Help! Someone, please!" A voice pierced through the chaos, and Lucy turned to see a woman desperately clawing at the charred remains of a structure, trying to reach a figure trapped beneath. The woman's clothes were torn, and her hair was a wild mess, but her determination was palpable. The panic in her eyes mirrored Lucy's own fear as she tried to process the nightmarish scene.

Lucy stumbled backward, the reality of her situation crashing down on her. This wasn't just a story anymore; it was a nightmare. The cries for help, the fear in the air—it felt all too real, and yet, she was nothing more than a bystander in this horror. She tried to comprehend what was happening, but the urgency of the moment made it impossible.

Then, as if in slow motion, she saw the framework of a nearby building begin to creak and groan. The sound was ominous, a low rumble that sent shivers down her spine. Lucy's instincts screamed at her to run, to escape this place of fire and despair, but her feet felt frozen to the ground. She was trapped in this moment, caught between the reality of her life and the history she had read about.

Before she could react, a section of the building gave way, crashing down toward her. Lucy's heart raced as she realised the danger she was in, the heat rushing over her as she turned to flee. But the ground was uneven, and panic flooded her veins as the weight of the collapsing structure bore down on her. She had to move, had to escape, but the flames danced closer, and the cries of the trapped filled her ears.

A deafening crack split the air as wooden beams collapsed. Flaming debris rained down around her, hissing as they hit the cobblestones. She stumbled backward, arms shielding her head, her socks slipping on the uneven ground. The air was a choking cocktail of smoke, soot, and ash that seared her lungs and stung her eyes. She could barely see, her vision blurred by tears and the swirling haze of embers.

The sound of the collapsing structure was deafening, a groan of tortured wood and stone, a sound that promised death.

"Run, girl! Move!" a man shouted as he barrelled past her, his face streaked with soot, his shirt half-burned. Others screamed, their voices barely audible over the roar of the inferno. Lucy tried to obey, tried to move her legs, but the ground felt like it was tilting beneath her. Her body wouldn't move, frozen by the impossibility of it all.

The fire consumed everything. Flames leapt from one building to another with voracious speed, the wooden facades igniting like dry kindling. Somewhere nearby, a woman's voice rose in a keening wail, her words lost in the chaos. A cart overturned in the street, spilling barrels that burst into flames. People shoved and tripped over one another, desperate to escape the unrelenting tide of destruction.

Lucy's ears caught the frantic cry of a child, and her head snapped toward the sound. A small boy was trapped beneath the cart, his terrified face smeared with dirt and tears. His mother clawed at the wreckage, her hands bloodied and trembling. Lucy's heart lurched as she took a step forward. Her every instinct screaming at her to help.

But the fire didn't wait. It surged toward them, a living, breathing thing that consumed all in its path. The mother looked up, her eyes locking onto Lucy's for one agonizing moment. There was no hope in them, only raw, animal terror and the flicker of startled confusion, as if Lucy's very presence didn't make sense in this world.

Before Lucy could react, the roof above her gave another deep, splintering groan. She looked up, frozen, as burning beams twisted overhead, the building's remains bending toward her like fingers curling into a fist. Her body finally obeyed, feet stumbling backward—but it was too late.

The heat punched into her like a wave. Not just hot— scalding, overwhelming, impossible. It clawed at her skin and dragged the air from her lungs. She tried to scream, but it came out as a gasp, swallowed by the roar of flame and collapsing wood.

Then something shifted. Not outside her, but around her.

The world once again became obscure

She felt it before she saw it, the strange, weightless drop, like missing a step in the dark. The edges of her vision bled, colours smearing as if someone had dipped a brush in fire and dragged it across the world. Her surroundings lost shape. The burning beams above her stretched, blurred, melted. The alley walls bent like wax.

It was as if reality itself had been soaked in water, and the lines were running.

The fire didn't go out. It bled away—orange and gold dissolving into grey, the sound of chaos thinning, fading, echoing from somewhere impossibly far.

The ground beneath her feet turned cold. The hard cobblestones softened, smeared into nothing. When she blinked, the shapes reassembled—just not the same ones.

Smoke gave way to shadows. Shadows gave way to stillness.

The kitchen came back slowly, like something remembering itself.

The sting of synthetic smoke. The faint hum of the fridge. A low car horn from the street below. Her feet pressed flat to cool plastic tiles. The scorched towel was on the floor beside her. The hob was still on. It was like no time had passed at all.

Her chest rose and fell in sharp, panicked bursts.

She didn't move.

She couldn't.

What had just happened?

Where had she just *been*?

The smell of burning began to hit her. A very different type of burning. A sharp stench that caught her attention. Her hands scrabbled against counter tops she collapsed into. The hard surface cold and unyielding compared to the uneven cobblestones she'd just left behind.

She lifted her head, her body trembling, and saw the flames on her pan. The dish towel was still burning, its edges curling into blackened ash. She forced herself into the here and now, turning the hob off and placing a fire blanket over the pan. Steam hissed as the fire died, leaving behind only smoke and the acrid scent of charred fabric. She threw the towel in the sink and turned on the cold water. And collapsed to her knees.

For a moment, there was silence. Her chest heaved as she struggled to process what had just happened. Her entire body felt like it had been wrung out, her muscles weak and shaking.

The smell of the Great Fire lingered in her nose, layered with the sharper, more chemical scent of her ruined kitchen. It was thick with soot and ash, the unmistakable aroma of wood reduced to embers. She inhaled deeply, or tried to at least. The dense smoke still filled her throat, making it feel like a blockage.

Slowly, she looked down at herself. Her faded green sweater, already fraying at the cuffs, was smeared with soot. Black streaks ran along the fabric, and small flecks of ash clung to the fibres. Her black leggings, though intact, were coated with dust. She thought she had put white socks on today. Closer inspection showed that she had, they were just deeply darkened by soot and ash.

Her hands shook as she brought them up to her face. They were filthy, blackened with soot, and under her nails was the grime of a city burning. She ran a hand through her hair, but even that felt wrong, it was sticky with sweat. She gently rose to her feet and walked to the mirror in her hallway.

When she glanced at her reflection she saw streaks of soot smeared across her pale face. Her hazel eyes were wide and rimmed with red from the smoke.

She looked like she had walked through hell. And somehow came back with it still clinging to her.

CHAPTER 2
The Stranger Who Knew My Name

Lucy hadn't slept much that night. Everything within her told her it wasn't possible. She must have imagined it. Maybe it was some kind of psychosis. Her Google searches returned little of use. She battled every possible explanation she could think of—stress, hallucination, memory lapse but none of them answered the glaring, inescapable elephant in the room: the physical. She had been covered in soot. Her eyes were red. The smoke still faintly clung to her lungs. Her once-white socks were now blackened beyond saving, not even worth washing. It took three showers before she even began to feel like her hair wasn't lined with ash.

This hadn't been a dream. It hadn't been some strange mental break. She had been *there*. She had come back with the evidence to prove it. Somehow, impossibly, she had slipped through time and landed hundreds of years ago, right in the middle of the Great Fire of London. And yet, no matter how many times she replayed it, she couldn't explain how. Or why. She questioned her own sanity, but not completely—because madness didn't leave you with smoke-scorched lungs and soot-stained skin.

That day had vanished in a haze of unanswered questions and ceiling-staring. She'd barely moved from the sofa. The tutor dating piece was a distant blur on her to-do list, and Natasha had been fobbed off with a vague *something's come up* text. She'd replied, of course—something passive-aggressive and thoroughly Natasha. One Lucy had yet to open, let alone give the headspace to acknowledge.

Lucy's eyes drifted around the room, searching for something—anything—that might stabilise her thoughts. Answer questions. Some sign. Some explanation. But all she found was the familiar family photo gathering dust on the shelf. She stood, brushed her thumb across the glass, then sank into her desk chair. As she looked down, it was like her parents smiled back at her from another lifetime. Her gaze lingered on her father. If he were here, he'd have known what to say. He always did. Somehow, he would've made sense of the impossible.

Her father, Edward, had always been a quiet presence. Calm, warm, and endlessly reassuring. He wasn't loud or overbearing, but he had a way of making people feel at ease, like they were the only person in the room worth listening to. Lucy remembered how safe she felt in his orbit, how his voice could ground her with just a few words.

He was tall, with a lean, athletic build, often dressed in a crisp white shirt and worn-in jeans. His dark hair fell just above sharp blue eyes that carried both kindness and a flicker of mischief. There was something timeless about him. The soft stubble, the scuffed boots, the laugh that filled their Devon home like music. In the few photos Lucy still had, he looked every bit the adventurer, and in her memories, he was always kneeling down to her level, engaging her in stories and games like she was the centre of his world.

He travelled often for work, though she never fully understood what that work was. He told stories of faraway places, lighting up with each tale, and she believed every word. It gave her a hunger for discovery she still carried.

Then one day, he was gone.

He'd said he was leaving for work, just like any other time. Nothing seemed abnormal. But he never returned. Search parties combed the woods and fields around their home. Weeks passed. His car had been found parked just off the track from Stonehenge but there had been no further leads. No sign of him. No answers. The official story settled somewhere between accident and disappearance, but Lucy and her mother were left in limbo, clinging to fading traces of a man who had been the heart of their family.

What lingered most wasn't grief—it was the not knowing. The silence. The unfinished goodbye. And over time, it changed Lucy and Evelyn's relationship in ways neither of them could undo.

Lucy's eyes drifted to her mother. Evelyn would've listened—really listened—but with a sharper edge than Edward ever had. She wouldn't have dismissed Lucy's story, just questioned it with that curious, focused energy she reserved for the unknowable. She'd have asked for details, not out of doubt, but fascination. *What did it feel like? What did she see?* For Evelyn, living through a time period would've been the ultimate gift, research in its purest form.

Not that she needed the help. Her peers often said her work read like she'd been there herself. Her descriptions so vivid, so immersive, it was as if she'd walked the streets and breathed the same air as the people she wrote about.

And with that, a small thought floated into the back of Lucy's mind, fragile at first, like a bubble drifting through still water. But it grew, expanding with quiet urgency until it demanded her full attention. She sat up suddenly, heart thudding.

What if Evelyn had experienced something like this? What if her descriptions weren't just vivid… but real? So intimate, so impossibly precise, because she hadn't just studied history. She'd lived it. It sounded ridiculous—completely impossible. But then again, hadn't Lucy just lived through a historical nightmare herself?

"No… *Now* you're really losing the plot," Lucy muttered to herself. But the thought didn't leave. It lingered—loud, insistent, immovable. No matter how hard she tried to dismiss it, it held its ground. It demanded something from her. Action. Proof. Or at the very least… to be humoured.

Lucy had read plenty of Evelyn's published work during university, and if she'd gone through something like this, surely someone—Lucy included—would've noticed. It wasn't exactly the kind of detail you could bury in the footnotes. If Evelyn had experienced what Lucy had, she hadn't written about it. Not directly. Not obviously.

But Lucy had access to more. And now that wild, intrusive thought was shifting, solidifying into something heavier. Something harder to ignore—a realisation she'd been avoiding for years. When Evelyn passed, Lucy had inherited all of her unpublished work. Boxes of notepads, loose documents, and miscellaneous components that had formed the backbone of her published triumphs. Somewhere in that chaos, Lucy knew, would be her mother's notes on the Great Fire of London.

Lucy had dreaded going back there. The thought of facing those boxes—her mother's life reduced to stacks of paper and dust-covered notepads—was overwhelming. When she'd first inherited them, she hadn't had the space, in her home or her head, to deal with it. So, she'd rented a small self-storage unit in Purley, just to keep it all out of sight until she could figure out what to do with it. It became one of many quiet expenses nibbling at her already thin payslip.

She'd never filed it properly, just dumped everything in a hurry, barely sorted or labelled—and even now, she clung to the same excuse: she was grieving. It needed to be done quickly. It was understandable. Justified. But that didn't make it any easier to go back.

But Lucy needed answers—even if this probably wasn't where they'd be. Still, she had to satisfy the biting curiosity at the back of her mind.

* * *

The next morning, the unit loomed just as it had the day before. Sealed, silent, and waiting. Small—no bigger than a single garage—and tucked at the far end of a dimly lit corridor, it looked exactly as she'd left it.

The door was made entirely of steel, painted a flat shade of blue that somehow made it look even more bland. The kind of colour that felt institutional. These doors had always reminded Lucy of the ones she'd seen in police stations on TV—impersonal and built to contain.

The only distinguishing feature was the black padlock she'd hastily bought when the storage company told her they didn't supply one. She'd set a combination on the spot and walked away without making a note of it.

Her mind drew a blank. She tried her birthday: **1.5.9.7.** No luck. Then Edward's. Evelyn's. Still nothing.

A sensible person would have written it down, she thought. But not Lucy. Of course not.

On a whim, she tried **1.2.3.4.**

Click.

She exhaled. "Genius," she muttered. "Truly, a fortress of security."

She pulled the door open, and a wave of stale air rolled out to meet her, thick with the smell of old paper, damp cardboard, and time left undisturbed. The overhead strip light flickered to life automatically, casting a pale glow over the chaos within.

The scale of it hit her instantly.

She'd known there was a lot. Dozens of boxes, stacked in haste, shoved in with the kind of urgency only grief could justify. But she hadn't expected *this*.

Some boxes were still neatly sealed, but most weren't. Sellotape had long since given up the fight, curling away at the edges or snapped entirely, leaving cardboard lids yawning open. Others were stacked in precarious towers, leaning dangerously to one side, threatening to topple if she so much as breathed too hard.

One pile looked like it had half-collapsed already, spilling loose notebooks and folded pages onto the floor in a fan of disorganised thought.

It wasn't an archive. It was a graveyard.

Lucy let out a slow breath. "Fuck me. This is gonna take months."

Lucy knew she could only take a small amount back with her. She didn't have a car, and lugging boxes onto the train—mercifully, a short journey—wasn't an option she had the energy for.

She lifted the lid on the nearest box, barely looking, already overwhelmed. Inside were loose papers and handwritten notes, most of them nearly illegible. With a sigh, she slid the box into the corridor to clear a space to work.

Then, some hope. Small, but unexpected.

Some of the boxes had been labelled in marker pen, scrawled in her own handwriting. It almost surprised her. Some past version of herself had made an effort. She assumed the unlabelled ones had been too dense, too chaotic to make sense of at a glance. The mess she couldn't face then… and wasn't quite ready for now.

She rummaged through the boxes, shifting piles and tugging at lids. A few collapsed as she moved them, but most held their shape… just about. Eventually, she spotted what she was looking for: a box labelled in thick black marker, *The Great Fire of London.*

She pulled it out from the Jenga tower she'd apparently constructed, wincing as the stack wobbled but didn't fall, and carried it over to her makeshift workspace.

Inside were old illustrations, annotated printouts, and rough drafts of Evelyn's article. All of it seemed depressingly, predictably normal. Research. Notes. Nothing magical. Nothing strange.

Lucy sighed. She'd known this was a fool's errand. And it was beginning to feel like exactly that.

Until she saw the notepad at the bottom.

Her eyes were drawn to it instantly. Without hesitation, she reached in and pulled it free.

As Lucy opened the notepad, the looping handwriting was instantly familiar—her mother's, without a doubt. Messy, fast, but unmistakably Evelyn.

The entries were rough, observational, as if scribbled down in a hurry. Descriptions of the fire. Patterns. Names. She skimmed through most of it, letting the words blur until a particular line caught her attention:

"Observed damage patterns inconsistent with recorded accounts. Fire spread too slowly. Confirmation needed at source (Pudding Lane)."

She frowned, reading it again.

Then another entry, written beneath it, just as casually:

> *"Spoke to a merchant at Hastings who claimed to have seen Harold's fall firsthand. Accounts align, but eyewitness impossible after retreat. Nexus Activity here? Investigate further."*

It didn't read like research. It read like experience. Like Evelyn hadn't just studied the aftermath—she'd *been there*. Spoken to people. Seen things.

She read on.

> *"Should the Nexus interfere with the fire's spread, huge risk of Quantum Time Collisions. Further observations required back at Pudding Lane."*

Lucy stared at the page.

"What's a Nexus?" she whispered. "Or a Quantum Time Collision?"

Lucy had never heard her mother mention anything about a *Nexus*, or *Quantum Time Collisions*. It read like science fiction. Jargon that made no sense. She couldn't make heads or tails of it.

But what it hinted at—with quiet, undeniable certainty—was that Evelyn had been there. Not just metaphorically. Not through dusty records or secondary sources.

She hadn't studied it. She hadn't imagined it. *She'd witnessed it.*

A voice in the back of Lucy's mind—sharp, cynical— reminded her she might just be seeing what she wanted to see. Bending her mother's notes to justify her own vivid hallucinations.

It wasn't a bad theory. But she wasn't ready to accept it.

The language Evelyn used was strange, unfamiliar. Terms she'd never shared. At least… not with Lucy.

If it was real, Lucy thought, *Dad must've known.*

She exhaled slowly, then muttered the old line she'd used to take the sting out of his absence, "he's still out getting milk." Crass. Automatic. Easier than admitting how much it still hurt.

Lucy glanced around the storage unit, notepad still in hand, as if another answer might be hiding in plain sight. She skimmed the tops of nearby boxes until one label caught her eye—*Cathars*. Notes from an old article Evelyn had co-authored with Dr Maureen Bellamy.

Evelyn had collaborated with dozens of historians over the years. Maybe she'd confided in one of them. Or maybe, just maybe—they'd noticed something odd themselves. Maybe Maureen had seen something—heard something—that hadn't made it to print. Either way, it was worth following up. Most of them would be listed in the footnotes of her published work.

With a plan forming and the notepad clutched tight, Lucy nudged the box she'd left in the hallway back into the unit and pulled the door shut behind her.

She clicked the padlock back into place, fingers spinning the dial to **1-2-3-4**.

She paused.

"…Right. That's definitely secure," she muttered, and turned away, already half-resigned to forgetting to change it… again.

                              * * *

By the time the afternoon arrived, Lucy had read the
notepad two dozen times. She was no longer trying to
convince herself—it felt real. Too detailed to be anything
else.

She'd gone through the footnotes of Evelyn's published
work and compiled a small list of former colleagues she
could try to contact. Now she sat on the floor against the
sofa, laptop on her knees, Evelyn's notepad beside her,
and a growing mess of notes and coffee cups around her.

Her first lead, Dr. Bellamy was easy to find. A quick
Google search brought up an old university profile
complete with a still-active email address. Lucy blinked at
it for a few seconds, unsure how to begin.

She couldn't exactly open with *"Hi, did my mum ever
mention casually bending the laws of time?"*

After muttering and writing a few terrible drafts, she
settled on something that felt… almost sane.

———

Subject: Inquiry Regarding Evelyn Calder
Dear Dr. Bellamy,
My name is Lucy Calder, and I'm Evelyn Calder's
daughter. I'm currently researching some of my late
mother's work and came across the paper you co-authored
with her on the Cathars. I was wondering if you might be
willing to share any memories or insights you have from
your time working with her.

I understand this is an unusual request, but your
perspective would mean a great deal to me.

Many thanks,
Lucy Calder.

———

Lucy put an asterisk next to Bellamy's name and moved on to the next.

Her second lead, Dr. Samuel Greene, was a younger academic who had worked briefly with Evelyn on a project about Tudor architecture. She managed to track down his phone number through his university directory and called, heart pounding as the dial tone buzzed in her ear.

"Hello?" A man's voice answered. Crisp, slightly impatient.

"Hi, Dr. Greene, my name is Lucy Calder. I'm Evelyn Calder's daughter." She hesitated, then rushed on. "I was hoping you might be able to tell me about your time working with her."

There was a pause. "Evelyn Calder," he repeated, his tone softening. "Yes, I remember her. We worked together briefly on a project about Hampton Court Palace."

"Yes, that's the one," Lucy said, a flicker of hope catching in her chest. "I've been going through some of her old research, and I was wondering if—"

"Miss Calder," Samuel interrupted, his voice kind but firm. "I'm afraid I didn't work with your mother long enough to be of much help. She was… remarkable, but also fiercely independent. Most of the time, she kept her own counsel."

Lucy's heart sank. "I understand. I just thought maybe you might have noticed something, or…"

He sighed. "I wish I could help, but I'm currently swamped with my own research and teaching responsibilities. I simply don't have the bandwidth right now. I'm sorry."

Lucy forced a polite smile, even though he couldn't see it. "Thank you for your time, Dr. Greene."

"Best of luck, Miss Calder," he said before the line went dead.

Lucy lowered the phone slowly, staring at the screen like it might offer a different ending. There was something cold about Dr. Greene's tone. Polite, yes, but distant. Dismissive. It caught her off guard.

He'd called Evelyn "remarkable," but there was no warmth behind it. No fondness. Just a vague respect wrapped in formality. And it made Lucy wonder—had her mother kept everyone at arm's length? Was it just her Evelyn had grown distant with… or was that simply who she'd become?

Before the thought could settle, her laptop chimed.

A new email. From Dr. Maureen Bellamy.

—

Subject: Re: Inquiry Regarding Evelyn Calder
Lucy,
While I am sorry for your loss, I cannot assist with personal inquiries regarding your mother's work. I am currently occupied with other projects and have no further insights to offer.
Regards,
Dr. Maureen Bellamy

—

Another curt dismissal. No warmth. No curiosity. Just a firm *no*.

How many bridges had her mother burned in her final years? What had Evelyn done to drive these people so far away that even *speaking* about her was too much?

She picked up her pen and drew a sharp line through both Bellamy and Greene's names on her ever-thinning list.

Next was a name that stood out for entirely different reasons. A historian Evelyn had mentored. He appeared often in her more recent work, described once as *"relentless in his curiosity."* St. Michael Olabode.

It was clear he had been one of her favourite protégés. His name came up again and again.

That alone was enough for Lucy.

She found him through a historian networking platform. His profile showed a warm smile, neat braids, and a wall of accolades behind him. But what really jumped out was his specialism: Nazi Germany, particularly the years leading up to World War II.

Lucy opened a new email window and began to type. Although, it wasn't clear whether he was *actually* a saint. Lucy played her first line safe.

—

Subject: Inquiry Regarding Evelyn Calder
Good Afternoon,

My name is Lucy Calder, and I'm Evelyn Calder's daughter. I've been revisiting my late mother's work and noticed your name in connection with some of her projects. I would love the opportunity to discuss your experiences working with her, as your perspective would mean a great deal to me.

Warm regards,
Lucy Calder.

—

She moved on to the last name on her list.

Dr. Harold Trent had also been easy to find. An obituary tucked into the archives of a prestigious academic journal. The short notice outlined a distinguished career in Renaissance history, along with several collaborations with Evelyn.

Lucy stared at the grainy black-and-white photo that accompanied the article: a severe-looking man with wire-rimmed glasses, a furrowed brow, and the inscription: *1940–2024.*

He'd died just seven months ago—taking whatever knowledge he had of Evelyn with him.

She lingered, falling into a wormhole of archived publications, accolades, and honorary titles. For a man who looked like he hadn't smiled since 1973, he had left behind a remarkable legacy.

Then her laptop binged.

——

Subject: Re: Inquiry Regarding Evelyn Calder
Dear Lucy,

Thank you for reaching out. It would be an honour to meet you. Evelyn was not only a mentor but an inspiration, and I would be happy to share my experiences.

I'm based in Finchley, and my office address is included below. Would you be available tomorrow at 10 AM?

Yours,
Michael.

——

Lucy read the message twice, her pulse quickening. She typed her reply:

——

Subject: Re: Inquiry Regarding Evelyn Calder
Dear Michael,

Thank you so much for your quick reply. Tomorrow at 10 AM works perfectly for me. I look forward to meeting you.

Best regards,
Lucy Calder

——

"Finally," she thought—someone willing to talk to her.

Of course, that meant she'd have to explain the unexplainable and hope—pray—she'd be believed. She glanced at the notepad. Proof, of a kind. She briefly considered bringing the ruined socks too, but quickly dismissed the idea. Dirty socks proved nothing and absolutely no one wanted to be handed a pair of them as evidence.

Still, this felt like progress. Real progress.

But the silence from Evelyn's colleagues lingered in her mind. Why had they been so quick to shut her down? So unwilling to even speak her mother's name?

What had Evelyn Calder really been like to work with?

And what secrets had she taken with her into the past?

* * *

Lucy spent most of her Northern Line journey the next morning spiralling inside her own thoughts. Would St. Michael see her as a curiosity? Or hysterical? What would she say if he challenged her account of what happened two nights ago? Or worse, what if he dismissed her entirely?

Was she about to discredit the name of Evelyn Calder?

She kept her backpack firm on her lap, fingers clenched around the notepad hidden inside as if it could shield her from the rising tide of doubt.

After a fifteen-minute walk from Finchley Station, she found the building easily enough. An unassuming structure wedged between a dry cleaners and a barber shop. Its faded sign simply read *Finchley Professional Offices,* and the frosted windows gave no clue as to what lay inside.

Lucy hesitated at the door, nerves gnawing at her.

What if he thinks I'm ridiculous? What if this is all a waste of time?

She shook her head and squared her shoulders. *You came this far.*

She pressed the buzzer for the second floor,
labelled *S.M.O.* Presumably for St. Michael Olabode.

Almost instantly, the main doors buzzed open with a
mechanical click. Lucy inhaled deeply and stepped inside.
Each flight of stairs seemed to weigh her feet down a little
more.

When she reached the door at the top, she lifted her
hand to knock on the door

but it opened before she could touch it.

"Lucy Calder?"

The man who greeted her was tall and lean, most likely
of African origin, with an almost boyish charm despite the
slightly dishevelled state of his vintage—but thoughtfully
composed—clothing. His hairline framed a warm,
intelligent face, and his dark eyes seemed to take her in
with a single, perceptive glance.

"Yes," Lucy replied, her voice a touch more uncertain
than she'd meant it to be.

Before she could offer her hand, St. Michael stepped
forward and pulled her into a firm but gentle hug.

"I'm so sorry for your loss," he said sincerely. "Your
mother meant so much to me."

Lucy froze, caught completely off guard. She hadn't
expected him to be so warm, nor the genuine emotion
behind his words. It was like stepping into someone else's
grief.

After a moment, she awkwardly patted his back.
"Thank you," she murmured, her throat suddenly tight.

St. Michael stepped back, his expression kind. "Come
in," he said with a soft smile. "I've been really looking
forward to meeting you."

The office was surprisingly spacious, though every
inch of it was used with meticulous intent. Shelves lined
the walls, packed with books, binders, and archival boxes,
each neatly labelled. Many of the titles dealt with early
20th-century Europe. Treatises on fascism, resistance

movements, and thick volumes on the rise and fall of Nazi Germany. Several shelves were dedicated entirely to primary sources and annotated documents, their spines marked in both German and English. Near the back, a sturdy oak desk stood, its surface scattered with open books and notes written in a precise, looping script. The room smelled faintly of aged paper and freshly brewed coffee. An odd but comforting mix that made it feel more like a scholar's sanctuary than an office.

But what caught Lucy's attention most was the mural.

It dominated one wall. A sprawling collage of photographs, articles, and handwritten notes, all arranged around a large black-and-white photo of Evelyn.

Lucy gasped as she stepped closer. "You made this?"

St. Michael nodded, his expression soft. "Your mother was an extraordinary mentor and an even better person. This is my way of remembering her."

At the centre of the display was Evelyn at her most commanding: dark hair swept back, eyes alight with determination, caught mid-gesture in what looked like a lecture or debate. Surrounding the image were clippings from her published works, snapshots of historical sites she'd studied, and fragments of her handwriting—familiar loops and flourishes scrawled across yellowing paper.

Lucy's eyes scanned the wall, her fingers itching to reach out and touch the fragments of her mother's life. Pieces of a woman she was still trying to understand. "I had no idea she meant so much to you," she said quietly.

"She shaped my career," St. Michael replied, his voice edged with emotion. "I wouldn't be who I am today without her. She pushed me, challenged me… believed in me, even when I didn't."

Lucy swallowed hard, emotions churning in her chest. Pride, guilt, and loss tangled together until she could barely separate them.

"She would've been so proud of this," she murmured.

St. Michael smiled gently. "She was proud of you too, you know."

Lucy looked away, her throat tightening. "I'm not so sure about that."

Trying to cut through the weight of the moment, she glanced at him with a crooked smile. "So… are you, like… an *actual* saint?"

St. Michael chuckled, the sound warm and genuine. "No, not quite. My parents named me after St. Michael the Archangel. It's a name to aspire to, not live up to."

Lucy grinned despite herself. "Still. It suits you."

St. Michael smiled and looked down in acknowledgment. "Honestly, just call me Michael."

"If you're sure." Lucy replied back.

"I'll make us some coffee," St. Michael said, nodding toward a small kitchenette in the corner. "Have a look around while I do."

As St. Michael busied himself with the coffee machine, Lucy's gaze drifted back to the mural. The emotions she'd been trying to keep down began to rise, uninvited and heavy.

Evelyn had been a giant in her field. Admired, respected and remembered. She'd left behind a legacy that felt impossibly vast. And Lucy? She couldn't even bring herself to finish a piece on Tudor dating trends for online engagement.

She would've been so disappointed in me, Lucy thought bitterly.

The guilt she'd carried since Evelyn's death flared up again, sharp and familiar, intertwining with the grief she still hadn't fully faced.

St. Michael returned with two steaming mugs and set them down gently on the desk. He gestured for her to take a seat, then settled into his own chair across from her.

"So," he said, his tone open and steady. "What brings you here?"

Lucy took a deep breath, steadying herself as she tried to find the words.

"It's going to sound crazy," Lucy began, her voice trembling. "But something happened to me. And I think it's connected to my mum or at least, to something she experienced."

She took another breath, then launched into the story, starting with the night in her kitchen. She described how she'd been reading Evelyn's article about the Great Fire of London, how the words had drawn her in, until it felt like she was inside them. Then came the pan catching fire. Her mistake with the water. The panic.

"I remember reaching for the fire blanket," she said, hands curling slightly in her lap. "But before I could put it out, everything changed. The air got heavy, like it was thickening around me... and then I wasn't in my kitchen anymore."

She spoke with growing urgency, painting the scene in sharp, vivid strokes: narrow cobblestone streets, the orange glow of flames devouring timber-framed buildings, smoke thick and choking in her lungs.

"There were people everywhere," she said, eyes wide. "Screaming, running. Some were carrying children, others trying to haul furniture or crates. I heard someone crying for water. Someone else shouted that their family was trapped."

Her voice faltered as she reached the worst of it. The collapsing building, the wave of heat that felt like it would consume her.

"I thought I was going to die," she whispered. "And then... I was back. Just like that. In my kitchen. The fire was still on the stove, like nothing had changed. But everything else had."

She swallowed. "I smelled like smoke. There was soot on my skin. On my socks. It was real."

Lucy sat back, her hands trembling slightly. "I don't know how it happened," she said quietly, "but it did. And I think my mum might've known something about it. Some of the notes I've found—they're vague, but it feels like she was writing from experience, not just research."

She reached for her bag, fumbling with the zip. "I can show you. Her notes. They're in here."

St. Michael hadn't spoken throughout her story. He'd listened—really listened—but with each sentence, a subtle tension had crept into his face. Not hostility, but the unmistakable edge of doubt.

Lucy pulled out the notepad and opened it to a familiar page. "Here. This is the part I'm talking about," she said, holding it out to him and pointing to the line about *Pudding Lane.*

St. Michael took the notebook carefully, his brow furrowed as he read. His eyes flicked across the page in silence.

"She mentions a few other things too," Lucy added. "Stuff I didn't understand. Terms I've never heard before."

When he finished, St. Michael closed the notepad gently and set it down on the desk. He exhaled through his nose, then rubbed a hand over his face before raising his eyebrows and shutting his eyes briefly.

"This… wasn't exactly what I expected you to say," he admitted, voice low, measured.

"Trust me, this wasn't on my bingo card this year," Lucy said, her voice dry as she tried to cut through the silence—and the disbelief settling between them. "I just want to know if Mum ever said anything. Described anything like that to you."

St. Michael gave a quiet, rueful smile. "She could definitely transport you through time with her words, but… she never claimed the source was from *actually* being there."

"But she did," Lucy said, motioning toward the notepad, palm open.

"Not really," St. Michael replied, cutting across her—gently, but firm. Lucy's brow creased.

"These are rough notes, Lucy," he continued, softening. "Written in a hurry, probably for a draft or early research. I do the same all the time—it doesn't mean I've lived it."

Lucy looked away, cheeks burning, her confidence slipping.

St. Michael leaned back, folding his arms as he studied her carefully. "I want to believe you, Lucy. I really do. But what you're describing… it's not just outside the realm of possibility. It's beyond what most people would even *entertain* as plausible." He paused. "You're talking about *time travel*."

"I *said* it would sound crazy. I *know* I sound crazy." Lucy paused, her voice unsteady but firm. "But it happened."

"I don't think you're crazy," St. Michael said gently. "I really don't. But Lucy… what you're describing… its… it's extraordinary. And I have to ask: are you absolutely certain? Could it have been a vivid hallucination? Stress can do strange things to us, especially when we're grieving."

That line. *That* line.

Lucy had heard it so many times over the years that it struck like a reflex. Her frustration flared.

"I'm not grieving," she snapped. "And I'm not stressed."

Her voice cut sharper than she intended, but she didn't take it back. She was done with that excuse.

"You said you were reading one of Evelyn's articles before this all happened?" St. Michael asked, trying to ease the moment.

"Yeah," Lucy muttered, leaning back in her chair and dragging her fingers through her hair.

"Lucy, I'm not saying you *are* grieving or stressed," he said, his tone steady, "but when we experience trauma, the brain sometimes latches onto things that offer meaning. Something that explains the chaos. Maybe—"

"No!" Lucy cut in, her voice rising. "Michael, this isn't about grief or stress or trauma. I *know* what I saw. I *know* what I felt. I was there. In 1666. I smelled the smoke. I felt the heat. My lungs *still* haven't caught up. I'm not here for sympathy. I'm looking for answers."

She stood abruptly, turning away as she felt the tears beginning to rise. She didn't want to cry, not here and not now. She didn't want to look any more unhinged than she already sounded.

"Like I said," St. Michael began gently, "I *want* to believe you, Lucy. I really do. But I just don't think it's possible. With the fire in your kitchen… I think maybe, just for a moment, your brain disassociated what you were reading from what was happening around you."

Lucy looked away, jaw clenched, frustration bubbling just beneath the surface. Her eyes drifted past him, to the wall behind his desk.

There, in stark black and white, was a photograph of a massive stone arena. Grand columns loomed under swastika-draped banners, hundreds of faces turned upward in chilling uniformity. And at the centre, on a high podium, Adolf Hitler stood mid-speech. The title above the image read: *The 6th Party Conference, Nuremberg, 1934.*

"I just think," St. Michael continued, "that maybe I'm not the right person to talk to about this. Have you spoken to your GP?"

That was it. Her composure cracked.

"I'm not asking you to *believe* it completely," she said, her voice strained and shaking. "I just need someone— *anyone*—to *try* and help me understand what happened!"

Her voice broke on the last word, and though she blinked rapidly, the tears spilled over anyway.

As Lucy stared at the images of the Nazi Congress, something shifted deep within her. A sensation stirred in her chest—faint at first, then spreading outward until it filled her completely, replacing the desperation to be believed with something else entirely.

St. Michael rose from his chair, brow furrowed. He glanced around the room, then froze. "Do you hear that?"

Lucy did more than hear it.

She *felt* it.

A low hum vibrated through the air, not loud but impossible to ignore. The atmosphere grew dense, heavy with static, like the charged stillness before a lightning strike. And she was at the centre of it.

The sound intensified, wrapping around her like a rising tide. Her expression went blank, eyes wide, fear flickering beneath the surface.

"Lucy?" St. Michael's voice cut through the growing haze. He stepped forward slowly, watching her with sharp, uncertain eyes. "What's going on?"

"I—" Her voice broke as the familiar sensation surged over her. The colours of the room began to blur, their edges softening, bleeding like watercolours in motion. Her limbs felt weightless, untethered from the floor.

St. Michael moved closer, now visibly alarmed. "Lucy, talk to me. What's happening?"

"I think…" she whispered, her voice shaking, "…I think it's happening again."

The distortion intensified. The air rippled and bent, as if the room itself was being twisted around her. St. Michael stood frozen, eyes wide with shock as reality warped before him. His scepticism shattered in an instant.

"Lucy—" St. Michael began, but before he could finish, she stumbled backward.

Instinctively, he reached out and grabbed her hand.

The moment their skin touched, the world unravelled.

The office dissolved in a swirl of light and shadow, the walls melting into a kaleidoscope of shifting colour and sound. Lucy felt the ground vanish beneath her, a rush of air tearing past her ears, a sudden pull deep in her chest,

like something had hooked into her and yanked her free.

When the spinning finally stopped, her feet hit solid ground. But the air was heavier here—thick, condensed, almost suffocating. Her lungs strained against it.

And then she saw them.

The swastikas. The towering stone columns. The massive podium looming overhead.

They weren't images from a photograph anymore—they were real. Solid. Imposing.

They were standing in the heart of a vast arena, surrounded on all sides by banners and stone, and by the oppressive hum of hundreds of indistinct voices. A low, thrumming murmur that seemed to pulse through the very air.

Finchley was gone. Completely. Something else had taken its place.

St. Michael released her hand like it had burned him. His voice, when it came, was barely a whisper.

"Lucy… what on earth just happened?"

But Lucy couldn't answer. The scene around them spoke louder than any words could.

CHAPTER 3
The Rally of Unity

The sound hit first.

A cacophony of rhythmic chants and shouts—*Sieg Heil! Sieg Heil!*—reverberated through the air like a drumbeat of inevitability. It surged and swelled, not a chant but a wall of noise. Lucy's chest tightened.

Then came the sights.

The arena stretched before her, impossibly vast and alien. Massive stone columns loomed like ancient sentinels, their edges sharp against the harsh lights that illuminated the scene. Red banners hung between them, emblazoned with the unmistakable black swastika on white, their stark contrast burning into her vision. Every detail seemed heightened, too sharp, too vivid, as if her senses couldn't keep up with what they were experiencing. Thousands of men stood in perfect formation, their uniforms pristine, their movements synchronised. Rows upon rows of soldiers, their polished boots catching the light as they shifted, created an effect that was almost hypnotic.

The air was thick, dense with heat and the collective energy of the crowd. It smelled faintly of sweat, leather, and something metallic, as if the atmosphere itself carried the weight of the moment. The cheers of the crowd were not just loud but the kind of sound that came from deep within, born of belief or desperation. It was suffocating.

At the centre of it all was the podium. Raised high above the crowd, it was framed by colossal stone steps, designed to elevate whoever stood there into something godlike. Lucy's eyes darted toward the structure, but her attention was quickly pulled back to the crowd. A sea of faces alive with belief and unwavering devotion. The sheer scale of it was paralyzing, a force of unity that felt almost unnatural.

The crowd erupted into cheers, their voices rolling across the arena like thunder.

Lucy's knees felt weak. Her chest heaved as she struggled to breathe, the sensory overload crashing over her like a wave. She gripped the cool stone of the column at her back, trying to steady herself, her fingers trembling as she fought to process the sheer scale of what was unfolding before her. It was impossible. Unreal. And yet it wasn't.

Somewhere, distantly, she heard her name.

"Lucy… Lucy!" The voice was familiar, urgent, but it felt far away, like a whisper from another world.

She closed her eyes, willing herself to focus. The sounds of the rally—the booming cheers, the chanting— faded slightly as she latched onto the voice calling her. Slowly, she opened her eyes and turned.

St. Michael stood beside her, his face pale, his expression a mix of confusion and barely-contained fear. "Lucy," he said again, his voice low but insistent. "What just happened? What did you do?"

Lucy stared at him, her heart still pounding. Her mouth opened to respond, but no words came. She shook her head, her voice caught somewhere between panic and disbelief. "I… I don't know," she managed finally, her voice trembling. "This can't be happening again…"

St. Michael's face went blank as he waited for answers.

Lucy swallowed hard, her eyes darting back to the crowd as if expecting them to turn and notice her at any moment. Her voice dropped to a hush. "Michael, I've done *it* again. Like I did before. To the Great Fire of London." Her hands were shaking, and she clutched them together to try to steady herself. "I don't know how, but we're… we're here. We're standing in your research, the one from your wall."

St. Michael looked at her, his face a mask of disbelief and growing alarm. "This is real," he said, more to himself than to her. "We're really here." He pressed a hand to his chest, his breathing uneven. "I feel… strange. Like I'm out of sync…"

St. Michael opened his mouth as if to speak again, but the words caught in his throat. His brow furrowed, and he turned his gaze away from Lucy, scanning the arena with wide, disbelieving eyes.

"I can't believe this," he murmured, almost to himself. His voice was low, filled with a mix of awe and dread. He blinked several times, his breathing shallow as he stared at the scene before him. "We're really here. This is… This is the Nuremberg Rally. 1934."

St. Michael took a deep, shaky breath, his historian's instincts warring with the panic rising within him. His gaze swept the arena, cataloguing every detail, his mind racing to piece together their exact location in time and history.

"This," he said finally, his voice quiet but steady, "is the 6th Nazi Party Congress. They called it the Rally of Unity. It's infamous—one of the most iconic moments of Nazi propaganda. This… this is history unfolding right in front of us."

Lucy stared at him, still struggling to process what she was seeing. "What does that mean?" She whispered.

He swallowed, gesturing subtly toward the grand stage dominating the arena. "This is the Zeppelinfeld, part of the

Nuremberg rally grounds. It was designed to intimidate, to inspire devotion. Look at it. Everything about this space is calculated—those banners, those columns, the way the soldiers are arranged like chess pieces. It's not just a gathering; it's a display of power, of control. It's… it's terrifying."

Lucy glanced around, her chest tightening at the sheer scale of the space and the deafening roar of the crowd. The faces in the crowd looked almost euphoric, their eyes fixed on the stage as though nothing else in the world existed.

St. Michael shook his head, his voice trembling slightly. "The Nazis used these rallies to sell their vision of Germany's future. They needed people to believe—to really believe—that they were part of something unstoppable. These events… they weren't just speeches or ceremonies. They were rituals. And they worked. They made ordinary people think they were part of something greater, something glorious."

Lucy's stomach churned. "And this is where it all starts, isn't it?" she asked softly. "The war, the camps, everything."

He nodded, his expression grim. "Not the beginning exactly, but close. The Nazis had taken power the year before, in 1933, but rallies like this helped cement it. They used these events to show off their strength, their unity. It was a warning to anyone who might oppose them—and an invitation for everyone else to join."

His voice caught slightly, and he turned away, running a hand over his face. "To see it like this, though… It's so much worse in person. You read about it, watch the old footage, but standing here, seeing their faces, hearing them cheer—it's horrifying how human it all feels."

Lucy nodded mutely, her throat tight. She didn't know what to say. She couldn't stop staring at the crowd. Their joy, their pride, their unwavering belief.

But for St. Michael, the danger wasn't abstract or distant, it was immediate and personal. He was a Black man of Nigerian heritage, standing in the heart of Nazi Germany among thousands of men and women who believed in racial purity and Aryan supremacy. He didn't need to hear the rhetoric from the podium to know that these people, with their cheers and salutes, saw him as less than human. They didn't just hate him. They believed he had no right to exist.

The knowledge of where he was and who he was among, wrapped around his chest like a vice. A primal urge rose within him, deep and instinctual: *Run*. It screamed in his mind, louder than the chants of the crowd. His body tensed as though bracing for a blow, his every nerve on high alert. He had to get out of here. He had to hide.

But he didn't say any of this. He couldn't. The words lodged in his throat, his fear too raw to vocalize. Instead, he clenched his jaw and forced himself to focus, trying to suppress the panic threatening to consume him.

Their attention was drawn to movement at the centre of the podium.

The man standing there, previously addressing the crowd, raised his hand to signal for silence. The thunderous cheers gradually died down, the crowd's collective focus shifting entirely to the figure on the stage.

St. Michael stiffened. "That's not him," he whispered, almost to himself.

Lucy frowned. "Not who?"

"The man at the podium," St. Michael clarified. "It's not Hitler. That's… someone else. A high-ranking official, introducing him, probably."

Lucy's heart raced as she turned her eyes back to the podium. The man there—tall, stern, and commanding— spoke with authority, though his words were indecipherable from where they stood. His body language, however, conveyed exactly what they needed to know. This was a prelude, a warm-up act for the main event.

And then it happened.

The man gestured to the side of the stage, his arm sweeping wide as he turned toward the shadowed edge of the platform. The crowd erupted into cheers once again, louder this time, their cries echoing through the massive arena. The energy in the air shifted, electric and almost unbearable, as all eyes turned toward the figure emerging from the shadows.

Lucy's breath caught as the man stepped forward, ascending the steps with deliberate precision. The spotlight caught him as he reached the centre of the podium, illuminating his face.

Her heart skipped.

There he was.

Lucy had seen his image countless times in textbooks, documentaries, and films. She knew his face as well as she knew any historical figure. But seeing him here, in the flesh, was something else entirely. The man who now stood before the crowd, raising his hand in greeting, was no longer a photograph or a footnote in history. He was real. Tangible. Human.

St. Michael exhaled sharply beside her, the sound somewhere between astonishment and dread. Lucy glanced at him, and in his expression, she saw the same conflicting emotions swirling within her: curiosity, disbelief, and an overwhelming sense of danger.

As a historian, St. Michael couldn't help but be captivated. This was his field, his specialty. To see it, to live it—this was something no historian could have imagined. And yet, another part of him, a far more primal part, screamed at him to get as far away from this place as possible.

But there was nowhere to go.

Hitler, standing at the podium paused, his gaze sweeping the crowd.

And then he spoke.

"Die Welt schaut auf uns," Hitler's voice rang out, sharp and deliberate, each syllable resonating with power. "Germany is no longer the defeated, fractured nation it was!" he continued, the words leaping seamlessly between English and German.

"Wir are not mehr das Land der humiliated," he declared, his voice rising as if daring the air itself to challenge him.

The words seemed to land oddly in Lucy's ears, some in crisp English, others in harsh, guttural German. They twisted and tangled in her mind, the switch between languages so fluid it was almost impossible to separate them.

Confused, she turned to St. Michael. "English. He's speaking English and German," she said, her voice unsteady.

St. Michael looked at her, his expression blank. "What are you talking about?"

"I didn't think Hitler could speak English," Lucy added as she turned back to the podium.

St. Michael's frown deepened, and his voice dropped to a whisper. "Lucy, he's not speaking English. He's only speaking German."

Lucy stared at him, her confusion deepening. "No, I'm hearing—" She stopped as a roar erupted from the crowd, drowning out her words. The energy of the arena surged like a thunderclap, shaking her to her core.

Hitler stood tall, commanding the crowd with nothing but his presence. His words had landed like a hammer blow, and the masses responded with a wave of frenzied devotion. Fists shot into the air, their chants reverberating through the space like a storm gathering strength.

Lucy turned back to St. Michael, whose eyes were scanning the crowd, his body tense. "Lucy," he said, low and urgent, "this is a really dangerous place to be."

She nodded mutely, but he wasn't finished. "Think about it," he continued, his tone growing sharper. "I'm a Black man with an accent that's about as far from German as you can get. Even if I wasn't…" He trailed off, glancing around at the sea of uniforms, banners, and swastikas. "Well, I think we both know what these people think of someone like me."

Lucy's stomach sank as his words hit home, but St. Michael pressed on. "You might have a better chance at blending in—at least until you start talking—but neither of us is dressed for this. These clothes are a dead giveaway we aren't from here." He gestured at their modern outfits, a stark contrast to the pressed uniforms and dated styles around them. "Lucy, we can't stay here. As much as I'd love to observe this for research, we don't have that luxury. We have to go. Now."

He paused, his eyes locking on hers. "Take us back."

"I can't," Lucy whispered, her voice barely audible over the hum of the crowd.

St. Michael's face twisted in confusion. "What do you mean you can't?"

"I don't know how," she admitted, her voice shaking. "I don't even know how we got here."

His eyes widened. "But you came back from the Great Fire of London," he said, the confusion and fear bleeding into his voice. "You made it home."

Lucy shook her head, her hands trembling. "I don't know how I did that either. I was about to be crushed, and then I just… I felt something, and suddenly I was back in my kitchen." She met his eyes, her fear mirrored in his expression. "I wouldn't even know where to start."

St. Michael let out a shaky breath, his lips quirking upward in a weak attempt at a smile. "Well, let's not hope it comes to that," he said, the humour falling flat in the suffocating atmosphere.

He glanced around the space, his sharp eyes darting over the details. Just behind the column where they stood, two dark coats hung from a rack, their lapels emblazoned with the unmistakable Nazi symbol. His jaw tightened, but he forced himself to focus. "Lucy," he said, motioning to the coats. "We need to put those on. It's our best chance at not getting noticed."

Lucy hesitated, her stomach churning at the thought, but she nodded. They had no other choice. As St. Michael reached for the coats, another deafening roar erupted from the crowd, drawing their attention back to the podium.

"We need to move," St. Michael said. He had already shrugged into one of the coats, its fabric stiff and scratchy, and was holding the other out to her. She hesitated for only a moment before taking it, slipping her arms into the heavy material. The swastika on her sleeve didn't just mark her, it stained her.

"Let's just get out of here," she whispered, her voice tight. "Then we'll figure out how to get back." Her eyes flicked to a nearby door, partially obscured by shadows. It wasn't far, but it might as well have been a mile.

As they moved closer to the exit, Lucy's emotions churned like a storm inside her. Fear gripped her chest, cold and unrelenting, but guilt gnawed at her as well. This wasn't just her life she had put in danger, it was St. Michael's. And for him, the stakes were so much higher. She felt the weight of that realisation pressing down on her, sharper than any physical threat.

And then there was the confusion. How had she done it again? Why had it happened now? And why was she hearing parts of the speech in English? The logical part of her mind whispered that this couldn't be real, that she had to be dreaming, hallucinating. But the air was too thick, the roar of the crowd too loud, the coat on her shoulders too heavy. It was real. All of it. And she didn't know how to stop it.

Lucy and St. Michael moved carefully along the shadowy edge of the arena, staying close to the towering walls. The roar of the crowd echoed behind them, broken only by Hitler's booming voice. The sound of his speech grew muffled as they approached the grand doors, their footsteps nearly inaudible beneath the oppressive din.

Every muscle in Lucy's body was taut with tension, her eyes darting constantly between the door and the crowd, praying no one would notice their retreat. St. Michael's expression was unreadable, but the tightness in his jaw and the stiffness of his movements betrayed his fear.

As they reached the grand double doors, Lucy pushed one open just enough for them to slip through. The cool air of the lobby hit her like a splash of water, but it didn't ease the anxiety knotting in her chest.

The room was grand and imposing, with high ceilings adorned with intricate mouldings. A sweeping staircase rose to the upper level, where guards patrolled the balcony above. A massive chandelier hung in the centre, casting an opulent glow over the polished marble floor. The red and black banners of the Nazi Party lined the walls, their ominous presence unrelenting.

Directly in front of them, another set of double doors led to the streets of Nuremberg. Lucy exhaled shakily, her hand tightening on the coat she wore. "Just a little further," she whispered.

They were halfway across the lobby when it happened.

"STOP!" The voice cut through the air like a whip.

Lucy froze mid-step, her breath catching in her throat. Slowly, she and St. Michael turned, their movements stiff and reluctant. A guard had spotted them leaving the arena. He now stood behind them, his piercing gaze fixed on them. He must have followed them through the door without their noticing.

He was tall and broad-shouldered, a starkly typical figure of the regime's ideal. His uniform was pristine, every button polished, the swastika on his armband a vivid reminder of their peril.

From the balcony above, other guards turned to look, their boots clicking as they moved to the edge to peer down. The atmosphere in the room grew heavier, the silence broken only by the faint murmur of distant speeches beyond the arena doors. As the guard approached Lucy and St. Michael, more guards descended the staircase, joining him. The small group now stood opposite them, their expressions a mix of suspicion and disdain.

The first guard's voice boomed again, colder and more accusatory: "And why are du gehst during the Mitte of the Führer's address?"

Lucy flinched at the sudden shift, her confusion mounting as the German words broke the rhythm of the otherwise English sentence. She hesitated, glancing at St. Michael, whose wide eyes silently begged her for answers.

Thinking quickly, Lucy forced a polite smile and replied seamlessly, "Es tut mir leid. Es war stuffy da drinnen, und ich… I felt schlecht. Wir wollten nur etwas water holen." She explained calmly that it was stuffy inside and that she hadn't been feeling well, so they were heading out to get some water.

Her tone was steady, and she gave no indication she was aware she was slipping between German and English. To St. Michael, however, her words were an odd jumble, mostly German with scattered English that made no sense. He turned to her, his mouth slightly agape in confusion.

The first guard's eyes narrowed as he shifted his attention to St. Michael. His gaze hardened, disgust flickering across his face. He took a deliberate step closer, his boots clicking against the marble. "And what," he sneered, "ist dieses Ding mit Ihnen?" (is this… thing… with you?)

Lucy kept her composure, though her stomach churned at the venom in his tone. Without hesitation, she replied, "Es tut mir leid für meine rudeness. Wir sind Akademiker aus London, und wir wollten diese monumentale Gelegenheit sehen." She politely apologized for being impolite, explaining that they were academics from London who had come to witness the monumental event.

The guard's suspicion only deepened. He tilted his head, eyes narrowing as her speech continued to flow between languages. "Sprechen sie Deutsch!" He barked, his voice echoing through the room. (Speak German!)

Lucy didn't flinch, but her heart was racing. She was completely unaware of how effortlessly her words transitioned between German and English. The tension in the guard's voice, however, made it clear he had noticed. St. Michael stiffened beside her, his fear radiating in waves.

The other guards murmured amongst themselves. Lucy caught fragments of their conversation—words that came through to her in perfect English, sharp and chilling:

"Look at their attire."

"British spies."

"A Black man."

"Hold for questioning."

Lucy's breath quickened. She leaned slightly toward St. Michael, her voice barely audible. "We need to run," she whispered.

His head snapped toward her; his voice just as quiet but laced with disbelief. "Are you insane?"

Before she could respond, the sharp, chilling words rang out from the group: "I say we just shoot them."

Lucy's eyes widened in horror. Without thinking, she grabbed St. Michael's arm and shouted, "Run!"

They spun around, lunging for the main doors. Lucy's hands fumbled desperately with the handles, but the heavy doors refused to budge. They were locked.

Behind them, shouts erupted as the guards gave chase. The echo of boots on marble grew louder, the tension in the room suffocating. Lucy turned back, as she saw the guards raising their pistols, the barrels aimed directly at them.

Her vision blurred. The walls seemed to close in, the air growing thick and heavy. Her mind raced, panic overwhelming every coherent thought. *This is my fault*, she thought. *I brought him here. I put him in danger*.

The shouts grew louder, the guards closing the distance between them. Lucy's chest heaved as the familiar sensation began to build. A pull deep within her, like the world around her was shifting out of focus. The air hummed with an unnatural charge, the edges of her vision blurring as light began to glow faintly around her.

The guards froze, their eyes widening at the sight of the strange luminescence. One bellowed an order, stepping forward as the light pulsed around them: "Stop whatever you're tun!" (doing!)

Lucy's body was shaking now, her heart hammering in her chest as the sensation intensified. The light around her grew brighter, distorting her outline. She instinctively reached out, grabbing St. Michael's arm just as the guards opened fire.

The bullets passed harmlessly through their bodies, the projectiles dissipating like smoke as they struck the now-translucent figures of Lucy and St. Michael. The guards' shouts of alarm faded into muffled sound as the world dissolved around them.

The pull reached its peak, and then, with a rush of air and a blinding flash, they were gone.

Lucy hit the floor with a thud. She gasped, disoriented, her surroundings coming into focus. The familiar clutter of St. Michael's office greeted her. The same papers on his desk, the same bookshelves lining the walls. The faint aroma of coffee still hung in the air, and the mugs on the desk were still steaming.

They were back.

CHAPTER 4
Devoid Of Certainty

Lucy turned to look at St. Michael, her chest heaving, and saw him slump into his chair as though the air had been knocked out of him.

"Well," St. Michael finally said, his voice breaking the silence, "I didn't plan on coming that close to being shot when I got out of bed this morning."

Lucy let out a shaky laugh, though there was no humour in it. "I—" she began, but her voice faltered. She sank into the chair opposite him, burying her face in her hands. "I don't even know where to start."

"You could start by explaining how you speak fluent German," St. Michael said, his tone sharper than she'd expected. It wasn't anger, not exactly, but there was an edge to his words, a result of adrenaline and fear still coursing through his veins. "That might have been useful to know before we were nearly executed by a firing squad."

"What?" Lucy's head snapped up, confusion knitting her brow. "I don't speak German."

St. Michael stared at her. "Lucy, I just heard you. You spoke it. Perfectly, I might add—to those guards. You even managed to calm them down for a moment. Don't tell me that wasn't you."

Lucy shook her head, her confusion deepening. "No, I… I heard them in English, Michael. The guards were speaking English. well, mostly. There were some words I didn't recognise, but I could understand them. And Hitler—he was speaking English too. Didn't you hear him?"

St. Michael leaned forward, his gaze narrowing. "He wasn't speaking English, Lucy. Not a single word. It was all German. And you—" He paused, his voice softening as the memory replayed in his mind. "You spoke German back to them. Almost flawlessly. But… every so often, you slipped in an English word, like it was second nature."

Lucy stared at him, her pulse quickening. "That's not possible. I've never studied German. I mean, I barely passed GCSE French. How could I—"

"Lucy." St. Michael's voice was calm but insistent. "It wasn't just German. It was like you were… pulling from two languages at once. You understood them, they understood you, but it was strange. Unnatural."

She sat back, her hands trembling. "I don't understand," she whispered. "I know what I heard. I heard them in English. You're saying I spoke German, but… I didn't feel like I was translating anything. It just… came out. Like as if I were speaking English."

The room fell silent again, the weight of the revelation settling over them. St. Michael studied her carefully. "Lucy, whatever's happening to you, it's more than just traveling through time. There's something… deeper at play."

Lucy opened her mouth to respond, but her eyes landed on the coat still draped over his shoulders, the red-and-black swastika patch glaring back at her like an accusation. She let out a shuddering breath, ripping off her own coat and tossing it onto the floor.

St. Michael followed her gaze, realising he was still wearing his as well. "Ah," he said, his voice tinged with dry humour. "Right. Probably not the best look for me, all things considered."

Despite herself, Lucy let out a breathless laugh. "Probably not. You'd make a *terrible* Nazi."

"Well, I guess that's a good thing," he replied, shrugging out of the coat and draping it over the back of his chair.

St. Michael leaned back, rubbing his temples. "All right. Let's try to make sense of this. Walk me through everything again, from the beginning."

Lucy nodded, her voice trembling as she recounted the events leading up to their slip through time. She described the fire in her kitchen, the way Evelyn's article had drawn her in, and the overwhelming sensation of being pulled into the past. Then she moved on to Germany, to the rally, to the moment they had been caught—and to the strange way she had understood and spoken a language she didn't know.

When she finished, St. Michael leaned forward, his elbows resting on his knees as he processed her words. "Two slips through time," he said slowly. "Both times were stressful—once during the fire in your kitchen, and then again when you were trying to explain it to me."

St. Michael placed a hand under his chin before continuing. "Yet, both times you were thinking about, or at least aware of the event you ended up in. The Great Fire of London and the rally. And both times, you were focused on something connected to those events. Your mum's article, my research. That can't be a coincidence."

Lucy frowned, her mind racing. "So, you think it's not just about the emotional state I was in—it's about what I was focused on?"

"Potentially," St. Michael said. "The emotional state might have acted as a catalyst, but it might not necessarily be the trigger. The connection seems to be what you're thinking about—consciously or unconsciously—when it happens."

Lucy blinked, her heart pounding. "So, what? You think I can... aim where I end up?"

"I think it's possible," St. Michael said, his voice steady. "But we won't know for sure unless we test it. If focus is the key, then maybe you can control where and when you slip through time."

Lucy shook her head, panic rising in her chest. "No. Absolutely not. I can't—I don't know how to stop it, Michael. What if I can't come back next time? What if I drag you into another dangerous situation?"

"Then we'll figure it out together," St. Michael said firmly. "You're not alone in this, Lucy. Whatever this is, we'll take it one step at a time. I'll be with you for all of it."

Lucy swallowed hard, tears pricking her eyes. She wanted to believe him, to trust that they could figure this out, but the fear was still too raw. "I need time," she said softly. "I need to go through more of my mum's work. There's so much I haven't read yet."

St. Michael nodded. "Then we'll start there."

Lucy hesitated, biting her lip. "It's not that simple. Most of her stuff is in a self-storage unit near Croydon. I don't have a car, and even if I did, there's no way I could fit it all in my flat."

"Then we'll bring it here," St. Michael said without hesitation. "I've got a car. We can make as many trips as we need. My office is hopefully big enough to hold everything, and it'll give us a proper base to work from."

Lucy stared at him, her heart swelling with gratitude. "You'd do that for me?"

"Of course," he said, smiling. "We're in this together, remember? You're not doing this alone anymore."

She nodded, her resolve strengthening. "Thank you. There's a lot of shit in there as well, so I'll go through that tonight and work out what we need to bring. Then we'll go from there. Meet back here tomorrow?"

"Deal," St. Michael said, rising from his chair. "And Lucy, call me. Day or night, if you find anything, if anything happens. Don't try to handle it on your own."

"I won't," she promised.

As Lucy was just about to walk through the door to leave the office, she stopped and leant back to look at St. Michael. "I take it this means you believe me now?" she said, with a slight grin on her face.

St. Michael smiled back at her. "I suppose I do."

"Thank you, Michael," Lucy said just before she closed the door behind her.

The door clicked shut behind her, but the weight of what they'd seen lingered.

* * *

Lucy had left St. Michael's office with a thousand questions, but one clear instruction: find answers. By the time she reached the unit, the afternoon light was already fading.

The storage unit seemed quieter than before, except for the faint buzz of the overhead strip light. She sat on the floor, surrounded by open boxes and scattered notebooks. Most of the journals were carefully labelled, others with loose pages spilling out the sides. She'd arranged a section of her mother's work into a rough semicircle around her, trying to make sense of the chaos.

One journal rested in her lap. She turned the pages slowly, scanning each line with growing frustration. Evelyn's handwriting was familiar—steady, looping—but the contents weren't as clear. Some entries listed names, places, and dates. Others read more like personal thoughts, scribbled quickly, almost like someone keeping track of what they'd seen rather than what they'd read.

"Come on, Mum," Lucy muttered. "You left breadcrumbs, but where's the fucking loaf?"

She closed the journal and let it rest beside her. The unit felt heavier than when she'd first arrived, like the air had thickened around her. Somewhere in all of this, there had to be a clue. Something that explained what she'd seen in Nuremberg, what was happening to her. But the more she read, the more it felt like chasing shadows.

Her eyes landed on another journal near the back of the pile. It was older, the leather worn and the spine cracked. She pulled it free and flipped through the pages, letting them fall open where they wanted.

She stopped flipping when she noticed how much had been written.

Most of the entries so far had been short—notes, fragmented thoughts. But this one stretched across nearly a full page. The handwriting was faster, more uneven, like it had been written in a rush. Lucy frowned, adjusting the journal in her lap.

She hadn't been looking for anything specific, but something about the way the entry spilled across the page made her pause.

She began to read.

"2nd December 1805.

*Napoleon's victory at Austerlitz. A
turning point of destiny. The speech
after the battle. It was haunting,
electrifying. The air itself seemed to
hum with possibility, as though time*

Lucy leaned forward, the tone was unmistakably personal, as though Evelyn had stood there, in the aftermath of Austerlitz, surrounded by the echoes of history. Her descriptions were vivid—too vivid to be imagined. Evelyn wrote about the chaos of the battlefield, the blood-streaked faces of soldiers, and Napoleon standing on a makeshift platform, addressing his troops.

Her notes grew more cryptic as they continued:

Lucy sat back, the journal trembling slightly in her hands. Her mind raced with questions. The Order of the Nexus—her mother had never explained them, at least not in the entries Lucy had read before.

The Nexus sounded familiar to Lucy. She rummaged through her bag and pulled out the notepad Evelyn had filled out at the Great Fire of London.

"Where is it?" she muttered to herself as she flipped the pages until she landed on it. Her fingers traced her mother's writing as she read her scribbles aloud.

"Should the Nexus interfere with the fire's spread, huge risk of Quantum Time Collisions. Further observations required back at Pudding Lane."

Who were they? Lucy thought. Evelyn's notes painted them as shadowy and enigmatic, their motives unclear. If Evelyn had been at Austerlitz, monitoring them, then it must have been important.

A dark thought crept into Lucy's mind. What if The Order of the Nexus weren't just observers? What if they were involved in something bigger? And if her mother had been following their movements, had it been dangerous? Could it have even had something to do with Evelyn's death?

Lucy closed the journal, her heart pounding. She didn't have all the answers, but one thing was clear. She knew where she and St. Michael had to go next.

She grabbed her phone from the coffee table and called St. Michael's number. It rang twice before his voice, brimming with a mix of excitement and curiosity, came through the line.

"Lucy! Have you found something?"

Lucy couldn't help but smile at his eagerness. "I have… at least I think I have," she said, her tone urgent.

"In one of my mum's journals. It's about Austerlitz. Napoleon. She was there."

There was a brief pause. "She was where?" His voice sharpened, though it carried an edge of disbelief. "Are you saying Evelyn…?"

"Yes," Lucy interrupted. "Her notes—they're not just research. They're firsthand accounts. Like the Great Fire, she writes about being there, after the battle, watching Napoleon give a speech. And she mentions something else, although I'm not too sure what it is: The Order of the Nexus. She mentioned them in her notes about the fire, too."

"The what?" St. Michael's voice was confused. "Lucy, you've lost me. What's the Order of the Nexus?"

"I'm not entirely sure," Lucy admitted, flipping back through the journal. "She wrote about them being at Austerlitz, watching the speech. She described them as being drawn to 'moments of great significance,' moments that ripple through history. She didn't explain much about who they are or what they want, but it sounds like they're more than just historians."

St. Michael let out a low whistle. "That's… ominous. You think they were a threat to her?"

"I don't know," Lucy said quickly, though the thought had crossed her mind more than once. "But if she was watching them, it means this speech is important. We need to see it."

There was rustling on St. Michael's end of the line, as if he were already preparing for their next move. "All right," he said. "If we're going back to 1805, let's try not to be seen. If we are though, we're going to need to look the part. I don't think my everyday tweed is going to fit in somehow."

Lucy smirked despite herself. "What do you suggest? Maybe something Napoleonic?"

"Well," St. Michael said, dragging the word out with theatrical flair, "I might have a coat or two that could pass as early 19th century. And a cravat. You know, just in case."

"Of course you do," Lucy said, rolling her eyes. "You'd better bring a spare for me. I don't exactly have anything in my wardrobe that screams 'Austerlitz chic.'"

"Consider it done," he said. Then his tone softened. "Are you all right, Lucy? I know this is a lot."

She paused, her gaze drifting to the chaos of her surroundings. "I don't know," she admitted. "I feel like I'm unravelling everything I thought I knew about my mum—and about myself. But I can't stop. I need to understand why this is happening to me. And why it happened to her."

"And we will," St. Michael said firmly. "We'll figure it out. Together. But listen," his voice became more serious, "bring everything you found about this tomorrow. Her notes, journals, anything about Austerlitz or the Order of the Nexus. It might help trigger the slip—or at least help us understand how it works."

Lucy nodded, even though he couldn't see her. "Alright. I'll bring everything."

Lucy felt a flicker of hope, fragile but real. "Thanks, Michael. For everything."

"Anytime," he said. "And listen, if you find anything else tonight, call me. If not, I'll see you tomorrow."

Lucy smiled faintly. "Of course. Goodnight, Michael."

"Goodnight, Lucy."

As the call ended, Lucy set her phone down and looked around the unit. The mess still overwhelmed her, but now it felt purposeful, like pieces of a puzzle waiting to be assembled. She picked up Evelyn's journal again, flipping back to the entry on Austerlitz. Her mother's words seemed to leap off the page, filled with urgency and warning.

Lucy's determination hardened. She didn't know what they would find at Austerlitz, but if the Nexus had been there once… who was to say they wouldn't be again?

CHAPTER 5
The Warning

Lucy clutched the straps of her backpack tightly as she stepped out of Finchley station and into the cool morning air. Evelyn's notes were zipped inside, pressing reassuringly against her back. The straps dug into her shoulders, but she didn't mind; it was a small discomfort compared to the unease that began to creep into her chest.

The street was quiet, the usual hum of the morning commute subdued by the soft mist curling around the buildings. Lucy pulled her coat tighter against the chill as she turned down a narrow alley. A shortcut she'd discovered on her way back the day before. It was only a couple of minutes from St. Michael's office, and though the alley was a little eerie, it halved her walk. The quicker she got there, the better.

Her boots tapped against the uneven pavement, the sound too loud in the hush of the alley. The fog clung to the air like a heavy curtain, muffling everything around her. Normally, she wouldn't have thought much of it, but this morning felt… different.

The sensation crept in slowly, like the faintest ripple in the air. It was the same strange energy she had felt before her previous slips. A hum she couldn't quite hear, a pull she couldn't quite resist. Lucy froze mid-step, her chest tightening. Her fingers gripped the straps of her backpack, her knuckles white. Evelyn's journals, tucked inside, seemed to pulse with significance, though she knew it was just her imagination. She scanned her surroundings, heart pounding.

Is it happening again? Panic prickled at the edges of her mind. The idea of slipping without St. Michael—without anyone—terrified her. She didn't feel in control. She didn't know where she might end up. And worse, she didn't know if she'd be able to return. But this time, the sensation felt distant, almost muted. It wasn't like before. It wasn't centred on her. Relief flickered—then vanished.

The charged air shifted, giving way to something colder, heavier. She felt it like a weight pressing down on her chest. The unmistakable feeling of being watched.

Lucy quickened her pace, her pulse hammering in her ears. The alley felt impossibly long. She told herself it was nothing, that the silence wasn't unnatural. But her instincts screamed otherwise.

Before she could make sense of it, the hum intensified, the air rippling in front of her. Lucy's gaze snapped to the distortion forming in the mist ahead. Her stomach dropped as she watched the space ripple and bend, the mist swirling unnaturally around a single point. It was the same way the world had shifted when she slipped. Only this time, someone else was stepping through.

The ripple solidified with an eerie smoothness, and a man emerged. He didn't stumble or hesitate like she had when returning from the Great Fire or Nuremberg. He moved with fluid precision, as if the transition had been entirely under his control. His figure became clear as the mist settled back into place: a tall man dressed in a black zip-up hoodie, cargo trousers, and boots. Hood up. But what caught Lucy's eye was his face—or rather, the stark white mask that obscured it.

The mask was ancient-looking, its surface smooth and solid, with inlets for the eyes and mouth. It contrasted jarringly with his modern clothing, giving him an unsettling presence that seemed to belong both everywhere and nowhere.

Before Lucy could react, he crossed the short distance between them in three quick, deliberate strides. His gloved hand shot out, gripping her arm and slamming her against the rough brick wall. The straps of her backpack dug painfully into her shoulders, and the edge of Evelyn's notes pressed sharply into her back.

"Lucy Calder," he said, his voice calm but cutting. The way he said her name sent a chill down her spine.

She winced, her breath coming in short gasps. "Who are you?" she demanded, her voice laced with fear but steady.

He tilted his head slightly, the gesture both curious and mocking. "You're playing with forces you don't understand," he said. His voice was low, deliberate, each word precise. "And you've drawn attention."

"Let me go," Lucy snapped, struggling against his grip. "I don't know what you're talking about!"

The man ignored her protest, his masked face close to hers. "The Order of the Nexus is watching," he said sharply. "You're walking a path far more dangerous than you realise."

Lucy froze at the mention of the Nexus. Her heart thudded painfully against her ribcage. "What do you know about them?" she demanded, her voice trembling. "What do you mean, 'watching'?"

The man didn't answer. Instead, he tightened his grip just enough to make her wince. "Your mother knew when to stop," he said, his tone a mix of disdain and warning. "She understood the cost."

The mention of her mother's name hit Lucy like a blow to the chest. Her mouth went dry. "What do you know about her?" she whispered, her voice barely audible. "What cost?"

The man leaned back slightly, his head tilting again as though appraising her. "Evelyn knew better than to challenge us. You would do well to follow her example."

Lucy's fear gave way to anger, her pulse hammering with frustration. "You don't know me," she spat. "You don't know anything about what I'm doing!"

"The Nexus knows enough," he replied coldly. "You've been warned."

Before she could respond, his grip loosened, and he stepped back, his movements calm and deliberate. Lucy pressed herself against the wall, her breathing ragged as she watched him.

"What do you want from me?" she shouted, but the man didn't answer. Instead, the air around him began to shift again. The ripple returned, this time centred on him. The mist swirled, the edges of his figure blurring as though he were dissolving into it.

Lucy's eyes widened as she realised what was happening. He was leaving. Slipping through time. The distortion grew, the ripple consuming him entirely, and with a faint hum, he disappeared, the mist swirling back into place as if he had never been there.

Unlike her own chaotic slips, his departure was precise, controlled—effortless. He knew what he was doing.

Lucy stood frozen for several seconds, her mind racing. Her hand flew to the straps of her backpack, clutching them tightly as if Evelyn's notes could somehow ground her. He had slipped the same way she had. He could do what she could do, only better.

The mention of Evelyn—her mother's knowledge of the Nexus—only left Lucy with more questions. Her chest heaved as she tried to steady her breathing, the chill of the alley sinking into her skin.

Her fear finally gave way to urgency. She had to get to St. Michael. Tightening her grip on her bag, she pushed off the wall and broke into a sprint, her boots pounding against the uneven pavement.

When she reached the office building, she jabbed at the buzzer frantically, her breath coming in short, sharp gasps.

"Come on, come on," she muttered, glancing over her shoulder at the misty street as if expecting the masked man to reappear.

The speaker crackled. "Lucy?" St. Michael's voice came through, calm but tinged with confusion.

"It's me! Let me in!" she said breathlessly, leaning heavily against the wall.

A second later, the lock buzzed, and she pushed through the door, taking the stairs two at a time. She burst into St. Michael's office, her chest heaving, her face pale.

The sound of the door slamming shut made St. Michael, seated behind his desk, look up in alarm.

"What happened?" St. Michael asked, standing immediately.

Lucy didn't answer at first. She dropped her backpack onto the desk with a thud, gripping the edge of the table as though she needed to steady herself. Her wide, panicked eyes met St. Michael's, and he saw something different this time. Raw fear.

"Lucy?" he prompted gently.

She ran a hand through her hair, pacing back and forth like a caged animal. "I— He— Someone followed me," she stammered. "No, not just followed. He travelled through time, Michael. Like me."

St. Michael froze. "What do you mean, travelled through time?"

Lucy turned sharply to face him. "I mean, he literally came through time. I saw it happen. He stepped out of nothing, like… like he tore through the air and appeared in the alley."

St. Michael's eyes narrowed, his mouth opening to question her, but Lucy was already continuing, her voice trembling. "He was wearing a mask, this white, solid mask. It looked old, but the rest of him—" She gestured wildly, searching for the words. "He was dressed like us. A hoodie, cargo trousers, boots. But he wasn't from here,

Michael. He could do what I could—but he knew what he was doing. It was controlled."

St. Michael rubbed his chin, "and what did he do? Did he say anything?"

Lucy let out a shaky breath, nodding. "He grabbed me, shoved me up against the wall. I couldn't get away. And then he said my name." She swallowed hard. "He said my name. He knew exactly who I was."

St. Michael's concern deepened, but he kept his voice calm. "And then?"

"He warned me. He said I was 'playing with forces I didn't understand,' and that the Nexus is watching me." Her voice cracked on the word 'Nexus.' "He said I was on a dangerous path and that I needed to stop. But the worst part—" She broke off, glancing at her bag.

St. Michael took a step closer, his tone gentle but urgent. "What?"

"He mentioned my mum," Lucy said softly. "He said she 'knew when to stop.' Michael, he knew her. Not just of her. He knew her."

St. Michael let out a low whistle, running a hand over his head. "This Nexus again…" He trailed off, his voice growing grimmer. "It sounds like he's tied to them."

Lucy nodded slowly. "He has to be. But why me? Why now?"

St. Michael gestured to her bag. "Maybe the answers are in there. Let's go through what your mum left behind."

Lucy unzipped her backpack, pulling out Evelyn's journals and spreading them across the desk. She flipped to the page she'd marked the night before, the one describing Austerlitz and Napoleon's speech. "Here," she said, sliding the notebook toward him. "This is what I found last night."

St. Michael leaned over the desk, reading Evelyn's words carefully. His brow furrowed as he traced a finger under her descriptions of the speech. "'A turning point of destiny.'" He muttered. St. Michael looked up at Lucy. "She really was there, wasn't she?"

Lucy nodded. "She had to be. And if she could do it… Michael, she could do what I can do."

St. Michael straightened, letting out a long breath. "And now this man shows up, warning you to stop. You think they're connected?"

Lucy hesitated. "I don't know. But he seemed certain in what he was saying."

"Well, I think I might have found something too," St. Michael said, turning back to his desk. He rummaged through his shelves, pulling out a battered book. He flipped through the pages before stopping abruptly. "Here—Nuremberg," he said, passing the document to Lucy.

"I had a look through accounts of the Nuremberg Rally after we had been there. I've never seen this before. I'd almost be certain to say this didn't exist before we went there." He said, pointing to a passage.

Lucy leaned forward, frowning as she read aloud.

"'*During the rally, guards reported firing at unknown intruders who disappeared without a trace. Witnesses described the intruders as a woman and a Black man. The guards, deemed unfit for duty, claimed they had encountered ghosts.* '" She looked up, her face pale. "That was us." she said softly.

St. Michael held his gaze on Lucy. "We left a mark. That could be how they know about you."

Lucy stared at him, her thoughts racing. "He said I'd drawn attention… if you're saying you've never seen this before, do you think we changed history?" Lucy asked.

"I think so," St. Michael said, leaning back on his desk.

"We have to be more careful," Lucy said, placing the document back down.

"Agreed," St. Michael said. "And we'll start with Austerlitz. If we're going to slip again, we need to be prepared."

St. Michael stepped away from the desk, holding up the two outfits he had prepared with a theatrical flourish. "On that note of being prepared, Voilà! Authentic-ish 1805 attire, as promised."

Lucy raised an eyebrow at the garments. "Wow. Did you raid a costume shop?"

"Hardly," St. Michael replied with mock indignation. "I have a friend at the National Theatre who owed me a favour. These are the real deal—accurate down to the buttons. Or so he said."

He handed Lucy her outfit: an elegant empire-waist gown in soft blue, complete with delicate lace trim and a matching bonnet. A pale shawl draped over the ensemble, its soft texture surprisingly warm against her fingers. "Very genteel," she remarked, holding the dress up in front of her. "But there's so much fabric. I'm gonna trip over myself."

"You'll manage," St. Michael said with a grin, unfolding his own outfit. His consisted of a dark, double-breasted military-style greatcoat, tailored breeches, a white cravat, and polished leather boots. The outfit exuded authority, though it looked slightly out of place draped over his modern stance.

Lucy snorted. "You look like Napoleon's right-hand man. I should probably start saluting."

St. Michael struck a mock-serious pose, straightening his coat. "Perhaps you should, Miss Calder. A little respect for history never hurt anyone."

"Respect is earned, not worn," Lucy teased back. She turned toward the office bathroom with her bundle of clothing. "Give me a minute to wrangle this monstrosity."

"Same here," St. Michael said, disappearing behind a partition in the office.

When Lucy emerged, she found St. Michael adjusting his cravat in the reflection of a windowpane. He turned to her, his expression slipping briefly into surprise before softening into a smile.

"Well?" Lucy asked, twirling awkwardly to display the gown. "Do I look like I belong in 1805?"

"You look perfect," St. Michael said earnestly. Then, with a sly grin, he added, "Although I think you'll need to work on your posture if you want to pass as a refined lady of the era."

"Excuse me?" Lucy retorted, placing a hand on her hip in mock offense. "I'm plenty refined."

"Oh, absolutely," St. Michael said with a laugh, straightening his greatcoat. "You'll fit right in—assuming you don't trip over your hem."

Lucy shot him a playful glare. "Let's hope I don't take you down with me." She gestured at his boots. "A bit shiny for the battlefield, aren't they?"

St. Michael glanced down, feigning indignation. "These boots are historically accurate, I'll have you know."

"Sure they are," Lucy said, smirking. "Let's just hope they're comfortable for time travel."

Back at the desk, Lucy had laid out Evelyn's journals. Her meticulous handwriting spread out like a map to the past. Lucy adjusted the bonnet nervously, staring at the notes, as if they might leap off the page and guide her directly to Austerlitz.

"So," she began, her voice betraying her nerves, "how do we actually… start?"

St. Michael leaned against the desk, arms open. "You focus. Focus on the time. You've done it before," St.

Michael said gently, gesturing to the journals. "Everything you need is here. Let it guide you."

Lucy took a deep breath and nodded. She pulled Evelyn's notes closer, her fingers brushing the familiar paper. Her mother's words stared back at her, a mixture of academic observation and deeply personal insight. "Austerlitz," she whispered, letting the name settle in her mind. "Napoleon's victory. The speech."

She closed her eyes, focusing on the descriptions Evelyn had left behind. The cold air of the battlefield, the tension of the soldiers, the cheers of triumph mingled with the groans of the dying. She let the imagery build in her mind, willing herself to connect with it.

Nothing happened.

Lucy opened her eyes, frustration creeping in. "It's not working."

St. Michael stepped closer, his voice calm and steady. "Take your time. I don't think it's a switch you can just flip. You're not doing this alone, remember? I'm right here."

Lucy inhaled deeply, calming herself. She adjusted the notes, centring the page that described Napoleon's speech. She ran her fingers across her mother's handwriting, grounding herself in the tangible connection to Evelyn. "Concentrate," she muttered to herself. "You can do this."

She closed her eyes again, this time focusing on the sensation she remembered from her previous slips. The strange hum in the air, the pull deep in her chest, the way the world seemed to fold in on itself before unravelling into something new. She thought of Austerlitz—the frozen air, the sound of war, the triumph etched into the faces of soldiers. She thought of Napoleon's voice, carrying through the chaos like a beacon.

Her pulse quickened as the air around her began to shift. It started as a faint ripple, a subtle disturbance at the edge of her awareness. Her breath hitched. "It's happening," she whispered.

St. Michael straightened, stepping closer. "Are you sure?"

Lucy nodded, her hands gripping the edge of the desk as the sensation grew stronger. The hum intensified, vibrating through her body. The edges of the room began to blur, colours bleeding into one another like a watercolour painting left in the rain. Her heartbeat thundered in her ears, matching the rhythm of the distortion around her.

"Michael…" Her voice trembled. "It's pulling me."

St. Michael reached out and grabbed her hand, his grip firm and reassuring. "Together, then," he said, tightening his grip. "Wherever this leads."

The distortion deepened, the room folding and twisting around them. Evelyn's journals shimmered on the desk, their ink glowing faintly before dissolving into the swirling light. The pull became overwhelming, dragging Lucy and St. Michael into its grip.

And then, with a rush of air and a burst of light, the office was gone.

CHAPTER 6
Burned Truths

The pull this time was different. Where before there had been chaos—sights and sounds blurring into one another as Lucy hurtled through time—this slip was almost serene. She could feel the tug in her chest, firm but not overwhelming, as if an invisible tether were guiding her instead of dragging her. The swirl of colours around her was softer, more fluid, and her breathing remained steady.

When the world solidified again, Lucy staggered but managed to stay on her feet. The sharp, biting air hit her lungs immediately, and she gasped, clutching St. Michael's arm for support. They were standing on uneven, frost-coated ground, the smell of smoke and iron heavy in the air. Around them, the world slowly came into focus: rolling hills dusted with snow, a battlefield scarred by cannon fire, and the murmur of voices carried on the cold wind.

St. Michael steadied her, his face breaking into a wide grin. "You did it, Lucy! You actually did it."

She looked up at him, her breath fogging between them. Relief and pride surged through her, and she flung her arms around him in a fierce hug. "We did it," she whispered, her voice shaking with exhilaration. "We actually made it."

He chuckled, squeezing her shoulders before stepping back to look her over. "And look at you! No soot, no singed hair. That was basically professional."

Lucy laughed, the sound light and genuine. For a brief moment, the weight of everything—the danger, the questions about her abilities, the encounter with the masked man—seemed to lift. "Maybe I'm finally getting the hang of this," she said, though her tone was tinged with cautious optimism.

The reality of their surroundings quickly settled back over them. The battlefield was a solemn landscape of ruin, stretching out in all directions under the muted grey sky. Patches of frost clung to the churned earth, stained dark with blood and ash. Broken weapons lay scattered across the ground, their jagged edges catching the faint winter light. Cannonballs lay half-buried in mud beside shattered carts, their cracked wheels frozen in place. Bodies, some frozen in contorted positions, were scattered across the expanse, their uniforms tattered and stiffened by the cold. The air was sharp and heavy, carrying the faint smell of smoke and decay.

St. Michael's expression turned grim as he surveyed the scene. "The battle's over," he said softly. "This must be just after Austerlitz."

Lucy nodded, her gaze drifting to the distant ridge where clusters of soldiers were gathered. At the centre of it all, standing on a makeshift platform, was a figure she recognised instantly: Napoleon. His presence was commanding, even from afar, and the soldiers around him watched with a mixture of awe and exhaustion.

"Come on," St. Michael whispered, tugging her arm. "We need to stay out of sight."

They moved carefully toward a cluster of broken carts near the edge of the ridge, crouching low to avoid drawing attention.

From their hiding place, they had a clear view of Napoleon and his officers. The emperor was speaking to his men, his voice carrying faintly over the distance.

St. Michael glanced at Lucy. "He'll be speaking French, of course. Let me know if you catch anything."

Lucy frowned, her heart pounding as she focused on the scene. Napoleon stood tall, his greatcoat billowing slightly in the cold wind. His voice was steady and commanding, carrying an undercurrent of triumph that resonated even across the language barrier.

"Soldats!" Napoleon's voice rang out, strong and clear. Lucy froze. She didn't *process* the words in French—they arrived in her mind already mostly translated, like memory instead of understanding. "I am satisfied with you," she murmured, translating instinctively.

St. Michael turned to her, his brows furrowing. "What did he say?"

Lucy hesitated, the realisation hitting her. "He said he's… satisfied with them. He's addressing the soldiers." She frowned, trying to reconcile what she was hearing. Most of the speech sounded like perfect English, but certain words—like soldats—remained in French, as if her mind couldn't quite make the leap.

Napoleon continued, his voice rising in intensity. "You justified everything I expected of your courage." Lucy blinked. The words were clear as day.

"What now?" St. Michael asked, his voice low.

Lucy didn't look at him. "He's praising their bravery," she said softly.

Napoleon's speech flowed on, the rhythm of his words captivating. "An army of 100,000 men, commanded by emperors, has been… déchirée." Lucy heard him say the word but didn't understand it. "Something about being torn apart," she guessed, frustration creeping into her voice.

Napoleon gestured grandly, his soldiers cheering as he spoke. "The results of this day will be immortal." The word came through clearly, as though it were spoken directly to her.

St. Michael glanced at her, his expression unreadable. "You're hearing all of that?"

"Most of it," Lucy admitted, her voice tinged with frustration. "It's like it's being translated in my head, but not completely. A few words don't make sense."

Napoleon's speech reached its climax, his voice swelling with emotion. "Let it be a lesson for the world that, as long as you defend me, no enemy can defeat us."

The soldiers erupted into cheers, their voices filling the cold air. Napoleon stood tall on the platform, basking in the adoration of his men. Lucy felt a strange mix of awe and unease as she watched him.

St. Michael leaned closer, his brow furrowed. "All I heard was French," he said quietly. "Every word."

Lucy turned to him, her pulse racing. "I don't know what's happening, Michael," she said, her voice barely above a whisper. "But I understood most of it. Not all, but enough. It's like… it's just there in my head."

Before St. Michael could respond, the soldiers began to disperse, their cheers fading into the distance as they marched off the ridge. Napoleon and his officers climbed down from the platform, their voices lost in the hum of activity.

"They're leaving," Lucy said, watching the scene unfold. The battlefield emptied as the soldiers retreated into the fog-draped hills.

St. Michael straightened, brushing frost from his coat. "No sign of Evelyn," he said grimly. "And no sign of the Nexus."

Lucy nodded, her jaw tightening. "Then we keep looking," she said firmly, though a shiver ran through her as the wind bit through her thin gown. "There has to be something here."

They exchanged a wary glance, the tension between curiosity and caution hanging in the air. As the last of Napoleon's troops disappeared into the distance, they stepped out of their hiding place and began to search the battlefield, the cold biting into their skin and the weight of unanswered questions pressing heavily on their shoulders.

Lucy pulled her shawl tighter around her shoulders, her breath visible in the biting cold. Every step she took felt deliberate, her boots crunching softly against the icy ground. St. Michael walked beside her, his eyes scanning the aftermath with a careful intensity.

"It's surreal," he said quietly, his voice barely above a whisper. "To see all of this. The end of one of the most famous battles in history."

Lucy nodded, her gaze lingering on a nearby cannon, its barrel cracked from the force of the battle. "It doesn't feel like history. It feels… wrong. Like we shouldn't be here."

St. Michael paused, crouching to examine a fallen soldier. The man's uniform was caked with mud, and his eyes, though frozen open, were unseeing. St. Michael stood, brushing frost from his gloves. "Your mother must have seen this," he said, glancing at Lucy. "She wrote about it. But why? Why here, out of all the battles she could've observed?"

Lucy sighed, her breath fogging in the air. "She must've thought it was important. Something about this moment—Napoleon's victory, his speech, the aftermath— it mattered to her. Maybe she was looking for someone, like the Nexus."

"Or she might have been looking for something else entirely," St. Michael added. "We don't know how much she understood about the way these moments work—or how they might connect to you."

They walked on in silence for a while, the sounds of the battlefield fading into the background. A few distant figures moved through the haze—soldiers gathering the wounded or salvaging supplies—but the area around Lucy and St. Michael remained eerily quiet.

"Do you think we're even looking in the right place?" Lucy asked after a few minutes.

"I'm not sure we'll know until we find something," St. Michael replied. "We might not even know what we're looking for until it's in front of us."

The air between them grew heavy, their steps slow and deliberate. Finally, St. Michael broke the silence. "Lucy," he said, turning to her. "You need to realise how incredible you are."

Lucy blinked, surprised by his sudden shift in tone. "What do you mean?"

He stopped walking and faced her fully. "What you can do—the time slips, the way you understood Napoleon's speech, it's not just unusual. It's extraordinary. There are people who study history their entire lives, people like me, and we'll never get as close to it as you have. And you're doing it with barely any preparation, barely any understanding of how it works. Do you realise how remarkable that is?"

Lucy shifted uncomfortably, her fingers clutching the edges of her shawl. "I don't feel remarkable. I feel like I'm stumbling through all of this. Half the time I don't even know what's happening, let alone how to control it."

"And yet," St. Michael said, his voice softening, "you keep going. You're learning. You brought us here, didn't you? On purpose. That's not stumbling. That's progress."

Lucy looked at him, his words sinking in. She gave a small, hesitant smile. "Thanks, Michael. I'm just… trying to figure it all out."

"You're not alone in this," he said. "You've got me, and we'll figure it out together."

They resumed walking, their pace slower now as they took in the desolation around them. St. Michael's gaze seemed distant, his steps less purposeful. Lucy noticed the shift and glanced at him.

"What is it?" she asked.

He hesitated before speaking, his voice quieter than before. "I was just thinking about how much my son would love this."

Lucy's steps faltered. "Your son?"

"Theodore," St. Michael said, a faint smile tugging at the corners of his mouth. "Teddy, for short. He's eight. Smart as a whip and loves history. He'd be fascinated by all of this. The cannons, the uniforms, even the mud. He'd probably be asking me a million questions right about now."

Lucy felt a pang of sympathy. "Does he know about your work?"

"He knows I'm a historian," St. Michael said. "But not this—this is a bit beyond what I could explain to an eight-year-old. And the truth is… I don't see him as much as I'd like."

Lucy frowned. "Why not?"

St. Michael's expression darkened slightly. "His mum—Michelle—and I… we didn't end well. We were happy at first, but after Teddy was born, things started to unravel. We argued. We argued a lot. We said things we couldn't take back… She eventually left, taking Teddy with her.

"That's awful," Lucy said softly.

"It is," St. Michael admitted. "I try to visit when I can, but it's never enough. Michelle and I… we've both made mistakes. But Teddy—he's the one who pays for it. He doesn't deserve that."

Lucy looked at him, her own memories surfacing. "That sounds a lot like me and my mum," she said quietly.

St. Michael turned to her, his gaze curious. "You and Evelyn?"

"We were close—once," Lucy said. "But after my dad disappeared, everything changed. She threw herself into her work, and I… I pulled away. I resented her for it. The last time we talked, we argued. It was so stupid, but I said awful stuff. I never got the chance to make it right."

"Lucy…" St. Michael began, but she shook her head.

"Don't wait too long, Michael," she said, her voice trembling. "You still have time to fix things with Teddy. Don't let resentment or pride get in the way. He needs you, even if you can't see him as much as you'd like. Just… make sure he knows you're there."

St. Michael stared at her for a long moment, her words settling heavily in the air. Finally, he nodded. "You're right," he said softly. "I can't change the past, but I can do better for him. I owe him that."

Lucy gave him a small, sad smile. "That's all that matters. Just… don't let it slip away."

They walked on in silence, the cold air swirling around them. Despite the desolation of the battlefield, Lucy felt a flicker of warmth between them. A shared understanding that eased the weight of their regrets, if only for a moment.

St. Michael walked a few paces ahead, his eyes scanning the area. Neither of them spoke much, their conversation from earlier leaving them both lost in thought.

Then, something caught Lucy's eye.

Amid the churned mud and trampled frost, a slip of paper lay pinned beneath a broken wheel. It looked out of place—too clean, too deliberate, as though it didn't belong in this desolate scene.

"Wait," Lucy said, stopping.

St. Michael turned back as Lucy knelt and reached for the paper. The moment her fingers brushed the edge, her breath caught. The writing was unmistakable—precise and looping, written with the same care and purpose as the notes she'd spent hours poring over.

"This is hers," she whispered, standing and holding it up.

"Your mother's?" St. Michael asked, stepping closer.

Lucy nodded, her fingers trembling as she unfolded the paper. "I'd recognise her handwriting anywhere. This must have been what she was working on here."

The words were faded in places, smudged slightly, but still legible. Lucy's eyes darted over the page, reading fragments that made her pulse quicken:

"This moment is pivotal. The victory shifts the balance of power across Europe. But it's more than that. The Nexus doesn't simply observe; they intervene. Napoleon's victory here is tied to something larger—something connected to the Universal Timeline itself. If my previous fears are true, then this place is…"

Lucy's words trailed off as she turned the page. "It's about why she was here, what the Nexus wanted—"

A sudden ripple in the air made her stop mid-sentence.

The hum was faint at first, barely noticeable, but then it grew louder, like a resonating vibration that seemed to ripple through the very fabric of reality. Lucy froze, her eyes snapping to the space directly in front of her as the air distorted and bent.

"Oh no," she breathed.

St. Michael tensed beside her. "Lucy…"

The distortion deepened, swirling and twisting until two figures stepped through, their movements smooth and deliberate, as though they had rehearsed the act countless times.

They were dressed the same as the last, modern, practical clothing—black hoodies, cargo trousers and boots— the unmistakable white masks. One of them carried a slim, confident posture, while the other loomed larger, his shoulders squared in silent authority.

Lucy stepped back instinctively, clutching the paper to her chest. St. Michael moved with her, his body tense, his eyes darting between the two figures.

The two Nexians turned toward each other, their movements deliberate and almost synchronized. The taller one spoke first, his voice sharp and guttural:

"Zalith n'kael. Fikran thal'marak vekthar gathil."

The second Nexian inclined his head slightly and replied in a lower, harsher tone:

"Morae velar nalar thil'mak. Kreth vekra zarath."

The words hung in the cold air, cutting through the silence with an otherworldly rhythm. Lucy froze as the unfamiliar sounds reached her ears. Unlike other languages she had encountered since her abilities awakened, this one was impenetrable. No meanings formed in her mind, no instinctual understanding bridged the gap. It was utterly alien.

Her confusion began to tighten her chest. *What is this?* she thought, her heart pounding. *Why don't I understand it?*

It wasn't just strange, it was unsettling. The words were sharp, their intent clear even without comprehension, and yet they were cloaked in an impenetrable veil of secrecy.

The Nexians turned their attention back toward her, their masked faces unreadable, but the air seemed to grow heavier with their gaze.

Before Lucy could react, the taller Nexian strode forward with unnerving precision. His masked face tilted slightly, as if studying her, and then his gaze dropped to the paper in her hands.

"Drop it," he said, his voice low and calm.

Lucy hesitated, her pulse racing. She took another step back, but her foot slipped slightly on the icy ground.

The Nexian didn't wait. He extended his gloved hand, his fingers splayed, and the air around him seemed to shimmer. A flicker of orange and yellow light danced at his palm, growing brighter as it twisted into the shape of a small flame. The fire glowed unnaturally, its edges rippling like liquid, and for a fleeting moment, Lucy caught the faintest flicker of colour in his eyes behind the mask, a deep, fiery orange.

"Lucy," St. Michael said sharply, grabbing her arm.

Before she could process what was happening, the Nexian thrust his hand forward, and the flame shot toward the paper in her hands. The fireball was small, fast, and precise. Lucy barely had time to drop the note before it ignited.

The flames consumed the paper in seconds, leaving nothing but ash that scattered in the cold wind.

"No!" Lucy shouted, her voice trembling with anger. She stepped forward, but St. Michael held her back.

The second Nexian tilted his head, his voice carrying a quiet menace. "You were warned," he said. "But you didn't listen. Now you've gone too far, Custodian."

The word sent a chill through Lucy. "Custodian?" she repeated, her voice low.

The first Nexian ignored her question. "This ends now," he said simply, raising both hands. The air around him shimmered again as twin orbs of fire began to take shape, one in each palm. His companion mirrored the action, their movements perfectly synchronized.

The flames were brighter this time, pulsing with heat that Lucy could feel even from several feet away. The Nexians' eyes behind their masks glowed brighter, matching the fire in colour and intensity.

"Lucy," St. Michael said urgently, his voice tight with fear. "We need to—"

Before he could finish, both Nexians thrust their arms forward, the fireballs crackling as they prepared to launch.

Panic surged through Lucy. Her anger and fear twisted together, building into something she couldn't contain. She felt it first as a low hum in her chest, then as a rush of energy that shot through her veins like lightning. It wasn't like slipping through time, this was different. It wasn't pulling her; it was pushing outward, a force she couldn't control.

She gasped, clutching her hands as the energy surged toward them. Her vision blurred, and for a moment, everything turned white.

The next thing she knew, her hands were raised, and a powerful gust of icy wind and snow erupted from her fingertips. The freezing air howled as it struck the Nexians with incredible force, knocking them backward and extinguishing their fire. They hit the ground hard, the frost clinging to their clothing as they struggled to rise.

Lucy staggered, her vision clearing. Her hands were shaking, her breath ragged. She turned to St. Michael, her voice trembling. "What just happened?"

He didn't answer. His eyes were wide, his expression a mix of awe and terror. "We need to go," he said finally, grabbing her arm. "Now."

The Nexians were already beginning to recover, their movements slow but deliberate. Lucy's heart pounded as she focused on the office, willing herself to slip back there.

The pull came almost immediately, the familiar distortion enveloping them. The last thing Lucy saw before the battlefield vanished was the Nexians, their masked faces turning toward her as the world dissolved into light.

The transition back to St. Michael's office was smoother than Lucy had anticipated. For the first time, she felt in control as the pull overtook her. It wasn't the chaotic rush she'd experienced before—it was purposeful, almost calm, as though the slip recognised her focus and obeyed.

The familiar hum took over her senses, and the battlefield dissolved into a swirl of light and sound. Before she could process it, the warmth of the office replaced the bitter chill of Austerlitz. Lucy stumbled slightly as her boots hit the polished wooden floor, her breath fogging in the office's cozy air.

They had returned.

* * *

St. Michael's desk was still strewn with Evelyn's journals. The contrast between the frigid battlefield and the office was almost overwhelming. Lucy still felt the frost biting at her skin and the weight of mud clinging to her boots. She glanced down, her footprints leaving a trail of damp grime across the floor.

St. Michael, shaking the snow from his coat, looked at her with wide eyes. "Lucy," he said, his voice still carrying the urgency from the battlefield. "What... what just happened out there?"

Lucy dropped into the nearest chair, her hands trembling. "I don't know," she said, her voice barely above a whisper. "I didn't even think. It just... happened."

St. Michael sat across from her, his expression a mixture of awe and concern. "You didn't think?" he pressed. "Lucy, you conjured—whatever that was—with your bare hands."

"It wasn't something I chose to do," Lucy said, gripping the armrests of the chair as if anchoring herself to the moment. "I was scared, angry, and it felt like... like something inside me snapped. The energy—it built up so fast, and before I knew it, I was throwing snow and wind at them. I didn't even know I could do that!"

St. Michael leaned forward, "you've slipped through time, Lucy. And now you've… summoned something. Energy, elements—I don't even know what to call it. Do you have any idea what it means?"

"No," she admitted, shaking her head. "It didn't feel like slipping."

St. Michael let out a long breath, leaning back against the wall. "And those people," he said, his voice dropping lower. "The fire—they summoned fire, Lucy. What do they want with you?"

Lucy's gaze dropped to the floor. "They called me a custodian," she said softly, the word unfamiliar yet weighted. "I've heard that word before, but not like this. Not directed at me. What does it even mean?"

"I don't know," St. Michael said, rubbing his temples. "But it's clear they don't want you knowing any of this. They burned your mother's note before you could finish reading it. Whatever Evelyn was trying to tell you—it's something they're desperate to keep hidden."

Lucy exhaled shakily, staring out of the window from the chair she was slumped in. "She was there," she murmured. "She wrote that note for a reason. If the Nexus wanted it gone, then it must've been important."

"Lucy," St. Michael said cautiously, his voice breaking the heavy quiet. "Back there—what were they saying to each other?"

Lucy lifted her head, her face pale and drawn. "I don't know," she said slowly, her voice tinged with frustration. "I didn't understand any of it. Not a single word."

St. Michael stepped away from the wall. "Nothing at all? Not even a phrase?"

She shook her head, her hands gripping the arms of the chair. "Nothing. And that's… that's never happened before, Michael. The other languages we've come across, I've been able to get at least something. Even when I didn't know the words, I could at least feel the meaning. But this…" She trailed off, her eyes narrowing in confusion. "This was completely different."

St. Michael began pacing the room, his boots leaving faint marks on the wooden floor. "It didn't even sound like anything I've ever heard," he muttered, almost to himself. "Not a dialect, not a regional accent, not even something ancient or obscure. It was… I don't know. Like it was from somewhere else entirely."

Lucy leaned forward, resting her elbows on her knees. "It wasn't just unfamiliar. It felt… wrong," she said quietly, her voice trembling. "I can't explain it. It was like it didn't belong—not there, not anywhere."

St. Michael paused mid-step, turning to face her. "Do you think it's… older? I mean, older than anything we know about?"

Lucy shrugged helplessly, her frustration bubbling to the surface. "I don't know, it could be literally anything."

"I don't like it," she admitted, her tone dropping to a whisper. "I don't like not being able to understand."

St. Michael moved closer, his expression softening. "It doesn't mean you've lost your abilities, Lucy," he said gently. "You've been thrown into things you weren't prepared for, and this is just… something new. Something we haven't encountered before."

Lucy looked up at him, her eyes searching his face. "But what if it's more than that?" she asked. "What if this is just the start of things I can't do? What if there's more out there—more that I'll never be able to… to grasp?"

St. Michael shook his head firmly. "Lucy, you've done things no one else has even dreamed of. If there's more out there, we'll figure it out. Together."

She leaned back in the chair, her gaze drifting to the frost-streaked window. The weight of the unknown pressed down on her chest, but St. Michael's words stayed with her, steadying her in the midst of her confusion.

St. Michael moved to his desk. Lucy heard the faint shuffle of paper, followed by a sharp intake of breath.

"Lucy," he said, his voice unreadable. "Come here."

She stood reluctantly, moving to his side. On the desk, where there had been nothing bar Evelyn's journals, now also lay a single folded piece of parchment.

Her stomach tightened. "What is that?"

"It wasn't here before we left," St. Michael said quietly. He hesitated for a moment, then picked it up. The handwriting was elegant, precise, yet completely unfamiliar and certainly not that of Evelyn's. He read aloud:

"Lucy Calder,

If you wish to uncover the answers you seek, meet me at Kilchurn Castle, Lochawe, Scotland. The 2nd of March, 1802. The truth awaits you there.

Alaric Vale."

The name hung in the air between them like an unspoken question.

"Alaric Vale," Lucy repeated, frowning. "Who the fucks that?"

"I don't know," St. Michael said, his gaze flicking back to the parchment. "But this—" He gestured to the note. "This isn't random. He knows your name, Lucy. He knows about us."

Lucy took a step back, her arms crossed tightly over her chest. "It's a trap," she said flatly. "It has to be. The Nexus just tried to kill us. They could've left this here to lure us out."

St. Michael shook his head, already moving to his laptop. "If they wanted to kill us, why not do it when we slipped back here? Why leave a note at all?" He opened the laptop and began typing. "Whoever this Alaric is, I don't think he's with them."

"You don't know that," Lucy argued, her voice rising. "This could be their way of messing with us. Of leading us into something we can't handle."

St. Michael glanced up from the screen, his expression steady. "Lucy, think about it. They had the chance to ambush us—here, where we're vulnerable. Whoever this Alaric guy is, I don't think he's working with the Nexus. It sounds like he wants to help us. To help you."

Lucy faltered, her gaze dropping to the parchment. The name "Alaric" seemed to pulse in her mind, its meaning elusive yet significant.

"And Kilchurn Castle?" she asked finally.

St. Michael turned the laptop toward her, displaying an image of the castle. Its crumbling walls and eerie silhouette stood against the backdrop of a misty loch. "Abandoned by the late 1700s, but still intact enough to hide in," he said. "If he's asking you to meet him there in 1802, there's a reason."

Lucy's jaw tightened. "Or it's the perfect place for an ambush."

St. Michael stepped closer, his tone softening but steady. "Lucy, you've been looking for answers since this all started. This—" he pointed to the note in her hands, "—this is the first real lead we've had. If there's even a chance Alaric can tell us something about Evelyn, about the Nexus, about why you're at the centre of all of this… don't you think it's worth it?"

She hesitated, her eyes flicking between him and the note. "It's a risk," she said quietly.

"It is," St. Michael agreed. "But what's the alternative? Sit here and wait for the Nexus to come for us again? At least if we go, we might get the upper hand. We'll be prepared this time."

Lucy exhaled shakily, staring at the elegant script. The truth tugged at her, insistent and unrelenting. Finally, she nodded. "Fine," she said, her voice steady but low. "We'll go. But if it's a trap…"

"We'll figure it out," St. Michael interrupted, offering her a faint smile. "Together."

"Together," Lucy echoed, tucking the note into her coat pocket. She glanced back out the window, her reflection staring back at her. Uncertain, but resolved.

And somewhere in the distance, Kilchurn Castle awaited.

CHAPTER 7
The Ties That Bind

"It's settled, then. We're going," St. Michael said, his voice steady, but his eyes searched Lucy's for confirmation.

Lucy bit her lip, her heart pounding as she stared at the note in her hand. The elegant script seemed to mock her hesitation, the name "*Alaric*" carrying both promise and threat. Every instinct screamed caution. *This could be a trap. It probably was a trap.* But beneath the fear, something stronger gnawed at her: desperation. Desperation to understand her abilities, to make sense of the strange, uncontrollable power that had upended her life. She needed answers—not just about her mother, but about herself.

She looked up at St. Michael, her fingers tightening around the parchment. "If this goes wrong…"

"It won't," he interrupted, his tone leaving no room for argument. "But if it does, we'll handle it."

Lucy nodded, exhaling slowly. "Fine. Let's do it."

St. Michael brought up the image of Kilchurn Castle, its crumbling walls and jagged silhouette sharp against the misty backdrop of Lochawe. He turned the screen toward her, and Lucy leaned in, studying every detail.

"This is where we're going," she murmured, half to herself. She tried to picture it. The cold air, the sound of waves lapping at the shore, the creak of wooden beams within the castle walls. Slowly, she closed her eyes, letting the image fill her mind.

St. Michael stood beside her, silent but watchful. "What do you need from me?" he asked.

"Just… stay close," Lucy replied, her voice low. She reached for his hand, her palm brushing his. The contact steadied her, his grip firm and reassuring.

She focused on the visual in front of her mind's eye. She willed the image to sharpen, to take shape. And then, with a slow inhale, she felt it: the hum.

This time, it wasn't a chaotic pull. It didn't crash over her like a wave or drag her into its grip. It began as a soft vibration, growing steadily, responding to her focus. She steadied herself, matching her breathing to the hum's pulse.

"It's beginning," she whispered, opening her eyes briefly to meet St. Michael's. He gave her a small nod, his face calm despite the tension in his posture.

The air around them rippled, bending and twisting at the edges of her vision. Colours bled together, muted and soft, as if the world was being painted anew. The office began to dissolve, its lines blurring as light seeped in from all directions. Lucy tightened her grip on St. Michael's hand, the hum growing louder but never overwhelming.

For the first time, she felt control. The slip obeyed her, bending to her will rather than the other way around. It was like guiding a current instead of being swept away by it.

She smelt damp earth first, then wood smoke, then the distant scent of the loch. Then came the sound: the whisper of wind through crumbling stone, the faint lap of water against the shore.

When the world solidified, Lucy found herself standing on uneven ground. Frost crunched beneath her boots, the chill biting through the fabric of her gown. Around them, Kilchurn Castle loomed, its weathered walls rising like a jagged crown against the grey sky. The loch stretched out behind it, dark and glistening, framed by the shadowed outline of distant hills.

She released St. Michael's hand and turned to him, her breath visible in the cold air. "We made it," she said, her voice trembling slightly, not with fear, but with exhilaration.

St. Michael glanced around, his expression a mixture of awe and relief. "Ayy you're getting the hang of this," he said, with a smile of reassurance.

For the first time, she hadn't been dragged through time. She had led. Controlled it. The fear was still there—but so was something stronger. Hope.

From the outside, the castle looked as it should for this period in history, abandoned. Weathered by storms and neglect. Yet, faintly glowing from within, a warm light flickered through the cracks in the shutters of a tall window, casting long, wavering shadows across the frosted walls.

"Someone's definitely home," Lucy muttered, gripping her shawl tightly around her shoulders.

"That's not right," St. Michael murmured, glancing up at the battlements. "Kilchurn was left to ruin by the late 1700s. No one should be here—especially not like this."

Lucy's unease grew, but she pushed it to the back of her mind. Answers were inside. Whether it was a trap or not, she couldn't walk away now. St. Michael, as if sensing her resolve, gave her a reassuring nod before stepping forward to push open the heavy oak doors.

They creaked loudly as they swung inward, the sound reverberating through the vast hall beyond. Lucy and St. Michael exchanged a nervous glance, then stepped in.

The air within was cool but not as biting as outside, carrying the faint scent of burning wood and dried herbs. The grand entry hall was nothing like the abandoned ruin she had imagined. The stone walls, though weathered, were adorned with tapestries, their colours muted but vibrant against the flickering glow of wall-mounted lanterns. A large hearth at the far end roared with a lively fire, casting dancing shadows on the worn stone floor.

St. Michael frowned, his eyes narrowing as he surveyed the scene. "This is… not right," he whispered. "None of this should be here. By now, this place should be cold, empty. But it's—"

"Lived in," Lucy finished for him, her voice low.

The pair moved further into the hall, their footsteps echoing off the high, vaulted ceiling. The space was both grand and unsettling—anachronistic in its warmth and care. Heavy wooden furniture lined the walls, worn but clearly used. Shelves were filled with books, their spines gleaming faintly in the firelight. A half-empty goblet sat forgotten on a nearby table, the faint smell of wine still lingering in the air.

Lucy's unease deepened as they wandered further into the castle's depths, the hall opening into a series of smaller rooms connected by narrow stone corridors. Each was just as alive as the last: beds with neatly folded linens, a desk cluttered with ink pots and quills, a corner where cloaks and boots hung, dustless and well-worn.

The two stopped suddenly, frozen by the sound of footsteps.

Slow.

Measured.

Not rushed like a guard, not cautious like an intruder. They were confident. Certain.

Lucy's eyes lifted to the grand staircase that curved along the far wall. The flickering firelight painted the stone in moving shadows, and for a moment, it was impossible to tell if they were alone.

Then a figure emerged—first a silhouette, tall and upright, haloed by the orange glow behind him. His presence filled the space long before his face became clear. There was something in the way he moved: not just grace, but control. Power held in reserve.

And when he descended, each step echoed with quiet purpose, as though he were descending not into a hall, but into history itself.

By the time his features sharpened—silver-streaked hair, black beard, piercing eyes—Lucy already knew.

This was Alaric Vale.

"Lucy Calder," he said, his deep, calm voice filling the hall. "I'm so glad you came."

Lucy first glanced at St. Michael, who stood tense and watchful at her side.

"Are you Alaric?" she asked, her voice steady despite the rush of her pulse.

The man nodded, reaching the bottom of the staircase. He stepped closer, though his movements were slow, deliberate, unthreatening. "I am. And you must be St. Michael." He gestured lightly toward Lucy's companion, a faint smile tugging at his lips. "Your reputation precedes you."

St. Michael raised an eyebrow, glancing at Lucy before replying. "Not the kind of saint you're thinking of, I'm afraid. It's just a name my mother decided to saddle me with." He smiled wryly, adding, "Not that I'm not flattered by the assumption."

Alaric chuckled softly. "A name like that does lend itself to certain expectations. But I'm glad to see that Lucy has found such... dependable company."

Lucy relaxed slightly, though her guard was still up. "You're not surprised to see us," she said, watching him carefully.

"Of course not," Alaric replied warmly. "I invited you, didn't I? And it seems you've accepted. Welcome to my home—or at least, my home for now. In a few more years, it will be abandoned again, but I've made use of it. It's a good place to think, to work... to stay out of sight."

"You live here?" Lucy asked, surprised.

"For now," Alaric repeated. "That's the beauty of our abilities, isn't it? We can choose where—and when—to make ourselves comfortable."

His words hung in the air, the implication unmistakable. "You can slip through time?" Lucy asked.

Alaric nodded, his expression calm. "Of course. Just as you can, Lucy. Although, it's actually called Traversal. *Time Traversal*"

"It has a name?" St. Michael asked, raising his eyebrows.

"Well, of course it has a name." Alaric replied jovially. "Everything has a name."

Lucy exchanged a glance with St. Michael, who looked more curious than concerned now. "You said you wanted to help," Lucy said cautiously. "To explain things."

"And I will," Alaric assured her. "But first, let's get out of this drafty hall, shall we? My study is much more comfortable."

He gestured for them to follow, and though Lucy hesitated for a brief moment, the warmth in Alaric's tone and the inviting ease of his demeanour calmed her nerves. She glanced at St. Michael again, who gave her a small nod, and together they followed Alaric deeper into the castle.

* * *

Alaric's study felt like stepping into a sanctuary untouched by time. The fire crackled warmly in the corner, casting flickering shadows across the walls lined with bookshelves. Each shelf seemed to tell a story, packed with volumes from every conceivable era, artefacts resting among the tomes like forgotten histories. Lucy's eyes wandered over a gleaming Roman coin, a Viking arm-ring, and a compass that looked as though it had sailed with explorers centuries ago.

Alaric motioned toward two chairs placed opposite his desk, their leather upholstery worn but inviting. "Please, sit," he said warmly.

The heat from the fire seeped into Lucy's chilled bones, but her muscles remained tense, her mind brimming with questions as she eased into the chair.

Alaric folded his hands on the desk and regarded her with a smile that was equal parts kind and knowing. "I imagine you're feeling a bit overwhelmed," he began. "But let's start with the most important question. Do you know who you are, Lucy Calder? Or more importantly, what you are?"

Lucy's fingers tightened on the armrest. "I know I can slip—sorry, traverse—through time," she said cautiously. "But I don't know why—or how. And I don't understand what it means."

Alaric nodded, his expression empathetic. "You, Lucy, are a Time Custodian. A protector of the Universal Timeline."

Lucy blinked, leaning forward slightly. "A protector? What does that even mean?"

Alaric's voice softened, his words deliberate. "Time Custodians have existed since the dawn of mankind. We were chosen—or perhaps gifted—with the ability to traverse the fabric of time.

St. Michael straightened. "Time Custodians? You mean there are more of you?"

"There were," his tone tinged with melancholy. "Once, we were many. Now, we are but a small few." Alaric said, taking a brief pause before continuing "Our purpose is not to alter history but to preserve it. To ensure the Universal Timeline, the natural flow of events, remains intact."

"Why?" Lucy asked, her voice edged with scepticism.

"Because history is fragile," Alaric explained. "Every moment is connected, a thread in a vast tapestry. Even the smallest change can send ripples cascading through time, creating Quantum Time Collisions. These are disruptions in the Universal Timeline, and they can lead to catastrophic consequences."

St. Michael frowned. "You mean like alternate realities?"

"Not exactly," Alaric said, shaking his head. "Think of it as two rivers colliding. The waters don't flow neatly together—they churn, creating chaos. That's what happens when the timeline is disrupted. Events overlap, diverge, or collapse entirely. It's why the Codex exists."

"The Codex?" Lucy asked.

"A set of principles by which all Custodians live," Alaric said. "The most important rule is non-interference. Custodians observe, document, and ensure that history unfolds as it should. Intervening can destabilize the timeline."

Lucy thought back to the soldiers in Germany. "That explains what happened when we slipped into Nuremberg," she said. "The guards shot at us, and when we came back, St Michael's research into the event had changed. It said they'd gone mad, claiming they'd seen ghosts."

Alaric nodded. "A minor collision, but collision nonetheless. The Universal Timeline absorbed it, but larger, spontaneous disruptions could tear the fabric of history apart."

Lucy frowned, her mind racing. "So you're saying I'm supposed to protect history? How am I supposed to do that when I barely understand what I'm doing?"

Alaric's expression grew sympathetic. "Your abilities were meant to be nurtured, Lucy. Most are trained by other Custodians or their parents. But your circumstances…" He hesitated, his gaze softening. "Your parents were both Custodians—brilliant ones, at that. Evelyn and Edward Calder were legends among our kind."

Lucy froze, the weight of his words sinking in. "I guessed about my mum having the same abilities," she said slowly. "But my dad? He never… I didn't know."

Alaric inclined his head. "Edward was a gifted Custodian, as was your mother. Together, they were a force to be reckoned with."

"Then why didn't they tell me?" Lucy demanded, her voice rising. "Why didn't they prepare me for this?"

"I'm afraid only they could tell you that," Alaric said, his tone heavy with regret. "But it raises questions, doesn't it? Why keep you in the dark? Why leave you unprepared for the legacy you were born into?"

"Do you know how they died?" Lucy asked, the weight of the question filling the room.

"Your parents were extraordinary," Alaric said firmly. "It's almost certain their deaths were tied to their work as Custodians and not whatever story you were given. As for the details, I cannot help you there."

Lucy leaned forward in her seat. "And how would their work lead to their deaths? Was their work dangerous?"

Alaric's eyes held Lucy's with an intensity that made her chest tighten. "Not innately. There was a time of peace."

"Then how could their deaths be tied to their work?" Lucy asked, probing Alaric.

He let out a gentle sigh. "Custodians have always existed to protect the timeline, to ensure history flows as it's meant to. But… not everyone sees preservation as the right path."

St. Michael straightened in his chair, his brow furrowed. "You're talking about a divide," he said, watching Alaric closely. "A conflict."

Alaric inclined his head slightly, a faint, almost imperceptible smile tugging at his lips as if he appreciated St. Michael's quick deduction. "A schism," he said quietly, the word carrying a weight that settled heavily in the room. "A time when Custodians were united by purpose—until they weren't."

Lucy leaned forward, her pulse quickening. "What happened?"

Alaric hesitated for a moment, his fingers tracing an invisible line on the desk as if organizing his thoughts. When he spoke again, his voice was softer, almost wistful. "There are—and I believe always were—those who thought Custodians could do more than observe, more than protect. They believed they could change the course of history—rewrite tragedies, erase suffering. They wanted to create a world that was cleaner. Fairer. Free of suffering. They believe the timeline is a tool, a canvas for a greater vision."

"And you?" Lucy asked, narrowing her eyes slightly. "What did you believe?"

Alaric held her gaze for a moment longer than felt comfortable. Then he said, calmly, "I believed—and still believe—that time is fragile. Every change, no matter how small, carries risks. But to some, the risks were worth it."

St. Michael frowned, his voice sceptical. "And I take it this disagreement didn't end with a debate over tea?"

Alaric let out a quiet breath, his lips curving into a faint, fleeting smile. "No. It ended in chaos. Custodians gathered to settle the matter—a meeting meant to heal the divisions. But instead…" He shook his head, the shadows of the firelight deepening the lines on his face. "It fractured The Custodians forever. Those who believed in preservation remained true to the Codex. But the others… they broke away. They formed their own faction."

Lucy's stomach twisted. She already knew what was coming. "*The Order of the Nexus*," she said, her voice low.

Alaric didn't flinch. If anything, his expression softened, though there was a flicker of something else there, something almost imperceptible. "Yes," he said simply. "The Nexus. They believed their vision of a perfected timeline was worth the cost of disruption. And they had the conviction—and the power—to pursue it."

Lucy stiffened at the name. "We've met them," she said grimly.

"Then you know their methods," Alaric said, his voice calm but heavy. "The Order believes in using our abilities to rewrite history, to create a better world. Their vision is… ambitious."

"But you're against them?" Lucy asked, searching his face.

Alaric hesitated, his expression inscrutable. "The Nexus's ideals are not without merit," he said carefully. "But for over a decade, since the Great Schism, I've been avoiding their attention, trying to stay one step ahead."

Lucy nodded slowly, accepting of his answer.

Alaric shifted, his tone lightening slightly. "But enough about them. There's more you should know about your abilities."

Lucy sat up straighter, eager for answers.

"I take it on your travels so far you've heard other languages, yet they came through in perfect English to you?"

Lucy nodded. "Well, mostly although at points it's been a mix."

This is your Innate Understanding," Alaric said. "It's a skill unique to Custodians. It allows you to comprehend and communicate in any language, spoken or written, from any era. It's an essential tool for navigating history."

Lucy's eyes widened. "I can read, too?"

"Indeed. You've already been using it without realising. It just takes some practice," Alaric said with a smile.

"There's something else you can do," St. Michael said, gesturing toward Lucy. "Back in Austerlitz. You summoned a-"

Alaric cut him off. "A form of elemental energy?"

"Yeah, it was strange," Lucy said turning her attention back to Alaric. "It was like it was pushing out of me. And the Nexians, they could do it too—though theirs was fire, and mine was more like wind."

"These are called Temporal Incants. Like I mentioned earlier, everything has a name," Alaric said with his lips turning at their corners.

"Right… and what are they?" Lucy asked.

"Temporal Incants are a manifestation of your connection to time. Custodians can summon elemental forces by channelling energy from specific moments in history. Fire, wind, water and lightning to name a few— all drawn from the fabric of the Universal Timeline itself." Alaric continued with a lowered tone. "But it's a skill that requires training and control. Unchecked, it can be as dangerous to you as to those around you."

Lucy Thought back to the fireballs and the icy gust she had conjured. "So I can do that too?"

"Yes," Alaric said. "But such power must be used with caution. It's a tool, not a weapon. The Codex has strict rules around their usage as in the wrong hands, they could be devastating."

Lucy nodded slowly, the pieces of her identity slowly falling into place.

Then a thought struck her, and she sat forward, her voice filled with urgency. "I need to speak to my mum," she said. "I can go back—back to before she died—and ask her why she didn't tell me any of this."

"No," Alaric said sharply, his warmth replaced by
alarm. "This would interfere with your own timeline
which is forbidden. It's one of the Codex's most sacred
rules. Such interference could create a catastrophic
quantum time collision."

"But—"

"It's not worth the risk, Lucy," Alaric said, his voice
firm but not unkind. "The timeline is fragile, and you've
already seen what even minor disruptions can do. Trust
me, you don't want to know what happens when the
disruption is personal."

Lucy hesitated, her shoulders slumping. "Fine," she
muttered, though the longing in her voice was
unmistakable.

Alaric's expression softened. "You'll find your
answers, Lucy. But they must come in their own time."

Lucy listened intently, her doubts about him ebbing
with each answer he provided.

Alaric leaned in toward Lucy. "All your abilities—
Traversing, the Innate Understanding, Temporal Incants—
are like muscles," Alaric explained. "Without training,
they respond instinctively, often in unpredictable ways.
Your traversals, for example, have likely been triggered
by a combination of thought and heightened emotion. An
unconscious reflex."

"I knew it! Didn't I say it would be something like
that?" St. Michael said, his voice bright with satisfaction.

Alaric's voice softened. "This is why most Custodians
are trained from childhood. It's not just about control, it's
about understanding what you're capable of. Different
Custodians are capable of much more than others, it's a
wide spectrum. Some… far exceed expectation."

Lucy frowned, her mind racing. "So, you're saying I've
been traversing by accident? Just… reacting?"

"Not entirely," Alaric replied, a faint smile tugging at
his lips. "You've already started to learn control, even if

you didn't realise it. Guiding yourself and St. Michael here, for instance, was no small feat. You focused on a time and place and held that focus. That's the foundation of mastery. It's been a long time since someone Traversed without guidance."

St. Michael tilted his head. "And the other abilities? Like Temporal Incants? Or that… innate understanding of languages?"

"Both require practice and refinement," Alaric said, his gaze flicking to Lucy. "Your innate understanding is already active, but there's more to it than you've explored. And as for Incants… they demand precision. Reckless use of such power could be catastrophic. But with proper guidance, I believe you could master them."

Lucy's shoulders tensed as she took this in. "It sounds like you think I'm meant to be… exceptional," she said hesitantly.

Alaric's smile grew warmer. "You are, Lucy. Your lineage is proof enough of that. Both Evelyn and Edward were extraordinary Custodians. With their bloodline and the right training, your power could become almost limitless."

Lucy couldn't find the words. Not out of fear, but something closer to hope. There was weight to his words, but instead of crushing her, it steadied her. She felt, for the first time, like her abilities weren't just an uncontrollable curse. They were part of her, something she could hone.

"If you ever have questions," Alaric continued, his tone gentle, "or need further guidance, return to this time. I will always be here, ready to help."

Lucy met his gaze, a faint smile breaking through her guarded expression. "Thank you," she said quietly. "I… I appreciate it."

Alaric dipped his head, a gesture of understanding. "You'll do great things, Lucy Calder. I can see it."

The fire crackled softly, filling the pause as their conversation came to a natural close. Lucy glanced at St. Michael, who gave her a small nod. It was time to go.

"We should head back," Lucy said, rising from her chair. "There's still so much to figure out."

"Of course," Alaric said, standing as well. "Safe travels. And remember, Lucy—trust yourself. You're capable of far more than you realise."

Lucy hesitated, then extended a hand toward him. Alaric clasped it firmly, his touch steady and reassuring. "Thank you," she said again.

"Until we meet again," he said with a faint smile. And something in his tone made Lucy wonder if he already knew exactly when that would be.

The air in the study shimmered faintly as Lucy and St. Michael prepared to slip back to the present day. Lucy closed her eyes, focusing on the image of St. Michael's office. The hum began to build, softer this time, as if the slip recognised her growing confidence.

The warmth of the fire faded into cool neutrality. The smell of parchment and old wood gave way to the faint tang of ink and paper. Colours shifted, the golden light of the castle dissolving into the muted tones of the office.

* * *

When Lucy opened her eyes, she was standing in the familiar chaos of St. Michael's workspace. The sharp contrast between Kilchurn's timeless atmosphere and the modern world left Lucy slightly breathless, but she steadied herself.

St. Michael dropped into his chair, rubbing the back of his neck. "Well," he said, exhaling deeply. "That was… enlightening."

Lucy perched on the edge of the desk, her expression thoughtful. "It was," she agreed. "And now we know a lot more than we did before."

St. Michael raised an eyebrow. "So, what's next? Where do we go from here? Or do we take a breath for once?"

Lucy met his gaze, her expression resolute. "He said I couldn't interfere in my own timeline," she began, her voice steady. "But there's nothing stopping me from finding my mum whilst she was traversing."

St. Michael straightened, alarm flashing in his eyes. "Lucy, we just talked about this. Alaric warned you about the risks—"

"He warned me about interfering with my own timeline," Lucy interrupted. "But this isn't about that. If I can find her while she's traveling, while she's outside of her timeline, it won't cause a collision... I think."

St. Michael leaned back in his chair. "Do you even know that for sure? Do you know where to start? Or when? Evelyn could have gone to hundreds of times."

Lucy tilted her head, her confidence growing. "We need to go through everything again. There has to be a time where we can find her."

St. Michael hesitated, clearly torn. "Lucy, I'm not saying this isn't important. But what if—"

"I know it's a risk," Lucy said firmly. "But this might be my way of getting the answers to questions I've asked for four years. There has to be a reason she didn't tell me about any of this."

St. Michael studied her, his scepticism softening into reluctant admiration. For the first time, she wasn't reacting out of desperation or fear. She was leading, her determination balanced by thoughtfulness.

He sighed. "Alright," he said finally. "If we're going to do this, we do it right. Alaric mentioned your dad was a

Custodian, too. Maybe that gives us a starting point. Somewhere they went together?"

Lucy frowned, shaking her head. "In everything I've seen so far, it was her most recent work. Dad was dead by then. We need to look further back."

St. Michael ran a hand through his hair. "Then we go back to square one. The self-storage unit. We get everything out, bring it here and go through it."

Lucy nodded, her resolve unwavering. "Let's do it. But first let's get back into our normal clothes," She added, half-smiling.

As St. Michael began gathering his things, Lucy stood by the window, staring out at the city below. Her thoughts were clear for the first time in days. The doubt, the chaos—it hadn't disappeared, but it no longer consumed her. She was beginning to see the path ahead, not as a series of insurmountable obstacles, but as a challenge she could face.

Evelyn—and now Edward's—legacies weren't just mysteries to solve. They were responsibilities to embrace. Truths waiting to be found.

CHAPTER 8
The Weight of What Remained

The road stretched out ahead of them, pale ribbons of grey under a cold January sky. Lucy sat in the passenger seat of St. Michael's car, gazing absently out the window as trees and buildings blurred past.

The car was spacious, almost too spacious for just the two of them. Its modest interior was clean and meticulously organized. Everything in its place, except for an old, half-empty water bottle rattling softly in the cup holder. Lucy's eyes wandered to the back seat, where a child seat sat quietly, its straps neatly arranged as if waiting for its occupant.

She glanced at St. Michael, who kept his eyes firmly on the road. His knuckles were relaxed on the steering wheel, but his jaw was set, a faint tension radiating from him. The child seat sat between them, unspoken but undeniable. A quiet reminder of the parts of his life that remained just out of reach.

The silence lingered, comfortable but thoughtful, until Lucy finally spoke. "I keep running through everything he said," she murmured.

St. Michael didn't look away from the road but gave a small nod. "Alaric?"

"Yeah," Lucy said. "It's just… it all makes sense, doesn't it? Everything about the Codex, the Custodians, The Nexus. It lines up with what we've seen."

St. Michael adjusted his grip on the wheel, his expression unreadable. "It does," he said. "More than I expected, honestly. It's like he filled in all these gaps we didn't even know were there."

Lucy glanced at him. "But do you think he's right? About the Codex being the key to holding everything together?"

"I think he's got a better understanding of it than we do," St. Michael said, his tone careful. "And if the timeline's really as fragile as he says, then it's probably not something we can take lightly."

Lucy nodded, her fingers tracing the edge of her coat sleeve. "He seemed… grounded about it, though. Like he wasn't just repeating rules for the sake of it. He actually believes in what he's saying."

St. Michael hummed thoughtfully. "He's been at this a lot longer than us. And if he's been fighting The Nexus all this time, he'd have to believe in something to keep going."

"You're not wrong," Lucy said with a faint smile, turning back to the window as the trees gave way to rows of houses. "It's funny, though. For someone who's been through so much, he seems… steady. Like he's already worked through all the questions we're just starting to ask."

"He does," St. Michael agreed. "And that's what I keep coming back to. Alaric's been honest with us, hasn't he?"

Lucy tilted her head, considering this. "I mean as far as I can tell. And the way he talked about my parents…" Her voice trailed off, a flicker of emotion passing over her face. "He knew them. Really knew them. And he's taken a risk in reaching out to us."

St. Michael's gaze softened, though he kept his attention on the road. "And your parents trusted him. Your mum trusted him. That says a lot."

"Yeah," Lucy murmured. "It does."

"What about The Nexus?" Lucy asked after a moment. "Do you think they ever followed the Codex? Or were they always…"

"Reckless?" St. Michael finished for her.

Lucy nodded.

"It's hard to say," he admitted. "From what Alaric told us, they were Custodians who wanted to fix things, make things better. But somewhere along the line, they lost sight of the consequences. Or maybe they decided the consequences didn't matter anymore."

Lucy frowned. "It's such a fine line, isn't it? Between wanting to help and doing more harm than good."

"It is," St. Michael said. "And I think that's why the Codex exists in the first place. To keep people from crossing that line."

Lucy leaned back in her seat, letting his words settle. "It's a lot to take in," she admitted. "It's crazy really, I always used to think history was something you could study. Read about. Now it feels like something that can break you, if you're not careful."

"It's a lot," St. Michael said, trying to ground Lucy. "But at least we've got a clearer picture now. That's something," he added.

The car fell into silence again as the storage facility came into view.

St. Michael slowed the car, pulling into the small car park near the entrance.

"Here we go," he said, unclipping his seatbelt.

Lucy followed suit. "Let's see what else my mum left behind," she said softly.

* * *

Lucy put in the combination on the lock. 1.2.3.4. "That's the combination?" St. Michael asked with a smirk.

"I do keep meaning to change it," Lucy chuckled as she pulled the door.

As the contents of the unit came into view, St. Michael let out a low whistle. He stood behind Lucy, his arms crossed, a mix of amusement and awe on his face. "I know you said it was a lot of stuff," he remarked, tilting his head, "but I didn't realise it was *this* much!"

Lucy couldn't help but laugh, shaking her head. "I swear it didn't seem this bad over the last few days," she said, though she knew it was a lie.

"It's a bit of a mess," Lucy admitted, stepping inside and moving a box off a leaning pile.

St. Michael stepped in behind her, crouching to inspect a box labelled "1792-1801." He raised an eyebrow, glancing at her. "This is how you keep your priceless historical accounts? Tossed into whatever box was closest?" he said with a smile.

Lucy shrugged with a small grin. "I mean, when I first put it all in here I wasn't exactly in the mood to colour-code. At least some of the boxes are labelled," she said ironically.

The air inside felt cooler, with a faint smell of cardboard and dust. Lucy's expression softened as she glanced around the unit. The first time she had been back here after this all began, she had felt defeated, unsure of herself, and utterly alone. Now, as she looked at the chaotic collection her mother had left behind, she felt none of that despair. There was a sense of purpose in her now, a confidence bolstered by what she'd learned and who stood by her.

"Right," St. Michael said, brushing his hands together. "Let's dig in. We're gonna need a plan if we want to get all of this back to the car without breaking anything, or ourselves."

Lucy opened a nearby box and glanced inside. "No plan," she said lightly. "Just grab and hope for the best."

He chuckled. "Efficient."

They set to work, sifting through the boxes as they carried them back and forth to the car.

"This is incredible," St. Michael said as he lifted a folder of yellowed papers, his voice tinged with awe. "She documented *everything*. I mean, look at this—dates, names, footnotes in the margins. And they're so… accurate."

"Now you know where I get it from," Lucy quipped, though her voice softened with fondness.

St. Michael smiled as he placed the folder carefully in the back of the car. "I worked with Evelyn for years, but I never fully appreciated just how detailed she was. She had this way of seeing things, finding the stories in the smallest details."

Lucy carried another box to the car, balancing it against her hip. "She did love a good story," she said. "Sometimes I'd catch her staring off into space like she was somewhere else entirely. I used to think it was because she was overworked, but now…" She trailed off, her gaze distant.

"She was probably reliving something she'd seen firsthand," St. Michael finished for her, his tone reflective. "She never mentioned it, though. At least, not directly. I always thought her accounts were just… exceptionally vivid."

Lucy smiled faintly, opening the car door to load the box. "She was a good storyteller. Kept me locked in, even when I was a toddler."

St. Michael paused and looked up at Lucy. "She was a good mentor, too," he said quietly. "Patient and sharp. She had this way of making you feel like every little thing you did mattered. I owe a lot of what I know to her."

Lucy looked at him, her expression softening. "I know she thought the world of you," she said.

St. Michael glanced at her, a flicker of emotion crossing his face. "That means more than you know," he said, his voice low.

St. Michael picked up a smaller box with the words *"Schism Notes"* scrawled across the top in Evelyn's neat handwriting. "This might be important," he said, his voice thoughtful. "The Schism. Alaric talked about it, remember? We should probably keep this somewhere easy to grab before we sort through the rest."

Lucy glanced at the box and nodded. "Good idea. We'll go through that first when we're back," she said, taking it from him carefully. The weight of the box felt heavier than it should have, and she ran her fingers over the label. "If there's anything in here about how this all started, we need to know."

They worked in companionable silence for a while, the car filling steadily with the rest of Evelyn's legacy. With the seats folded down—except for the one with the child's seat, they managed to make room for most of the boxes. Lucy ended up with one on her lap, the weight pressing down but not enough to bother her.

"That everything?" St. Michael asked, closing the boot.

"I think so," Lucy said, adjusting the box on top of her.

As he got in the driver's seat, St. Michael turned to Lucy with a grin. "You'd make a terrible removalist, by the way."

"Good thing I've got other career options," Lucy shot back.

Behind them, the storage unit stood empty, its treasures now on their way to where they belonged.

* * *

The drive back to St. Michael's office was quiet, the rhythm of the road filling the space between them.

St. Michael broke the silence first. "Teddy's turning seven soon," he said, his voice subdued but steady. He adjusted his grip on the steering wheel, eyes fixed on the road ahead. "Seven already. Feels like I blinked and those years just… disappeared."

Lucy turned to look at him, catching the tension in his jaw. "Do you get to see him for his birthday?" she asked softly.

St. Michael hesitated, the silence stretching just long enough to speak volumes. "I hope so," he admitted. "Michelle hasn't said anything about it yet. She usually just sends me a message about what he's up to, maybe a photo or two if I'm lucky."

Lucy frowned, shifting the box slightly to ease the weight on her lap. "Do you ever push back? Ask for more time with him?"

"It's… complicated. Michelle doesn't trust me to be reliable. She always says I'm too consumed by work to be a consistent presence in his life. And maybe she's not entirely wrong. I've made mistakes, gotten caught up in things I thought were important at the time…" He shook his head, his grip tightening on the wheel. "But none of it mattered compared to him."

Lucy nodded, her gaze drifting back to the road. "Does he know that?"

"I hope so," St. Michael murmured, his voice thick. "I really do. But it's hard, you know? Not being there for the big stuff. When he lost his first tooth, it wasn't me he showed it to. I just got a message about it later." He laughed bitterly, the sound hollow. "Sometimes it feels like I'm just this… observer in his life. Like I'm looking through a window at someone else's world."

Lucy glanced at him, her heart tightening. "That must be hard. Not being there."

"It's brutal, but really, I only have myself to blame," St. Michael admitted, his voice raw with emotion. "He used to grab my hand every time we crossed the road, like he thought I was the only person who could keep him safe. Now I don't even know if he'd recognise me as someone he could count on."

Lucy searched for the right words, but nothing felt adequate. Instead, she settled for honesty. "It sounds like you're trying, though. And that counts for something."

"Does it?" he asked, his voice tinged with doubt. "Because from where I'm standing, it feels like too little, too late. He's growing up without me, and I'm just here... stuck."

They fell into silence for a moment, the hum of the car filling the space between them. The streetlights cast fleeting shadows over St. Michael's face, deepening the lines of regret etched there.

Lucy finally spoke, her voice soft. "It's not too late. You've got time to show him you're there for him, even if it's not as often as you'd like. He's not even seven yet, Michael. There's so much left."

St. Michael nodded slowly, a faint smile ghosting his lips. "Yeah. Maybe."

The car continued its steady pace, London growing quieter. Lucy was about to say something more, a reassurance forming on her lips, when—

"Michael, watch out!" she screamed, her voice sharp with panic.

A man had appeared in the middle of the road. Sudden, impossible, wrong.

He stood perfectly still, as though he'd been there the entire time, his feet planted in the exact centre of the lane. He wore black cargo trousers, a dark hoodie pulled up over his head, and the unnervingly familiar white mask that seemed to catch the light in all the wrong places. The mask was expressionless, but somehow... watching.

There was no movement. Not a twitch. Not a breath.

St. Michael's hands tightened on the wheel as he slammed the brakes, the tyres screeching. The car jolted violently, and Lucy braced herself against the dashboard. But there was no impact. No sound of flesh hitting metal. Nothing.

The car skidded to a stop. For a moment, silence engulfed them, broken only by their ragged breathing and the idling hum of the engine.

"What on earth was that?" St. Michael managed, his voice shaky.

Lucy's hands trembled as she fumbled with the door handle. "I… I don't know," she said, but the dread pooling in her chest told her otherwise.

They climbed out of the car, the cool night air rushing against their flushed faces. The side road was empty, eerily still under the dim glow of the streetlights. Lucy took a hesitant step forward, her eyes scanning the empty road. There was no one there.

"I saw him," St. Michael said, his voice low. "I know what I saw."

"So did I," Lucy whispered. Her gaze swept the area, and that's when she felt it—the faint hum in the air, the same subtle vibration she always noticed before or after a slip.

Her stomach churned. "He traversed," she said, more to herself than to him.

St. Michael turned toward her, his expression grim. "You're sure?"

Lucy nodded slowly. "Yeah. That energy… it's the same. And his clothes, that mask—it's them, Michael. It's fucking them."

St. Michael's jaw tightened as he exhaled sharply. "A Nexian."

They exchanged a look, the weight of the realisation settling over them. Neither said it outright, but the implication was clear: the Order of the Nexus was watching them. Whether it was a warning or something more sinister, they couldn't be sure.

"We need to go," St. Michael said firmly, ushering her back toward the car.

They climbed in quickly, shutting the doors in unison. St. Michael started the car again, the engine roaring to life as he pulled away from the eerie stretch of road. Lucy glanced out the rear window, her heart hammering.

The quiet tension hung between them as the car sped away. Lucy clutched the box on her lap, her fingers tightening on the edges. She wanted to say something, to break the oppressive silence, but her mind was racing too fast to form coherent words.

Just as they disappeared into the distance, the air behind them shimmered faintly. The Nexian reappeared exactly where the car had stopped, his masked face tilted slightly as he watched the car's rear lights fade. He stood motionless for a long moment before traversing again, vanishing into the night.

* * *

When they arrived at the office, neither of them moved. The weight of the encounter with the Nexian still hung heavily over them, leaving a silence that felt like it might stretch on forever. Lucy finally broke it.

"We can't leave anything in the car," she said, her voice quiet but firm.

"Agreed," St. Michael replied, stepping out and moving to the boot.

They worked in tense silence, hauling box after box out of the car. Each one seemed heavier than the last, not just with their physical weight but with the emotional and historical significance they carried. By the time they'd cleared the car, it looked almost empty, its interior now filled with scuff marks and faint impressions where the boxes had been stacked.

St. Michael glanced up at the stairs leading to his office, then at the boxes piled around their feet. "This is going to take a while," he muttered.

Lucy nodded, already picking up one of the larger boxes. "Let's just get it done."

The staircase was narrow and steep, and the weight of the boxes made each trip a slow, gruelling process. By the fifth trip, beads of sweat were forming on both their foreheads, and St. Michael's shirt was sticking to his back.

"Bet you didn't think time traveling would involve this much manual labour," he said, attempting a bit of humour to cut through the tension.

Lucy huffed a short laugh, shifting her grip on a particularly heavy box. "Not exactly what I imagined, no."

After several more trips up and down, they had finally moved the last box into the office. St. Michael leaned against the doorway, catching his breath as he surveyed the chaos they had just unleashed. His once-pristine office now looked like a storage room, with boxes stacked haphazardly on every available surface. Papers and books were already slipping out of the boxes, adding to the clutter.

"Well," St. Michael said, straightening up and placing his hands on his hips, "we've officially ruined my office."

Lucy smirked faintly. "It's temporary, I promise," she said, though the sheer volume of boxes suggested otherwise.

St. Michael stepped over to the desk and pulled the box labelled *Schism Notes* toward him, clearing a space for it. "Here we go," he said, almost to himself.

Lucy joined him by his side.

Taking a deep breath, St. Michael pulled the sellotape from the lid and carefully lifted out the first item: a slim notebook, its leather cover worn and cracked with age. He turned it over in his hands, and as he opened it, the faint, precise handwriting inside immediately caught Lucy's eye.

"That's her handwriting," Lucy said, her voice barely above a whisper. She leaned in closer, her gaze fixed on the delicate script.

Evelyn's words were concise yet deeply personal, detailing her years of following the Order of the Nexus in the aftermath of the Great Schism. She described the subtle ways they were working to manipulate history. Not through grand, obvious gestures, but through small, calculated changes that most would overlook.

St. Michael read the passage aloud, his voice steady but grim. Lucy listened intently, her mind racing as she tried to absorb the implications of her mother's words.

"The Nexus believes they can reshape the world, not in sweeping strokes but in small, deliberate corrections.

They intervene at moments no one would think to protect, creating 'corrections' that align with their vision of a utopia. But they don't dissipate. They compound, layering over one another, and the cumulative effect will be just as catastrophic as any single large-scale intervention. Their intentions may be noble, but their methods are reckless. I fear they may move on to larger interferences next.

"She was still following the Codex," Lucy said quietly. "Even after everything that happened, she still believed in it."

St. Michael nodded. "She understood the risks better than anyone. And she knew how dangerous the Nexus had become."

As they continued to read, it became clear that the notebook wasn't just a record—it was a warning. Evelyn hadn't explicitly addressed Lucy, but the way she described her thoughts, her fears, and her discoveries felt deeply personal, almost as if she had been speaking directly to her daughter.

After a long moment of silence, St. Michael set the notebook aside and reached for the larger book in the box. Its cover was embossed with the words *Account of the Great Schism.* He ran his hand over the title, then glanced at Lucy.

"Are you ready for this?" he asked.

Lucy nodded, her expression resolute. "Let's see what she wanted us to know."

They opened the book together, the weight of Evelyn's legacy and the mystery of the Nexus pressing down on them as they turned to the first page.

The answers Evelyn left behind wouldn't begin with Lucy. They started with the day everything changed.

CHAPTER 9
Through Edward's Eyes

Thirteen years ago

Edward Calder sat at the wide oak kitchen table of his family home near Woolacombe Bay, Devon, leaning over Lucy's workbook. The golden light of the setting sun poured through the large windows, casting soft shadows across the room. Outside, fields of lush green stretched towards the horizon, framed by hedgerows, wildflowers, and the occasional bleating sheep.

"Right then," Edward said, tapping the page with the end of his pencil. "This question's asking for three differences between rivers and streams, not a dissertation on how lovely they look."

Across from him, 13-year-old Lucy groaned and let her head flop dramatically onto the table. "But they *are* lovely," she mumbled into the table. "I mean, *all the world's a stage*, right? So, rivers should get points for looking nice."

Edward chuckled, the sound warm and easy. "I reckon you'd be top of the class if your teacher was marking on poetic Shakespearean flair. But for this, let's stick to facts, eh?" He gently lifted her head, straightening her workbook in front of her. "Come on, what do we know about rivers and streams?"

Lucy sat up with a sigh, twirling her pencil between her fingers. "Rivers are bigger?" she ventured, glancing at him out of the corner of her eye.

"Spot on," Edward said, jotting it down for her. "That's one. What about how they move?"

"Streams are faster?"

"Good," he said, writing that down as well. "Now, one more. Think about the depth."

Lucy frowned, her nose scrunching up in concentration. "Streams are shallower?"

"There you go," Edward said with a grin. "Now, all you need to do is turn those into proper sentences."

Lucy let out a theatrical groan, slumping back in her chair. "Can't I just leave it as bullet points? It's the same thing!"

"Nice try," Edward said, raising an eyebrow. "But your teacher's looking for proper sentences, not a shopping list."

Lucy rolled her eyes but picked up her pencil again, muttering under her breath as she scribbled down the answers. "I bet other kids' dads don't turn homework into an interrogation."

Edward leaned back in his chair, arms crossed. "Other kids' dads probably don't know the difference between a tributary and an estuary. You're lucky, really."

"Lucky," Lucy muttered, though there was a hint of a smile tugging at her lips.

The kitchen, much like the rest of the house, was a blend of old and new. Heavy oak beams crisscrossed the ceiling, and a stone fireplace dominated one wall, its mantel lined with Evelyn's collected trinkets. Modern touches—the induction hob, steel appliances, and brightly coloured mugs—stood out against the old-world charm. The scent of wood polish mingled with the faint sea breeze drifting in through the half-open window.

Outside, the fields stretched towards the cliffs that overlooked Woolacombe Bay. On quieter days, you could hear the distant roar of the waves crashing against the shore. The fields, owned by the Calder's, were home to a handful of sheep, a small vegetable garden, and a scattering of wildflowers. It was a peaceful place, chosen not just for its beauty but for its isolation. A sanctuary where they could carry out their duties as Custodians without drawing too much attention.

Edward smiled as Lucy scribbled, her tongue poking out in concentration, a sight that always stirred a bittersweet pride.

"You're doing brilliantly, you know," he said after a moment, his tone softer.

Lucy glanced up, her pencil pausing mid-word. "Really?"

"Really," Edward said firmly. "You've got more brains in you than I had at your age. Don't tell your mum I said that, though—she'll never let me hear the end of it."

Lucy giggled, a bright, infectious sound. "You think she'd make you take a test?"

"Oh, she'd write the test herself," Edward said with a mock grimace. "And mark it, too. Harshly."

They both laughed, the sound filling the room and spilling out into the fields beyond. The light outside was beginning to fade, casting long shadows across the rolling hills.

Edward glanced out of the window, his gaze lingering on the horizon. These quiet moments—helping with homework, listening to the wind in the fields, teasing Lucy about her reluctance to write proper sentences— were the moments he treasured most. Moments where the weight of the Codex and the responsibilities of being a Custodian felt far away.

But he knew how fragile that peace was.

"Right," he said, clapping his hands together and standing up. "Finish that off, and I'll see if your mum's finishing work soon."

"Cool beans," Lucy said as Edward got up.

Edward chuckled, pausing in the doorway to glance back. She was already writing again, utterly focused.

Edward climbed the wooden staircase, his footsteps slow and deliberate on the creaking boards. The house was quiet now, the warmth of the evening settling into the cottage's thick stone walls. As he reached the landing, the faint golden glow of Evelyn's office spilled into the hallway. He pushed the door open gently, the familiar scent of old books, lavender, and something faintly metallic meeting him.

The room was unmistakably hers. A
n eclectic mix of modern functionality and the timeless weight of history. Bookshelves lined the walls, sagging slightly under the weight of tomes, journals, and scrolls collected over decades. Maps were pinned to corkboards alongside timelines, annotated with Evelyn's precise looping handwriting.

The large oak desk in the centre of the room bore the scars of time, its surface marked with faint rings from countless cups of tea and the grooves of a restless pen. Evelyn sat behind it, her head bowed over an open notebook. The faint lines on her forehead deepened as she ran her fingers through her auburn hair, which had loosened from its usual knot. Her hazel eyes, framed by the soft glow of the desk lamp, were narrowed with thought.

"Hun," Edward said softly as he stepped inside. "You've been hiding up here for hours. What's going on?"

She looked up, startled, though her expression softened immediately at the sight of him. "Oh hey," Evelyn said softly.

"I didn't hear you come up." She straightened, setting her pen down carefully. "It's… there's news from the council."

He crossed the room, leaning against the edge of her desk as he often did, his hands braced on the smooth wood. "What sort of news?"

Evelyn hesitated, her fingers tracing the edge of the notebook. "The council's been summoned to the Sanctuary," she said finally. "An address is to be made tonight by a group of Custodians."

Edward raised an eyebrow. "An address? That's not exactly common. Do we know what it's about?"

"No names have been given officially," Evelyn said, her voice calm but clipped. "But there's been talk— rumours, mostly—that some Custodians are questioning the Codex. They believe it's… restrictive. That it's holding us back."

Edward frowned, folding his arms across his chest. "Holding us back? From what?"

"From interfering," Evelyn replied, leaning back in her chair. "From making changes to the timeline. From—what was it one of them said?—'reshaping history for the greater good.'"

He studied her closely. "You're worried."

Evelyn let out a slow breath. "I don't know, Edward. I don't know what to think yet. Addresses at the sanctuary are rare enough. But the fact that this one was granted at all…" She shook her head, her gaze distant. "It suggests that whoever is behind it has significant support. Enough to warrant being heard."

Edward watched her for a moment, his expression softening. He reached out, tucking a stray strand of hair behind her ear. "You've been pacing up here for hours, turning this over in your mind, haven't you?"

"I have," she admitted, her lips curving into a faint smile. "You know me too well."

"I should hope so," Edward said warmly. He cupped her cheek, his thumb brushing lightly across her skin. "Let's not jump to conclusions. They'll make their case, and the council will listen, but the Codex has guided The Custodians for centuries. It's kept the timeline intact. That kind of stability doesn't just disappear because a few people have doubts."

She leaned into his touch, closing her eyes for a moment. "I know you're probably right," she said softly. "But I can't shake this feeling, Ed. If the Custodians are as divided as they seem… it could get messy. It could even—" She hesitated, her voice faltering.

"Go on," Edward urged gently.

"It… if this spirals, I don't know what will happen," she whispered, barely audible.

Edward pulled her into a firm embrace, wrapping his arms around her as if to shield her from her own fears. "Listen to me," he murmured, his voice steady and warm. "We'll face whatever comes, together. But let's not borrow trouble. If there's one thing I know, it's that fear rarely helps us see clearly."

She held onto him tightly, her head resting against his chest. "I know. I know," she murmured, her voice tinged with affection.

"I'm probably overthinking it anyway," she said, almost confirming to herself.

"Most likely," Edward teased, kissing the top of her head. He pulled back slightly, meeting her gaze. "Now, do they need both of us?"

Evelyn sighed, shaking her head. "Only one of us needs to go. There'll be enough of the council present to proceed without us both."

"Good," Edward said, his tone firm. "Then you'll stay."

Her brow furrowed. "Edward—"

"No, listen," he said, his hands settling on her shoulders. "If you're right—and let's say, for argument's sake, that this does escalate and becomes drawn out—we can't both be there. One of us should stay home with Lucy."

Evelyn searched his face, her expression softening. "Yeah, you're right."

"Plus, she's better with the parent who knows how to calm her down when she starts quoting Shakespeare to win an argument," Edward said, grinning. "And let's face it, love, that's not me."

Evelyn laughed despite herself, the sound breaking through the tension like sunlight. "You have a point there. Really nice guy though, wasn't he?"

"Surprisingly nice!" Edward said, his voice gentling. "Look, Eve, I'll go. You stay here, keep Lucy grounded. If anything happens, I'll let you know straight away."

She hesitated, then nodded slowly. "All right. But Edward…"

He tilted his head, waiting.

"Promise me you'll be careful," she said, her voice trembling slightly.

"I promise," he said without hesitation. He kissed her forehead again, lingering just a moment longer than usual. "And you know I always keep my promises."

The tension in the room softened as they stood together in the lamplight. Outside, the fields stretched into the dark, and the sea hummed in the distance. Whatever awaited Edward at the Temporal Sanctuary, neither of them could truly imagine the storm it would bring. But for now, their home was still safe, and they held onto that fragile peace for just a little longer.

* * *

Later that evening, the house had settled into its nighttime rhythm, the warmth of the evening giving way to the quiet chill that crept through its old walls. The sound of the wind outside had picked up, brushing against the ivy that clung stubbornly to the stone exterior. Upstairs, Lucy's footsteps thudded softly on the wooden floorboards, the telltale creak of the second-to-last step marking her journey to bed.

Edward stood in the living room, nursing a cup of tea he didn't particularly want. The fire in the hearth had burned low, the embers glowing faintly in the dim room. He was staring out of the window, his reflection faintly visible against the glass. Evelyn's words from earlier hung in his mind like a persistent fog.

"You're brooding," Evelyn's voice cut through his thoughts as she stepped into the room, her arms crossed.

"Just thinking," Edward replied, setting the mug down on the mantle. "Lucy's heading up."

Evelyn nodded, her face softening. "She asked if you were coming up to tuck her in."

A small smile touched Edward's lips. "She's thirteen going on thirty. I'd best take the chance while I've got it."

Evelyn smiled faintly, but there was worry in her eyes. Edward didn't mention it; he didn't need to. Instead, he gave her arm a reassuring squeeze and made his way upstairs.

Lucy's bedroom was at the far end of the landing, tucked away beneath the eaves. Edward knocked lightly on the door before stepping inside. The room was a chaotic blend of childhood innocence and burgeoning independence. Posters of bands he didn't recognise competed for wall space with bookshelves crammed full of novels, and her bed was piled high with a mismatched assortment of cushions and blankets.

Lucy was sitting cross-legged on the bed, scrolling through her phone, her pyjamas rumpled and her hair slightly messy. She looked up when he entered, tucking the phone under her pillow with a sheepish grin.

"Caught me," she said lightly.

"Not the first time," Edward teased, pulling the blanket over her legs as he sat on the edge of the bed. "You'll burn your eyes out staring at that thing."

"That's what Mum says," Lucy countered. "And yet she's always squinting at her notes. Double standards really."

Edward chuckled. "Fair point. But I'm your dad. It's my job to harp on about these things."

Lucy flopped back against her pillows, stretching out like a cat. "You're not too bad at it."

"Well, thank you for the glowing review," Edward said, smiling as he reached out to smooth her hair.

Lucy peered up at him, her brow furrowing slightly. "You've got that 'I'm going somewhere' look."

Edward tilted his head, impressed despite himself. "What's that supposed to mean?"

"You're all… I don't know. Serious. You only look like that when you've got work stuff." She paused, then added with a knowing grin, "And Mum's worried about it."

Edward sighed, shaking his head. "You're too observant for your own good, you know that?"

"So where are you going?" Lucy asked, propping herself up on one elbow.

"Just something for work," Edward replied, keeping his tone light. "It's nothing you need to worry about. I'll be back later tonight, or tomorrow at the latest."

Lucy shrugged, clearly unbothered. "Okay. Just don't forget to bring me back something cool if you're gone for ages."

Edward laughed. "I'll see what I can do. Goodnight, Lucy."

"'Night, Dad," she said, already reaching back for her phone.

Edward hesitated for a moment, watching her as she became absorbed once more in the little glowing screen. He leaned down and kissed her forehead, a rare moment of quiet affection. Lucy smiled without looking up, and Edward left the room, closing the door softly behind him.

Back downstairs, Edward found Evelyn standing by the fireplace, arms wrapped tightly around herself. She glanced up as he entered, her worry etched plainly across her face.

"Everything all right upstairs?" she asked.

"She's fine," Edward said, reaching for his coat draped over the back of a chair. "Still asking me to bring her souvenirs as if I'm off to the pyramids, not a meeting."

Evelyn didn't smile. She watched as Edward slid on his coat, her fingers twitching at her sides.

"You don't have to go, Edward," she said quietly. "The council would understand. You could stay."

"You said yourself we need to be represented," Edward replied gently, moving to stand in front of her. "This is probably nothing, Evelyn. An address, some heated debate, and a lot of sighing about protocol. I'll be back before you know it."

Evelyn shook her head. "I don't like it. The Codex has always been clear, but if even a fraction of what I've heard is true..." She trailed off, unable to finish.

Edward placed his hands on her arms, drawing her closer. "It'll be fine," he said firmly, looking her directly in the eye. "I promise."

She searched his face. "I wish I could believe that as easily as you do."

"Hey," he murmured, pulling her into a tight embrace. "You're the brilliant one in this family. I'm just the optimist."

Her laughter was soft, muffled against his chest. "You're impossible."

"And you love me for it," Edward said with a smile.

Evelyn pulled back just enough to look at him, her eyes soft and filled with something deeper than worry. "I do. Always."

Edward kissed her, slow and deliberate, as if trying to reassure her without words. When they finally broke apart, he rested his forehead against hers for a moment before stepping back.

"I'll let you know if there's any delay," he promised, reaching for his bag and keys.

Evelyn nodded, but her expression remained strained. "Be careful," she said again, her voice barely above a whisper.

"I will," Edward said with a smile, though his heart felt heavier now than it had earlier.

He stepped out into the cool night, the door closing softly behind him. As he climbed into his car, the unease that had taken root in his chest grew. But Edward shook it off, forcing himself to focus on the road ahead. He had promised Evelyn everything would be fine, and Edward Calder never broke his promises.

Evelyn stood by the window, watching until the car's lights vanished into the night. Then, with a heavy sigh, she turned away, letting the shadows of her fears settle into the quiet corners of the room.

* * *

The long, winding roads of the Devon countryside stretched out before Edward, bathed in the silver glow of the moonlight. His car's headlights cut through the darkness, the hum of the engine the only sound accompanying him. His thoughts swirled with Evelyn's earlier concerns, but he kept his gaze steady on the road.

Duty called, and he had never been one to shirk responsibility.

After a few hours, the countryside gave way to open plains, the night sky expansive above him. His car bumped along a rough grass verge as he pulled off the main road, coming to a stop just short of the ancient stones. He switched off the engine, the sudden silence almost deafening, and stepped out into the cool night air.

Before him stood the Timebound Altar, a gateway to the Temporal Sanctuary. Edward felt a sense of reverence every time he stood before it, aware of its true purpose.

The site was steeped in history, both mundane and extraordinary. To the casual observer, it was a marvel of ancient engineering, a relic of prehistoric Britain. But to the Custodians of Time, it was something far more profound: a bridge between worlds, a site where the flow of time could be stabilized and accessed.

Normally, during the daytime the site would be full of tourists and passing cars slowing down to marvel at its wonder. For the world knew the site as Stonehenge.

Stonehenge had been constructed by the first Custodians, who recognised this site as one of the most potent temporal locations on Earth. Located on the intersection of powerful leylines, the altar had been designed to channel and focus temporal energy, creating a stable gateway to the Temporal Sanctuary. A space existing outside the normal flow of time.

The Temporal Sanctuary was the heart of Custodian society, a timeless realm where the Universal Timeline could be studied, preserved, and debated without the interference of the physical world. It was here that the Codex of Time was written, where councils convened, and where Custodians trained to master their abilities.

The construction of the Timebound Altar was a feat of both engineering and temporal mastery. The massive sarsen stones and smaller bluestones were not merely chosen for their durability but for their unique ability to channel temporal energy. Arranged with precision, the stones created a natural harmonic resonance that connected the physical and temporal realms.

Though its true purpose was hidden from the public, the altar's presence in the mortal world was no accident. The Custodians had allowed the site to pass into legend, believing that its fame and mystique would protect it from destruction. Over the centuries, it had been studied, revered, and misinterpreted by countless generations, but its true function remained a closely guarded secret.

Edward stood before the towering stones, his breath visible in the crisp night air. The altar was bathed in moonlight, the pale beams casting long shadows across the grass. The stones loomed above him, silent and imposing, their ancient presence a reminder of the legacy he had sworn to protect.

As he stepped closer, the air seemed to shift, growing heavy with an almost electric charge. Edward raised his hand, his fingers tracing the cool surface of the stone as he focused his mind.

A deep hum began to resonate through the air, low and vibrating, as if the stones themselves were stirring from slumber. Edward stepped back, holding his hand aloft, and the space between the stones began to shimmer.

It started as a faint distortion, but it quickly intensified. The shimmer deepened into an ominous, swirling void, dark and pulsating with faint streaks of light. The hum grew louder, resonating deep in Edward's chest, until the gateway fully materialized. The once-empty space between the stones now held a rippling portal, its surface like liquid streaked with faint, golden veins that pulsed rhythmically, as if alive.

Edward hesitated for a moment, standing on the threshold of two worlds. He couldn't help but think back to the first time he had stepped through this very portal, his heart pounding with a mix of awe and trepidation.

A small smile tugged at his lips as he imagined one day taking Lucy through it. She had no idea what awaited her, but Edward dreamed of the day he could show her the sanctuary, the heart of everything their family had devoted their lives to. The thought filled him with both pride and a pang of regret.

"Not yet," he murmured to himself, stepping closer to the portal.

With a steadying breath, Edward stepped forward, his body enveloped by the rippling surface of the gateway. The sensation was unlike anything else. Both weightless and heavy, as if he were being stretched and compressed simultaneously. A faint ringing filled his ears, and for a moment, he felt suspended in a void, the concept of up and down irrelevant.

Then, as quickly as it had begun, the sensation passed. Edward emerged into the Temporal Sanctuary. The air here was warm, vibrant and alive with something ancient and eternal.

* * *

Edward strode through the Temporal Sanctuary, his footsteps echoing faintly against the polished stone beneath him. The sanctuary was a marvel, both ancient and futuristic. Celestial Bridges connected the Sanctuary, the faint hum of temporal energy ever-present. Above, the eternal sky glimmered in shades of gold and deep indigo, streaked with veins of light that pulsed in rhythmic harmony. The air felt alive, charged with the essence of time.

Custodians moved with purpose, their robes trailing behind them like ripples in still water. Some exchanged quiet greetings with Edward as he passed, others bowed their heads in deference to his position on the council.

The path to the council chambers was one Edward knew well. The chambers were housed in a tall, cylindrical spire that loomed above the other structures of the sanctuary. The spire's surface was a blend of gleaming obsidian and gold, etched with flowing script from the Codex of Time. It was both a symbol of authority and a reminder of the responsibility borne by the council.

Upon entering the council chambers, Edward's gaze fell on the pair of robes hanging on one side of the room. The *Robes of the Timeless* were ceremonial attire worn by council members, their design intricate and steeped in tradition.

Edward's robes were a deep, midnight blue trimmed with fine gold thread that shimmered faintly under the warm light of the chamber. The chest bore an embroidered symbol of the Codex. A circle with three concentric lines radiating outward, representing the balance of past, present, and future. The sleeves were long and flowing, their edges adorned with silver filigree depicting constellations.

Next to his robes hung Evelyn's. They were similar in design but tailored to her form, with an elegance that mirrored her own grace.

He donned his robes with care, fastening the golden clasp at his neck and smoothing the fabric over his shoulders. As he adjusted the sleeves, he glanced at Evelyn's robes once more, silently vowing to return home to her and Lucy as soon as this was over.

Exiting the council chambers through a separate door, Edward stepped into the Temporal Assembly Hall. The sheer scale of the space never failed to humble him, even after years of service. The hall was vast, a cavernous expanse capable of holding hundreds. Its walls were smooth and bare, constructed from a seamless stone that gleamed faintly, as if imbued with its own light.

The ceiling arched high above, its surface a swirling mosaic of time itself. Moments from history and glimpses of the future played out in abstract patterns, shifting and reforming like living art. The room was empty of decoration, yet its grandeur was undeniable. It was a place designed to inspire awe and reverence.

At the centre of the hall stood a circular platform, raised slightly above the ground. Surrounding it were the council's ten podiums, each carved from the same shimmering stone as the walls and inscribed with the name of the Custodian it belonged to.

At the heart of the platform rested The Codex of Time, a massive tome bound in black leather and adorned with golden clasps. Its pages were said to contain the first laws of timekeeping, written by the First Custodians. The Codex radiated an aura of authority, its presence a silent reminder of the responsibility borne by the council.

As Edward approached, the other council members turned their attention to him. He noted their faces, some familiar and reassuring, others tinged with tension.

Of the ten council members, only seven were present, including Edward. Evelyn was absent, as they had agreed she would remain home. Two others, Alaric Vale and Solric Avanir, had sent word that they were tied up with pressing work and unable to attend. That left the remaining six council members, each one representing a vital aspect of the Custodians' collective leadership.

Directly across from Edward, at the central podium behind the Codex, stood the Time Sovereign, Thaloc Eryndor. His crimson robes, edged with intricate platinum thread, shimmered under the glowing light of the hall. A mantle of white and gold draped his broad shoulders, and his silver hair fell in long waves, framing a face both stern and compassionate. His golden eyes, almost unnervingly sharp, scanned the room with an intensity that made it clear no detail escaped his notice. Thaloc, the highest-ranking Custodian, was both a leader and a symbol, repeatedly elected to guide them through the most complex and trying times with his unparalleled wisdom and resolute demeanour. It was no wonder he was a direct descendant of the very first Time Custodian.

To Thaloc's left stood Maris Veyra, her deep green robes flowing around her tall frame. Maris was known for her sharp intellect and meticulous attention to detail, a Custodian who could weave the threads of seemingly insignificant moments into a coherent narrative of immense significance. She met Edward's glance with a small nod, her expression calm but focused.

Next to Maris was Kellan Drayce, a man of imposing stature who exuded an air of quiet authority. His dark grey robes, practical and less adorned than the others, reflected his role as the Custodians' most skilled practitioner of Temporal Incants. A faint scar cut across his cheekbone, a reminder of the dangerous situations he often found himself in. Though Kellan rarely spoke unless necessary, his mere presence commanded respect.

On Thaloc's right, Lyra Kaelith stood with an almost regal poise. Her soft lavender robes were tailored perfectly, the silver circlet on her brow catching the light with every movement. Lyra was the Voice of the Council, her gift for diplomacy and her ability to mediate disputes among Custodians unmatched. Her sharp blue eyes darted across the room, reading the tension with an almost supernatural precision.

Further down the line was Darion Foln, his muted gold robes trimmed with delicate geometric patterns. Darion was a strategist by nature, always several steps ahead in his planning and deliberations. His analytical mind made him a cornerstone of the council, though his overthinking sometimes tested the patience of others. He adjusted his robes with his characteristic precision before offering Edward a fleeting, knowing glance.

Finally, Ishara Ventin stood with an ethereal grace, her black robes shimmering faintly with silver constellations. Ishara, the council's mystic, was deeply attuned to the metaphysical currents of time. Her insights, though often cryptic, were invaluable, her words often lingering in the minds of those who heard them long after she spoke.

Edward's eyes lingered on each of his fellow council members in turn. Together, they represented a balance of strengths and perspectives, each Custodian bringing a unique element to the leadership of their order. Though the council was not complete, the room still felt heavy with the gravity of their collective presence.

Edward's attention returned to Thaloc, whose golden gaze swept across the room, pausing on those gathered to witness the proceedings.

Below the council, on either side of the vast chamber, stood the Custodians who had gathered to witness the proceedings. They were arranged in two groups, flanking the hall's centre, their positions slightly below the council's raised platform. Each side held barely ten to twenty members. A noticeably sparse turnout for an assembly of this magnitude.

Between the two groups of spectators was a vast open space, polished to a mirror-like sheen, deliberately left bare. This space, where those addressing the council would later stand, felt almost like an arena. A stage where words would soon carry the weight of action. The emptiness of the floor contrasted starkly with the gathered Custodians, creating a sense of foreboding as if the absence of bodies only amplified the importance of what was to come.

Beyond the chamber's doors, more Custodians waited, the ones here to present their case before the council.

Their absence from the room served as a reminder of how many sought to address the assembly directly.

The grandeur of the hall—the sweeping ceilings and the carved stone reliefs depicting the history of the Custodians—seemed to accentuate the silence. Though the sanctuary had always been a place of unity and purpose, the atmosphere now carried a palpable tension. Edward's gaze flicked across the empty floor and toward the grand doors at the far end of the hall, where the first speakers would soon be called in. The weight of the moment pressed against him, a quiet certainty that this was no ordinary council meeting.

The stakes of this meeting were clear, and though he had reassured Evelyn earlier, he now felt the weight of what might lie ahead pressing down on him.

CHAPTER 10
The Great Schism

The chamber remained silent as Thaloc stepped forward to address the assembly. His presence commanded the room, his voice resonating with an air of authority honed over centuries of leadership.

"Time Custodians," he began, his deep baritone echoing off the stone walls. "It has come to our attention that a significant number of our order have petitioned for a revision to the Codex of Time. Such unity in appeal is rare, and as per our traditions, the council has agreed to hear their grievances. Tonight, we open the grand doors to those who wish to address this assembly."

He gestured toward the towering double doors at the far end of the hall. A faint creak reverberated as they swung open, revealing the silhouettes of figures standing beyond. Edward, from his position at the council's podium, instinctively straightened, his gaze fixed on the threshold.

One by one, they entered, forty Custodians in total. They moved with deliberate precision, their footsteps perfectly synchronized. The robes they wore were black and flowing, identical to the ceremonial attire of the council but devoid of any embellishment or insignia. Most striking, however, were the masks. Each Custodian wore a stark white mask, featureless except for subtle contours that hinted at eyes, noses, and mouths. The effect was unnerving—human and yet not.

Murmurs rippled through the gathered spectators on either side of the hall. Edward felt his chest tighten as he took in the sight. He couldn't help but think of Evelyn's earlier concerns.

Thaloc raised a hand to quiet the murmurs. "Why do you conceal your faces?" he demanded, his tone sharp. "This council is a place of transparency and trust. Masks have no place among Custodians."

From the group, a single figure stepped forward. Their voice, calm yet firm, carried an undercurrent of defiance. "We conceal our faces not out of shame but necessity, Sovereign," they replied. "Our plea is deeply personal, and we wish to shield ourselves from potential prejudice—from this council and those observing."

Thaloc straightened, his expression darkening. "Prejudice? You insult this assembly by suggesting that we, who are sworn to fairness, would stoop to such pettiness. Your words are unwarranted and unbecoming of our order."

The spokesman did not waver. "Forgive me, Sovereign, but we have seen how dissent is treated among the Custodians. We do not wish for our identities to overshadow our message."

The tension in the room grew palpable. Edward noticed his fellow council members exchanging uneasy glances, their discomfort mirrored in their stiffened postures.

After a long pause, Thaloc exhaled slowly. "Very well," he said, though his displeasure was evident in the clipped edge of his words. "You may keep your masks. But understand this: we will not entertain baseless accusations against this council or its principles. Now, speak your piece."

The spokesman bowed their head slightly before retreating into the group. Another masked Custodian stepped forward, their movements fluid and deliberate. "We come before you, Sovereign, to plead for change. The Codex, as it stands, binds our hands while the universe watches us suffer. We are sworn to observe, to protect—but at what cost? How many of us have buried

loved ones, watched lives crumble, all because we refuse
to act?"

A murmur of agreement rose from the masked
Custodians. "My son died in a fire last year. I could have
traversed just seconds earlier, Sovereign—just seconds—
and pulled him from that inferno. Instead, I was unable to
save him, while he screamed for me." The Custodian's
voice cracked, and they stepped back into the crowd,
trembling.

Another moved forward. "The Codex is flawed. It
clings to an outdated belief that we must preserve history
at all costs, ignoring the advancements we have made. We
understand time better than our predecessors ever did. We
can calculate the quantum time collisions, mitigate the
quantum time collisions. Sovereign, we are no longer
helpless stewards. We are architects. Let us shape the
timeline to reflect the better world we know is possible."

As Edward listened, his jaw tightened. Every plea,
every impassioned cry, was another affirmation of
Evelyn's warnings. She had seen this coming, the
fractures within their order widening into a chasm.

A third masked Custodian stepped forward. "This is not
about our personal pain alone. Once we master this, we
could go further. We could rewrite history's greatest
wrongs. Wars, genocides, atrocities—we could stop them
before they begin. Imagine a timeline where none of these
horrors ever occurred. Countless lives would be saved. Is
that not the purpose of our power?"

The gathered Custodians murmured in agreement, their
masked faces turning toward the council with expectancy.

Thaloc's voice cut through the chamber like a blade.
"The purpose of our power is not to wield it recklessly,
Custodian. What you propose is not compassion—it is
hubris."

The masked Custodian did not falter. "And yet you call
it reckless to prevent suffering? What greater good is there

than ensuring history itself is a reflection of the best we can achieve?"

Ishara Ventin leaned forward from her podium. Her voice was icy with conviction. "You speak of rewriting history's wrongs, yet you ignore the lessons it has taught us. Every tragedy, every war, every loss has shaped the world we live in today. You would erase that, claiming to create perfection. But perfection, Custodian, is an illusion."

Lyra Kaelith added her voice to the debate. "The Codex exists because we learned—through sacrifice and failure—that even the smallest interference can create chaos. You believe you can control the quantum time collisions, but you are wrong. History is not yours to manipulate."

The masked Custodians bristled, their leader stepping forward once more. "With respect, Sovereign, this council clings to fear. We are not advocating reckless manipulation. We propose measured intervention— calculated acts of compassion. Surely you see the difference?"

Thaloc's gaze hardened, and he stepped closer to the edge of his podium. "The difference," he said, his voice cold, "is arrogance. You believe you can outwit the universe itself. You cannot. The Codex is not a mere set of rules—it is the foundation of our order, the anchor of time itself. To discard it is to invite catastrophe."

The chamber was heavy with tension as the masked Custodians continued to voice their demands, each plea blending into the next. Edward found himself leaning forward slightly, his mind catching on a strange detail. Every voice that emerged from behind those white masks was eerily similar—calm, measured, and unnervingly uniform.

It struck him suddenly: the masks didn't just conceal their faces. They muffled their voices, altering the pitch and cadence in subtle ways, making it impossible to identify who was speaking. He scanned the group, trying to discern any differences among them, but there were none. They moved, spoke, and even gestured as one. It was deeply unsettling.

Edward cleared his throat and raised a hand to interject. "A question for those who wear the masks," he said, his voice firm but curious. "Your voices—why are they altered? Is it not enough to hide your faces?"

The spokesman turned their blank, featureless mask toward Edward. "We have taken every precaution to ensure our anonymity, Custodian Calder," they replied. Their voice was as indistinct as the rest, the words hollowed of any personal inflection. "The purpose is to protect us from the prejudice we fear even now."

"Prejudice?" Thaloc's voice thundered across the hall before Edward could respond. He stepped closer to the edge of his podium, his commanding figure casting a shadow over the masked group. "You keep invoking this word, yet you offer no proof. No Custodian here has judged you or dismissed your concerns. You undermine your own credibility with these baseless accusations."

The spokesman tilted their head, a gesture that seemed almost mocking. "Do we not? Even now, Sovereign, you call our demands reckless. You label us misguided. You accuse us of arrogance for daring to challenge the Codex. Is that not prejudice?"

Thaloc's expression darkened, his hands gripping the edge of his podium. "I call you disillusioned fundamentalists because that is what you are! You stand here, cloaked in secrecy, demanding that we abandon the very principles that define our order. And for what? For your egocentric belief that you can outthink the universe itself?"

A murmur of agreement rippled through the council members behind him, but the masked Custodians remained unmoved. Another of their group stepped forward, their voice identical to the spokesman's, adding to the unnerving uniformity. "We are not fundamentalists, Sovereign. We are innovators. We see a future where suffering is no longer an inevitable truth, where the Universal Timeline reflects the best of humanity, not its failures."

"You speak of suffering," Ishara Ventin interjected, her icy tone slicing through the room. "And yet you ignore the suffering your actions will create. Do you think history will bend neatly to your will? That you can calculate every consequence, every ripple? You would undo tragedies only to cause others far greater in scale."

"We would mitigate those ripples," another masked Custodian insisted, their identical voice ringing out. "We would make the Universal Timeline better, stronger—"

"Stronger?" Thaloc cut in sharply, his booming voice silencing the masked Custodian. "The timeline is not a puzzle for you to solve! It is a living entity, fragile and unpredictable. To tamper with it is to risk its collapse. Do you not understand that your so-called solutions will unravel everything we have worked to protect?"

A masked figure at the back of the group stepped forward, their movements deliberate and slow. "And do you not understand, Sovereign, that your inaction is just as dangerous? You call us reckless, yet you are the ones clinging to an outdated ideology, refusing to evolve while the universe demands change. You have become the very thing the Codex warns against—rigid, unyielding, blind to the suffering around you."

The room was electric, the tension between the two groups crackling in the air. Edward glanced at his fellow council members, their faces lined with unease. He could see it in their eyes—this was more than a debate. It was a fracture in their order, one that would not be easily mended.

"We are blind?" Thaloc's voice was low now, dangerous. "It is you who refuse to see reality. You believe yourselves saviours, but you are nothing more than arrogant children playing with fire."

The spokesman raised their hands in a placating gesture, though the movement felt almost mocking. "Sovereign, we are not children. We are Custodians, just as you are. And we believe it is time for our order to embrace its potential—to wield its power for the greater good."

"Enough!" Thaloc roared, his voice reverberating through the chamber. He pointed an accusatory finger at the group. "You speak of the greater good, yet you hide behind masks. You claim righteousness, yet you refuse accountability. Your actions, your words—they are not the path of Custodians. They are the path of destruction."

The masked Custodians shifted, their movements synchronized, the featureless masks turned toward Thaloc in eerie unison.

The spokesman stepped forward again, their voice cutting through the silence. "We do not seek destruction, Sovereign. We seek evolution. We seek a future where Custodians are more than passive observers, bound by fear and tradition. We seek a world where we can act—where we can save lives, rewrite wrongs, and fulfil the true potential of our power."

The room felt on the verge of shattering. Edward could feel it in the air, the precarious balance tipping, the lines being drawn. The next words spoken would define their future. He held his breath as Thaloc stepped out of his podium, his towering presence commanding the hall.

"You seek a world that does not exist," Thaloc said, his voice low but seething with fury. "And in your arrogance, you would destroy this one to build it."

The masked Custodians stood their ground, their silence as defiant as their words had been. Edward's heart pounded in his chest as he braced himself, sensing that the boiling point was just moments away.

Thaloc's face, stern and imposing, now burned with barely restrained fury as he stared down the masked Custodians. His voice erupted, sharp and commanding, echoing across the vast hall.

"Enough of this farce!" he bellowed, his voice reverberating with a force that seemed to shake the very air. "You dare accuse us of prejudice while skulking behind masks, concealing your identities like cowards? If you have grievances, you will air them as Custodians, not as shadowy masked men!"

He stepped forward, pointing an accusatory finger at the masked spokesman, the motion both a challenge and a command. "Remove those masks and leave this hall at once! Your audience is over, and your presence here dishonours everything we stand for."

The masked spokesman stood motionless, his hands calmly folded in front of him. The faceless mask turned slightly toward the others in his group before returning to face Thaloc. Then, slowly, he raised a single hand, the movement deliberate and almost reverent. His voice, as hollow and featureless as the mask, emerged, sending a chill through the hall.

"You misunderstand, Sovereign," the spokesman said, his words slicing through the tension with a precision that made the gathered Custodians hold their breath. "This was never merely an address. We will have our order… no matter the cost. The era of the Time Custodians ends tonight, and from the ashes, the Order of the Nexus will rise. A utopia forged not by passivity, but by action."

Thaloc's expression shifted to one of disbelief, then cold fury. He began to step toward the spokesman, his robes billowing behind him like a storm. But Edward, who had remained silent at the edge of the council, suddenly caught something—a faint glimmer in the eyes of the masked spokesman. They had turned a sickly yellow, glowing faintly with an unnatural light.

Edward's heart dropped as realisation struck him. "Thaloc!" he shouted, his voice desperate. "Stop—!"

The warning came too late. The spokesman's hand shot out, and a swirling orb of fire, immense and blazing with deadly intent, erupted from his palm. It roared across the hall with the force of a cannon, colliding with Thaloc in an instant. The Sovereign barely had time to react before the fireball consumed him, engulfing his form in a searing, incandescent blaze. He was dead before he hit the ground, his robes and flesh reduced to ash.

The hall descended into chaos.

The masked Custodians behind the spokesman moved as one, raising their hands toward the Custodians gathered along the sides of the chamber. Edward could only watch in horror as a massive storm cloud materialized above them, swirling with black and silver energy. The air vibrated with an otherworldly hum before jagged bolts of lightning rained down in rapid succession. The gathered Custodians, unable to react in time, were struck with merciless precision. The lightning incinerated them instantly, leaving nothing behind but scorch marks where they had stood.

"Fatal incants," Edward whispered, his stomach twisting in revulsion. The Codex strictly forbade such usage of temporal incants, powers that manipulated the elemental forces of time and nature to devastating effect. These masked Custodians had abandoned the Codex entirely, their actions a grotesque betrayal of everything the Time Custodians stood for.

The council sprang into action, each member conjuring their own temporal incants. Maris Veyral thrust her arms forward, summoning twin jets of water that surged across the hall, dousing the edges of the fire left in the masked Custodians' wake. Kellan Drayce unleashed a cascade of jagged rocks that hurtled toward the attackers, aiming to force them back.

Lyra Kaelith's hands glowed as she raised a shield of wind, deflecting a stream of fire hurled by one of the masked Custodians. Ishara Ventin countered with bolts of lightning, her attacks precise and ferocious, but for every strike, the masked Custodians responded in kind, their fatal incants cutting through the council's defences with alarming power.

Edward joined the fray, raising his arms and summoning a jagged arc of lightning that streaked across the chamber. It collided with one of the masked Custodians, forcing them back but not defeating them. He moved quickly, darting between attacks, but the masked group was relentless.

One by one, the council members began to fall.

Edward saw Maris Veyral collapse as a fireball struck her directly, the impact sending her lifeless form crumpling to the ground. Kellan Drayce let out a pained cry as a jagged spike of rock impaled him, leaving him sprawled amidst the rubble of the shattered podium. Lyra and Ishara fought valiantly, their combined wind and lightning weaving a symphony of resistance, but they, too, were overwhelmed, their bodies consumed by the fatal force of the masked Custodians' incants.

Edward's breaths came in ragged gasps as he struggled against the overwhelming force of the masked Custodians. He was still locked in a vicious clash of lightning with the figure before him, the crackling arcs illuminating the carnage in the chamber. His hands shook under the strain, sweat dripping from his brow as the blinding energy between them surged and hissed. His opponent's power was immense, far beyond anything he'd encountered before, and the sheer intensity of their incant was driving him backward, inch by inch.

But Edward refused to yield.

With a roar of defiance, he pushed back with everything he had, his own lightning crackling louder as it surged forward. For a moment, he thought he might overpower them, but then another masked Custodian joined the fray, hurling a wave of fire at his side. Edward barely had time to react, spinning away and deflecting it with a desperate flick of his hand, the fireball exploding against the wall with a deafening roar.

The room was alive with chaos—fire raining down, the ground shuddering as jagged rocks erupted from the floor, wind howling through the chamber like a vengeful spirit. Edward dodged and countered with every ounce of his strength, sending arcs of lightning and bursts of wind hurtling toward his enemies. He moved with the precision of a master Custodian, his incants weaving a shield of elemental fury around him.

But they were too many.

Another masked Custodian advanced, conjuring a massive boulder from the ground and sending it hurtling toward him. Edward threw out his hand, shattering it midair with a bolt of lightning, but the fragments rained down, cutting into his robes and skin. He staggered, blood seeping through the ceremonial fabric.

More incants followed—fireballs exploding around him, gusts of wind forcing him off balance. He countered each one, but every movement drained him further, his strength ebbing with every passing second. The masked Custodians surrounded him now, their attacks relentless, coordinated, and utterly merciless.

He could see the bodies of his fellow council members strewn across the chamber. Maris. Lyra. Ishara. All of them. Gone. He was alone. His heart clenched at the thought of Evelyn and Lucy at home, unaware of what was happening. Unaware that this would be his last stand.

A masked Custodian lunged toward him, unleashing a torrent of flames. Edward thrust both hands forward, summoning a gale of wind to extinguish it. The flames flickered and died, but the effort left him staggering. Another strike came. A jagged bolt of lightning from his left—and he barely managed to deflect it, the energy grazing his shoulder and sending searing pain down his arm.

He dropped to one knee, his breathing laboured. His vision blurred as sweat and blood mingled, dripping into his eyes. Still, he forced himself upright, summoning another arc of lightning that crackled toward his attackers. It struck one of the masked Custodians, knocking them back with a grunt, but the others pressed forward, their incants coming faster, more brutal.

"I won't fall to you," Edward growled through clenched teeth. "Not here. Not like this."

But the truth was, he was losing. He could feel it in the tremble of his limbs, the ache in his chest, the way his incants were slower to form. And they knew it. The masked Custodians encircled him now, their hands raised, their elemental forces crackling and churning in the air.

Edward let out a roar, summoning a final surge of power. Lightning erupted from his hands, spreading in a brilliant web that forced the masked figures to step back, shielding themselves from the onslaught. For a brief, shining moment, Edward held them all at bay, his defiance blazing as brightly as the lightning itself.

But then, one by one, they retaliated.

Fire, wind, rock, lightning all converged on him at once. Edward fought to deflect them, his hands moving in frantic motions as he conjured barriers of wind and bolts of his own lightning. But the attacks kept coming, their combined force driving him to his knees. His arms trembled under the strain, his strength waning with every second.

As the final masked Custodian raised their hand, a fresh surge of power erupted from the group—a torrent of elemental fury that Edward could not withstand. The combined force struck him with devastating impact, the energy slamming into him and hurling him across the chamber. He hit the wall with a sickening crack, the impact knocking the air from his lungs. His body crumpled to the ground, broken and burned.

Edward lay there, pain radiating through every inch of him. He could barely move, his strength completely spent. His vision blurred, the edges of the room fading into darkness. But his thoughts were clear.

He saw Evelyn's face, her soft smile as she kissed him goodbye. He saw Lucy, her laughter echoing in the fields outside their home, her eyes shining with curiosity and wonder.

"I should have stayed," he whispered, his voice barely audible. "I should have protected you."

Tears slid down his face, mixing with the blood and ash. His heart ached with the weight of everything he would leave behind. His family, his life, his love. The realisation that he would never see Evelyn again, never hold Lucy in his arms, was a pain greater than any wound.

"I love you," he murmured, his voice breaking. "Both of you... more than anything."

And with that final thought, Edward Calder's world faded to black.

The hall was silent now, save for the crackling of dying flames and the faint hum of dissipating energy. The once-grand chamber was a ruin, its pristine walls scorched, its floors littered with ash and debris. The masked Custodians stood amidst the devastation, their silent forms a chilling testament to the violence they had unleashed.

The Time Custodians, at the peak of their power mere hours ago, had fallen. And with them, Edward Calder.

The Order of the Nexus had risen.

* * *

Evelyn paced by the fireplace, the flames casting flickering shadows on the walls of their cosy Woolacombe home. Her arms were crossed tightly over her chest, and her teeth worried her lower lip. It had been hours since Edward had left. Too many hours. The familiar warmth of the fire, the comforting creak of the wooden beams above, none of it could settle the unease clawing at her chest.

She froze suddenly. A cold shiver ran down her spine as if the world itself had shifted beneath her feet. A hollow ache settled in her chest, and she instinctively pressed a hand to her heart. Something was wrong. Something catastrophic.

Evelyn closed her eyes, falling to her knees while the feeling only intensified. A harrowing sense of loss, of devastation. She knew in her soul that something had happened, and she had no doubt it was at the Temporal Sanctuary. For a moment, she faltered, torn between staying to protect Lucy and the overwhelming need to investigate.

Her mind raced. She couldn't leave Lucy, not now—not when everything felt so precarious. But the thought of doing nothing, of waiting in ignorance, was unbearable.

"I'll be back," she whispered, though the words felt hollow even to herself.

She moved quickly, her bare feet barely making a sound as she ascended the stairs. Lucy was fast asleep, her small frame curled beneath the thick duvet and assortment of blankets. Evelyn knelt by her daughter's bedside, brushing a stray lock of hair from her face. She bent down and pressed a kiss to her forehead, her lips lingering as tears threatened to spill from her eyes.

"Stay safe, my love," she murmured softly, her voice trembling.

Evelyn stood, her gaze lingering on Lucy for a moment longer, then hurried back downstairs. She grabbed her coat, her keys, and her resolve before stepping into the cold night air. Her car roared to life, and she drove with a reckless urgency, the quiet roads blurring around her as she sped toward the Timebound Altar.

* * *

When she arrived at the familiar sight of Stonehenge, Evelyn didn't pause to admire its usual majesty. The ancient stones stood stark against the night sky, their silent presence almost foreboding. She approached the central arch, raising her hand as Edward had earlier. The air around her seemed to hum, and the portal materialized with an ominous glow.

Evelyn hesitated for just a moment, the weight of her decision pressing down on her. Then she stepped through.

The Temporal Sanctuary was unrecognisable.

What had once been a bastion of order, a shining symbol of the Custodians' unity and power, was now a ruin. Evelyn stopped as she took in the destruction around her. The grand walkways were cracked and blackened, the pristine marble scorched and splintered. Smoke lingered in the air, mingling with the faint, acrid smell of burned fabric and stone.

She hurried forward, her boots crunching on debris as she called out into the suffocating silence. "Ed! Thaloc! Is anyone here?"

Her voice echoed back to her, a lonely sound swallowed by the devastation. The sanctuary was silent, eerily so, save for the distant groan of settling stone. She felt her heart thumped as she pushed deeper into the ruin. She passed through the shattered remains of the council chambers, her eyes darting to the walls where the insignias of the Codex once stood proudly. They were smeared with soot, marred by whatever horrific incants had torn through this place.

Then she reached the assembly hall.

Evelyn stopped dead in her tracks. The grand hall, once a place of awe and reverence, was a hollowed shell. The podiums were in pieces, scorched black and barely standing. The walls were riddled with cracks and burns, ash drifting like snow in the still air. The space where the Codex of Time should have stood was conspicuously empty, the pedestal toppled and broken. It was gone. Most likely taken. Stolen.

Her legs trembled as she stepped forward, tears streaming freely down her face. Her earlier fears, the whispers of dissent among the Custodians—everything she had dreaded had come to pass. This wasn't just a disagreement or a schism. It was annihilation.

"Edward!" she called again, her voice breaking. She stumbled over the debris, her eyes scanning frantically. "Edward, where are you? Please!"

And then she saw him.

For a moment, she couldn't move. Edward's body lay crumpled against the far wall of the assembly hall, his robes of the Timeless ripped and bloodied, the once-grand fabric now scorched and blackened. He looked small, too still, so unlike the vibrant man who had kissed her goodbye only hours earlier.

"Ed?" Her voice was barely a whisper, trembling as though saying his name aloud might shatter what little hope she clung to.

She stumbled forward, her boots crunching over shattered stone and ash. When she reached him, she dropped to her knees, her hands shaking as she reached out to touch him. "Edward… no, no, no…"

Evelyn's voice broke as she leaned over him, her hands cradling his face. His skin was still faintly warm beneath her fingers, but his body was limp, unresponsive. "It's okay," she whispered, her voice trembling as tears streaked down her cheeks. "I'm here now. I'm here. It's going to be okay."

Her thumb traced the familiar lines of his jaw, the same way she always did when she wanted to comfort him. She smoothed back his hair, now matted with blood, and pressed her forehead to his, rocking slightly as if willing her warmth, her presence, to pull him back to her.

"Wake up, Edward," she pleaded, her voice breaking as sobs wracked her chest. "Please, darling, open your eyes. It's me. I'm here. You're safe now."

The silence of the ruined hall was deafening. Evelyn clung to him, shaking him gently at first, then more desperately. "Edward, look at me. Please, just look at me. It's okay. You're going to be fine. We'll go home, and Lucy's waiting… she's waiting for you. Please…"

Her voice trailed off into broken sobs as she pressed her face into his shoulder, her body trembling with grief. She clutched him tightly, as if holding him close might somehow pull him back. "You promised me," she whispered, her voice barely audible through her tears. "You promised you'd always come back. You promised, Edward…"

Her hands moved to his chest as she searched for any sign of life—a breath, a heartbeat, anything—but there was nothing. She leaned over him, her tears soaking into the tattered fabric of his robes as her sobs grew louder. "Please, don't leave me," she begged, her voice raw. "I can't do this without you. Lucy needs you. I need you. Please, Edward, come back to me."

The sight of him was unbearable. The strong, steady man who had been her partner in everything, now reduced to a broken shell. Her mind raced with memories: his laugh, the warmth of his embrace, the way he would brush her hair behind her ear when he thought no one was looking. She could still feel his lips on her forehead from earlier that night, the promise of safety in that small, familiar gesture.

"I'm so sorry," she whispered, her voice trembling as she held him close. "I should've come with you. I should've been there. I—"

Her words dissolved into sobs, the weight of her loss crashing over her like a tidal wave. She clung to Edward's body, rocking him gently. "It's okay, love," she murmured. "I'm here now. You're not alone. You're not alone…"

Her words hung in the air, unanswered, as the reality of his death settled over her. The strong, steady heartbeat she had once felt beneath her fingertips was gone, and the light that had always shone in his eyes was extinguished.

Evelyn pressed her lips to his forehead, lingering there for a long, agonizing moment. "I'll take care of her," she whispered, her voice raw with grief. "I'll keep her safe …"

The silence was unbearable. Evelyn's cries echoed through the ruined hall, her voice breaking as she poured every ounce of her love and anguish into her pleas. But Edward remained still, his body lifeless in her arms.

As the cold reality settled in. She stayed there, holding him, until the fire in her heart felt extinguished, leaving only an aching void where her love for him still burned.

"It's okay, my love," she murmured one final time, her voice breaking. "I'm here. I'll always be here…"

CHAPTER 11
Fury And Focus

The room was silent, the kind of silence that pressed on the chest and made the air feel heavy. Lucy and St. Michael sat surrounded by Evelyn's notepads and the broken pieces of a legacy neither of them had fully understood until now.

Lucy stared at the desk, her hands resting in her lap, motionless. St. Michael sat beside her, his gaze steady but cautious as he studied her profile. He could see the tension in her jaw, the way her fingers twitched like she was suppressing the urge to curl them into fists.

Neither of them spoke.

Lucy stood abruptly, her chair scraping against the floor with a jarring screech. She turned on her heel and strode toward the window, her movements stiff, mechanical. Her reflection was faint against the glass, her breath fogging the surface. The evening lights of London sparkled, oblivious to the storm brewing within her.

She pressed a hand to the window, her fingers trembling as her other hand tightened into a fist. When she finally spoke, her voice was low, but her words were searing, laced with fury.

"They killed him." Her voice cracked slightly, but it only seemed to fuel the anger that followed. "The Nexus killed my dad."

The words hung in the air, sharp and brittle. St. Michael leaned back slightly in his chair, his arms crossing defensively. He didn't respond, he didn't think she wanted him to but he couldn't look away from her.

Lucy's hand curled against the glass, her knuckles white as she gritted her teeth. "All this time," she said, her voice rising with each word. "All these years, I thought he just… disappeared. That maybe he'd left us, or that something—" Her voice broke, and she pressed her forehead against the glass, her breath fogging it as she tried to regain control.

"They fucking killed him," she repeated, her tone trembling with restrained rage. She turned sharply, her eyes flashing as she met St. Michael's gaze. "And Mum knew."

St. Michael's expression softened. "Lucy—"

"She *knew*," Lucy interrupted, pacing now, her arms crossed tightly over her chest. "She fucking knew, and she didn't tell me. She didn't tell *anyone*. She just… what? Pretended everything was fine? Tried to carry on like our lives haven't fallen apart?"

Her voice cracked again, but this time it wasn't anger, at least, not entirely. It was pain, raw and undeniable. "Thirteen years, Michael. I spent thirteen years thinking he might come back. That he might walk through the door one day and tell me he'd been stuck somewhere, or that he'd lost track of time, or… something."

She stepped away from the window and now looked blankly toward the ceiling. Her voice softened, trembling with the weight of her grief. "Every time the phone rang, every time I heard footsteps outside—I thought it might be him. But no, he was *dead*. He was dead, The Nexus killed him, and she knew."

St. Michael opened his mouth, but Lucy cut him off, her voice rising again. "Why didn't she tell me?" she demanded, her fists clenching at her sides. "Why didn't she prepare me for this? For *any* of this?"

"Maybe she was trying to protect you," St. Michael said carefully, his voice soft but steady.

Lucy turned on him, her eyes blazing. "Protect me? By keeping me in the dark?"

"Think about it," he said, meeting her gaze evenly. "If Evelyn knew the Nexus was behind your dad's death, she would've done anything to keep you away from them. To keep them from coming after you next."

Lucy hesitated, her anger wavering as his words sank in. She turned back to the window, her reflection blurred by the fog her breath had left behind. "Maybe," she murmured, her voice subdued. "Maybe that's why she kept me at arm's length after he died. I thought she just didn't want to deal with me, but now…"

Her voice trailed off, and the room fell silent again.

St. Michael shifted in his chair, his tone cautious but firm. "Your mum didn't leave you unprepared, Lucy. Not completely. She left you bits. Her notepads, her accounts. All of it was for you. Maybe she knew you'd work it out when you were ready."

Lucy's shoulders slumped. "But why wait? Why let me stumble through this on my own?"

"Because if you'd known everything from the start, the Nexus might've known too," he said simply. "She was protecting you the only way she knew how."

Lucy didn't respond. She stayed by the window, her arms wrapped around herself as if trying to hold the pieces of herself together.

After a long moment, she spoke again, her voice low and thoughtful. "Why didn't the Nexus come after me before? If they killed him, why not me?"

St. Michael rubbed the back of his neck, his brow furrowed. "Maybe they didn't know you existed. Or maybe they didn't think you were a threat."

Lucy frowned, her gaze distant. "They've confronted me now. Why wait until after this all began?"

St. Michael exhaled slowly. "I don't know, but surely the two are linked?"

"It doesn't make any sense," Lucy muttered.

She turned back to him, her expression shifting. "Alaric said they think they're creating a better world. That they're doing this for the greater good."

St. Michael nodded, his voice grim. "What is it they say? 'The path to hell is paved with good intentions'."

Lucy didn't respond, but the weight of his words lingered in the air.

After a long silence, she straightened, her expression hardening into one of determination. "I need to see Alaric again," she said firmly. "We know how dangerous the Nexus is now, and I need to learn to control these… Incants, or whatever he called them. If we have to face them again, I need to be ready."

St. Michael didn't hesitate. "Alright. Let's go."

"No," Lucy said quickly, holding up a hand. "You've done so much already, and we're both exhausted. Go see Teddy tomorrow. Take some time for yourself. I'll meet you the day after."

St. Michael frowned, shaking his head. "Lucy—"

"You need this," she insisted. "And I'll be fine. I'll meet Alaric, get some answers, and traverse back to my flat after. I'll be careful, I promise."

He hesitated, torn, but the determination in her voice was clear. Finally, he sighed, relenting. "Alright. But you come back the second anything goes wrong. Understand?"

Lucy smiled faintly. "I understand."

She closed her eyes, picturing Kilchurn Castle in 1802. The image came to her easily. The frost on the ground, the cold air, the flicker of firelight inside its walls.

The hum began, soft and steady. The air around her shimmered as the colours of the room shifted and blurred. Lucy felt it take hold, her focus unwavering.

And then she was gone.

St. Michael stood alone in the now-quiet office, staring at the space where she'd been. He ran a hand over his face, sighing heavily before pulling out his phone.

He hesitated for a moment, then brought up Michelle's contact.

It rang a few times before a warmly familiar voice answered.

"Michelle," he said, voice faltering. "I know this is extremely short notice, but can I see Teddy tomorrow?"

* * *

The air inside Kilchurn Castle was still and cold, yet it carried a faint hum of something ancient yet familiar. Lucy stood just inside the heavy oak doors, the same ones she'd passed through hours ago—or centuries ago, depending on how one measured time. The castle seemed unchanged, yet its weight pressed on her differently now. This time, she wasn't here with curiosity or trepidation. She was here with purpose.

Her boots clicked softly against the stone floor as she stepped into the hall. Torchlight flickered along the walls, casting restless shadows that seemed to dance in the quiet. Lucy stopped in the middle of the space, her voice cutting through the silence.

"Alaric?"

She took another step forward, her pulse steady but expectant.

"Alaric," she called again, more firmly.

From the far end of the hall, a voice emerged, calm and measured. "I thought you might return soon."

Lucy turned sharply, her eyes narrowing slightly as she spotted him stepping into view. Alaric moved with the same quiet grace she remembered, his silver-streaked hair neatly tied back, his dark clothing sharp and tailored, and his blue-grey eyes unreadable as they met hers. He looked as though he had been waiting for her.

"I need to ask you some more questions," Lucy said without preamble.

Alaric studied her for a moment, his gaze thoughtful. Then he inclined his head. "Walk with me," he said simply, turning toward the corridor that led deeper into the castle.

They walked side by side through the familiar halls, their footsteps echoing softly. Lucy found herself glancing around at the castle's timeless details. The worn stone, the intricate tapestries, the faint smell of damp earth and wood smoke. It all felt heavy with history, as though the walls themselves had been witnesses to every moment that had passed here.

She broke the silence first, her voice steady. "I've read my mum's account of the Great Schism," she said, choosing her words carefully. "I know what the Nexus did. And I know now that they killed my father."

Alaric's stride faltered ever so slightly, though he didn't stop. His eyes remained fixed ahead, and when he finally spoke, his voice was quiet. "Yes."

Lucy stopped walking, forcing him to turn and face her. She searched his face, her tone soft but tinged with confusion. "You knew," she said. "You knew all along. Why didn't you tell me?"

Alaric's gaze dropped for a moment before meeting hers again. His voice, when it came, was steady but tinged with regret. "Because it wasn't my place to tell you, Lucy. It's not the kind of truth you deliver lightly—or from someone you barely know."

Lucy frowned, trying to reconcile his explanation. "But if you'd told me earlier… maybe I would have been more prepared. Maybe—"

Alaric raised a hand, gently interrupting her. "Prepared for what? For grief? For anger? Nothing could prepare you for learning how you lost him—not from me. It needed to come from someone who could carry the weight of that truth with you. Someone who loves you." He hesitated, his voice softening. "But I see now… you didn't have that. And for that, I'm truly sorry."

Lucy's shoulders sagged slightly, her expression flickering with a mix of frustration and understanding. "It still hurts," she admitted quietly.

"It always will," Alaric said. "But you're stronger than you realise, Lucy. And that strength will guide you."

They resumed walking, the silence between them heavy with unspoken emotion. Lucy's thoughts churned, her questions multiplying with each step. Finally, she broke the quiet again.

"What happened after?" she asked. "After they killed him?"

Alaric's expression darkened, and his pace slowed. "The Nexus began seeking out other Custodians who weren't present during the Schism. They sought those who would see from their perspective and asked them to join," he explained.

"And what of those who refused?" Lucy asked with trepidation.

Alaric stopped walking and held Lucy's gaze. He raised his eyebrows and then solemnly looked toward the floor. He didn't answer. He didn't need to. His expression spoke answers Lucy had already guessed.

"Some fought The Nexus, others hid, and the rest seemed to simply vanish."

"What did you do?" Lucy asked softly.

"I survived," Alaric corrected, though his voice lacked conviction. "I traversed from one time to another, always staying ahead of the Nexus. While your mother and others fought to stop them, I… hid."

"You feel guilty," Lucy said, her tone less questioning than certain.

"I am guilty," Alaric replied, his voice heavy with regret. "I wasn't there when your father needed me. Or your mother. Or any of the others. I told myself I was preserving what was left of the Custodians. That I could do more good by staying alive. But the truth is… I was afraid."

Lucy searched his face, her expression softening despite herself. "But you're not afraid anymore?" she said.

"No," Alaric admitted. "But that doesn't mean I can undo what's been done."

She turned to Alaric, her eyes blazing with determination. "Then don't try to undo the past. Help me change the future. Fight with me, Alaric. We can stop the Nexus before they cause any more damage."

Alaric's gaze dropped, and he shook his head slowly. "I can't, Lucy. My time has long since passed. Yours is just beginning."

Lucy's jaw tightened. "You can't just sit here while they tear apart the timeline. You know more about them than anyone—you could make a difference!"

"You will make the difference. That I am certain of," Alaric said quietly. "But it's not my fight anymore."

"I need to learn more," she said as she stopped. "About the Temporal Incants. You mentioned them last time, but you didn't explain everything. I need to understand how they work. How to use them."

Alaric nodded, gesturing for her to follow him. "I thought you might ask about that," he said, his voice calm. "Which is why I brought you here," he said, gesturing toward the castle grounds through the archway ahead. "But before I teach you, there's something you need to understand." He added.

Lucy's eyes narrowed slightly, but she nodded.

"Temporal Incants are not ordinary abilities," Alaric began, his tone shifting into something more measured and serious. "They are an extension of your connection to time itself. They draw their power from the very fabric of the timeline—moments of energy, change, and momentum. That's what makes them so powerful… and so dangerous."

He turned to face her fully, his gaze steady. "The Codex once governed their usage, permitting them only in dire situations. Life and death. Now though, those times are very much gone."

Lucy tilted her head, steady and curious. "What are the rules?"

Alaric began pacing, his hands clasped behind his back.

"First," he said, voice even, "Custodians were never to use Incants against one another. Trust held us together. To turn our powers inward was to risk everything we protected."

Lucy caught the faint emphasis on '*were*', but said nothing.

"Second," he continued, "Incants were forbidden against civilians. We were meant to preserve history, not shape it through force."

As Alaric spoke, it was as if the wind began to bite colder.

"And the third?" Lucy asked, her voice low.

"Incants were a last resort. Their power—unstable, volatile—was not meant for casual use. A single reckless act could fracture entire timelines."

He stopped pacing and turned to face her fully.

"And the final rule," Alaric said, his voice heavy, almost bitter, "was the most sacred: no Custodian was ever to take a life with an incant."

He held her gaze for a moment longer than necessary, and for the first time, Lucy sensed it. These rules had once been sacred.

But now, they felt like memories of a world already lost.

Lucy's expression tightened. "And what happens if someone breaks these rules?"

Alaric hesitated, his gaze darkening. "Then they cease to be a Custodian," he said simply.

A chill ran through Lucy, but she forced herself to meet his gaze.

Alaric's expression shifted, the lines of his face etched with something close to regret.

"During the Schism, the rules weren't simply broken—they were abandoned. What was once sacred became… expendable."

Lucy tensed, her hands tightening into fists.

"The Nexus," Alaric continued carefully, "saw the Codex as a chain, not a guide. They chose to break it, believing they were forging a better path."

"And now?" Lucy asked, her voice cautious.

Alaric's gaze turned distant, almost unreadable. "Now, the rules survive more in memory than in practice. Some cling to them. Others… barely remember they existed."

Lucy hesitated. "And you? What do you believe?"

He let the question hang for a moment, then added, voice softer, almost thoughtfully, "I believe the rules were written for a simpler time," he said. "But time doesn't stand still. Nor should we."

Lucy studied him, her instincts tingling with unease. But she pushed it aside, focusing on the task at hand. "Then show me," she said firmly. "Teach me how to use them."

Alaric nodded slowly, gesturing to the open field before them. "Very well," he said. "Let's begin."

Alaric gestured toward a fallen tree, its massive trunk lying crooked on the frosted ground. "That," he said, his voice calm and steady, "will be our first target. Now, watch closely."

He raised one hand, palm open and facing forward, his fingers slightly curled as if cradling an invisible flame. His eyes sharpened with focus, and Lucy felt the air around him shift, charged with an invisible energy. A soft, flickering glow ignited in his palm, growing brighter and hotter until a ball of fire materialized, its core white-hot and its edges licking outward in golden tendrils.

With a smooth motion, Alaric thrust his hand forward, releasing the fireball. It streaked through the air like a comet, illuminating the darkened grounds in a flash of orange light. It struck the tree with a loud *crack*, splitting the bark and setting the wood ablaze. Flames climbed the trunk, consuming it in moments, their heat radiating outward and warming Lucy's cheeks.

She stared at the burning tree, her heart pounding. Alaric lowered his hand and turned to her, his expression calm but expectant. "Now, it's your turn. Extinguish the fire."

Lucy blinked. "Extinguish it? With water?"

"Precisely," Alaric said, stepping aside to give her space. "Summoning water isn't as instinctive as fire, but it follows the same principle. Focus on the element. Visualize it. Think of a rushing river, a torrential downpour—any source of water you can picture. And then, *will* it to come to you."

Lucy swallowed hard and nodded, raising her hand as Alaric had. She closed her eyes for a moment, conjuring the image of water in her mind. The roar of a waterfall, the cool spray of a stream, the endless expanse of an ocean. She reached for the hum of energy she'd felt before, the connection to time itself.

A faint shimmer appeared around her hand, and a small stream of water trickled forth, barely more than a drizzle. It splashed onto the ground, dampening the frost but falling far short of the blazing tree.

Alaric's voice was patient but firm. "Good. You've made the connection, but it's weak. You need more focus—more intent."

Lucy frowned, frustration bubbling beneath the surface. "I summoned a gust of wind before," she said, her tone defensive. "When St. Michael and I were attacked by the Nexus. But that was… instinct. It just happened."

"That's because your survival was at stake," Alaric explained. "In moments of great danger, your abilities will respond instinctively. But instinct alone won't save you. To master Incants, you need control. Intent. Now, think back to that moment. Remember the fear, the urgency—but don't let it overwhelm you. Channel it."

Lucy closed her eyes again, her breathing steadying. She pictured the fire in front of her, the roaring flames threatening to spread. She let herself feel the urgency, the need to act. Her hand tingled with energy, and this time, when she reached for the water, it came more readily.

A stronger stream burst forth, arcing through the air and striking the edge of the fire. The flames hissed and sputtered but didn't go out entirely. Lucy grimaced, lowering her hand.

"You're improving," Alaric said, stepping closer. "But you're holding back. You're afraid of failing, of losing control. Let go of that fear. Trust yourself."

Lucy took a deep breath, determination hardening her expression. She raised both hands this time, her fingers trembling as she focused. The image of the roaring waterfall returned, stronger now. She imagined the force of the water, its relentless power.

The air around her grew cold and damp, and then, with a sudden surge, a torrent of water erupted from her hands. It struck the fire with a deafening roar, dousing the flames and sending the charred remains of the tree skidding backward across the ground. Lucy staggered slightly, the effort leaving her breathless, but she couldn't suppress the small smile that tugged at her lips.

Alaric nodded approvingly. "Now *that* is progress."

"You've taken your first step," he said, his voice steady. "But controlling one element is just the beginning. Each has its own nature, its own personality, if you will. Mastering them is not simply about power—it's about understanding. Let's see how well you can adapt."

He motioned for her to follow him further out toward a rocky outcropping. The moonlight caught the edges of the stones, casting sharp, jagged shadows. Alaric's hand hovered briefly over the ground before he straightened.

"Lightning is next," he said, his tone quieter now, as if the very air demanded respect. "It's the most unpredictable of the elements. It requires both confidence and precision. Hesitate, and it will either fizzle out… or consume you."

Lucy glanced at the skies. "And how exactly do I pull lightning out my arse?"

Alaric's lips curved into the faintest smile. "It's not out of nowhere. You're reaching into the past, pulling from storms that raged centuries ago. The energy is there—your job is to bring it forward and make it yours."

He raised his hand, and Lucy saw the faintest flicker of light dance along his fingers, like static electricity waiting to be unleashed. A moment later, a bolt of lightning surged from his palm, striking the rocks with a deafening explosion. The sound echoed across the grounds, and Lucy jumped despite herself.

"The key," Alaric said, turning to her, "is to feel the power without letting it overtake you. Picture the energy building in your hand. Focus it. Control it. Now, try."

Lucy hesitated, staring at her palm, trying to feel the hum of power Alaric described, but nothing happened. She exhaled sharply, frustration bubbling to the surface.

"Don't force it," Alaric said gently, stepping beside her. "Think of a storm—not just the lightning, but the wind, the rain, the way the air seems alive before the first strike. Feel that in your chest, then guide it to your hand."

Lucy closed her eyes, imagining the storm. The roar of thunder filled her mind, the sharp crack of lightning splitting the sky. Her chest tightened as she reached for that energy, her fingers tingling. Slowly, a faint spark flickered in her palm, followed by a sharper jolt that made her wince.

"Good," Alaric said. "You're starting to feel it. Again."

With each attempt, the spark grew stronger until, finally, Lucy unleashed a jagged bolt that struck the rocks, splitting one cleanly in two. She gasped, staring at the destruction.

"You see?" Alaric said. "Lightning answers to confidence. Never hesitate."

* * *

They moved to an open area of the grounds, where the wind whispered through the grass and over the ruins. Alaric stood with his arms outstretched, letting the breeze rustle his coat.

"Wind," he said, his voice carrying like a soft gust itself, "is about movement. It's not something you command—it's something you guide. You can't trap the wind, Lucy, but you can steer it."

He raised a hand, and the breeze around them grew stronger, rustling the grass and tossing loose leaves into the air. With a sharp motion, he sent the wind rushing past her, almost knocking her off balance. Lucy turned, wide-eyed.

"How did you—"

"You feel it," Alaric interrupted, his gaze fixed on her. "It's all around you. It's constant. You don't summon wind, Lucy. You simply direct it. Close your eyes and listen to it. Where is it coming from? Where does it want to go?"

Lucy closed her eyes, letting the soft currents of air wash over her. It was subtle at first, like the faintest touch on her skin, but as she focused, she began to feel its presence more clearly.

"Now," Alaric said, "turn it toward me."

She raised her hand, imagining the breeze bending to her will. A gentle gust swirled around her but barely ruffled Alaric's robes. He raised an eyebrow.

"Stronger," he urged. "Don't be polite, Lucy. The wind doesn't care about delicacy."

Gritting her teeth, she pushed harder, and this time, the gust roared past her, sending a cluster of leaves spiralling toward Alaric. He nodded approvingly, steady against the force.

"Good. You're learning to guide it. Wind isn't as destructive as fire or lightning, but it can be just as powerful when used wisely."

* * *

Their next stop was a patch of loose stones scattered across the field. Alaric knelt and pressed his palm to the ground.

"Earth," he said, his voice quieter now, almost reverent. "It's the most grounded of the elements—steady, unyielding. But it requires patience. You can't rush the earth, Lucy. You have to respect it."

He rose to his feet and raised his hand, and the ground trembled slightly beneath them. A boulder rose from the earth, hovering for a moment before slamming down with a resounding thud.

"Like the ground beneath your feet, it's always there," Alaric continued. "But to move it, you have to dig deep. Feel your connection to it. Draw from your roots."

Lucy stepped forward, mimicking his stance. She pressed her hand to the ground, trying to feel that connection, but the earth remained still. She frowned, her frustration mounting again.

"Patience," Alaric reminded her. "Breathe. You're not pulling the stone—you're asking it to move."

She closed her eyes, exhaling slowly. She pictured the stone beneath her hand, its weight, its strength. Her fingers tingled as she reached deeper, and then, slowly, a smaller rock lifted from the ground, hovering unsteadily. Lucy grinned, but her focus wavered, and the rock tumbled back to the earth.

"Good start," Alaric said as he gestured for her to walk beside him. "But the earth won't tolerate hesitation. Trust your connection, and it will answer."

* * *

Returning to their starting point, Alaric pointed toward the log he had earlier set ablaze.

"You've already seen what fire can do," he said. "It's the easiest to summon but the hardest to control. It's wild, destructive. It feeds on emotion, so you must temper it with discipline."

He extended his hand, and flames burst forth, their orange tongues dancing with a life of their own. With a flick of his wrist, the fire leapt into the air, forming a perfect arc before dissipating.

Lucy raised her hand, and almost immediately, a small flame flickered to life in her palm. But it wavered, unsteady, as her concentration faltered.

"Good," Alaric said. "But don't let it rule you. Fire thrives on chaos, but you must give it purpose. Focus on what you want it to do—no more, no less."

Lucy exhaled, steadying herself. The flame grew brighter, more defined, and when she thrust her hand forward, it shot out in a small but precise arc, striking her target.

"Better," Alaric said, a hint of pride in his voice. "You're beginning to understand."

As Lucy stood amidst the remnants of her training, her chest heaving with exertion, Alaric's voice cut through the still night air with a calm, deliberate weight.

"You've done well tonight, Lucy. You're beginning to grasp the fundamentals of each element, but understanding them in isolation isn't enough." His gaze settled on her, sharp but not unkind. "In the real world, these powers are not wielded in peace. You must know how to use them when confronted by an opponent."

Lucy's brow furrowed, her unease evident. "You're talking about fighting? With you?"

Alaric hesitated. "No Lucy, sparring. It's essential. Theoretical knowledge will only take you so far. To truly master these abilities, you need to understand how they behave in a clash, how they respond to force, intent, and resistance."

She hesitated, her arms crossed protectively over her chest. "I don't know if I'm ready for that. What about if I fuck it up? What if—?"

"You won't," Alaric interrupted, his tone firm but reassuring. "And even if you do, that's why I'm here. To guide you. To ensure nothing goes awry. Sparring is not about winning or losing. It's about learning. Trust me, Lucy, this is critical. One day, this knowledge could save your life."

Lucy exhaled deeply, her hesitation still evident. "Alright," she said reluctantly, glancing at the ground. "But you'll stop it if it gets out of hand?"

Alaric smiled faintly. "I won't let anything happen to either of us. Now, listen carefully—before we begin, there's something you need to understand about what happens when two Incants collide."

He gestured for her to stand beside him, his voice lowering, as if imparting a secret known only to a select few. "When two Custodians unleash Incants against one another, the elements don't simply cancel each other out. They meet, and the stronger force pushes the weaker one back toward its caster."

Lucy's eyes widened. "Wait—you mean if I can't hold my ground, my own Incant could… turn on me?"

"Precisely," Alaric said, his expression grave. "Not only will your opponent's power reach you, but your own Incant will rebound as well. The impact is… significant. It's why control and focus are paramount. The stronger Custodian's energy will dominate, overwhelming the weaker."

Lucy's shoulders tensed at the thought. "So, if I'm not strong enough, I could end up taking the brunt of the attack—twice over."

"Yes," Alaric confirmed, his gaze unwavering. "But that's why we're doing this. To prepare you. To strengthen your resolve and your control. This isn't just about power, Lucy. It's about discipline, strategy, and precision. The stronger mind, not just the stronger hand, determines the outcome."

He stepped back, giving her space. "This lesson isn't designed to harm you. It's designed to prepare you for the moment harm finds you. The reality of what it means to face another Custodian in battle. And I'll be here to stop anything before it goes too far."

Lucy nodded slowly, her expression a mixture of apprehension and determination. "Okay," she said, lifting her chin. "Let's do it."

Alaric's faint smile returned, though there was a flicker of something unreadable in his eyes. "Good. Now, take your position. This is your first step toward truly understanding the power you possess."

Lucy stepped into position across from Alaric, the cool evening air brushing her face, carrying the faint scent of singed bark and damp earth from their earlier training. Her heart raced as she glanced at her hands, still faintly tingling from the energy of the elements she had summoned. She could feel the weight of Alaric's gaze, steady and unreadable, his stance relaxed but purposeful.

"Ready?" he asked, his voice calm, almost soothing.

Lucy swallowed hard, her nerves coiling tighter. "As I'll ever be," she replied, forcing her voice to remain steady.

"Good," Alaric said, his lips curving into the faintest hint of a smile. "Then let's begin."

Without hesitation, he raised his right hand, extending his arm toward her. A spark flickered in his palm, bright and crackling, as if he were holding the very essence of a storm. The spark grew into a mass of pure lightning, swirling and alive, illuminating his face with a pale, cold light. It buzzed angrily, sending tendrils of energy dancing along his forearm.

Lucy's hands tingled with anticipation as she raised them, summoning the memory of fire. The roaring heat, the consuming blaze. She focused on the sensation, and within moments, a flicker of flame sparked in her palm. It grew, feeding on her determination, until a steady plume of fire writhed and twisted in front of her hand, its orange glow painting her features.

With a sharp thrust of his arm, Alaric's bolts of lightning surged toward her, a streak of blinding, crackling energy. The air hissed and popped in its wake, the sheer force of it making Lucy flinch.

She reacted instinctively, throwing her fire forward to meet the oncoming lightning. The two elements collided with an explosion of light and sound, forming a glowing nexus of energy between them. Fire and lightning twisted and churned, neither willing to give way, creating a radiant sphere of raw power.

Lucy's face tensed as the collision held. Her arms trembled under the strain, and sweat beaded on her forehead. The sheer force between them was overwhelming, yet she could feel the push, the tension of her flames fighting against the lightning.

Alaric's power began to overtake hers, the ball of energy inching closer to her. Her flames faltered, pushed back by the unrelenting strength of the lightning. The heat and crackle of the combined forces grew unbearable, and panic flared in her chest.

"Focus, Lucy!" Alaric called, his voice cutting through the chaos. "Don't let fear control you!"

She gritted her teeth, willing herself to hold on, but the strain was too much. Her arms burned, and the lightning was dangerously close. She could feel the hum of its energy against her skin, the threat of its power about to engulf her.

Just as the lightning was a breath away from striking her, Alaric dropped his hand sharply. The energy between them dissipated instantly, dissolving into harmless sparks that scattered into the air.

The sudden release of tension left Lucy staggering. Her knees buckled, and she collapsed to the ground, her breath coming in heaving gasps. Every muscle in her body ached, and her arms felt like they'd been weighed down with lead.

Alaric approached her, his movements steady and unhurried. He crouched beside her, his expression calm but laced with approval. "You did well," he said, his voice soft yet firm.

Lucy shook her head, her breaths still ragged. "I felt like I was going to lose it," she admitted, her voice tinged with frustration. "Like it was all going to hit me."

"That's because you're untrained," Alaric said, his tone even. "However, you did well," his voice softening. "What you're feeling now is natural. Using Incants is like exercising a muscle. The more you train, the stronger you'll become. But for a first attempt? You've done far better than most."

She looked up at him, her exhaustion warring with a flicker of pride. "It didn't feel like I did well."

Alaric chuckled lightly, the sound warm but measured. "It rarely does at first. But trust me, Lucy—you're stronger than you realise. You just need to learn how to harness that strength."

He stood, extending a hand to her. Lucy hesitated for a moment before taking it, letting him pull her to her feet. Her legs wobbled slightly, but she steadied herself, determination flickering in her eyes.

"You're going to be powerful, Lucy," Alaric said softly, his tone filled with both pride and something deeper, more elusive. "I can see it already. You're stronger than you know."

Lucy looked up at him, her breath still coming in shallow gasps. "I didn't think I could do it," she admitted.

"You can," Alaric said, "You have a gift, Lucy. And with time and training, I have no doubt you'll surpass even the strongest Custodians who came before you."

Despite her exhaustion, Lucy felt a flicker of pride. She wasn't there yet, but for the first time, she believed she could be.

Lucy took a step back to gather herself before meeting Alaric's gaze once more. "Again, let's do it again," she said with determination that almost surprised herself.

Alaric smiled. "What you've achieved tonight is beyond what most Custodians would ever attempt during their first lesson. You've pushed your limits—and then some. To push further would only do more harm than good."

Lucy swallowed, the tension in her shoulders easing slightly at his words. "But—"

"No," Alaric interrupted again, stepping closer to her. "Go home, Lucy. Rest. Your mind and body need it.

You'll find that tonight, after what you've done, exhaustion will hit you."

The promise of rest was tempting, but Lucy still lingered, unwilling to leave so much unresolved. Alaric's gaze softened as he seemed to read her hesitation.

"You have questions," he said gently. "I know. But you need time to process what you've learned, and that's not something I can teach you. When you're ready, when you're rested, I'll be here. You can always come back, and we'll continue. But for now, get some rest."

Lucy bit her lip, her resistance wavering. She felt a pang of frustration at her own exhaustion, but Alaric's calm reassurance grounded her. Finally, she nodded, though her reluctance was clear.

"Alright," she said quietly.

Alaric's face was one of both approval and pride. "Good," he said. "You've done something extraordinary tonight, Lucy. You've proven your strength, your potential. You're a force to be reckoned with, and I have no doubt your mother and father would be immensely proud of you."

His words struck a chord deep within her, filling her chest with a mixture of pride and emotion. Her exhaustion didn't fade, but it suddenly felt more bearable, as though his encouragement had given her just enough strength to keep going.

Lucy stepped back, preparing herself for the traversal. She pictured her flat in Brixton. The familiar sight of her bedroom, the comfort of her bed waiting for her. Her mind's eye sharpened the image, and she took a deep breath, focusing.

"I'll be back," she said softly, managing a faint smile despite her weariness.

"I'll be here," Alaric replied, his voice steady. "Whenever you're ready. Whether it's to practice or to ask more questions, this place is yours as much as mine."

Lucy nodded, her confidence returning just enough to carry her through. She took another step back, closing her eyes as the hum began to build.

Alaric watched her, his expression calm but proud. "Well done tonight, Lucy," he said as the air around her shimmered faintly. "And remember—you're stronger than you know."

Those words lingered in her ears as she felt the familiar pull, the world bending and reshaping itself around her. With a final exhale, she was gone.

* * *

Lucy landed in her living room with a soft jolt, the familiar surroundings of her flat grounding her instantly. She opened her eyes, blinking at the sight of her laptop still sitting on her desk, the pile of books stacked neatly beside it. The transition back to the present day was almost seamless, and for a moment, she just stood there, letting the stillness of the room wash over her.

Her legs felt like lead, and her mind was foggy with exhaustion, but she forced herself to step forward. She opened her laptop, the faint glow of the screen illuminating her face as she checked the date and time.

Relief washed over her as she confirmed everything was as it should be. She was back in her time, back where she belonged.

She turned sharply into her bedroom. Without bothering to undress or even pull back the covers, she collapsed onto her bed, the mattress enveloping her like a warm embrace. Her body felt impossibly heavy, and her eyes fluttered shut almost immediately.

The events of the day and night she had lived played faintly in her mind. The clash of fire and lightning, the horror of the Great Schism, the weight of Alaric's words and the pride she'd felt at his encouragement. But those thoughts were fleeting, drowned out by the all-encompassing pull of sleep.

Within moments, she was gone, lost to the deepest, most restful sleep she'd had in years.

CHAPTER 12
The Distance Between Us.

The next morning

The sun hung low in a sky streaked with soft pastel grey, casting a crisp light over the frosted streets of London. St. Michael's car hummed steadily along the nearly empty road as he made his way toward Kingston. The heating was on, but the chill still clung to him, burrowing beneath his coat like an unwelcome reminder of how far he felt from the warmth of home.

A gift for Teddy sat on the passenger seat, still in its shiny carrier bag. It was a history-themed puzzle set. Medieval castles, knights, and siege equipment. He'd grabbed it on impulse from a nearby shop late the night before, a half-hearted attempt to seem thoughtful when his mind had been consumed by everything else. It wasn't bad, he supposed. But St. Michael couldn't shake the nagging thought that it wasn't enough. Not for a boy who deserved so much more than hurried, last-minute gestures.

St. Michael's gaze flicked to the rearview mirror, where the pristine child seat sat unused, its straps neatly fastened, its surface immaculate. He'd bought it as a small, hopeful act of preparation. Perhaps a part of him had believed that having it there, waiting, might make the possibility of more time with Teddy feel more real. Instead, it had become a silent reminder of all the promises he hadn't yet fulfilled.

He exhaled sharply, his breath fogging faintly in the cool air, and turned his attention back to the road.

His thoughts spun, unrelenting and chaotic, each one bleeding into the next.

Teddy. Michelle. Lucy.

Their names carried their own weight, pulling at him from different corners of his mind. The last few days had been a whirlwind. Too fast, too chaotic, too utterly surreal. He'd stood on Napoleon's battlefield at Austerlitz, watched Hitler's address in Nuremberg, and been hunted by Nexians wielding impossible power. He and Lucy had pieced together fragments of her mother's life, unravelling truths that stretched far beyond anything he'd thought himself capable of understanding.

And now, here he was. Driving down the North Circular Road on a quiet Saturday morning, preparing to see his son for the first time in weeks.

The dissonance was suffocating.

He could still hear the muffled roar of the crowd at Nuremberg, feel the icy wind of Austerlitz cutting through his coat, see the flicker of light as a Nexian destroyed Evelyn's note. Every detail clung to him like smoke, impossible to shake.

His chest tightened at the thought of his son. Teddy, with his quick grin and boundless energy, who had once run to greet him with outstretched arms and a shout of "Daddy!"—a sound so full of love it had almost undone him every time. But lately, those moments had become rarer, the bond between them stretched thin by distance, time, and mistakes he couldn't undo.

And then there was Michelle.

Her name was like a bruise. Tender, aching and impossible to ignore. He could still picture her clearly, even now. Her soft brown eyes, so full of warmth and fire, the way she used to look at him when she thought he wasn't paying attention. He hadn't seen that version of

Michelle in a long time. The woman he saw now was guarded, her voice sharp and efficient, her expressions carefully controlled. She wielded her words with precision, every conversation a quiet reminder of how much had been lost between them.

But the love was still there. God, it was still there.

Every time he saw her, the ache of it returned, sharp and unrelenting. It lived in the spaces between them, in the silences they couldn't quite fill. He wanted to bridge the gap, to reach out and touch the part of her that still felt like home. But he didn't know how. And the fear of making things worse always stopped him before he could try.

A horn blared, jarring him back to the present. He realised, too late, that he'd drifted slightly into the other lane and quickly corrected, his heart pounding. "Pull yourself together, man," he muttered under his breath, shaking his head.

The last thing he needed was to show up shaken. Teddy deserved better than that.

Still, his mind wouldn't quieten. The day ahead felt heavy with significance, like a crossroads he wasn't prepared for. Seeing Teddy always left him feeling both elated and hollow, a reminder of everything he had and everything he'd lost. And now, with the weight of what he and Lucy had uncovered, the stakes felt even higher.

His thoughts drifted once more, unbidden, to *the Nexus. The Custodians. The Codex.* It was staggering to think how much power existed in the shadows, wielded by forces no one even knew existed. The world kept turning, oblivious to the wars being fought beneath its surface.

And yet, for all the danger, all the monumental implications of their discovery, it was the thought of Teddy that gripped him most tightly.

Because if the Nexus was as dangerous as Alaric had hinted, and the account of the Great Schism suggested, then none of them—not Teddy, not Michelle, not anyone—was truly safe.

The thought clawed at him, threatening to spiral out of control. He shook his head, gripping the wheel tighter. *Focus.* Today wasn't about the Nexus or the Custodians. It was about Teddy.

* * *

The landscape shifted as St. Michael drove into Kingston, trading the dense traffic of central London for its busier high streets and open, tree-lined roads. He let his gaze wander briefly, taking in the familiar surroundings.

As the park where he and Michelle had agreed to meet came into view, St. Michael slowed the car, his stomach twisting with a mix of nerves and anticipation.

He pulled into a parking space and turned off the engine, the silence in the car suddenly deafening. His hands rested on the steering wheel for a moment, his grip loosening as he exhaled deeply.

The gift bag rustled faintly as he picked it up, turning it over in his hands. It wasn't perfect, but it was something. And for now, that had to be enough.

St. Michael stepped through the heavy iron gates, the distant sound of children's laughter cutting through the stillness. His breath misted faintly in the crisp air as he slipped his phone out of his pocket.

No messages from Lucy.

He'd checked three times on the drive over, willing some kind of update from her. He was hoping Lucy would let him know how her meeting with Alaric had gone, but there'd been nothing. The silence weighed on him, but he knew he couldn't afford to let his mind drift. He needed to be here—*fully here*—for Teddy.

The park stretched out before him, sprawling and open, the paths glistening faintly where the frost hadn't yet melted. To his left, by the metal railings that separated the park from the quiet road beyond, he spotted a bench. Michelle was there, sitting with her legs crossed, her posture effortlessly poised. St. Michael's heart lurched, as it always did when he saw her.

For a moment, he froze. She looked as though she'd been lifted straight from one of his memories, a version of her he'd always carried in his mind. Her dark brown hair fell in loose, flowing waves that brushed against the collar of her coat, the rich chestnut strands catching the winter sunlight. Her skin, always glowing with a natural warmth, seemed to defy the chill of the season. A patterned scarf looped elegantly around her neck, its soft fabric complementing the sleek black coat that hugged her figure.

She wore sunglasses. Oversized, the kind most people wouldn't even think to put on in the middle of January. But Michelle could wear anything and make it look deliberate, as though winter itself had bent its rules just for her. St. Michael felt a knot in his stomach as he took her in. *She was stunning.* She always had been, but there was something about seeing her here, so close yet so far, that made it all the more painful.

He glanced toward the playground and spotted Teddy, darting between the climbing frame and a low slide. The sight of his son—his wild, carefree movements—filled him with a complicated mix of joy and grief. For a moment, he wasn't sure where to go first. The decision felt weighted, as though it carried more significance than it should.

Finally, he adjusted his scarf, straightened his coat, and made his way toward Michelle.

She noticed him as he approached, turning her head slightly but keeping her posture relaxed. Her smile was polite, almost hesitant, but it didn't quite reach her eyes. "Morning," she said, her voice calm and even.

"You alright?" St. Michael replied, his tone quiet but a little too fast.

He stopped a few feet from the bench, unsure whether to sit or hover. He opted for a slightly awkward lean against the bench's armrest, his hands shoved deep into his coat pockets.

"It's cold, init," he said, gesturing vaguely at the park around them.

Michelle nodded, her lips twitching into a faint smile. "Looks like the sun's trying to break through though," she replied, tilting her chin up slightly.

"Yeah," he agreed, his breath fogging faintly in the air. He glanced at her again, unable to help himself. "You, uh… you look good."

Her head turned toward him, and even through the sunglasses, he could feel her eyes on him. "Thanks," she said, her tone neutral.

There was a brief pause, the silence between them awkward but charged. St. Michael shifted his weight from one foot to the other, glancing toward the playground. "Where's Teddy?" he asked, though he already knew the answer.

Michelle inclined her head toward the climbing frame. "Over there," she said simply.

"Right. Of course." St. Michael nodded quickly, glancing toward the boy before turning back to Michelle. He felt clumsy, as though his words weren't landing properly.

"I've got him something," he said, reaching into his coat pocket and pulling out the small bag from the passenger seat earlier. "You know… just a little something, something."

There was something guarded in Michelle's expression. "That's nice of you," she said, her voice carefully measured.

He swallowed, feeling the tension in the air between them. "Yeah, thought he might like it. It's a history puzzle—castles, knights, all that jazz. It looks right up his street."

Michelle tilted her head slightly, her expression softening just enough to take the edge off her words. "You didn't have to," she said quietly.

"I wanted to," St. Michael replied quickly, his voice earnest.

Before the silence could stretch any further, Michelle turned toward the playground. "Teddy!" she called, her voice carrying just enough authority to cut through the chatter of children.

Teddy's head popped up from behind the slide, his sandy brown hair messy and windswept beneath his hat. For a moment, he hesitated, looking toward Michelle and then toward St. Michael before reluctantly making his way over.

St. Michael straightened as Teddy approached, his heart thudding heavily in his chest. When the boy finally reached them, he stopped just short, his hands tucked into his pockets and his gaze flickering between the two adults.

"Hi, mate," St. Michael said, crouching slightly to meet him at eye level. "You all okay?"

Teddy shifted his weight from foot to foot. "Yes thanks," he said, his voice quiet.

The interaction hung in the air, awkward and stilted. St. Michael searched for something—anything—to bridge the gap between them. He held up the bag, offering a smile he hoped didn't look as nervous as he felt.

"I got you something," he said, glancing at Michelle for confirmation. "If that's alright?"

She nodded once. "Yeah, go ahead," she said, her voice softer now.

Teddy took the bag and pulled out the puzzle box. He studied the cover, his expression carefully neutral. "It's cool," he said after a moment, though his tone betrayed a lack of genuine interest.

St. Michael smiled, ignoring the sting. "Thought you might like it. It's got castles, and you can build the catapults yourself. Pretty cool, huh?"

"Thanks," Teddy mumbled, glancing at Michelle as if for reassurance.

"Teddy," she said gently, her voice carrying just the faintest edge. "Say thank you properly."

"Thank you," Teddy said, a little louder this time.

"You're welcome mate," St. Michael replied quickly.

Teddy glanced back toward the playground. "Can I go play now?" he asked, his tone a mix of impatience and politeness.

Michelle nodded. "Go on, then."

Teddy handed the puzzle back to St. Michael before darting back toward the climbing frame, his small figure disappearing among the other children.

St. Michael stood, holding the box awkwardly for a moment before slipping it back into the bag. He handed it to Michelle, his expression resigned.

"Sorry," he murmured.

"It's fine," she said, taking the bag from him. Her voice was calm, but there was something unreadable in her tone. "He's just… distracted. That's all."

"Yeah," St. Michael replied, his voice quieter now. "I get it."

They fell into a tense silence, the sound of children playing filling the air around them. St. Michael's gaze drifted toward Teddy, watching as the boy climbed the steps to the slide. There was a lump in his throat that he couldn't seem to swallow, an ache in his chest that refused to ease.

St. Michael sank onto the bench beside Michelle, the cool metal biting through his coat. He sat to her right, leaving a respectful distance between them, though it felt like an insurmountable chasm. Michelle's eyes were fixed on the playground where Teddy climbed the steps to the slide with a confidence that tugged at St. Michael's chest. He wanted to say something, anything, but the words tangled in his throat.

Instead, he stared at his son, drinking in the sight of him. The way his hair caught the sunlight, the bounce in his step as he reached the top. Teddy looked taller than the last time he'd seen him, more self-assured, less like the small boy who used to cling to his hand whenever they crossed the road.

"He's changed," St. Michael said finally, his voice quiet but warm. "He's grown so much."

Michelle turned her head slightly, as though debating whether to respond. For a moment, she said nothing, her profile serene but unreadable behind her sunglasses. Then she let out a short, bittersweet laugh.

"Yeah, he has," she said, her tone measured but with an edge to it. "Kids tend to do that when you're not around to see it."

St. Michael flinched at her words. He tried to muster a response, but she cut him off before he could speak.

"It's been what—weeks? Months?" she continued, her voice rising slightly. "And then, out of the blue, you text me asking to see him like it's nothing. Like it doesn't matter that you're never here."

"Michelle, that's not fair—" St. Michael began weakly, but she didn't let him finish.

"Isn't it?" she interrupted, turning to face him fully now. Her sunglasses couldn't hide the intensity in her voice. "You come and go whenever it suits you, and it's not good for him, Michael. He needs more than that. He needs you to be consistent. To actually be a part of his life, not just some random visitor."

St. Michael's shoulders slumped, her words hitting harder than any argument they'd had before. He knew she was right. He had no defence, no justification that didn't sound hollow even to his own ears.

"I've been busy," he said weakly, the excuse barely leaving his lips before Michelle shook her head, cutting him off again.

"It's always work," she said, her voice quieter now but no less firm. "Something always comes up, doesn't it? History. Research. Whatever it is. It's all so important to you. You're so caught up in that past that you're missing the present."

She gestured toward Teddy, who was now laughing with another child on the roundabout. "He's here, Michael. Right here. And you're letting these moments slip through your fingers. Do you even realise how much he needs you? Because I'm telling you, he's becoming a stranger to you. And you to him."

St. Michael stared at Teddy, his heart breaking under the weight of her words. He wanted to argue, to explain that his work wasn't just a job, that it had become something far greater, far more dangerous than she could understand. But what could he say that didn't sound like another excuse?

"I know," he said finally, his voice cracking. He leaned forward, resting his elbows on his knees and staring at the ground. "I know I haven't been there. And it kills me every single day."

Michelle softened slightly, though her expression remained guarded. "Then change it, Michael," she said gently but firmly. "Don't just say it. Do it. He deserves that."

St. Michael took a deep breath, the air catching in his throat as he nodded. "I will," he said, his voice stronger now. "I swear I will."

For a moment, they sat in silence, the tension between them easing slightly as they both watched Teddy climb onto the swings. Michelle was the one to break the quiet.

"So," she said, trying to break the tension, "what's been keeping you so busy? Your research was never exactly the lightest of reading."

St. Michael hesitated, glancing at her before replying. "Actually, do you remember Evelyn Calder?"

Michelle frowned slightly, the name sparking recognition. "Of course. She was amazing for you. Why?"

"I'm working with her daughter now," St. Michael said, letting a soft smile creep in. "Her name's Lucy. She's… she's incredible, honestly. Smart, determined, reminds me so much of Evelyn."

Michelle raised an eyebrow, surprised. "I didn't know Evelyn had a daughter."

"Not many people did," St. Michael said. "She's a lot like her mum—sharp, relentless. We're working on something big together. It's… complicated, but she's brilliant."

Michelle gave a small nod, her curiosity satisfied for now. "Well, if she's anything like Evelyn, I'm sure you've got your hands full."

St. Michael chuckled softly. "You could say that."

The conversation tapered off naturally, and for a while, they simply watched Teddy, his laughter carrying on the breeze. St. Michael felt a flicker of something—hope, maybe—at the ease between them, fragile as it was.

"Look," he said, turning toward her. "I know things have been hectic lately, but it won't always be like this. Once things settle down, I was thinking… maybe the three of us could go away somewhere. Barcelona, Venice, Rome—wherever you and Teddy want."

Michelle hesitated, her expression shifting as she looked down at her hands.

"I don't know, Michael," she said softly. "I don't think that's a good idea."

St. Michael frowned, leaning closer. "Why not? It'd be good for Teddy to spend time with both of us. And for us… it'd give us a chance to—"

"Michael." Her voice was quiet but deliberate, cutting him off gently this time. She hesitated, as though searching for the right words. "I'm… I've started seeing someone."

The world seemed to tilt beneath him, her words landing like a blow to his chest. For a moment, he couldn't breathe.

"Oh," he said finally, the word hollow and small. He cleared his throat, forcing himself to look at her. "I didn't realise."

Michelle nodded, her expression careful but kind.

"Is it… serious?" St. Michael asked, his voice unsteady.

"Yeah," she said softly.

He swallowed hard, his chest tightening painfully. "Who is he?"

"It doesn't matter," Michelle replied gently, glancing at him briefly. "You don't know him."

St. Michael's jaw tensed as he nodded slowly. But before he could say anything else, Michelle continued.

"He makes me happy," she said, her voice quieter now, as though admitting it to herself as much as to him. "He's… he's been there for me, Michael. And he's been there for Teddy too."

St. Michael's head snapped toward her at that, his expression shifting. "Wait—what? He's met Teddy?"

Michelle turned to face him fully, her tone calm but firm. "Of course, he has. He's a part of my life, and Teddy's a part of my life. It wouldn't make sense to keep them apart."

St. Michael's chest tightened further, the weight of her words almost unbearable. This man—some stranger—was everything he had failed to be. Everything he wanted to be.

Michelle hesitated, as though sensing the turmoil in him. "But," she added, her voice soft, "that doesn't mean he's replacing you. He's not. He never could. You're still Teddy's dad, and you always will be."

St. Michael nodded numbly, his gaze fixed on Teddy as his son laughed on the swings, blissfully unaware of the storm brewing in his father's chest.

The bench beneath them had grown colder, the chill seeping through St. Michael's coat as the weight of the conversation settled between him and Michelle. Her words had softened, the sharp edges of her frustration dulled as she noticed his hurt expression. St. Michael hadn't said much since she mentioned her new relationship, but the silence spoke volumes. His shoulders slumped, his gaze fixed downward, and the defeat etched into his features told her everything she needed to know.

For a moment, Michelle just watched him. Seeing him like this—so small, so lost—stirred something tender in her. Against her better judgment, she spoke gently. "Michael," she said softly, her tone free of its earlier bite. "Look at me."

He hesitated before reluctantly turning to meet her eyes.

"Teddy loves you," she said, her voice firm but kind. "He still loves his dad. That hasn't changed, no matter what's happened. And it won't change."

St. Michael nodded faintly, his throat tight as he swallowed the lump that had been forming for the past few minutes. He wanted to thank her, to acknowledge her kindness, but the words wouldn't come. Instead, he just blinked, his eyes slightly glassy.

Michelle's voice softened further, quieter now, almost as though she were thinking aloud. "It's just… hard, you know? I've had to make a lot of decisions on my own.

And sometimes it feels like…" She trailed off, searching for the right words, but St. Michael wasn't listening anymore.

Something behind her had caught his attention.

Over her shoulder, on the far side of the park, stood a man.

Dressed in a black hoodie pulled tightly over his head, black cargo trousers, and a distinctive white mask. *That mask.* The same mask he had seen before—it's rough, aged texture like weathered bone, its inlets for eyes and a nose eerily blank, as if no one human could exist behind it.

The world seemed to shift, the sounds of the park dulling, Michelle's voice becoming a distant sound. His focus was completely consumed by the figure, standing motionless beneath the shadows of a tree, its stillness unnerving.

Then, deliberately, the Nexian tilted his head to one side. A calculated, taunting gesture that sent a chill down St. Michael's spine.

The Nexian shifted his gaze. Toward the play park. Toward Teddy.

St. Michael's blood ran cold. A primal fear gripped him, twisting in his chest.

"Michael?" Michelle's voice cut faintly through the haze, confusion lacing her tone. "Michael, what are you looking at?"

Her words barely registered. St. Michael couldn't take his eyes off the figure. The Nexian didn't move, didn't make any other gesture, yet his presence alone screamed danger. His gaze was fixed on Teddy, and the meaning was unmistakable. A threat. A challenge. A warning.

Michelle's voice sharpened. "Michael? What's wrong?"

He snapped into action, his body moving on instinct.

"Teddy!" he shouted, springing to his feet and sprinting toward the play park.

Teddy, midway up the steps to the slide, looked up, startled.

St. Michael ran, his heart pounding, the world narrowing to the single focus of reaching his son. "Teddy!" he called again, his voice raw with panic.

Teddy froze, confusion flashing across his small face. He barely had time to react before St. Michael reached him, scooping him up into his arms and holding him tightly.

"Dad?" Teddy's voice was small, uncertain. "What's happening?"

St. Michael didn't answer. His eyes darted back to where the Nexian had been. The figure was gone. As if he'd never been there.

Michelle came running behind him. Her face was a mix of anger and confusion, her voice sharp as she approached. "Michael! What are you doing?"

St. Michael stood in the middle of the play park, clutching Teddy against his chest. Around him, the other children had stopped playing, their faces filled with confusion and fear. Parents edged closer to the railings, some murmuring to each other, their expressions concerned.

"Michael!" Michelle repeated, reaching him. "What are you doing?" she demanded, now holding her sunglasses in her hand.

St. Michael turned, his breathing ragged. "There was someone," he said, his voice trembling. "Over there. Watching."

Michelle frowned, following his pointed hand. "There's no one there," she said, her tone clipped.

"There was," St. Michael insisted. "He was standing right there, Michelle. Staring at Teddy."

Michelle's expression shifted, a flicker of concern crossing her face before frustration took over. "You're scaring him," she said, her voice low but firm. "Look at him."

St. Michael glanced down at Teddy, who was clinging to him, his small hands gripping St. Michael's coat. Teddy's eyes were wide, his lower lip trembling.

"I'm sorry," St. Michael said softly, loosening his hold but still keeping Teddy close. "I just… I had to—"

"Had to what?" Michelle cut in, her voice rising. "Michael, you're not making any sense!"

"I can't explain it," St. Michael said, his voice faltering.

Michelle stared at him, her frustration giving way to something closer to pity. "Michael," she said quietly, her tone softening. "What's happened to you?"

He shook his head, unable to answer. How could he explain the Nexus, the mask, the danger he felt closing in around them? How could he make her understand?

"Give him to me," Michelle said gently, stepping closer.

St. Michael hesitated, his arms tightening slightly around Teddy. But the look in Michelle's eyes—firm yet compassionate—convinced him to let go. Slowly, he handed him over, his heart sinking as Teddy immediately clung to his mother.

Michelle held Teddy close, stroking his hair. She looked back at St. Michael, her expression unreadable. "I knew this was a mistake," she said, her voice quiet but cutting.

"No," St. Michael said quickly, reaching out toward her. "It's not safe. Neither of you are safe."

Michelle froze, her brow furrowing. "What do you mean?"

St. Michael opened his mouth to speak but faltered. He didn't know how to explain it, didn't know how to put into words the threat that felt so real and yet so impossible to prove. "I can't…" He shook his head, his voice breaking. "I can't explain it."

Michelle's eyes searched his, her concern deepening. For a moment, she looked like she might say something, but then she shook her head. "Michael," she said softly, almost pleadingly, "you need help."

And with that, she turned and walked away, holding Teddy tightly as they headed toward the gate.

St. Michael stood frozen, his eyes fixed on their retreating figures. Around him, the park emptied, parents pulling their children away with wary glances in his direction. The silence was deafening.

Finally, he turned and walked back to his car, the weight of everything crashing over him. Michelle's words etched into his mind, the thought of her with another man, the distance between him and Teddy feeling wider than ever. And then there was the Nexian. The mask that haunted his every thought.

Reaching his car, St. Michael lashed out, kicking the side of it. Pain shot through his shin, sharp and grounding, but it did nothing to ease the anger.

Leaning against the car, he pulled out his phone. His fingers trembled as he typed a message to Lucy.

He hit send and shoved the phone back into his pocket, staring out at the empty park. The Order of The Nexus had threatened his son.

And St. Michael wasn't going to let that happen again.

CHAPTER 13
Thresholds

Later that day.

Lucy woke with a sharp gasp, her entire body ached. Every muscle screaming in protest, her limbs refusing to move the way she wanted them to. Even breathing felt like work, each inhale dragging against the tightness in her ribs.

Her head throbbed faintly, the kind of pulsing ache that came from too much strain. She groaned, rolling onto her side, and blinked at the pale light filtering through the edges of her curtains.

"God," she muttered, her voice hoarse and dry, "this is worse than a hangover."

As her body caught up with her mind, the memories of the night before came rushing back. Alaric's voice. The roar of fire as it bent to her will. The searing heat of lightning as it cracked from her fingertips, lighting up the darkened castle grounds. The weight of her own power, raw and barely contained, surging through her veins like molten steel.

She sat up slowly, wincing as she did. It wasn't just the physical toll—though that was bad enough. It was the emotional weight of what she'd learned, what she'd done. She'd reached into the fabric of time and pulled something real from it, something elemental and ancient. And now, that power was hers to command.

Her phone buzzed faintly on the bedside table, its
vibration cutting through the silence. Turning toward it
with a groan, she grabbed it and squinted at the screen.

15:07

"Fucking three o'clock?" she said aloud and with
disbelief. "How—?"

She unlocked the phone, her heart sinking as the
notifications lit up the screen.

**St. Michael (10:44): Hi Lucy, I hope last night went
alright. Can you give me a call?**
**St. Michael (11:58): Are you up? Let me know when
you see this.**
**St. Michael (12:46): Lucy? It's important. Please call
me.**
**St. Michael (15:07): I need to hear from you, I'm
starting to worry!**

Missed Calls (2)

Lucy's concern deepened. St. Michael didn't seem the
type to panic easily. The growing urgency in his messages
sent a wave of unease through her. Whatever had
happened, it wasn't good.

Swinging her legs over the edge of the bed, she winced
again as her feet reached the floor. The air was stale,
carrying the faint scent of burnt wood, a lingering trace of
the fire she'd conjured with Alaric.

With a deep breath, she steadied herself and hit the call
button. The phone barely rang before St. Michael's voice
came through, sharp and immediate. "Lucy…"

The single word was enough to send her pulse racing.
His voice was tight, the edges frayed with something she
couldn't quite place.

"Michael," she said, trying to sound calm. "What's
going on? Are you alright?"

There was a pause on the other end of the line, and then his words tumbled out in a rush. "Am I alright? I've been trying to reach you all bloody day. I was starting to think—"

"Michael," she interrupted, her voice soft but firm. "I'm fine. I—last night with Alaric… it just knackered me out. I've only woken up now. What's happened?"

He hesitated, and Lucy could hear the sound of him pacing. When he spoke again, his voice was lower, more controlled, but no less urgent.

"I saw one of them," he said. "A Nexian. This morning, in the park."

Lucy froze. Her grip on the phone tightened, her breath catching in her throat.

"A Nexian?" she repeated, her voice sharp with disbelief. "Are you sure?"

"Of course, I'm bloody sure!" he snapped, the frustration in his tone masking something deeper. Fear. "The mask, Lucy. The same as the ones we saw before. He was just standing there, watching."

Her heart sank. "Watching who?"

"Teddy," Michael said, his voice breaking slightly. "He was watching Teddy."

The words hit her like a physical blow. "What—what did he do? Did he say anything?"

"No," Michael said tightly. "He didn't have to. The way he stood there… it was a message, Lucy. A threat. I ran to Teddy, but by the time I looked back, he was gone."

Lucy exhaled shakily, her free hand gripping the edge of the desk for support. "Gone as in traversed?"

"I don't know," Michael admitted, his voice raw. "But he saw Teddy, Lucy. And now I can't stop thinking— what if they come back? What if they come after you? Or—"

"Michael," she said sharply, cutting him off before his panic could spiral further. "Teddy's safe, yeah? Michelle's with him?"

"Yes," he said, though the faint tremor in his voice remained. "But—"

"Then we're okay," Lucy said firmly. "We'll figure this out. We also aren't exactly defenceless anymore."

Michael paused, his breathing slowing slightly. "The Incants," he said finally.

"Exactly," Lucy replied, her voice steadying. She moved toward the window, pulling the curtain aside to let in a sliver of light. "Alaric showed me last night. I know how to use them now. If the Nexus shows up again, I'll be ready."

"Are you sure?" Michael asked, his voice quieter now, almost hesitant. "I mean, really sure?"

Lucy smiled faintly, the memory of her training sparking a flicker of pride. "I conjured fire, lightning, water, and wind last night, Michael. Not by accident—on purpose. Alaric showed me how to control them. Trust me."

A long silence stretched between them. When Michael spoke again, his voice was heavier, filled with a quiet resolve.

"We need some more answers," St. Michael said.

There was a heavy silence on the line, the faint crackle of static filling the void as Lucy waited for Michael to continue. She could feel the weight of his hesitation, the way he seemed to be choosing his words carefully, as if afraid of what he might say next.

Finally, he exhaled, the sound weary and laden with something unspoken. "Lucy," he began slowly, his voice quieter now, almost tentative. "I've been going through your mum's boxes and notes again. Trying to find anything—anything at all—that might help us understand what the Nexus wants with us. But it's not enough."

Lucy frowned, her fingers tightening around the phone. "What are you saying?"

"I'm saying we need more," Michael continued, his tone gaining momentum now, the edges sharper. "We need to go to the source. To the one place where this all began."

She froze. "Do you mean—"

"The Temporal Sanctuary," he said, his voice firmer now, as though speaking the words gave him the resolve to commit to them. "It's their birthplace, Lucy. If there's any place that might hold the answers we need, it's there."

Lucy stared blankly at the floor, the weight of the name sinking into her chest like a stone. The Temporal Sanctuary. She'd read the fleeting descriptions of its halls—its role as a sacred place for the Custodians before everything fell apart. It was a place heavy with history, with tragedy.

And then realisation hit her. "Michael," she said softly, her voice tinged with unease. "You remember what that place is, don't you? What it means?"

On the other end of the line, Michael fell silent. She could hear the faint rustle of papers, the sound of him shifting as though the truth itself was too heavy to hold still.

"Oh, I'm so sorry, Lucy," he said finally, his voice strained.

The words hung, heavy and unrelenting. Lucy closed her eyes, the weight of them pressing down on her. Images of her father flashed through her mind. Faded memories of his laugh, the way his eyes crinkled at the corners, the warmth of his presence that had been stolen from her far too soon.

"I should've asked you first," St. Michael continued, his tone softer now, almost apologetic. "If it's too much, if you're not ready, we'll figure out something else. I can—"

"No," Lucy said firmly, cutting him off. "We're going."

"Lucy—"

"We're going," she repeated, her voice steady and resolute. "This isn't just about me, Michael. It's about stopping them. Stopping the Nexus. If it's possible the Sanctuary holds the answers we need, then that's where we'll go."

She drew in a breath. "We'll go to Stonehenge."

St. Michael hesitated, the silence on the line stretching as he weighed her determination. Finally, he sighed, the sound filled with equal parts relief and resignation. "Alright," he said quietly. "Don't worry about coming to the office, we'll wait for all the tourists to go, so I'll pick you up at ten tonight."

Lucy nodded, though he couldn't see her. "Cool. I'll be ready."

There was a pause, and when Michael spoke again, his voice was softer, almost hesitant. "Lucy… for what it's worth, I think your father would be proud of you. Of everything you're doing."

The lump in her throat rose too quickly for her to swallow it down. She closed her eyes, the edges of her composure cracking ever so slightly. "Thanks, Michael," she said, her voice thick but steady.

"See you at ten," he said, in confirmation.

"See you then," she replied, before hanging up.

When the call ended, Lucy stood in the stillness of her flat, her mind racing. She scrolled through the notifications on her phone and then—

Shit.

Double shit

She hadn't looked at her phone in over a day, completely forgetting about the responsibilities of the real world. The world where deadlines still mattered. Like the Tudor dating article she'd forgotten about.

There were over eight chaser text messages and six missed calls from Jade. Their tone became more and more irritated. The last one, sent late last night, simply read:

Jade (22:03): Lucy, I don't know what's going on but disappearing like this isn't okay. Please call me Monday morning. We need to have a proper conversation.

Jade could sometimes be prickly at the best of times, but never like that. But for now, it wasn't important. Not to Lucy. It could wait until Monday.

She lifted her head from her screen and opened her empty palm, thinking back to the surge of energy with Alaric. Closing her eyes, she focused.

A flicker of flame appeared above her palm, small but steady. It cast warm, golden light across her face, the heat comforting.

She stared at it, her lips curving into a determined smile. "Let them fucking try," she whispered.

The fire danced in her palm. Small, steady and defiant. Hers.

* * *

Later that night

Lucy stood in the middle of her living room, hands on her hips, surveying the space. The flat felt warmer now, quieter. One candle flickered on the coffee table, throwing soft shadows across the walls.

It was a stark contrast to yesterday. A mirror of how tangled her own mind had felt. Messy, tangled, overwhelmed. Now, it was ordered, tidy and calm.

The faint scent of lavender wafted in the air, soothing but not strong enough to dull the unease twisting in her stomach. All day, her thoughts had been churning beneath the surface, circling one inevitable truth.

The Temporal Sanctuary. The place where her father had been killed. Murdered. By the Order of the Nexus.

That word had repeated in her head for hours. Her dad had been murdered—by his own kind. The thought tormented her. How could people who claimed to protect the Universal Timeline do something so… vile? The anger flared when she thought about it, but it was the hurt that lingered. The betrayal.

She thought of her mum's account she had read. Evelyn had written so much about the Sanctuary, about its purpose, its grandeur, yet never once *actually* explained how to access it. The Timebound Altar—Stonehenge— had been a gateway her parents had opened seemingly instinctively. Lucy had no idea how to do the same. What if she and St. Michael got there and couldn't even step inside? What if after all this time it no longer worked? What if it didn't recognise her?

She exhaled sharply, pulling herself out of the spiral. This wasn't the time to second-guess. They had to try.

Her phone buzzed faintly on the counter, drawing her attention. She grabbed it, glancing at the screen.

St. Michael (21:43): I'm outside. No rush if you're not ready.

Lucy smiled faintly, shaking her head. Of course, he was early. She'd predicted as much.

She slipped on her navy puffer jacket, tugging it over her cream hoodie. It was a cozy outfit—functional, warm—but it did little to shield her from the chill settling deep in her bones. The rain fell in a fine, cold drizzle.

She pulled up her hood and took one last look at the flat. Everything was in its place now. Yet there was a sense of finality as she stood in the doorway, her hand lingering on the frame. She was leaving tonight to go to the Sanctuary, the same way her father had left all those years ago. He hadn't come back.

"Not me," she whispered aloud, as if saying it made it true. She pulled the door shut behind her and locked it.

The cold drizzle hit her face as she stepped onto the street. She spotted St. Michael's car at the kerb, the headlights casting long beams through the rain. The rhythmic swipe of the windshield wipers filled the quiet.

As she approached, the passenger-side window rolled down, and St. Michael leaned over. His face was shadowed by the dim interior light, but she could see the lines of tension around his mouth. "Hey," he said, his voice soft but tired.

Lucy opened the door and slid into the seat, the warmth of the car wrapping around her like a blanket. She turned toward him and, on impulse, leaned over and gave him a quick hug. He stiffened slightly, surprised, but then relaxed, patting her back awkwardly.

"How are you doing?" she asked as she pulled back, her voice gentle.

"You know," he said after a pause, his voice tight. "I think I'm just… angry now."

Lucy tilted her head, watching him closely. He wasn't looking at her, his eyes fixed on the rain-slicked street ahead. She stayed quiet, letting him continue.

"At the time, I was bricking it," he admitted, his voice growing rougher. "Mainly for Teddy. And don't get me wrong, I still am. But now I just think—how dare they? How *dare* they threaten him? He's totally innocent in all of this."

He laughed bitterly, the sound harsh in the confined space of the car. "I mean, what kind of monsters target a child? A child, Lucy. He doesn't even know what's going on."

Lucy placed a hand on his arm, her grip firm but reassuring. "It's not fair," she said quietly. "None of this is. But we're going to figure it out. I promise you."

He finally turned to look at her, his dark eyes shadowed with exhaustion and something rawer—fear, anger, and maybe even hope. "I know we will," he said, his voice quieter now. "We have to."

They sat in silence for a moment, the rain tapping softly against the windows. Then, with a deep breath, St. Michael turned the engine on.

"Ready?" he asked, glancing at her.

Lucy nodded, tightening her seatbelt. "Ready."

* * *

The road ahead stretched on as they approached the M3, shrouded in mist and darkness yet Lucy felt a flicker of optimism. Whatever waited for them at the Temporal Sanctuary, she wouldn't face it alone.

"What do you think we'll find?" she asked softly, breaking the silence.

St. Michael glanced at her, his jaw tightening. "Honestly? I've got no idea," he admitted. "Answers, hopefully. Maybe a way to stop them. Or… maybe nothing."

Lucy nodded, but it didn't ease the knot of tension in her chest. "My mum never explained how to access the Sanctuary," she confessed. "She wrote about it, but not the specifics. She and my dad could just… do it. What if I can't?"

"You can," St. Michael said firmly, his voice cutting through her doubt. "You're Evelyn Calder's daughter. And from what I've seen, you're more than capable."

She glanced at him, her lips curving into a faint smile. "Cheers," she said, her voice barely above a whisper.

St. Michael's hands gripped the wheel tightly. He glanced at Lucy, who now sat quietly in the passenger seat, her eyes fixed on the rain-slicked world outside.

"Are you sure you're happy with this?" he asked, his voice low but laced with concern. "We could try something else, another way—maybe even wait until we know more."

Lucy turned toward him, her expression calm but resolute. "I'm sure," she said softly. "It's not gonna be easy, I know that. But waiting isn't an option. The Nexus isn't exactly giving us breathing room."

"I just don't want you to feel like you're being pushed into this. What we're walking into…" He paused, struggling to find the right words. "It's not just some historical mystery we're trying to work out. It's where your dad…" His voice trailed off, but the weight of the word hung heavily in the air.

Lucy nodded, understanding his unspoken thought. "Where he died," she finished quietly, her tone soft but steady. "Believe me, I've been thinking about that all day. About how he must have felt, what he must have been thinking."

St. Michael glanced at her, his expression heavy with worry. "And you're still willing to do this?"

"I am," she replied, her voice growing stronger. "It's not just about him. It's about us stopping the Nexus. They keep showing up—first in the alley, then Austerlitz, then on the fucking road and now they're watching your son? We can't afford to hesitate."

St. Michael exhaled slowly. "It's like they've been one step ahead of us the whole time," he muttered, his frustration simmering beneath his words. "But what I don't get—what I can't stop thinking about—is why they haven't just killed us. After what we learned, I just assumed they wanted us dead. So why not just… do it? They've had plenty of chances."

Lucy tilted her head in thought. "Maybe they don't want us dead," she said, her voice cautious, as though testing the theory aloud.

St. Michael glanced at her sharply. "Then what do they want? To mess with us? To keep us guessing? Because I tell you what, they're bloody succeeding."

She shook her head. "I don't know. And that's the part that scares me the most." Her gaze dropped to her lap, her fingers fidgeting slightly with the cuff of her sleeve. "Alaric said that after the Schism, the Nexus rounded up other Custodians. Gave them an ultimatum. Either join or…" she trailed off, unable to finish.

"Be killed," St. Michael said, staring straight ahead.

A brief silence settled between them.

"But that still doesn't make sense." His voice picked up, as if the thought had only just clicked. "I mean, respectfully, you're not exactly their ideal recruit. You've only just started piecing this together now."

"The one who approached me in the alley more or less said 'stay out the way'—not really an ultimatum," Lucy replied, glancing over at him.

"And now they just keep appearing." A lower note crept into St. Michael's voice. "Did you ask Alaric about the language?"

Lucy blinked at him, confused.

"In Austerlitz. You couldn't understand anything they were saying." He sounded almost surprised she'd forgotten.

"Oh fuck," Lucy muttered, pressing her hands to her head. "No—once we got going, I was knackered and it completely slipped my mind."

"That's okay, we'll just ask next time we go," St. Michael said, offering a reassuring smile.

The sound of the rain intensified briefly, the drops drumming harder against the roof of the car. Lucy leaned her head against the window, watching the droplets race down the glass. After a moment, she spoke again, her voice quieter now.

"How was it with Teddy? Before… before the Nexus turned up, I mean."

St. Michael's expression darkened, "Difficult," he admitted, his words heavy. "He looks at me like I'm… I don't know. Like I'm that cousin you see once a year at Christmas. The one your mum forces you to be nice to because they're family." He let out a bitter laugh, shaking his head. "I used to be his whole world, Lucy. Now I'm just some bloke who turns up occasionally with a gift and pretends that makes up for everything."

Lucy winced, her heart aching at the rawness of his words. "That's not fair on you."

"It's not fair on him," St. Michael corrected, his voice sharp with self-reproach. "I wasn't there for him, Lucy. Not properly. And now he doesn't know how to let me back in. That's my fault."

"You're too hard on yourself," she said gently, turning to face him fully. "Teddy loves you. He's just a child, Michael. He doesn't know how to process all of this."

"Maybe," he muttered, though his tone was unconvinced. "But then there's Michelle. Apparently, she's seeing someone."

Lucy blinked, surprised by the shift in conversation. "Oh," she said, unsure how to respond at first. "How do you feel about that?"

St. Michael's laugh was bitter and self-deprecating. "From what Michelle says, he's everything I'm not. Everything I've failed to be. He's reliable, stable, present. And you know what? I can't even be angry about it. She deserves that. Teddy deserves that."

"Michael," Lucy said, her voice gentle but firm. "You're being too hard on yourself. You're trying. And that matters more than you realise."

He shook his head, his grip on the wheel tightening again. "It's not enough, Lucy. This bloke—I want to hate him, but I can't, because all I can think is—he's the kind of man I should be. The kind of dad Teddy deserves."

Lucy felt the raw emotion in his words. "Teddy doesn't need some perfect version of you," she said softly. "He needs *you*. The real you. The one who shows up, even when it's hard. The one who cares. That's what matters."

He glanced at her, his eyes glinting with something unspoken. "He's my reason for everything," he said quietly, almost to himself. "He's the only reason I keep going. But I don't know if it's enough."

Lucy gave his arm a comforting squeeze, her voice steady. "It's enough. And we're going to figure this out, Michael. For Teddy. For all of us."

St. Michael nodded. "Thanks," he murmured, his voice barely audible.

They fell into silence again. Both were lost in thought, the weight of their next destination pressing heavily on their minds.

The lights of the motorway stretched ahead, a glowing thread leading them toward whatever waited at the Timebound Altar. Lucy felt a smidge of determination stir within her. Whatever lay ahead, they would face it together.

* * *

The car rumbled quietly to a stop, its tyres crunching against the gravelly track just outside the looming silhouette of Stonehenge. Rain pattered softly on the windshield, a fine, misty drizzle that seemed to coat everything in a cold, damp sheen. Beyond the beams of the car's headlights, the stones stood like dark sentinels against the horizon, shrouded in shadow. Their massive forms loomed over the night, timeless and unyielding,

224

exuding an air of solemn authority that made the hairs on Lucy's arms prickle.

As St. Michael turned the car off, Lucy stared out at the ancient monument, her breath fogging slightly on the window. Her hands rested on her thighs, still and tense. She thought of her dad, of her mum, and everything they'd endured.

She exhaled sharply, the sound breaking the silence. Then, almost as if to dispel the weight in the air, she slapped her palms lightly against her legs and muttered, "Right," her voice low and filled with determination. She reached for the car door handle, the cool metal cold under her fingers.

Just as she began to push the door open, St. Michael's hand darted out, gently wrapping around her forearm. His touch was firm but not forceful, enough to make her pause.

"Lucy," he said, his voice quiet but steady, cutting through the drizzle tapping against the windows. "Are you absolutely sure about this? You've been through so much already, and this—" He glanced toward the shadowy outline of the stones. "This is something else entirely. I just want to make absolutely sure you're ready."

She turned to him, startled by the depth of concern in his voice. His eyes searched hers as if trying to find the answer for her. The lines of his face were tense, his usual calm demeanour softened by an undercurrent of protectiveness.

For a moment, she didn't speak. Instead, she studied him, her expression softening despite the knot of nerves twisting in her stomach. "Thank you," she said finally, her voice quiet but sincere. "For asking. For… caring. Genuinely."

St. Michael's grip on her arm loosened slightly, but he didn't pull away. His voice was a shade softer now. "I just don't want you to push yourself too hard."

Lucy offered him a faint smile, a flicker of warmth breaking through the tension etched into her features. "I appreciate that," she said, placing her hand lightly over his. "But I have to do this. I need to see it. We need to understand."

His lips pressed into a thin line, and he gave a small nod. "Alright," he said quietly. "But if you change your mind at any point, just say the word."

"I won't," Lucy said with a soft determination. She squeezed his hand briefly before letting go, her resolve solidifying. "But I know you've got my back if I do."

That seemed to ease him slightly. He gave her a faint smile, the edges of his tension softening. "Always."

They stepped out of the car into the cold night. Lucy pulled her puffer jacket tight around her as the damp air wrapped around them like a second skin. The drizzle was steady, fine enough to blur the edges of St. Michael's car and persistent enough to soak through her hair. The ground squelched underfoot as they stood side by side, staring at the towering stones ahead.

Stonehenge rose from the earth like a monument to another world, its weathered surfaces darkened by the rain. Lucy took it in. She'd seen it countless times. But tonight, knowing its true purpose, it felt like something entirely different. Something alive.

"It's strange, isn't it?" Lucy murmured, her voice barely louder than the rain. "How many people come here, year after year, marvel at it, take their photos… and they have no idea what it really is."

St. Michael nodded, his hands tucked into his coat pockets as he stared at the stones. "Millions of people, generation after generation," he said quietly. "And yet we're standing here, knowing it's not just a monument. It's… more. And we're some of the only ones who know."

Lucy glanced at him. "Do you ever wonder how many others do know? Or what they've done with that knowledge?"

His gaze didn't waver from the stones. "Ever since we found out its purpose," he admitted. "But I try not to think about it too much. It's enough to worry about what we're doing with it." He paused, his jaw tightening slightly. "And what it's done to us."

That last comment hit Lucy harder than she expected. She turned back to the stones, her eyes tracing their jagged outlines. "And what it's going to do to us," she murmured.

Neither of them spoke after that. Instead, they began walking, their boots sinking slightly into the wet earth with each step. The closer they got, the heavier the air seemed to grow. Lucy felt her heart rate pick up, a faint thrumming in her chest that wasn't just nerves.

She slowed as they reached the outer edge of the circle. The hum began as a faint vibration in her sternum, subtle and insistent. She stopped abruptly, pressing a hand to her chest.

"Michael," she said softly, glancing at him. "Do you feel that? Or… hear it?"

He frowned, glancing at her with concern. "Feel what?"

"There's a hum," she said, her hand still against her chest. "It's faint, but it's there. It's getting stronger."

He shook his head. "I don't feel anything," he said, watching her closely. "Are you alright?"

Lucy nodded, but her focus was already shifting back to the stones. The hum grew stronger with each step she took, resonating through her body like a tuning fork vibrating against bone. It wasn't just a sound, it was a feeling, a resonance that pulsed in time with her heartbeat.

By the time they reached the centre of the circle, the sensation was overwhelming. Lucy stopped again as the vibration swelled, filling her entire being. She felt as though she were standing on the edge of something vast and unfathomable, the weight of time itself pressing down on her.

St. Michael looked at her, his expression a mixture of concern and amazement. "Lucy, are you sure you're okay?"

Lucy closed her eyes, letting the sensation flood her senses. "Yeah, I'm fine, but it's just… I don't know how to open it," she admitted, her voice tight with frustration.

Lucy began to walk, her boots squelching softly against the wet ground as she circled the stones. Her hand brushed lightly against the cold, rough surface of each one, her eyes scanning them as though they might reveal their secret. The hum remained constant, guiding her.

As she approached one particular trilithon, the vibration surged, the resonance almost overpowering. She stopped abruptly, her breath catching. "It's this one," she said firmly, her voice steady.

"How do you know?" St. Michael asked, watching her closely.

"I just do," Lucy replied, her voice filled with conviction. She placed her hand against the stone, the cold surface rough under her fingertips. The hum grew louder, resonating through her arm, her chest, her entire being.

A surge of energy flooded her veins, different from anything she'd felt before. It wasn't like traversing or summoning an Incant, it was deeper, rawer, like the stones themselves were alive and willing her to act. Her hand rose instinctively. As it hovered between the stones, the air rippled and distorted.

The space beyond the trilithon shimmered, bending and warping as though reality itself was unravelling. The distortion deepened, solidifying into a shimmering gateway that pulsed with an otherworldly energy.

"I can see it," St. Michael said, his voice hushed with awe. "It's… it's changing."

Lucy didn't answer. Her focus was entirely on the energy surging through her, the timeline itself seeming to guide her movements. She lowered her hand, her breath coming in shallow gasps as the gateway stabilized. She turned to St. Michael, her expression resolute.

Without thinking, she extended her hand toward him. "Stay close," she said, her voice steady despite the weight of what they were about to do.

He hesitated only for a moment before taking her hand, his grip firm and reassuring.

Together, they stepped through.

The sensation was indescribable. It was as though their very essence was being unravelled, dissolved into pure energy before being rewoven into something new. Every thought, every sensation blurred into a kaleidoscope of light and sound. It wasn't painful, but it was overwhelming, a total surrender of self to the unknown.

When the world finally settled around them, they were standing hand in hand, their breaths coming in unsteady gasps. They turned slowly, their eyes widening as they took in the sight before them.

It was vast and unyielding. Its beauty and terror blurred together, vast and unknowable. Breath-taking.

Lucy's hand tightened around St. Michael's. Neither of them spoke.

They had arrived. The Temporal Sanctuary awaited them.

CHAPTER 14
Beneath The Broken Sky

The first thing Lucy noticed was the silence. It wasn't the kind of quiet she was used to. The soft hum of her flat when she was alone. No, this silence was oppressive, weighty, as if the very air held its breath. Her boots clicked faintly against the cracked marble beneath her, the sound swallowed almost immediately by the vast emptiness surrounding her.

She and St. Michael stood together at the edge of the Plaza. The once-pristine marble platform stretched out before them, but its grandeur was a ghost of its former self. Cracks veined the surface like spiderwebs. The faint light that once illuminated the plaza now pulsed erratically, casting long, wavering shadows across the expanse.

Lucy stepped forward hesitantly, her eyes drawn to the faint inscription carved into the edge of the plaza's central pedestal. Despite the wear, the words were still legible:

The Central Plaza: The Heart of Custodian Harmony.

"This must've been the centre of everything," Lucy murmured, her voice breaking the oppressive quiet. "It looks like a meeting place. Custodians must have come here to talk, plan, and reflect."

St. Michael nodded, his gaze sweeping across the ruined platform. "You can see how it was designed for that. The bridges—they all start here."

Lucy followed his gaze to the remnants of the Celestial Bridges, their translucent, glowing surfaces now cracked and unstable. A few still stretched out toward the horizon, their once-steady hum replaced by a faint, dissonant crackle. Others were broken entirely, their shattered ends sparking faintly as they hovered precariously in the air. One bridge leaned dangerously, its surface flickering like a dying ember.

"Do you think they were all destroyed in the schism?" Lucy asked, stepping closer to one of the flickering bridges.

"Maybe," St. Michael said, his tone grim. "Or maybe the sanctuary just couldn't hold itself together after what happened."

Lucy reached out, her hand brushing against the faint energy pulsing through the nearest bridge. The sensation was strange, like static electricity and a heartbeat all at once. She drew her hand back quickly, unnerved by the faint jolt it sent up her arm.

"Come on," she said, her voice tight. "Let's keep looking."

They crossed the cracked plaza cautiously, their steps echoing faintly in the vast emptiness. As they walked, Lucy's eyes caught glimpses of what the sanctuary must have once been: delicate carvings of constellations etched into the marble, now marred by scorch marks; faint traces of golden inlays that shimmered weakly in the fractured light. It was breathtaking even in its ruin, a testament to the Custodians' mastery and the price of their fall.

At the far end of the plaza, they came upon another inscription, this one carved into a massive archway leading to a shadowy grove.

The Garden of Tranquillity: A Place of Reflection and Clarity.

Lucy and St. Michael exchanged a glance before stepping through the archway. The garden stretched out before them, its once-vibrant flora now blackened and lifeless. Twisted branches reached toward the sky like skeletal hands, their leaves long since fallen and scattered across the cracked ground. Streams that had once flowed with crystal-clear water were now dry, their beds marked by jagged fissures.

"It's like walking through a graveyard," St. Michael said quietly, his eyes scanning the desolation.

Lucy knelt by one of the dried streams, her fingers brushing against the brittle remnants of moss that clung to the stones. "It looks like it used to be alive," she said. "Conversations from the past, decisions made here. But now…"

She trailed off, closing her eyes and focusing. For a moment, she thought she heard something. A faint, disjointed murmur, like a distant voice carried on the wind. But it was fleeting, fading before she could make sense of it.

"Did you hear that?" she asked, glancing at St. Michael.

He shook his head. "Hear what?"

"Never mind," she said, rising to her feet. The garden's emptiness weighed heavily on her, a sharp contrast to the vitality it must have once held. She couldn't help but wonder how many Custodians had sought solace here, only for their sanctuary to betray them in the end.

They moved on, their path leading them toward the Celestial Bridges. As they climbed the fractured steps that led to the first intact bridge, Lucy paused, her eyes drawn to the swirling void beyond the sanctuary's edge. The golden and indigo sky she had read about was gone, replaced by a churning chaos of black clouds and green lightning. It was as if the sanctuary itself had been severed from the Universal Timeline, left adrift in a storm of its own making.

The bridge beneath their feet was translucent, its surface etched with faint, glowing patterns that pulsed unevenly. It stretched out into the void, connecting to another floating structure in the distance. Lucy hesitated, her eyes tracing the flickering patterns.

"It doesn't feel stable," she said, her voice tight.

St. Michael tested the bridge cautiously, his shoes clicking against its surface. "It'll hold," he said after a moment, though his tone was uncertain. "For now, at least."

They crossed carefully, the bridge swaying faintly beneath their weight. The energy pulsing through it hummed discordantly, sending vibrations through their feet. Lucy kept her gaze forward, refusing to look down at the abyss below.

When they reached the other side, they found themselves on a platform overlooking the Assembly Hall. The building was a ruin, its grand entrance marred by jagged cracks and scorch marks. The mosaic ceiling, which had once displayed moments from history, was shattered, its fragments scattered across the ground.

St. Michael placed a hand on her shoulder, his expression sombre. "It's hard to believe this place was once... whole."

They lingered for a moment, taking in the devastation, before making their way toward the Council Chambers. The spire that had housed the chambers leaned precariously, its surface marred by deep cracks. Inside, the damage was just as severe. The flowing script from the Codex was faded, and the once-bright light that had filled the chambers was dim.

As they stepped into the main lobby, Lucy's eyes were drawn to a row of empty spaces along the wall where the Timeless Robes had once hung. Each space bore a nameplate, the inscriptions still faintly legible.

Edward Calder.

Evelyn Calder.

Lucy stared at the empty spaces. Her father's robes were gone. No surprise, given the circumstances of his death. But her mother's absence struck her.

"She wrote that they were here. At the start of the Schism," she murmured, her voice shaking. "Why are they gone?"

St. Michael looked at the inscription. "Maybe someone took them," he said, though his tone lacked conviction. "Or maybe…"

He didn't finish the thought, and Lucy didn't press him. Instead, she stepped forward, her fingers brushing against the plaque bearing her father's name. The metal was cold under her touch, a sharp reminder of the man she lost.

They looked around at the other empty spaces, names of the council members passing before their gaze until it settled on another familiar name.

Alaric Vale

"He's probably got his with him," St. Michael stated. However, Lucy didn't respond.

Taking a deep breath, she turned toward the doors leading into the Assembly Hall. "This is it," she said, her voice steady despite the weight in her chest.

St. Michael nodded, his expression grave. Together, they pushed open the heavy doors, the sound echoing through the silent hall.

The assembly hall was vast, its grandeur reduced to ruin. Lucy's eyes were drawn immediately to the ten podiums near the centre, their surfaces scorched with only a few still standing. She approached them slowly, her steps faltering as she saw the inscriptions on the two immediately in front of her.

Edward Calder.

Evelyn Calder.

Her fingers brushed against the edge of her father's podium. She could almost imagine him standing there, his voice calm and commanding, a symbol of everything the Custodians had once stood for.

Lucy glanced to her right and saw remains of the Codex pedestal, toppled and broken in the centre of the hall. "This is where it happened," she said softly, her voice barely above a whisper. "This is where the Nexus betrayed them."

St. Michael stood beside her, his eyes fixed on the shattered remains of the Codex pedestal. "It's gone," he said quietly. "The Codex. The heart of all of this. It's just… gone."

Lucy nodded, her eyes lingering on her parents' podiums. The weight of the sanctuary's fall pressed down on her, a heavy reminder of everything that had been lost.

They stood there in silence, the ruins of the sanctuary stretching out around them. For a moment, time itself seemed to hold still, as if the sanctuary were mourning its own downfall.

They stood together in the heart of the assembly hall, surrounded by the broken past.

And then they heard it.

A single footstep. Sharp and deliberate, the sound echoed across the chamber like a crack of thunder.

Lucy's head snapped toward the noise, her heart lurching in her chest. "You must have heard that?" she whispered, her voice tight.

St. Michael froze, his body going rigid as his eyes scanned the darkness. A second footstep followed. Then another. The sound wasn't steady. It darted from one side of the room to the other, as if the source was circling them, unseen.

"I heard it," he murmured, his voice low. "It's just one person. But they're… moving fast."

Lucy felt her pulse quicken, the weight of her unease settling heavily in her stomach. "You think it's a Nexian?" she asked, already bracing herself for the answer.

St. Michael didn't reply immediately. His jaw clenched as he stepped closer to her, his hand twitching at his side. "Who else would it be?" he said finally, his voice grim.

The footsteps grew louder, more deliberate, each one seeming to ricochet off the walls. Lucy's hand instinctively rose, her fingers tingling with the familiar surge of energy. She summoned it without thought, her mind focused entirely on the threat. A flame flickered to life in her palm, its light casting sharp shadows across her face. The fire danced and crackled, reflecting the turmoil simmering just beneath her surface.

"Get behind me," she said sharply, her voice cutting through the sound of steps.

St. Michael didn't argue. He moved behind her quickly, his eyes darting around the hall, trying to pinpoint the source of the noise. The footsteps seemed to circle them now, faster, more erratic, like a predator closing in on its prey.

And then came the voice.

"How dare you return here." The tone was harsh and filled with a righteous fury that made Lucy's blood run cold. "The archives remain locked!"

Lucy's grip on her fireball tightened, the flames flaring brighter. "Show yourself!" she demanded, her voice steady despite the fear prickling at the edges of her mind.

The footsteps stopped suddenly, the silence more oppressive than ever. Then, without warning, a figure stepped from behind one of the crumbling columns.

There was no hesitation as he raised his hand, and in an instant, fire erupted from his palm, streaking toward Lucy with deadly intent.

"Get down!" St. Michael shouted, but Lucy was already moving.

Her own fireball shot forward, meeting the man's head-on in an explosion of light and heat. The two flames collided mid-air, their energies snarling and writhing as they fought for dominance. The impact lit up the hall in flashes of orange and gold, the heat searing Lucy's skin even from a distance.

The flames hissed and crackled, locked in a fierce struggle that neither side seemed able to win. Lucy gritted her teeth, sweat beading on her forehead as she poured more of her energy into the incant, willing her fire to overpower his.

But the man was strong. His fire burned with a ferocity that matched her own, refusing to yield.

She couldn't hold this for long. The strain was already beginning to take its toll, her arms trembling as the two forces pushed against each other. She felt the anger rising within her, hot and consuming, and she let it guide her next move.

Without warning, she dropped her hand, extinguishing her fireball. The sudden absence of resistance sent the man's flames surging forward, but Lucy was already one step ahead. Both hands rose from her waist, her palms facing outward. She summoned the wind, pulling it from the very air around her.

A ferocious gust tore through the hall, howling like a tempest. It shattered what remained of the chamber's brittle windows and tore through the doors, sending shards of glass and splinters of wood flying. The wind slammed into the man, hurling him backward with a force that made him cry out. He collided with a column, the impact driving the air from his lungs in a sharp gasp.

Lucy advanced, her anger burning hotter than the fire she now summoned in her hand. The flame flared to life once more, swirling and twisting as if it had a mind of its own. She raised it high, her eyes locked on the man as she closed the distance between them.

"Lucy!" St. Michael called, his voice cutting through the haze of her rage. He reached out, his hand brushing against her arm. "Wait. Look at him."

She hesitated, her breath coming in short, sharp bursts. The fire still danced in her palm, casting an orange glow over her face. "He tried to kill us," she said through gritted teeth, her voice trembling with anger.

"Look closer," St. Michael urged. "He doesn't have a mask. He's not a Nexian."

The words cut through her anger like a blade. Her eyes darted to the man, taking in details she hadn't noticed before: an older figure with fine, curly white hair that caught the faint light filtering through the broken ceiling. His face was bare, his expression a mix of pain and shock as he pushed himself up against the column. There was no sign of the white mask that marked the Order of the Nexus. Instead, he wore a striking blue garment beneath a flowing blue robe, its design unmistakable: the Robes of the Timeless.

Lucy's fireball dimmed slightly, though it didn't disappear. She kept her distance, her voice sharp. "Then why the fuck did you attack us?"

The man coughed, wincing as he adjusted his position. "A Nexian?" he repeated, his tone exasperated. "You thought I was one of those lunatics?"

St. Michael stepped forward cautiously, his hands raised in a gesture of peace. "We're not Nexians either," he said calmly.

The man stared at them for a long moment, his expression shifting from anger to confusion. "Then who or what does that make you?" he demanded, his voice rising in frustration.

Lucy stood firm, her fireball extinguished but her hands still hovering near her sides, ready to summon another incant at the slightest provocation. Her eyes locked on the man who had just tried to kill her. St. Michael was tense beside her, his body angled slightly toward Lucy, as if ready to intervene.

"I'm Lucy," she said, her voice steady. "Lucy Calder. And this is St. Michael."

When she had introduced herself, his reaction had been unexpected. His eyes widened, his expression unreadable. And then he'd said it. One word, spoken almost under his breath.

"Unbelievable," the man murmured, almost as if he were speaking to himself. His gaze seemed to drift, as though he were staring through her rather than at her.

"I beg your pardon?" Lucy said, her voice cutting through the thick silence. There was a sharpness to her tone, a blend of confusion and frustration.

The man straightened slightly, though his grip on the column remained firm. "Solric Avanir," he said finally, his voice steady but laced with an air of gravitas.

Lucy's mind raced. She'd read the name in her mother's records of the schism. He had been a council member, one of the three who hadn't been present, along with Evelyn and Alaric. And now, here he was, standing before her.

Before she could say anything, Solric's voice broke through her thoughts. "I've been waiting a long time to meet you, Lucy Calder."

Lucy blinked, the weight of his words pulling her focus back to him. "You… you've been waiting for me?" she asked, her voice uncertain.

"It is as the Codex foretold," Solric said, his tone growing firmer. "Two would make eleven."

Her heart skipped a beat. "What's that supposed to mean?" she asked, her voice sharper now. "What are you talking about?"

Solric stepped away from the column, his movements slow and deliberate. His gaze never left hers. "Before it was stolen," he began, his voice carrying a quiet authority, "the Codex of Time would, on occasion, offer fragments of guidance. Prophecies, if you will. Most were cryptic, their meanings obscured until the right moment. But one of its final utterances before everything fell apart was this: *Two would make Eleven.*

One who rises when the breath stills.

One who chooses what none before could.

And from the Eleventh, balance returns… or ends forever."

Lucy shook her head, her confusion mounting. "And you think that has something to do with me?"

"It has everything to do with you," Solric replied, his tone unwavering. "The Codex never lies. Thaloc was unsure of its meaning, but now, seeing you here, I finally understand."

She stared at him, her mind reeling. "You're wrong," she said, shaking her head more firmly now. "That can't be me. You've got it wrong."

Solric stepped closer, his expression softening slightly. "I'm not wrong, Lucy. Your parents—Edward and Evelyn—they made you. They brought you into this world. They were the two. And you… you are the Eleventh. Ten council members, you make it eleven."

Lucy glanced at St. Michael, searching for some kind of reassurance, but he looked just as bewildered as she felt. "That doesn't make any sense," she said, her voice trembling. "I'm just—this isn't possible. I didn't ask for any of this."

"No one asks for destiny," Solric said, his voice gentler now. "But it finds you all the same. The Codex has chosen you, Lucy Calder. It always knew you would come."

Lucy opened her mouth to argue, but no words came out. She didn't know how to respond. The weight of Solric's revelation was suffocating, and she felt like the ground beneath her was slipping away.

Solric seemed to sense her turmoil. He tilted his head slightly, his expression thoughtful. "What brought you here, Lucy?" he asked, his voice calm but probing. "Why now?"

Lucy took a shaky breath, trying to steady herself. "I… I've been traversing through time," she said, her voice quieter now. "I tried to work out why it was happening and discovered the Time Custodians and that I apparently am one. I've been trying to understand my mother's disappearance after the Schism. And the Order of the Nexus… they keep appearing. We've been running through history in search of answers, with them chasing us."

Solric's expression darkened at the mention of the Nexus. He was silent for a moment, his eyes narrowing as if he were piecing something together in his mind. Finally, he spoke. "The Nexus," he said slowly, the word heavy with disdain. "I thought as much."

Lucy frowned. "You've dealt with them before?"

"They've tried to gain access to the archives more times than I care to count," Solric replied. "But I've made sure they never succeed."

"The archives?" St. Michael asked, his voice breaking the tension. "What archives?"

Solric turned to him, his expression softening slightly. "The Archives of Time," he said. "The library of the Universal Timeline. Every moment of human and Custodian history, accounted for and preserved. Since the Schism, I've dedicated my life to protecting it."

Lucy's eyes widened. "The Archives of Time," she repeated, almost in awe.

"It may hold the answers you're looking for," Solric said firmly.

Lucy stared at him, her heart pounding. "Can you show us?"

Solric hesitated, his gaze lingering on her. Then he nodded. "Yes," he said finally. "But you must promise me something."

"What?" Lucy asked cautiously.

"Whatever you find," Solric said, his voice low, "you must use it wisely. The timeline has already suffered enough."

Lucy nodded slowly. "I promise."

Solric stepped back, raising his hands. "Then stand clear," he said.

Lucy and St. Michael exchanged a glance before stepping back, giving Solric space. The older man closed his eyes, his hands moving in slow, deliberate motions. The air around them seemed to vibrate, the energy in the room growing palpable.

The floor beneath their feet began to shift, the ancient stone groaning as it pulled apart. It was like watching the earth itself split open, the centre of the assembly hall giving way to reveal a staircase descending into darkness. The steps were wide and curved, their edges glowing faintly with an otherworldly light.

Lucy stared in awe. "That's… incredible," she whispered.

Solric opened his eyes, lowering his hands and gestured toward the staircase. "Follow me."

He descended the steps without hesitation. Lucy and St. Michael exchanged one last glance before following, their footsteps echoing softly as they ventured into the unknown.

Solric led the way down the staircase, his robes trailing behind him as the air seemed to hum faintly in response to his presence. The steps were wide and smooth, carved from a dark, crystalline stone that shimmered faintly in the flickering light of the torches lining the walls. The flames weren't ordinary, they burned with a pale, ethereal light, turning on in sequence as Solric descended, as though responding to him.

Lucy followed close behind, her hand brushing lightly against the cool stone of the wall for balance. The silence was broken only by the soft echo of their footsteps, and she felt her nerves simmering under the surface. But before she could dwell on her unease, St. Michael gently tapped her shoulder.

"Oi," he whispered, his tone light and teasing. "That fireball and wind thing you pulled back there? That was insane. Are we sure you're not secretly Thor?"

Lucy blinked, caught off guard, before a faint grin tugged at her lips. "Thor doesn't do wind," she whispered back, her voice equally playful. "And anyway, I think that was more luck than skill."

"Luck?" St. Michael raised an eyebrow, smirking. "If that was luck, I'd hate to see what happens when you're trying."

Lucy stifled a laugh, shaking her head as they continued to descend. The warmth of the banter helped ease some of the tension knotting in her chest, though the hum in the air grew louder with each step, vibrating faintly beneath her skin.

At the bottom of the staircase, they stopped abruptly. Before them stood a massive, intricately carved door, its surface pulsing faintly with a purple and blue glow. The patterns etched into the metal seemed to shift and ripple like water, creating an ever-changing mosaic of light and shadow. Lucy couldn't take her eyes off the sheer beauty of the design.

Solric stepped forward, raising both hands. The light from the door responded instantly, surging toward his palms as though drawn to him. A deep, resonant hum filled the air, and a loud *click* echoed through the space as the mechanisms within the door unlocked.

"Stand back," Solric said, his tone calm but commanding. He placed both hands against the surface, pushing it open with a steady effort. The massive doors creaked as they swung inward, revealing the chamber beyond.

Lucy and St. Michael stepped forward cautiously, their eyes widening as they took in the sight before them.

The room was vast, far larger than it had any right to be. Row upon row of towering shelves stretched into the distance, their heights disappearing into a faint, swirling mist above. The walls shimmered faintly, their surfaces etched with glowing constellations and symbols Lucy didn't recognise. But what struck her most was the shelves themselves.

Instead of books, the shelves were lined with translucent, purple crystalline objects. They pulsed faintly, each one emitting a soft glow that shifted and flickered like a heartbeat. As Lucy stepped closer, she noticed that each crystal seemed to contain movement within— images, shapes, and colours swirling and shifting as though alive.

"It's…" Lucy began, her voice trailing off as she struggled to find the words.

"Beautiful," St. Michael finished for her, his own voice hushed with awe. He stepped closer to one of the shelves, leaning in to examine the crystals. "What… are these?"

Solric joined them, his expression calm but filled with quiet pride. "They are records," he said, his voice carrying the weight of centuries. "Every moment in history, every decision, every event—it is all preserved here. Everything that ever was or has been is recorded in the Archives of Time."

Lucy reached out tentatively, her fingers hovering just above one of the crystals. Within it, she could see faint, flickering images. Figures moving through a field of tall grass, the sound of wind whispering faintly in her ears as though the scene was alive.

"They're not just records," she murmured, her voice barely above a whisper. "They're… alive."

Solric nodded. "Indeed. These are not mere books or scrolls. They're imprints—snapshots of time itself. Each one captures not only the events but the emotions, the sounds, the very essence of the moment it records. To hold one is to experience the past as if you were truly there."

St. Michael pulled back slightly, his expression equal parts awe and caution. "That's… incredible," he said. "But why here? Why lock all this away?"

Solric's gaze darkened slightly, the weight of his years showing in the lines of his face. "Because knowledge is power," he said simply. "And power, in the wrong hands, is a dangerous thing. The Archives were meant to be a resource for the Custodians, a tool to guide us in protecting the timeline. But after the Schism…" His voice trailed off, and his expression grew heavy. "It became clear that not everyone could be trusted with such responsibility."

Lucy frowned, her fingers still hovering over the crystal. "And the Nexus? They've tried to get in, haven't they?"

"Many times," Solric said grimly. "They believe the Archives hold the key to reshaping the timeline in their image. And perhaps they are right. But as long as I draw breath, they will never have access to this knowledge."

Lucy exchanged a glance with St. Michael, the enormity of what they were standing in struck her all at once. The weight of history, of legacy, of everything that had been lost and could still be lost if the Nexus succeeded.

"Can we… use it?" she asked hesitantly, her voice tinged with both hope and fear. "To understand them? To stop them?"

Solric's expression softened slightly. "The Archives can reveal much," he said. "But be warned, Lucy Calder— knowledge is a double-edged sword. The answers you seek may not be the answers you wish to find."

Lucy opened her mouth to speak, but St. Michael beat her to it, gesturing broadly to the endless expanse of translucent shelves around them. "Alright, before we get into the nitty-gritty—who *built* all of this?" he asked, his voice tinged with disbelief. "This place is massive. How did it all appear here?"

Solric paused mid-step and turned to face them, raising a single eyebrow. "Appear? Hardly," he said, almost smugly. "I built it."

"You *built* this?" St. Michael repeated, incredulous. "All of it?"

"Centuries of work," Solric replied with a slight shrug, as though it were no more impressive than assembling a bookshelf. "Every shelf, every record. It's been my life's work."

"Centuries?" Lucy cut in, her voice rising slightly. "You've been working on this for *centuries*? How… how old are you?"

Solric turned to her, his expression shifting to one of faint amusement. "Centuries," he said again, as if that alone were the explanation.

Lucy frowned, crossing her arms. "That doesn't answer my question. How is that even possible?"

St. Michael leaned against one of the glowing shelves, folding his arms. "Yeah, I'd love to know that, too. Living for centuries doesn't exactly sound like a standard Custodian perk."

Solric chuckled, shaking his head. "Not for all, I assure you. But if you want to understand, let's start with the basics." He gestured for them to follow as he continued walking deeper into the archives. The glowing shelves seemed to stretch infinitely ahead, the faint hum of energy filling the silence.

"All Custodians," Solric began, his tone deliberate, "are connected to the Universal Timeline. It's the source of our abilities—the reason we can traverse through time, summon Incants, and perceive languages. For a few of us, this connection isn't just a source of power; it's also what keeps us alive for centuries, sometimes millennia."

"So, you're immortal?" St. Michael asked, still sceptical.

"Not quite," Solric replied. "We're not invincible and can still fall to injury or illness. But as long as we remain tethered to the timeline, our aging slows dramatically—sometimes halts altogether. It's a side effect of being so deeply attuned to time. Those of us who have that attunement are called Timeless Custodians, hence the name of our robes."

Lucy frowned, glancing at St. Michael before stepping closer to Solric. "But my parents weren't like that," she said firmly. "They were Custodians, too, and… well, they weren't exactly around for centuries."

Solric stopped walking, turning to face her. His expression grew more serious, the faint humour in his tone fading. "Your parents were unique, Lucy. They—and you—are what we call *Finite Custodians*."

"Finite?" Lucy repeated, the word feeling strange on her tongue.

"Yes," Solric said, nodding. "Timeless Custodians develop their abilities gradually over centuries, their connection to the Timeline growing stronger as they age. But your parents… they were different. They were born with a connection to the Timeline so powerful, it rivalled even the oldest members of the Council."

"Born with it?" St. Michael repeated. "What does that mean?"

"It means," Solric said, his tone carrying a weight of reverence, "that Evelyn and Edward Calder weren't just ordinary Finite Custodians. Their abilities weren't learned over centuries—they were *inherent*. Natural. It's as though the Timeline itself placed its mark on them from the moment they were born. That kind of connection… it burns brightly, but briefly."

Lucy tried to process his words. "And me?" she asked quietly. "Am I… the same?"

Solric's expression softened, and he nodded. "One would assume you are just like them. Perhaps your connection could even be stronger. But like them, you are Finite. Your time is precious. And that is why you must use it wisely."

Lucy exchanged a glance with St. Michael, who looked equally overwhelmed. "So, all Custodians aren't like you," she said, her voice tinged with both curiosity and frustration. "They don't all live for centuries."

"No," Solric confirmed. "The majority of Custodians are finite too. Mortal and deeply connected to humanity. They form the backbone of our society, patrolling the timeline, guarding and preserving history. They may not have the power of the timeless Custodians, but their contributions were no less vital."

"And the Council?" St. Michael asked. "They're all like you? Timeless?"

Solric hesitated before answering. "Not all," he admitted. "Your parents were an exception— unprecedented, actually. Their inclusion on the Council was necessary, but their finite nature made them a rarity."

Lucy nodded slowly, piecing it all together. "So, the Timeless Custodians have centuries to learn, to deliberate, to… perfect their abilities. But my parents—Finite Custodians—they have to act quickly, make decisions without the luxury of time."

"Exactly," Solric said, his tone tinged with admiration. "And that is why they are so vital. Their humanity—their ability to feel the urgency of time—is what grounds us. It reminds us what we're fighting for."

Lucy lingered in silence, her mind swirling with everything Solric had revealed. The air of the Archives felt heavier now, charged with a sense of awe and importance that made her next words difficult to find.

It was St. Michael who broke the tension, leaning against one of the glowing shelves with a sharp exhale. "Alright, so you've spent centuries building this… monumental, otherworldly library. That's impressive, don't get me wrong, but what exactly do you *do* with all of it? "

Solric raised an eyebrow, turning his gaze to St Michael. "The Archives are far more than a repository of history. Since the Schism, they've become my tool for monitoring and documenting changes to the Timeline."

"Changes?" Lucy asked, tilting her head. "You mean the disruptions caused by the Nexus?"

"Precisely," Solric replied, gesturing to the translucent shelves that seemed to stretch infinitely. "Every anomaly, every moment the Nexus has interfered—it's all recorded here. This is the one place in existence where the timeline's integrity can be observed in its entirety."

"And you're the only one who can do this?" St. Michael asked, scepticism creeping into his tone.

"Yes," Solric said simply. He raised his hand, brushing his fingers along one of the glowing shelves. The purple light seemed to ripple at his touch, as though responding to his presence. "The Archives were my creation. My design. As the Council's record keeper, it was my duty to ensure every moment in history was documented and preserved. After the Schism, when the Council was shattered and the Codex stolen, the Archives became my sanctuary—and my responsibility. I've been here ever since."

Lucy frowned. "So, no one else can use them? Not even the Council members who survived the Schism?"

Solric shook his head. "No. The Archives are bound to me and me alone. Only I can access their full functions or make changes to their records. That was intentional—part of the design."

"Why would you make it that way?" St. Michael asked, his tone curious but cautious. "I mean, no offense, but putting all that power in the hands of one person seems… risky."

"Because, like I have said, knowledge is power," Solric replied, his voice sharp. "And power, when wielded recklessly, destroys. The Schism proved that much. When the Nexus betrayed us, the timeline itself was thrown into chaos. I made the Archives this way to ensure that no one—*no one*—could exploit them."

Lucy stepped forward, her expression thoughtful. "But now… you're letting us in."

Solric's gaze softened slightly as he turned to her. "Desperate times call for allies, Lucy Calder," he said. "Since the Schism, I've worked alone. I've watched the Nexus grow stronger, their influence spreading like a disease through history. And now… I see something in you. Something your parents had."

Lucy swallowed hard, unsure how to respond. "But… why me? Why now?"

"Because I've spent too long fighting this battle in isolation," Solric admitted, his voice quieter now. "I believed I could protect the Timeline on my own from afar, but the Nexus is relentless. They've grown bolder, more dangerous. And you—you've already faced them and lived to tell the tale. That alone speaks volumes."

"So, you want *us* to help you?" St. Michael asked.

"I'm saying," Solric said, his gaze fixed on Lucy, "that it's time to share the burden. For centuries, I've been the only one allowed within these walls. Even when our society was at its strongest. But you—Lucy—you have the potential to do what I cannot. You're Finite, yes, but that makes you bold, decisive. I believe you should have access to the Archives. It's time they served a greater purpose."

Lucy blinked, the enormity of his statement sinking in. "You'd trust me with this? After… everything?"

Solric smiled faintly. "The Nexus is relentless. They adapt, they evolve, and they are no longer content to remain in the shadows. If we're going to stop them, I need someone who can act. Someone who doesn't just record history but shapes it."

Before Lucy could respond, Solric turned and gestured to the glowing shelves around them. "The Archives have already been helping me monitor their activity. When the Order of the Nexus attempts to change the Timeline, the room notifies me."

That caught St. Michael's attention. "Notifies you how?"

Solric gestured to the pulsating lights that lined the shelves. "Through colour. Each disruption sends a ripple through the Archives, and the room responds. A Quantum Time Collision triggers the room to turn red. It's my way of keeping watch."

"That's… genius," Lucy said, her voice filled with wonder. She glanced around, imagining the room alive with shifting hues.

"It was genius," Solric admitted, his tone grim. "But it's getting harder. The Nexus has learned to mask their actions. They're no longer causing overt, explosive disruptions. Instead, their changes are subtle—delicate enough to slip past the Archives' detection until it's too late."

Lucy's expression hardened. "So, they're learning."

"They've been learning for years," Solric confirmed. "And they've become frighteningly good at it. Their disruptions are quieter, more insidious.

Lucy tilted her head. "So, you just watch the Timeline fall apart?"

Solric's expression grew heavier. "I observe. I document. But I do not fight."

"Why not?" Lucy asked, her voice edged with disbelief.

Solric hesitated, his eyes scanning the glowing shelves. "Because I can't," he said quietly. "I lack the mastery needed to create Incants that could rival theirs. My strength lies here, in preservation. It was never in combat."

"And the Nexus knows that," St. Michael guessed.

"Of course," Solric said grimly. "They're masters of deception. They've ensured that even someone like me—someone who dedicates their life to protecting the Timeline—cannot stop them."

Lucy's voice softened. "What kind of deception?"

Solric gestured toward the shelves. "It's not just their subtle disruptions. It's everything about them. Their masks, for example—those infernal things make every member of the Nexus sound identical. Their voices are indistinguishable, which makes identifying individuals impossible."

Lucy shivered. "That's… unsettling."

"It's more than unsettling," Solric said. "It's deliberate. And that's not their only trick. They've developed something far more dangerous—something that makes them nearly impossible to track."

St. Michael raised an eyebrow. "What?"

Solric looked at Lucy, his expression darkening. "Their own language."

"We've heard," Lucy interjected. "But I couldn't understand it. Any of it."

"And that's exactly the point of it," Solric said. "It was designed specifically to block out the innate understanding that Custodians possess. Even the most experienced among us cannot decipher. Every word, every phrase is designed to confuse and mislead, to keep their plans hidden from us."

St. Michael let out a low whistle. "A language Custodians can't crack. That's… terrifying."

"And brilliant," Solric added, his voice heavy with reluctant respect. "By using Nexian, the Order ensures that their strategies remain hidden. Even when spoken aloud, their intentions are veiled. The Nexus thrives on secrecy and manipulation. It's how they've stayed ahead of us for so long."

Lucy's voice was quiet but firm. "And you think I can stop them?"

Solric's gaze softened. "I believe you can help turn the tide, Lucy. The Nexus cannot predict you. They cannot anticipate someone like you."

Solric's sharp gaze softened, and he tilted his head toward Lucy, a hint of curiosity creeping into his expression.

"You seem to have a strong grasp of your abilities," he said, breaking the silence. "Your mastery of Temporal Incants already feels… advanced. How did you come to learn them so quickly? Most Custodians require years of training with experienced mentors, something I imagine you've not had?"

Lucy hesitated for a moment, glancing briefly at St. Michael before meeting Solric's gaze. "Honestly, some of it's been by accident," she admitted. "When I first started traversing through time, I had no control over it. It just… happened. But I've been reading through my mum's accounts, piecing together bits of what she left behind. And—" She paused, her voice steady but cautious. "Another Custodian reached out to me. Alaric Vale."

The name hung for a moment before Solric's face twisted into a look of pure disgust. He let out a low, bitter laugh and shook his head.

"Of course that rat survived," he said, his voice dripping with disdain.

Both Lucy and St. Michael froze, their eyes wide with surprise. Lucy's mouth opened slightly as if to respond, but St. Michael beat her to it.

"Rat?" he repeated, his tone a mix of confusion and disbelief. "What do you mean, 'rat'? Alaric's been helping Lucy."

Solric scoffed, crossing his arms over his chest. "Helping her? Alaric Vale doesn't help anyone. Not really. He's a coward. Always has been. If he's helping now, it's because he has a plan."

Lucy's brow furrowed. "That's… not the impression I've gotten," she said carefully. "He's been nothing but supportive. He's helped me understand how to control my powers—he even trained with me to use my Incants."

"That's because it serves his interests," Solric said sharply, his eyes narrowing. "Alaric is reckless, impulsive, and utterly incapable of seeing the bigger picture. He always made poor decisions, ones that put the rest of us at risk. And when things got difficult, he was the first to retreat. He is probably teaching you so you'll answer his call when the Nexus inevitably come for him as well."

Lucy exchanged a glance with St. Michael, her mind racing. "But he survived the Schism," she pointed out. "That has to mean something, doesn't it?"

Solric let out a bitter laugh. "It means he ran," he said flatly. "He cowered while the rest of us fought to preserve what we could. Alaric was harmless, yes, but he was also a liability—a weak link in the chain."

St. Michael leaned forward slightly, his curiosity piqued despite the tension. "You make it sound like you knew him well."

"I did," Solric replied, his tone clipped. "Too well. He had his moments of brilliance, I'll grant him that. But his lack of discipline, his inability to follow through… it cost the council more than once."

Lucy frowned, processing Solric's words. "He told me he's been hiding from the Nexus," she said carefully. "He's in Scotland, in the 1800s. That's where I met him."

Solric's lips curled into a faint sneer. "Scotland. The 1800s. Fitting," he said with a derisive shake of his head. "Hiding, as always. It's what he does best."

Lucy bristled slightly, feeling a twinge of defensiveness for Alaric despite Solric's words. "He's not hiding," she argued. "He's trying to stay off their radar so he can help me—and others, if they need it."

Solric raised an eyebrow, his expression sceptical. "Is that what he told you?" he asked. "Because if there's one thing Alaric is good at, it's spinning tales that make him look like the hero."

Lucy felt a flicker of doubt creep into her thoughts, but she pushed it aside. "Regardless of what you think of him, he's been helping me," she said firmly. "And that's made a difference."

Solric sighed, his shoulders relaxing slightly. "Perhaps," he said reluctantly.

The words lingered between them, heavy and unyielding. Lucy caught St. Michael's eye, who gave her a subtle nod, as if silently agreeing to let the topic drop for now. But in the back of her mind, questions swirled, nagging at her.

Solric exhaled as if to release the tension from their exchange about Alaric. His sharp gaze softened as he turned his attention back to Lucy and St. Michael, his tone serious once again.

"The Nexus," he began, his voice steady but heavy with implication. "They should have killed you by now."

St. Michael stiffened slightly, his arms crossing over his chest. "That's a cheery thought," he said dryly.

Solric's expression didn't waver. "I'm not saying it lightly. It's a miracle that all four of us—yourself, Lucy, Alaric, and myself—are still breathing. The Nexus doesn't leave loose ends. That they haven't ended you yet means one of two things: either they're toying with you, or there's something else at play that we don't yet understand."

Lucy felt a chill run through her, though she did her best to mask it. "Why haven't they come for you here?" she asked.

"Oh, they've tried," Solric said with a grim smile. "And they'll try again. It's only a matter of time before they come for me in earnest. But I've had centuries to prepare for that eventuality. My defences aren't impenetrable, but they've held… so far."

"You don't seem too worried about it," St. Michael said, narrowing his eyes.

"I'm worried, trust me," Solric replied. "But I've accepted the reality of it. I'm prepared to hold my ground for as long as I can, but this sanctuary isn't eternal. One day, it may fall." He paused, looking at Lucy. "That's why I'm sharing all of this with you now. It's no accident that you've come here. Whatever happens, you must be ready to continue the fight."

Lucy nodded slowly, the weight of his words settling heavily on her shoulders. "Thank you," she said, her voice quiet but sincere. "For everything. For sharing what you know, for helping us… I just don't know where to go next. How do we even start unravelling all of this?"

Solric studied her for a moment, his expression unreadable. Then, almost as if coming to a decision, he stepped away from them and began walking toward one of the countless shelves. "Perhaps I can offer a starting point," he said, his tone measured.

Lucy and St. Michael exchanged a glance before following him. Solric reached for a translucent purple record from the shelf, its edges glowing faintly as he pulled it free. He held it carefully, as though it were a fragile artifact, and turned back to face them.

"There's been an unusual pattern," he said, holding the record up. "The archives have detected numerous attempts to alter one specific point in history. "

"What point in history?" Lucy asked, leaning forward slightly.

Solric's eyes locked on hers. "The Taiping Rebellion. 1853."

For a moment, the world seemed to tilt. "The Taiping Rebellion?" Lucy repeated, her voice barely above a whisper. "That's… that's what my mother was working on before she disappeared."

St. Michael straightened beside her, his expression sharpening. "You're sure?"

"Yes," Lucy said, her voice gaining strength as her excitement grew. "She must have followed the Nexus there. That's where she went."

Solric nodded, his expression serious. "If the Nexus have been targeting that event, it's not without reason. Whatever they're trying to do there, it's significant enough that they've attempted to alter it multiple times."

Lucy didn't hesitate. She turned to St. Michael, her resolve clear. "We're going there. Now."

St. Michael nodded, falling in step with her. "Then let's not waste any time."

As they began to move toward the door, Solric stepped in front of them, his expression stern. "Wait," he said firmly. "If you're going there, you need to proceed with extreme caution. The Nexus are dangerous enough, but the Taiping Rebellion itself is a volatile time. You'll be walking into chaos."

Lucy nodded, her determination unwavering. "I understand. But we don't have a choice."

Solric studied her for a moment before stepping aside. "Very well," he said. "But don't let your confidence blind you. The Nexus are masters of deception, and they won't hesitate to exploit any weakness."

Lucy gave him a small, grateful smile. "Thank you," she said. "For everything."

As they reached the doorway, she hesitated and turned back to him. "One more thing," she said with a faint laugh. "How do we… like, leave? I didn't really think to ask that."

Solric raised an eyebrow, a faint smirk tugging at his lips. "Traverse as you normally would," he said. "Focus on the Altar. It will guide you out."

Lucy turned to St. Michael, who nodded in understanding. She took a deep breath, stepping into the centre of the room. She closed her eyes, focusing her thoughts on the Altar, the stones standing tall against the misty night sky. Slowly, she raised her hand, extending it toward St. Michael.

He took her hand without hesitation, his grip firm and steady. The hum began softly, a low vibration that coursed through the air. Lucy concentrated, channelling her energy. It grew stronger, smoother, until the room around them seemed to dissolve into light.

The last thing Lucy saw before they vanished was Solric, standing tall and unyielding amidst the archives, watching them with a mixture of caution and hope.

* * *

The air was damp and heavy as Lucy and St. Michael reappeared within the circle of Stonehenge. The familiar drizzle of rain greeted them, a stark contrast to the sanctuary they had just left. The ancient stones loomed around them, silent sentinels in the mist. In the distance, St. Michael's car sat on the nearby track exactly where it had been left.

For a moment, neither of them spoke. They simply stood, letting the rain bead on their jackets. Then, St. Michael spoke.

"That was… a lot to take in," he said, his voice tinged with disbelief but a touch of humour.

Lucy exhaled sharply, almost a laugh, as she started walking toward the car. "Understatement of the century," she replied. "Or maybe several, if we're going by Solric's timeline."

St. Michael glanced sideways at her. "Solric really doesn't like Alaric, does he?" he said, smirking.

Lucy chuckled despite herself. "Yeah, that was awkward," she said with a slight smirk. "But, I mean, tensions between those two probably date back literal centuries. You spend that long in someone's orbit, there's bound to be friction."

St. Michael shook his head, amused. "If you asked Alaric, he'd probably have some equally colourful things to say about Solric."

"Oh, definitely," Lucy agreed. "He'd probably call him a pompous, self-important fossil or something equally dramatic."

They both laughed lightly, the sound cutting through the cold drizzle. The tension from earlier began to ease as they reached the car. St. Michael unlocked the doors, and they slid into the relative warmth of the vehicle. Lucy shook the rain from her jacket before pulling her hood down.

As St. Michael started the engine, he turned to Lucy. "Alright, what's the plan?"

"The records," she said decisively. "The ones my mum left behind. They're at your office in Finchley, right? She was working on the Taiping Rebellion before she disappeared. If she followed the Nexus there, then I'll follow her."

St. Michael frowned, gripping the steering wheel a little tighter. "You know that was one of the most violent civil wars in history, right? Millions of people died, Lucy. You're absolutely not going there on your own."

Lucy turned to him, her expression softening but resolute. "Michael, you've been with me for everything. I know I can count on you—I always have—but I'm not going to put you in danger. Not again."

He scoffed, his tone firm. "Lucy, I'm already in danger. I've been in danger since the Nexus first came after us. You're not dragging me into this—I chose to be here. Besides, there's no way I'm letting you walk into the Taiping Rebellion alone. End of discussion."

Lucy sighed, crossing her arms as she looked away. "I can't go through losing someone again."

"You're not going to lose me," St. Michael said firmly, his voice softening. "And you shouldn't have to carry this on your own. You've been through enough as it is. I'm coming with you."

"You're annoyingly stubborn," Lucy declared with a chuckle. "You know that?"

"Part of my charm," he replied, smirking slightly as he turned the car onto the main road.

"Fine," Lucy said, relenting. "We'll go through my mum's records together at your office. Study everything she documented about the Taiping Rebellion. Then we'll follow her trail."

"Good," St. Michael said with a nod. "We'll get dry and start digging in. No point rushing off without knowing exactly what we're walking into."

Lucy leaned back in her seat, watching the rain streak across the window as they drove. She was used to him being there—always steady, always ready—but the thought of what lay ahead still left a knot of worry in her chest. Whatever came next, she didn't want to take his presence for granted.

CHAPTER 15
The Heavenly Kingdom

Lucy took a deep breath as she and St. Michael stepped into his dimly lit office. "Right," she said, scanning the chaos of boxes before her. "Where do we even start?"

St. Michael ran a hand through his damp hair, his eyes drifting over the sea of unopened boxes. "Somewhere in here is your mum's work on the Taiping Rebellion," he said, his tone matter-of-fact but laced with something heavier. An unspoken awareness that whatever they found could lead them straight into danger.

Lucy nodded, ripping open a box. "If the Nexus was involved, she must have left something—notes, theories, anything."

They moved quickly, sorting through Evelyn's research with the efficiency of people who had done this before. Notepads were pulled from folders, documents skimmed and discarded. Some were official published accounts, others handwritten entries, rushed as though Evelyn had been trying to record everything before it slipped away.

After several minutes of digging, Lucy pulled a thick leather-bound notebook from the bottom of a box. Its edges were frayed, the cover softened with use. She flipped it open, scanning the dense script of her mother's familiar handwriting. The date at the top of the first page caught her attention—*1853*.

"This is it," she breathed.

St. Michael leaned over, peering at the page. "What does it say?"

Lucy traced her fingers over the ink, skimming through lines of research before speaking aloud. "She was investigating Hong Xiuquan—the so-called 'Heavenly King.'"

St. Michael frowned. "I think I recognise the name. Some religious leader, wasn't he?"

Lucy nodded, flipping further. "More than that. He believed he was the younger brother of Jesus." She glanced at St. Michael, her expression unreadable. "He thought he was divinely chosen to overthrow the Qing Dynasty and establish a utopian kingdom—the *Taiping Heavenly Kingdom*."

St. Michael let out a low whistle. "That's a bold claim, init."

Lucy continued, her voice steady but urgent. "The Taiping weren't just a simple rebellion. They were a movement. It was a combination of radical Christianity, political instability, and military domination. Hong Xiuquan gathered thousands of followers—farmers, labourers, even soldiers—people who were desperate for something different." She flipped to another page, scanning her mother's notes. "They wanted equality, wealth to be distributed and ultimately an end to the Qing government. But it wasn't just about faith—it was war. And a bloody one."

St. Michael exhaled sharply, leaning against the desk. "I did say millions of people died."

Lucy nodded grimly. "It was one of the deadliest conflicts in history. Over twenty million people died; however, some have estimated that number could be well over forty million. Whole cities were destroyed. It was chaos." She turned another page, Evelyn's writing becoming more urgent. Then, she saw the words.

The Order of the Nexus.

The words were scribbled hastily in the margins of one page, underlined twice, standing out against the otherwise orderly text. The ink was darker, pressed into the page with force, as though Evelyn had written it in a rush, or in fear.

Lucy's pulse quickened. "Michael," she said sharply, flipping the page open fully.

He turned at once, pushing aside a stack of papers to get closer. "What?"

She pointed, her voice urgent. "Here. My mum wrote about the Nexus."

St. Michael leaned over, reading alongside her as she traced her fingers over the text, her mother's hurried words spilling out in fragmented urgency.

The Nexus is here. This is their first attempt at large-scale intervention. Their theory is that the Taiping Rebellion is the perfect testing ground. An era of destruction so vast that altering it at this precise moment could cause minimal Quantum Time Collisions, unlike past failed attempts. They are perfecting prevention. Not just small adjustments. This is something bigger. Something permanent.

Lucy swallowed hard. "They're not just disrupting history. They're trying to *rewrite* it."

St. Michael exhaled sharply. "That's what Solric meant. "

Lucy turned another page, her mother's notes becoming even more frantic.

She hesitated, reading the next lines aloud.

St. Michael stiffened. "They're planning an assassination?"

Lucy nodded slowly, her mind racing. "Not just any assassination. They're targeting him *during* the Battle of Nanjing. 1853." She said, turning the page to the last entry.

St. Michael let out a low whistle, running a hand down his face. "Well... *shit.*"

Lucy shook her head, her mind piecing everything together. "The Nexus has always framed themselves as the ones protecting the Timeline. But this? This is something else." She flipped back to Evelyn's last recorded entry on the subject.

"She went after them," Lucy murmured. "She must have. If she knew this was their plan, there's no way she would've just let it happen."

St. Michael's voice was tight. "And she never came back."

That reality settled between them.

Lucy's gaze drifted upward, her breath unsteady as her eyes locked onto the mural of Evelyn on the wall. It haunted her.

This was one of her mother's last recorded traversals through time before she vanished.

Before she was lost.

Lucy exhaled, the weight of it pressing against her ribs. *I have to go.*

She clenched her fists, grounding herself before turning back to St. Michael. "We have to stop them."

His expression was unreadable, his arms crossed tightly as he leaned against the desk, but she could see the hesitation flicker in his eyes. "Lucy…" he started, his voice careful, measured. "If we go back—if we interfere—*isn't that* a time collision in itself?"

Lucy hesitated, her throat tightening. "I don't know."

St. Michael let out a slow breath, rubbing his hands over his face. "That's not exactly reassuring."

"I know," she admitted. "But this isn't just about stopping the Nexus anymore. I need to know what happened to my mum. I need answers." She gestured to the scattered documents between them. "She went back to stop them, Michael. And she never came back. *I have to find out why.*"

"Alright," St. Michael said, scanning the brittle pages with sharp focus. "Let's at least make sure we know what we're walking into."

Lucy nodded, stepping closer as he opened his laptop and began searching for information on the battle.

"*It was brutal*," St. Michael said grimly, his fingers tracing along his screen. "Nanjing wasn't just some minor city in this rebellion—it was *everything*. Hong Xiuquan and his followers stormed it, and when they won, they declared it their capital."

Lucy leaned over, reading alongside him.

"This victory let them push out further," she murmured. "They launched full-scale invasions into the north and west from here." She hesitated for a moment. "If the Nexus succeeds in killing him now, the whole war shifts."

"Or stops completely," St. Michael added.

They both knew the stakes. This wasn't just history playing out. This was a powder keg moment, one that could redefine *everything*.

Lucy exhaled, glancing at her mother's notes once more. "We need to move."

St. Michael nodded. "Agreed."

For all the danger they had faced so far, this felt different. This wasn't traversing through time to observe or to gather knowledge. This was stepping straight into the heart of a war. And the Nexus would be there.

Lucy exhaled slowly, her fingers drumming against the edge of the desk as she forced herself to meet St. Michael's gaze.

"You ready?" she asked, her voice quieter than she expected.

St. Michael hesitated for only a fraction of a second before nodding. "Yeah," he said, though the tension in his jaw betrayed his nerves. "You?"

Lucy swallowed. "Yeah."

Neither of them sounded convincing.

St. Michael turned back toward his desk and began typing again.

Lucy turned back and tried to glance over his shoulder. "What are you doing?"

"Getting a visual reference," he replied, eyes scanning the screen. "It's helped you before, remember? Nuremberg. Austerlitz. Seeing something from the era seems to make it easier."

Lucy watched him for a second. It was a logical step, one she would've taken without hesitation before. But something felt different now. She didn't need an image of the Taiping Rebellion to lock onto. She *knew* where they were going. She could feel it, sharp and electric, waiting just beyond the walls of the subconscious like it were drawing her in.

"I don't think I need it," she said, almost surprising herself with the certainty in her voice.

St. Michael's fingers hovered over the keyboard as he turned to look at her. "You sure?"

Lucy hesitated, not out of doubt, but because she wasn't entirely sure when this confidence had settled into her bones. It was just… there. The moment Evelyn's notes had revealed the Nexus' plan, something had shifted. There was no hesitation. No second-guessing.

She met St. Michael's gaze. "I'm sure."

He didn't question it. He just nodded once, pushed back from the desk, and stepped toward her.

Lucy felt the warmth of his palm against hers, steady and sure. His trust in her was absolute.

He would follow her to the end of the earth.

The hum of the slip was smooth, precise. Controlled. There was no jarring tug, no spiralling loss of sight. Just a seamless transition, the world around them melting away in quiet surrender. Time folded inward, wrapping around them like a tide pulling back into the ocean.

Evelyn had gone into the past to stop the Nexus. Now, it was Lucy's turn.

Then, reality reformed.

And it was *hell*.

* * *

The smell was thick and suffocating. The air was heavy with the stench of blood, sweat, and burning flesh. The scent of gunpowder clung to the damp earth, mingling with the unmistakable coppery tang of death. Smoke rolled through the battlefield like a living thing, curling around the fallen and the dying, obscuring what little light the sun had to offer through the overcast sky.

The screams, gunfire, and the relentless clash of steel against steel. The roar of cannon fire thundered across the field, shaking the very ground beneath them.

War cries, desperate and raw, travelled through the air. Some in fury, others in agony. The clang of blades meeting flesh, the sharp crack of musket shots, the wet, gurgling gasps of the wounded. It was a symphony of horror, unrelenting and merciless.

Lucy's vision adjusted to the chaos around them. The battlefield stretched before them, a writhing mass of bodies locked in combat. The outer walls of Nanjing loomed ahead, their once-imposing stone fortifications blackened and scarred by relentless cannon fire. Jagged craters marked the ground, evidence of the heavy artillery that had rained down upon the defenders. The walls were lined with ladders, hastily constructed by the Taiping forces, some still standing, others shattered, their broken remains strewn across the blood-soaked ground.

Bodies of both Qing and Taiping soldiers lay in tangled heaps, discarded like dolls. Some still clung to life, their blood seeping into the dirt, adding to the already vast pool of suffering. The Qing soldiers stood in their worn blue and green padded jackets, some covered in dented armour, their faces streaked with sweat, dirt, and blood. They moved together, hacking and stabbing in a desperate bid to hold their line.

The Taiping warriors surged forward, their simple tunics—red, blue, and white—stained with the grime of battle. Their cropped hair marked them unmistakably as soldiers of the Heavenly Kingdom. Their weapons were a mixture of captured muskets, long spears, and long swords. Some carried banners emblazoned with religious symbols.

Lucy barely registered the deafening roar of another cannon blast before she felt herself being yanked violently to the ground.

Boom.

The force of the explosion sent a shockwave through the battlefield, rattling her bones as debris rained down around them. Dust and smoke filled the air, blinding her for a moment as her ears rang from the concussive blast.

St. Michael had tackled her down, his arm still braced protectively across her back, his breath ragged. "Jesus

Christ, Lucy!" he gasped, his voice barely cutting through the ringing in her ears.

Lucy blinked rapidly, her hands pressing against the mud as she tried to make sense of everything. One moment, she had been frozen, caught in the horror of what surrounded her, and the next, she had nearly been blown apart.

St. Michael shook her lightly, his grip firm but not rough. "Are you alright?" His face was close, his dark eyes searching hers for any sign of injury.

"Yeah," she managed, though her voice was croaky. "I—I'm fine."

A lie.

Nothing about this was fine.

They weren't supposed to be here. not like this. Lucy had planned to land just outside the conflict, to observe from a distance, assess the situation before making any decisions. But something had gone wrong.

Her traversal had placed them in the heart of the carnage, right between the surging Taiping forces and the desperate Qing defenders.

Lucy turned her head slightly, eyes locking onto St. Michael's. He still held her close, his own breathing uneven, but his grip was steady-grounding.

"We need to move," he said, urgency thick in his voice. "Now."

She nodded, forcing herself to shove aside the horror clawing at the edges of her mind.

She could break down later. Right now, they had to survive.

She tightened her grip on his arm and prepared to run.

Her eyes locked onto the closest ladder leaning against the city walls, its wooden rungs slick with blood and rain. It was their best chance at getting inside—at getting their bearings.

"There," she said, tilting her head toward it.

St. Michael followed her gaze, nodding once.

No questions, no hesitation, just trust. They ran.

Lucy ducked instinctively as a musket shot rang out nearby, the bullet whistling past her ear.

Ahead, a Qing soldier on horseback let out a strangled yell as his horse reared violently, its eyes wide with terror. The rider lost control, the beast toppling sideways, hooves flailing.

"Move!" St. Michael shouted.

Lucy lunged forward, narrowly dodging the crashing weight of the horse as it hit the ground with a sickening crunch. The soldier beneath it didn't even have time to scream.

They kept running.

The air was thick with smoke and cannon fire, the battlefield shifting like a living beast beneath them. A deafening boom tore through the chaos, and Lucy turned just in time to see a cannonball rip through the ranks behind them, sending bodies flying in a grotesque spray of limbs and shattered armour.

She didn't stop. Neither did St. Michael.

They weaved through the melee, ducking low, dodging past swinging sabres and musket blasts, every step a gamble between survival and death. A Taiping rebel lunged at a Qing soldier barely a few feet away, his sword carving a brutal arc. Lucy didn't see how it ended. She didn't look back.

By the time they reached the base of the ladder, it was clear. No soldiers scrambling up, no archers positioned above. Yet the momentary relief was cut short by a brutal realisation.

St. Michael turned to her, voice low but urgent. "We're completely exposed climbing this."

He was right. From the moment they started up, they'd be sitting ducks. Musket fire, cannon blasts, anything could take them out before they reached the top.

Lucy opened her palms, her mind racing. They had seconds. Maybe less. Then, instinct took over.

She raised her hands, the pulse of the Universal Timeline surging beneath her skin, familiar, fluid, alive. She didn't have time to think about it. she just… felt.

A deep, rolling cloud coalesced above them, thick and heavy with moisture that obeyed her desire. Within moments, the battlefield dimmed as a blanket of fog descended, swallowing their ladder in a dense, swirling mist.

St. Michael exhaled sharply. "That's— "

"No time," Lucy cut in, already gripping the ladder.

St. Michael clapped a firm hand on her back. An unspoken "stay alive," and stood watch as she climbed first.

Lucy hauled herself upward, rung by rung, her breath coming in sharp and shallow gasps.

The wood was damp, worn smooth from countless hands before hers. The mist obscured everything, but she didn't dare slow down.

Her fingers scraped against stone. The top.

With a final heave, she pulled herself over the edge onto the parapet before turning back, reaching for St. Michael.

His hand found hers as he clambered up, his boots scraping against the stone ledge.

Lucy yanked him forward, and he collapsed beside her, chest rising and falling rapidly.

For a moment, neither of them spoke.

Then, slowly, they turned, taking in the city before them.

Nanjing.

A burning, ruined *nightmare.*

Thick plumes of smoke rose from the shattered rooftops, blotting out the sky in rolling waves of black and orange. The once-majestic city was barely recognisable, its grand boulevards now war-torn streets littered with bodies, broken carts, and fallen banners. Fires devoured entire buildings.

In the distance, the Taiping banners still flew high, their tattered silk whipping violently in the wind. The city was a patchwork of control-some districts held by the Qing, others by the rebels.

"This place is more than a war zone," Lucy said, taking a steadying breath. "It's a graveyard."

St. Michael pushed himself up, wiping sweat from his brow. "And we just merrily walked into it."

Amidst the ruin, Lucy's eyes caught something on the opposite side of the wall—another ladder, leading down into the city itself. Someone had placed it there, but it was currently unguarded.

She turned to St. Michael, "That's our way in."

His expression was grim but resolute. "You go first. I'll cover you."

Lucy gave him a short nod before moving fast, crossing the length of the wall in a low crouch to avoid any stray bullets or watchful eyes. The ladder was sturdy but weathered, its wooden frame creaking beneath her weight as she climbed over the ledge and began her descent.

She moved quickly. Hand over hand, foot over foot, she climbed down. The ladder swayed slightly, but it held.

Above her, St. Michael crouched, waiting, his dark silhouette tense against the dim firelight.

Lucy was halfway down when she heard a faint scrape above.

St. Michael was starting his descent.

She didn't look up, just focused on the ground drawing closer. The moment she hit the blood-slicked stone floor, she pivoted, scanning the immediate area. The alley was narrow, lined with abandoned buildings and half-collapsed stalls, but for the moment, it was empty.

She exhaled sharply, turning back toward the ladder. Just in time to see disaster unfold.

A cannon roared somewhere in the distance.

The air shuddered with the force of the blast.

And then, impact.

The cannonball struck the wall barely a few feet from the ladder, stone exploding inward in a deafening eruption of debris and dust.

Lucy barely had time to register the impact before she saw St. Michael's form jerk violently, the entire ladder wobbling beneath him.

Then, it gave way.

"Michael!" Lucy shouted, already moving, but there was nothing she could do.

The ladder snapped.

St. Michael fell.

His body twisted midair, flailing as he hurtled down. Not toward the ground, but toward a wooden rooftop jutting from the alleyway.

Lucy watched, helpless, as he slammed into the roof with brutal force.

The impact was immediate.

The brittle wooden planks gave way beneath him, splintering on impact, his body disappearing into the collapsing structure.

A sickening crack reverberated through the alley as the remains of the ladder split into two useless halves, both tumbling down.

"Michael!" she called, already racing forward, her boots kicking up dust and blood as she sprinted toward the walls of the building St. Michael had fallen into.

No answer.

The moment St. Michael disappeared beneath the wreckage, the world around Lucy seemed to collapse inward.

The distant gunfire, the screams of war. All of it faded way into inaudible background noise. Her entire focus narrowed to the building in front of her.

There was no clear way into the building from her side. No doors. No low windows. No way to reach him.

The panic that crept in began to take over her entire being.

"Michael!" she shouted again, stepping closer, boots crunching over shattered wood. "Michael, can you hear me? Fucking talk to me!"

Nothing.

No. No, no, no. He couldn't be—

"Michael!" she tried again, her voice breaking. She didn't care who heard her. She didn't care if the entire Qing army or the Taiping rebels turned their heads in her direction. Nothing mattered except hearing his voice.

The wreckage below remained motionless.

The edges of her vision blurred. *Oh god—had he hit his head? Had something collapsed on top of him?*

Then, a faint, pained voice cut through the silence.

"…I'm… I'm alright."

Lucy froze.

A sharp exhale tore from her lungs as she doubled over, planting her hands on her knees. "Oh, thank god."

Her head dropped forward, squeezing her eyes shut for half a second. Relief flooded through her so fast her limbs went weak, but it was short-lived.

Because the realisation slammed into her next.

They were stuck.

She forced herself upright, scanning the alleyway. The building that had swallowed St. Michael was between two massive concrete walls to its left and right. No entry point on her side. No obvious way for Lucy to get in.

"Michael?" she called, a little calmer now, but still breathless.

A few seconds passed before she heard him again. Closer this time, but not from within the building.

Her head snapped left.

His voice was coming from the other side of the building's left-hand wall.

Lucy spun, taking a few side steps toward the thick stone barrier, pressing a palm against it as if she could somehow see through. "You're out?"

"Yeah." His voice was strained but steady. "Literally through the front door."

Lucy exhaled sharply, tilting her head back to stare at the imposing wall separating them.

"Can you get over?" she asked, already scanning its surface for anything—a foothold, a ledge, something.

A pause. Presumably while St. Michael scanned the immediate area.

Then, "Nah, nothing that'll take my weight."

Lucy's stomach dropped.

They were separated.

She didn't want to leave him. Every instinct in her body screamed against it.

But there was no way over, no way through.

She had no choice.

"Wait there," she called, reluctant, her voice betraying every ounce of resistance inside her. "I'll find a way around."

The words felt like ash in her mouth.

But before she could turn, St. Michael's voice rang out—stronger this time, steadier.

"Lucy—go find your mum!"

Lucy stilled.

His words hit harder than they should have.

She knew he was right. She knew that wasting time trying to find a way through this wall—when the battle was raging and every second mattered—was reckless.

But she also knew what he wasn't saying.

He didn't want to slow her down. That was what this was really about.

Lucy's fingers curled into fists against the stone. Her jaw locked.

She hated this. Hated every second of it.

But she forced herself to swallow the instinct to argue, to fight him on it. *To stay.*

"Wait there," she said again, her voice lower this time, thick with reluctance.

St. Michael didn't respond right away. "I'll find somewhere to tuck myself into," he eventually said, calmer than Lucy expected.

"I'll be back," Lucy called out. As if not only to confirm to St. Michael, but herself. "I promise."

"I know you will," St. Michael said softly and trustingly. "Now go."

Almost immediately, she heard his footsteps retreating into the building. He was going back inside.

She exhaled sharply, glancing up toward the shattered roof. The building looked like it had once been a home. The remains of what might have been someone's sanctuary.

For a moment, she imagined the people who had once lived here. The family that had called it home before the war had torn their world apart.

Now, it was nothing but a hollowed-out ruin. A temporary refuge for a man trapped on the wrong side of history.

She forced herself to move.

Every step away from that wall felt wrong.

But she kept walking.

* * *

The battle was still raging. A brutal, chaotic blur of violence and blood. She had to be smarter than before. She couldn't afford any mistakes.

Keeping her head low, Lucy started moving through the war-torn streets, slipping from shadow to shadow, sticking close to collapsed buildings, piles of debris, anything that could keep her hidden.

Bodies littered the streets. Some fallen in battle, others—civilians caught in the crossfire, their lives stolen by a war that cared nothing for innocence.

Lucy crouched behind the crumbling wall of an abandoned shop, as a squad of Qing soldiers stormed past, their muskets raised, shouting orders to one another as they rushed toward the next skirmish.

She didn't move until their voices faded into the chaos.

She checked both directions were clear before emerging.

Lucy moved like a ghost. Silent, deliberate, pressing herself against the cold stone walls of the alleyway as she advanced.

The side streets had been eerily untouched by the carnage, as if the war had forgotten these narrow veins of the city. The only sounds were the distant sounds of war.

Then, as she turned a corner, the alley spilled out into a vast central square.

She stopped dead.

This place had once been sacred.

She could see it, what it must have been before. The bones of its past still lingered beneath the ruin.

The charred remains of a temple gate stood at the square's edge, its once-intricate carvings blackened and broken. Statues of holy beings, their faces now shattered beyond recognition, lined the perimeter, half-buried beneath rubble. This had been a place of worship. A place where prayers had once been whispered into incense-laden air.

Now, it was a battlefield.

At least fifty soldiers fought in the centre of the square, their bodies locked in a vicious, unrelenting struggle. Qing and Taiping clashed, their war cries blending into an animalistic roar. Musket shots cracked through the chaos, spears glinted in the firelight, swords carved through flesh, sending blood spattering against the ground.

The dead and the dying were everywhere. While some still twitched, others had long gone still. The once-pristine stone beneath them was now slick with the thick, claret stain of war.

Lucy swallowed hard, forcing herself to push past the horror, push past the pile rising in her throat.

And then—she saw *them*.

At first, they were just shadows in the smoke. Two figures moving against the backdrop of chaos. They walked side by side, cutting through the battlefield untouched. Unchallenged.

No one looked at them.

No one stopped them.

They moved with purpose, deliberate in their steps, their presence unnatural in a way Lucy couldn't explain.

Then—a break in the smoke.

A single, unobscured glimpse.

And she saw everything she needed to.

They wore black robes. Not unlike those of the era, their garments tailored to blend seamlessly into the time they were trespassing in. But it wasn't their clothing that confirmed Lucy's suspicions.

It was the masks. White. Bone-pale. Devoid of emotion. *The Order of the Nexus.*

Lucy felt a cold chill claw down her spine as the figures continued forward, unbothered by the battle raging around them.

She had been right to come here.

Whatever was happening in this city, they were at the centre of it.

The two Nexians disappeared down a side street to the right.

Lucy moved without thinking.

She couldn't lose them. She wouldn't.

Because they were going to lead her to the answers she sought.

* * *

Back inside the building where St. Michael had taken cover, he watched the war unfold through a splintered crack in the wall.

Smoke clung to the air like a ghost of the city's former self as it twisted through the skeletal remains of buildings. Lifeless bodies scattered across the streets. St. Michael stayed low, his breath slow and measured, his fingers lightly resting against the rough wooden beams of the ruined home he had taken shelter in.

Civilians, women and children ran for their lives, their ragged cries swallowed by the roar of the flames consuming their city. Mothers clutched their infants tightly against their chests, fathers shielded their families with shaking hands, but there was nowhere to run. The Qing defenders had been caught off guard, outnumbered, and overwhelmed.

It was clear now. The battle was lost.

The Taiping swept through the streets like raging fire, cutting down anyone who stood in defiance of their vision. Their ideology left no room for opposition, no place for those unwilling to submit to their utopia. The way they moved, with unshaken purpose, with an enthusiasm that bordered on the fanatical—

It reminded him of *them*. The Nexus.

Different beliefs, different worlds, yet the same unwavering certainty. The same merciless conviction.

His train of thought shattered when movement pulled his focus back to the street outside.

A woman, barely in her mid-thirties, stumbled into view. She wore the plain, earth-toned robes of a peasant woman. Long, loose-fitting, tied at the waist with a simple sash, her feet wrapped in cloth shoes that had seen too many miles. Dust and soot stained her clothes, but the true marker of her suffering was the terror painted onto her face.

A boy—no older than ten—clung to her side. They were lost. Disoriented.

They must have taken a wrong turn, St. Michael realised. Trying to escape, only to find themselves at a dead end.

The woman spun around, looking to the destroyed building in front of her, where St. Michael remained hidden. Then to the outer wall to her left. A sheer, unscalable barrier. There was nowhere left to go.

She turned toward the building's door.

St. Michael barely held his breath as her hand reached for the wooden latch.

Then—

Her head snapped to the right, toward the city's inner streets.

Slowly, she backed away from the door, retreating toward the wall, her arms instinctively pulling the boy behind her.

St. Michael saw why. A Taiping soldier approached.

He moved slowly, deliberately. Like a wolf toying with its prey. His long, curved sword hung loosely in his grip, the blade darkened with fresh blood. His robe—red and blue, was torn at the edges, but his posture was relaxed.

He wasn't in a hurry. He was enjoying this. The woman pleaded.

St. Michael couldn't understand the words, but he didn't need to. He could hear it. The desperation, the raw terror in her voice. She pressed her child closer against her, shielding him with her own body.

The soldier smirked. He raised his weapon. His intent was clear.

St. Michael had an understanding of the Codex. He knew the rules. Its demands.

History had to take its course. He had no place in this moment nor to intervene.

But then his vision blurred.

For a split second, it was no longer the woman and the boy kneeling before the soldier.

It was Michelle. It was Teddy. In their place.

He saw Teddy's tiny fingers clutching at Michelle's robes, trembling as she placed herself between him and the soldier's blade.

The fear in her eyes. The instinct to protect. The terror of knowing it wouldn't be enough.

Something inside St. Michael broke. His hand closed around a jagged slab of broken stone beside him.

He didn't think. He acted.

The woman let out a strangled gasp as he burst through the door, sprinting at the soldier with everything he had.

He swung the slab.

It connected with the back of the soldier's head with a gruesome crunch.

The force shattered the concrete into fragments.

The soldier crumpled.

His body hit the ground, unmoving.

St. Michael stood there, his hands still trembling from the impact. His mind screamed at him.

Somewhere, at some point in time, a Quantum Time Collision had just occurred. He had altered history. But none of that mattered, not yet. Not in this moment.

He looked up. The woman stared at him, wide-eyed, her expression torn between horror, confusion and gratitude.

The boy clung to her side, gripping at her sleeve.

Then her face shifted. Her gaze lifted, looking past him.

St. Michael felt it before he saw it.

Something was behind him. Slowly, he turned.

Three Taiping soldiers.

They had been drawn by the sound, the impact of his attack, the disturbance in the street.

They stood at the edge of the alley, their expressions flat. Focused.

One carried a spear, the other two curved swords glinting beneath the flickering firelight.

They were staring directly at him.

The woman and her child took their chance. Without hesitation, they turned and ran, hugging the buildings, slipping past the soldiers unnoticed.

St. Michael barely registered it. His legs locked.

He stepped back but his foot caught on something—

The soldier he had struck. His body buckled.

He hit the ground hard, struggling against the surge of adrenaline keeping his limbs from working properly. He tried to push himself up, but his back hit something solid.

The outer wall. Nowhere left to go.

The soldiers spoke words he couldn't understand, but their intent was clear.

Their weapons rose.

St. Michael's mind filled with one thought.

Teddy. Michelle. They would never know. Never know he died in a war over a hundred years before he was even born.

He shut his eyes.

And then—light exploded.

CRACK.

A bolt of lightning split the air.

St. Michael's eyes opened in time to see the first soldier drop.

Then the second.

Then the third.

All three hit the ground, smoke emitting from their bodies.

Their weapons clattered against the stone.

St. Michael looked up. Someone had done this. Whoever it was, they had saved him. But there was no one.

He scanned the rooftops, the walls, the buildings. Nothing. No Lucy. No figures. No movement. No one.

St. Michael's breath steadied, confusion gnawing at his thoughts.

Then, slowly, he pushed himself up, his hand closing around one of the fallen soldiers' swords.

If he was still alive, then he sure wasn't going to die unarmed.

St. Michael gripped the sword in his hand, adrift in his own thoughts. Lost in the impossible moment he had just survived.

* * *

Meanwhile, Lucy moved deeper into the city.

Her steps were careful. Measured. She kept a precise distance behind the two Nexians, trailing their movements through the twisting alleys and ruined pathways.

They walked with purpose.

Lucy had to fight the instinct to recoil every time her eyes landed on them. There was something deeply unnatural about their presence. About the way they seemed to exist outside of the carnage.

They approached the end of a tight junction, the walls of ruined homes pressing in around them.

Then, abruptly, they stopped.

Lucy ducked behind a wall, praying they didn't turn around.

The Nexian on the left turned to the one on the right.

And then—they spoke.

"Gathil moran."

The second Nexian replied immediately, his voice exactly the same. *"Kithor vashan, zalith n'kael zarath moran."*

Lucy clenched her teeth, frustration bubbling up, "That fucking language," she whispered bitterly.

That cursed, impenetrable, impossible-to-translate language that blocked Custodians from understanding them.

She had no idea what had just been said.

And then, in unison, the two figures turned to their right and carried on, disappearing deeper into the city.

Lucy adjusted her stance before continuing.

The chase led her further in.

Lucy forced herself to focus. The Nexians never slowed. Never looked back.

They moved through narrow alleys, past burning shopfronts, over fallen banners once proudly raised by the Qing Dynasty.

Lucy kept pace.

But then, they were gone.

She came around a corner and they had vanished. A flicker of panic sparked in her chest.

She moved forward, more urgently now, turning down another tight alley, then another.

Still no sign of them.

Had she lost them?

Had she followed them too cautiously? Had she given them too much space? Or, had they known she was there?

Lucy slowed as she reached the end of the alley. A narrow junction unfolded before her A small intersection where the path split three ways.

Left. Right. Straight on.

She peered down each route. No tracks. No movement. No flicker of black robes disappearing into the dark.

Nothing.

Which way? Which way had they gone? Where should she go?

Had she just lost her one chance at answers? Had she come all this way only to find nothing?

Then, a voice.

Soft. Like a whisper. Distant yet close. Echoey but clear.

"Turn left."

Her head straightened up. But no one was there.

The voice had been so faint. Had she imagined it? It was like she had heard it within her own mind.

Had it been just a trick of her own thoughts? Her mind playing games with her?

Then, the voice came again.

Louder. Commanding. Unmistakable.

"Lucy. Turn left."

Her pulse stopped. She knew that voice.

She knew it.

It was her mother's.

Undeniably. Unquestionably. That tone. Firm but warm. A voice that carried weight but never lacked care.

She had no time to question it. She turned left.

And she ran.

The alley was narrow, choked with debris from the war-torn buildings that loomed above. The air was thick with smoke, with fire… with death.

A sudden clatter of boots on stone made her freeze.

Taiping soldiers.

They emerged from a nearby alleyway, their long spears glinting dully.

Lucy took a glance to her left and hopped over a broken wall into the remains of a shop. She sank lower behind the debris, barely daring to breathe.

The soldiers halted in the centre of the alley, their voices carrying over the distant roar of battle.

And as she listened, their words came to her in perfect English. Her innate understanding was reaching perfection.

"Nanjing is falling."

The voice was low, gravelly with exhaustion.

A second soldier—a younger man, his voice sharp with urgency—replied immediately.

"Yes, but we must ensure Qing forces do not reach the temple, for the King requests an audience with the gods."

Lucy's pulse spiked.

The King. *The Heavenly King*.

They were talking about Hong Xiuquan. The same man the Nexus had come to kill.

A third voice, hoarse and wary cut in.

"We must be vigilant. I've heard whispers of demons present. They wear white masks… and cast vengeful spirits from their hands."

The Nexus. Even here, even now, they had made themselves ghosts in history, twisting fear to their advantage.

The first soldier scoffed.

"That is nonsense. The gods of this world favour us."

The others murmured in agreement, but there was hesitation in their tones.

The Nexus had always thrived in the shadows, their presence unknown to history, yet somehow their existence had still bled through the cracks.

They had been seen.

The soldiers continued their discussion in hushed tones, but their voices began to drift as they walked back the way Lucy had come.

She waited. Still. Silent.

Then when the last flicker of their torches disappeared around the corner she finally exhaled.

Lucy knew what she had to do.

Find the King. Find the Nexus.

That was the path forward.

Lucy pushed off the rubble and sprinted further down the alley.

Up ahead, another path split.

Straight, left and right.

She didn't slow. She was about to charge straight through when—

A voice. That same voice.

"Right."

Lucy's feet faltered.

Her momentum carried her forward, but at the last second, she planted her heel and turned.

Her boots skidded against the dust-covered stone, her body jolting with the abrupt change in direction.

And then she ran. She didn't need to look back. She knew.

It was her mother. Guiding her. Still.

The alley widened, the ruined buildings giving way to an enormous temple. A towering Buddhist monastery, its golden roofs catching the glow of the fires raging through the city. The structure stood resilient against the devastation, its wide stone steps leading to an entrance flanked by ornate red pillars.

And at the base of those steps—Nexians.

Lucy came to a stop, watching as the masked figures strode forward, their movements eerily controlled, inhumanly precise.

The Nexians had been noticed.

Soldiers emerged. Taiping and Qing alike.

They had been slaughtering each other moments before, but now—now, they turned to a greater threat. Weapons were drawn. Spears levelled. Rifles cocked.

A Qing officer barked an order in a voice raw from battle. The soldiers hesitated only for a moment before charging forward.

The Nexians didn't even pause.

The one on the left raised his hand, fingers curling into a loose grip. And then—fire.

A roaring, torrential wall of flames erupted from thin air, scorching the air with blistering heat.

The soldiers in the front barely had time to scream.

Their bodies ignited instantly, the flames devouring them whole—consuming flesh, metal, bone—leaving behind nothing but charred remains. The heat rippled through the air, distorting the space around them.

Lucy flinched, her skin prickling with the intensity of the summoned inferno.

The Nexian on the right extended both arms outward, and in an instant, the winds howled.

A gale unlike anything Lucy had ever seen tore through the battlefield.

It wasn't just a strong gust, it was a force of nature, a wind pulled from the deepest storms of history.

Qing soldiers were hurled into the air like leaves caught in a hurricane. Their bodies twisted unnaturally, flung against the temple's stone steps with sickening cracks.

The Nexians moved forward with eerie calm, stepping over the dead as if they were merely obstacles in their path.

More soldiers rushed forward. Muskets raised, shaking hands fumbling to pull their triggers.

The Nexians didn't even turn to face them.

A hand flicked—a bolt of lightning cracked through the air.

It struck a soldier dead in the chest, his body convulsing as the current surged through him. His screams rang out for only a second before his charred corpse collapsed into a smoking heap.

Another wave of fire followed, incinerating anyone still foolish enough to stand against them. Lucy watched in horror.

It was effortless. Not a battle. Not even an execution. Just annihilation.

They moved like gods among men, their Temporal Incants weaving death with an unnatural elegance. It was as if they were merely swatting flies.

The Nexians ascended the temple steps, untouched.

The doors yawned open before them, and they disappeared into the shadows within.

She checked the ruins around her. No soldiers stirred, no more gunfire rang out. The battlefield had fallen silent.

It was clear. She sprinted forward, dodging the corpses that still smouldered, her mind forcing down the horror of it.

The grand doors loomed ahead, massive and unyielding. She hesitated for only a breath, then pushed them open.

Inside the temple was a scene of devastation.

Lucy stepped forward, taking in the ruin before her.

This was not the elegant, surgical destruction of the Nexus.

No, this was something else entirely.

The walls, once adorned with intricate golden murals of the Buddha's past lives, were now defaced. Scarred with deep gouges, burned until the figures were unrecognizable. Charcoal smudges and blackened streaks crawled up the temple's great columns, the aftermath of fires deliberately set to erase what once stood here.

Lucy's eyes travelled to what remained of the statues.

Some were beheaded, their expressions shattered upon the floor, their hands—once held in gestures of peace—severed at the wrists. Others had been toppled entirely, their golden bodies lying twisted amidst the rubble. The great central Buddha, which had surely once stood as the temple's heart, was unrecognizable.

The face had been completely destroyed.

Not simply broken, but struck repeatedly, over and over, until nothing but a hollow crater remained where the divine expression once was.

Lucy let out a slow, measured breath.

This wasn't chaos.

This was deliberate.

Hong Xiuquan's rebellion had sought to tear out the roots of Buddhism from China, to replace it with his own twisted vision of Christianity, one where he stood divine as king.

Every destroyed Buddha, every defaced inscription, every shattered relic—they weren't just remnants of war. They were acts of persecution.

Lucy carefully stepped over the remains of a broken incense burner, her fingers trailing over a nearby pillar, feeling the deep cuts left by blades, the violent strikes of men determined to erase centuries of faith in mere days.

Then—a sound.

A scream.

Sharp. Fearful.

It came from above.

Lucy looked toward the sound, her pulse rising.

She moved quickly, her footsteps light as she navigated through the ruined temple. She passed beneath shattered chandeliers, past scrolls of Buddhist scripture trampled into the dust, past what had once been altars, now desecrated, their offerings long since destroyed.

Then—a stairway.

At the side of the temple, half-hidden behind a collapsed wooden beam, she spotted the narrow stone steps winding upward.

Without hesitation, Lucy ascended.

The scream came again, closer this time.

She reached the upper balcony where a great archway stood ahead, leading beyond the temple's ruined interior. Leading to the roof.

Lucy pressed her back against the stone and to the right of the archway. The wind howled softly over the temple's rooftop.

She cautiously leaned forward, peering out.

The roof stretched before her. A wide, flat structure, worn by time and the elements, overlooking the destruction of Nanjing.

Hong Xiuquan was on his knees. He was trembling.

The self-proclaimed Heavenly King, the so-called brother of Jesus Christ, was reduced to nothing more than a desperate, pleading man.

Lucy's eyes took him in immediately.

A slender man with a pale complexion. His forehead was high and thin goatee framed a face that had once commanded thousands with unwavering conviction—now twisted in fear.

His robes, once symbols of divine authority and imperial grandeur, were ornate and flowing, embroidered with golden dragons and celestial symbols, marks of the utopian kingdom he had sought to forge. Yet here, on his knees before the Nexus, they meant nothing.

He bowed deeply, his hands pressed against the cold rooftop tiles, his voice shaking with desperation.

Lucy couldn't hear him fully over the wind, but she could see the raw panic in his movements, the way his shoulders shook with each breath.

The two Nexians loomed over him.

They stood tall, elegant in their stillness, their long black robes fluttering slightly in the wind. Their white masks—devoid of emotion, of mercy—tilted downward, fixated on the kneeling man before them.

Hong Xiuquan's lips moved rapidly, his words frantic, his hands trembling as he clasped them together in supplication.

Lucy knew what begging for one's life looked like.

The Nexian on the right took a step forward, his black robes shifting with the motion, and spoke in flawless Cantonese. His voice cool, deliberate, utterly devoid of emotion.

"Your reign of terror will lead to the death of millions."

Hong Xiuquan's shoulders tensed. He clasped his hands together in front of him, his fingers tightening as if he could will himself into divine protection.

"Famine, disease, and starvation will claim even more." The Nexian's voice didn't waver. "Innocent men, women, and children—sacrificed to your vision of a heavenly kingdom."

Hong Xiuquan shook his head violently, his expression twisted somewhere between defiance and terror. His voice was high-pitched, defensive, desperate.

"No! I am doing the Lord's work!" His breath came short, shallow. "He has bestowed this upon me! I am purifying our land in his name!"

Lucy swallowed hard as she watched.

She scanned the rooftop again, her muscles coiled with anticipation.

Her mother was here.

She had to be.

If Evelyn had come to stop the Nexus, if she had risked everything to intervene in this moment—then where was she?

The second Nexian moved, his head tilting ever so slightly, his mask catching the firelight from the streets below.

And when he spoke, his voice was different.

Sharper. Angrier. Whilst sounding exactly the same.

"Your conquest has already led to the deaths of thousands," he spat. "Cities lie in ruin. The streets are filled with corpses. Your people—your own followers—will be driven to cannibalism before this war is through."

Hong Xiuquan flinched, his lips parting as if to argue, but no words came.

Lucy felt a cold sweat creep over her skin.

Her gaze darted frantically across the temple rooftop. *Where was Evelyn?*

Why wasn't she here?

The first Nexian moved now, slowly, purposefully.

His black robes shifted like ink against the stone as he raised one hand.

A fireball ignited in his palm.

The flames erupted from nothingness, swirling and twisting, crackling in the night air. The heat from it rolled across the rooftop, its glow reflecting off the white masks of the Nexians, bathing them in an eerie, hellish light.

Hong Xiuquan let out a strangled gasp, his hands trembling as he scrambled backward.

The Nexian's voice was final. "This all ends now."

And he raised his hand to strike.

Lucy couldn't wait for Evelyn any longer.

She launched herself from the archway, boots slamming onto the rooftop, the weight of her sent loose tiles skittering down the edge.

Her hands surged with heat, time itself bending to her will as she summoned the inferno.

It exploded from her palm. A roaring, spiralling mass of flame, searing through the darkness like a meteor. The fireball twisted violently, its core a molten white-hot blaze, streaking across the rooftop in a brilliant arc.

The Nexian didn't react. Couldn't react.

The fire struck him head-on.

The force engulfed him instantly, flames consuming his robes, his mask, his very presence. The impact was merciless. his body lifted from the roof, hurled backward as if he weighed nothing.

With a crash, he struck the temple's edge.

For a brief, agonizing second, his silhouette burned beneath the sky, his form wreathed in fire.

Then—he was gone.

His body slipped from the rooftop, plunging into the chaos below.

The second Nexian spun on her, his white mask focused entirely on Lucy.

Her voice was steady. "Enough!" she declared.

The Nexian stepped forward, his voice calm but cold. "You do not understand what is at stake, Lucy Calder."

His words carried no anger, only conviction, the kind of unshakable certainty that came from absolute belief.

Lucy held her ground, steady despite the rage boiling in her chest. "No. I understand exactly what's at stake."

She gestured sharply to Hong Xiuquan, still cowering on his knees, his ornate robes dirty and dishevelled. "You think you're fixing history by killing him? You're not. For all you know, you could be tearing it apart."

The Nexian's posture never wavered. He merely tilted his head, his masked face unreadable.

"This man is a plague," he stated, as though it were an indisputable fact. "His rebellion will lead to the deaths of over twenty million people. Starvation will claim millions more. War will leave entire provinces in ruin. Do you know how many lives could be saved if he died tonight?"

"And what happens if you do kill him?" She shot back. "What about the Quantum Time Collisions? Millions of people alive that aren't meant to be. It could lead to worse. It could lead to better—I don't know. But, neither do you."

The Nexian took another step closer.

"We have studied this timeline extensively." His voice was measured, almost patient. "We have calculated the stress points. The loss of this man at this exact moment is one of the few interventions that will not cause catastrophic instability. The Codex clings to the illusion that history must remain untouched, but the reality is—it's flawed. It has always been. We have the power to make it better. Tonight."

Lucy felt the anger rise like a tide inside her.

The flames from her earlier incant still smouldered nearby, casting her shadow long across the temple rooftop.

"You think you can predict the outcome of rewriting history? That you can just choose which lives matter and which don't?" She shook her head, her voice sharp with disbelief. "It's not for you—any of us, to decide that."

The Nexian's voice did not waver. "And yet, we try. Because if we do nothing, then the suffering continues."

Lucy stiffened. "We don't get to decide that."

The Nexian exhaled slowly, as if disappointed. "The Nexus believes differently."

Lucy took a step closer, standing her ground, unwavering. "The Nexus is playing god in a world where it has no right to do so."

The Nexian remained silent for a long moment, then finally spoke, his tone measured but unyielding.

"So, tell me, when you look at history—the endless wars, the massacres, the atrocities—do you truly believe that all of it was meant to be? That we should simply stand by and let it happen?"

Lucy knew the weight of that question. She had asked herself the same thing countless times.

But she had her answer.

"Yes. Because it's not for us to decide."

The Nexian scoffed, incredulous. "Even when you know that with one small action, tens of millions could be spared?"

Lucy's gaze hardened. "Because that one action could be a death sentence to billions more."

The Nexian shot back instantly, as if he had predicted her answer. "So, The Codex would have you believe."

Lucy's voice was firm, unyielding to their ideology. Her lineage of a Time Custodian filling her being. "The Codex isn't about inaction. It's about preservation. You must see that?"

Lucy opened a palm and pointed it toward Hong Xiuquan. "You think you're creating a perfect world, but in doing so, you're just creating more chaos. And one day, your changes will collapse on top of you. On all of us."

The Nexian remained unmoved. "And if that day comes, we will bear that burden. But at least we try."

Lucy shook her head, again, in disbelief, her voice quieter but just as sharp. "I won't let you do this."

The Nexian stood in silence for a moment, the firelight dancing across his featureless mask.

He slowly stepped back. "Then you leave me no choice."

The Nexian's feet lifted from the ground, his black robes billowing unnaturally, untouched by the wind. It was as if the air itself recoiled from him, bending to his presence rather than the elements. His levitation was not clumsy or hesitant. It was absolute. It was a display of command over the forces he wielded.

As he ascended, the sky above them convulsed, shifting in an instant from the warm hues of firelight to a swirling, violent abyss. Dark clouds formed from nothingness, rolling in with a force that defied nature, twisting overhead in a vortex of shadow and fury. The world itself seemed to shudder beneath the weight of his power.

Then came the lightning.

A blinding bolt tore through the heavens, so close Lucy felt the static prickle against her skin. The crackling white-hot energy split through the clouds, illuminating the Nexian's hovering form in sharp relief. The storm responded to him, not as an effect, but as an extension of his will, like a painter commanding a brushstroke, or a sculptor shaping stone.

Another lightning bolt struck, this time the very edge of the temple roof, obliterating a section of the ornate railing in an eruption of shattered wood and stone. The storm was alive with energy that pulsed through the atmosphere, tangible and suffocating.

The Nexian remained still, poised like a god, his arms slowly outstretched. The sky rumbled in response, the storm growing denser, the winds howling around them.

"And now…" He paused, his mask catching the flickering light, its empty gaze a void in the storm's fury.

"You will feel the full force of the Nexus."

Lucy opened both palms, summoning the heat of the Timeline's fire. The energy built fast and volatile as the inferno took form. A fireball blazed into existence, its light reflecting off the temple's ruined stone.

Across from her, the Nexian lifted both hands in unison, his fingers spreading wide as the storm answered his command. The sky convulsed. The air turned suffocatingly dense.

Then—lightning.

A massive bolt erupted from his fingertips, jagged and searing, a concentrated arc of white-hot power that split the very air between them.

Lucy hurled her fireball, but the moment it left her palm, she knew it wouldn't be enough. The fireball wasn't just fire, it was a concentrated torrent, a stream of flame trailing behind it like the breath of a dragon. It crashed against the bolt of lightning mid-air, creating an explosion of elemental chaos, sending wild currents of fire and electricity whipping around them.

Lucy staggered as the impact sent a shockwave through her body. The sheer force made her arms tremble, her boots scraping against the rooftop as the lightning's power pushed her back.

The Nexian did not move.

He did not waver.

He simply pressed forward, his lightning bearing down against her fire like a force of nature.

Lucy gritted her teeth, channelling everything she had into holding the fire steady, forcing it forward, but she felt it. The inevitable loss.

The lightning was too powerful.

It didn't just match her fire, it consumed it. The collision of energy shifted, the sheer force of his attack pushing her back, inch by inch, her feet dragging helplessly across the stone.

She let out a strangled gasp as the crackling core of the two forces inched closer and closer toward her.

Then—it stopped.

The Nexian lowered his hands, snuffing out the lightning without effort. Lucy's flames vanished instantly, her arms falling limp.

The reprieve lasted less than a second.

With an effortless gesture, the Nexian swept both arms outward, and the air itself howled in response.

A massive gust of wind slammed into Lucy like a battering ram, hurling her off her feet and skyward. The world spun violently around her, the temple's roof a dizzying blur below.

And then—pain.

A lightning bolt lanced down from the storm, the blinding white energy striking her mid-air.

The agony was instant, electricity ripping through her body, setting every nerve ablaze. A scream tore from her throat, but the storm swallowed the sound.

Before she could even process the pain, another gust of wind slammed into her again, sending her hurtling downward.

She crashed into the stone with brutal force. The impact stole the breath from her lungs, the rough surface scraping against her skin as she barely managed to turn onto her side, coughing, gasping for air.

It didn't stop.

The Nexian raised his hands again, summoning another gust of wind that flung her back into the air.

Another lightning bolt.

Another shockwave of agony, the raw energy searing through her muscles like molten metal.

Another merciless crash to the rooftop, her body slamming against the stone with a sickening crack.

This time, she didn't move.

Her limbs refused to respond, her body aching too much to even try. Her fingers twitched weakly, but nothing more.

She heard him before she saw him.

The whisper of fabric as the Nexian descended, lowering himself gracefully back to the rooftop, his feet touching the stone with an eerie, weightless silence.

Lucy could barely turn her head, but she saw it.

Not a single sign of exertion. Not a single mark of battle upon him.

Her mind reeled. *This wasn't a fight. It was a lesson.*

The Nexian moved with terrifying precision, each step measured, deliberate, as he closed the distance between them. He barely made a sound against the stone, but his presence was deafening.

She lay sprawled at the centre of the rooftop, her limbs heavy, her breath shallow. Every inch of her body screamed in pain, the aftermath of his relentless assault leaving her too weak to rise. But she refused to look away. Even as he loomed over her, towering, his mask as expressionless as ever, she held his gaze.

With a casual flick of his wrist, the wind howled to life once more.

It struck her like a hammer, sending her tumbling uncontrollably toward the edge of the roof.

She came to a jarring stop just short of the precipice, her fingers curling instinctively against the ledge. Below her, the ruins of the temple stretched out into the chaotic battlefield of Nanjing, the fires flickering hungrily in the distance.

Slowly, the Nexian turned to face her.

The storm still raged above him, the darkened sky flashing with erratic bolts of lightning, illuminating the white, emotionless mask that hid his face. His back was to the archway, but his full attention was fixed on Lucy.

He took a slow, measured step toward her, his tone as cold as the grave.

"I was under strict instruction not to kill you," he mused, his voice carrying a mocking edge, as though the very idea of restraint amused him.

He tilted his head ever so slightly, studying her.

"However…" A pause. Calculated. Inevitable.

"Imagine the hero I'd be—destroying the Eleventh."

The Eleventh.

Lucy didn't move. She couldn't. But she did the only thing she still had the strength for. Staring back, refusing to let him see an ounce of fear.

Even as he took another step closer.

Even as the storm moved like a living thing, answering his call.

Even as the edge of the roof was all that separated her from the fall below.

The Nexian did not hesitate.

With a slow, taunting raise of his hand, the storm above
roared to life, a maelstrom of chaos responding to his
command. Thunder cracked, deafening and absolute, as a
bolt of lightning ripped from the clouds, drawn to his
fingertips like a serpent eager to strike.

And then he unleashed it.

The lightning exploded from his palm. A raw, blinding
energy that crashed into Lucy's body with brutal,
unrelenting force. Agony tore through her. It was unlike
any pain she had ever known, a searing, unholy torment
that didn't just burn. It consumed.

The electricity ripped through her veins. It crawled
inside her bones, burrowing deep, burning from the inside
out. Her muscles seized, her spine arched, her scream
never even making it past her lips as the shock stole the air
from her lungs.

She could feel herself unravelling.

The force of it held her in place, pinning her to the
rooftop. Her vision blurred. A violent, convulsing
darkness clawed at the edges of her mind, ready to pull her
under.

This was it.

Her body couldn't take anymore.

Her life was slipping, draining out of her as though
time itself was being torn from her grasp.

And then—

It stopped.

The lightning cut off instantly.

For a fraction of a second, there was only silence. A
hollow, ringing void where there should have been death.

Lucy, barely conscious, blinked through the haze of her
agony, her body still twitching from the residual charge.
The Nexian still stood above her, his mask angled down,
white and empty.

Unmoving.

Then, he fell.

The motion was almost unnatural, as though his body had only just realised it was dead. The Nexian crumpled forward in a slow, spiralling descent, his black robes catching the wind as he collapsed in a heap beside Lucy.

And behind him—

St. Michael.

His breath was heavy, his grip firm on the hilt of the sword he had taken earlier. Both hands locked around it, the blade still extended in the finality of a slicing downward motion. A warrior's stance.

The storm above them began to dissipate as normality took its place.

St. Michael stood over the fallen Nexian, his stance unwavering, his presence a force all on its own.

Lucy, still reeling, stared up at him, the world spinning, her body barely able to comprehend what had just happened.

He had saved her.

As soon as Lucy's body stirred, as soon as she even attempted to push herself up, he was there.

He practically slid across the rooftop, dropping the sword without a second thought. It clattered against the stone, forgotten. His only focus was on her.

His hands found her shoulders with the gentlest urgency, steadying her, grounding her, his touch firm but not forceful.

"I've got you," he breathed, his voice low, raw with something unspoken. "I've got you."

Lucy coughed, aching from the aftermath of the lightning's wrath. Her body felt like it had been shattered and pieced back together wrong, but St. Michael's presence was a lifeline.

His face was tight with worry, his eyes scanning her, checking for damage. His brows were furrowed so deep it looked like he was holding back something fierce.

"H… How…" her voice was barely a whisper, but she forced the words out, "how did you find me?"

St. Michael exhaled sharply, like he'd been waiting for her to ask. "I went looking for you."

Lucy huffed a small, exhausted laugh, shaking her head slightly. "Of course, you did."

St. Michael's lips twitched, but the relief in his expression overshadowed any humour. "I saw the lightning over the roof," he admitted, voice still laced with tension. "The whole city must've seen it. It was—" He swallowed, shaking his head slightly. "I knew it had to be them. Had to be you. So I ran."

He tilted his head slightly, his gaze sweeping over her burnt and torn clothes, the reddened streaks of pain along her face.

"And it's a good thing I did," he added, his voice quieter now.

He had risked everything to get here. For her.

With a slow, aching effort, she pushed herself up further. St. Michael helped her immediately, his arm sliding under hers, taking on some of her weight. She let him.

Lucy's gaze drifted past St. Michael, toward the lifeless body on the ground.

The Nexian.

The one who had nearly killed her.

She stared for a long moment, her exhaustion momentarily numbed by something else. Curiosity. Uncertainty. Dread.

Slowly, she pulled away from St. Michael just enough to crouch down beside the fallen figure.

Her fingers, still trembling slightly, reached for the white mask.

For so long, the Order of the Nexus had been a faceless nightmare. Their masks had become their identities, their presence an omen of disruption, of chaos.

But now, this one had a face.

Lucy's fingers hooked beneath the smooth edges of the mask, and with a careful, deliberate motion, she pulled it away.

What she saw shocked her.

The man—the boy—beneath the mask had pale, smooth skin, his features still soft with youth. Mousey brown hair fell across his forehead. His expression, even in death, was almost peaceful.

He looked… so young.

St. Michael let out a breath beside her, one of disbelief. "Christ," he muttered.

Lucy glanced at him, watching as his dark eyes widened with the same realisation sinking into her.

"He's just… a kid," St. Michael said, almost to himself. His voice was quieter now, like he wasn't sure how to process it. "He can't be any older than twenty."

Lucy swallowed hard, still staring. Someone so young who wielded enough power to bring her to the edge of death.

A boy who had been willing—eager—to rewrite history itself.

"He was so powerful," Lucy murmured, still gripping the mask in her hand. "More powerful than anything I've ever felt."

Slowly, she looked back at St. Michael, their eyes locking.

A sharp, panicked shout broke through the tense silence, cutting off whatever thoughts Lucy and St. Michael were having about the fallen Nexian.

It was in a language St. Michael couldn't understand, but Lucy did.

"Demons!"

She looked up, her eyes locking onto Hong Xiuquan.

She had completely forgotten he was still there.

The Heavenly King remained kneeling several feet away, his face pale as he pointed at them with wide, horrified eyes. His lips trembled as he repeated himself, louder this time, more frantic.

"Demons!"

His voice was thick with both fear and astonishment.

St. Michael turned to Lucy. "What's he going on about?"

Lucy, despite her exhaustion, despite everything they had just gone through, felt the corners of her lips twitch into a smile.

She exhaled sharply, shaking her head. "He called you a demon."

St. Michael blinked. Then, as if processing this revelation in real-time, he turned his gaze to Hong Xiuquan, who was still pointing at them as if he were staring at an omen from the underworld.

St. Michael gave him a nod of mock reassurance and said, completely deadpan - "You're all good, bruv."

Lucy snorted.

She tried to suppress it, she really did, but a genuine laugh bubbled up. It wasn't just about what he said, but how he said it—so casual, so unfazed, as if they hadn't just fought a temporal warlord on a temple rooftop.

Hong Xiuquan, of course, looked even more bewildered.

St. Michael, seeing her laugh, grinned slightly before turning back to her. "So," he said, brushing some debris off his sleeve, "are we done here?"

Lucy let out a breath she hadn't realised she was holding. "Absolutely."

She stepped closer, placing her shaking but determined hand on his arm.

The familiar hum began. Soft at first, then growing in intensity.

Even fatigued, even drained, it was controlled. Steady. Hers.

The roof beneath them started to melt away. The smells of burning wood, blood, and gunpowder faded.

The roar of battle, the distant cries of soldiers, the screams of history. Gone.

The air changed.

When Lucy opened her eyes, she was no longer staring at a battlefield lost to time.

They were back home.

* * *

Lucy stumbled away from St. Michael. Her mind raced, replaying everything over and over again, but one thought burned brighter than the rest.

St. Michael took a step toward her, his voice soft but urgent. "Did you manage—"

She cut him off.

"She was there, Michael."

Her voice wasn't just certainty, it was conviction.

St. Michael stilled. There was something else in his expression. A flicker of realisation.

Lucy was only just piecing it together herself. "My mum was there."

St. Michael's expression shifted, his shoulders tensing in quiet anticipation. "Did you see her?" he asked, his voice carrying a breath of something close to hope.

Lucy shook her head. "No, not quite." She let out a slow breath. "But I heard her. I felt her."

She turned toward him, searching his face. "She guided me to the temple. She told me which way to go."

Lucy braced herself for scepticism, for some kind of rational argument from St. Michael about how that wasn't possible. But instead—

"Yeah," he said, his voice steady, like he had been expecting this.

Lucy's brows knitted together. "Wait, what?"

St. Michael exhaled, running a hand through his hair before meeting her gaze. "Yeah, me too."

Lucy stared at him. She hadn't expected that. Not at all.

"What do you mean?" she asked, almost taken aback.

He sighed, shifting his weight slightly, as if unsure how to even put it into words. "Before I found you, I got backed into a corner. Three of the Taiping had me. I thought that was it."

"But then—" St. Michael hesitated for just a second, like he didn't quite believe it himself. "Just before they attacked, they were hit by lightning."

Lucy's eyes narrowed slightly. "Lightning?"

"Not just bad luck," he clarified. "Not a storm, not a stray bolt. It was targeted. Like—" He gestured vaguely, frustration flickering in his features. "Like someone was aiming. Like someone was protecting me."

Lucy didn't have an answer for that.

She had felt her mother's presence, guiding her through the city, but this—this was something else. Something she couldn't explain.

"But her records," Lucy murmured, grasping at logic, at something solid. "Her accounts—" She exhaled sharply, frustration bleeding into her tone. "It was worded like she was actually there."

She must have been.

St. Michael nodded slightly before he exhaled, puffing out his cheeks. He didn't have the answers either.

Lucy paced the room, her hands running through her hair as she tried to make sense of it all. The past still clung to her. The smoke, the fire, the weight of her mother's presence, the brutal fight against the Nexian. It was all still there, beneath her skin.

St. Michael, meanwhile, had settled into his chair, absently reading through a website about the rebellion still open on his laptop, before letting out a quiet chuckle.

Lucy stopped and looked at him, one eyebrow raised. "What?"

St. Michael shook his head, the irony of it all sinking in as he read aloud: "During the rebellion, Hong Xiuquan is said to have declared that he fought spiritual demons and won. This further cemented his belief that he was the brother of Christ and the Son of God."

He looked up smirking. "You reckon that was us and the Nexus he was on about?"

Lucy let out a breathless, fatigued chuckle. Not because she found it funny, but because she was too exhausted to process it properly.

St. Michael watched her carefully. She was still so pale, still wincing every now and then, still clutching her arms like she was trying to ground herself. He had seen Lucy battle briefly before, had seen her walk away from impossible things, but this—this had left a mark deeper than the burns on her skin.

His smirk faded, replaced with something softer. Something genuine.

"You're not going home tonight," he said simply.

Lucy blinked, caught off guard. "What?"

St. Michael stood, stretching his back before nodding toward the sofa. "You're staying here."

Lucy immediately shook her head. "I'm fine, Michael. I just need to—"

"You're not fine." His voice wasn't harsh, but it was firm.

Lucy opened her mouth, but he didn't give her a chance to argue.

"You literally got hit by lightning tonight," he continued, walking over to the sofa and grabbing the side of it. He pulled the extension, the old mechanics of the pull-out bed groaning in protest as he set it into place. "And don't think I didn't notice you barely holding yourself up since we got back."

Lucy sighed, too drained to fight him on this.

St. Michael continued as he grabbed a pillow from his desk chair. "This thing's actually not terrible. I promise"

"I'll take the chair," he added, already grabbing his coat to drape over it like a makeshift blanket.

Lucy sat down on the edge of the sofa, rubbing her temple. "Michael—"

"Lucy," he cut in, turning to face her properly. "After everything, do you really think I'm letting you go back to your place alone tonight?"

Lucy looked up at him, searching his face. He wasn't just saying this out of concern—this was something deeper. Something like responsibility.

She didn't say anything else. She just nodded.

St. Michael exhaled, a small sign of relief passing over his face before he clapped his hands together. "Alright then."

Lucy barely had time to kick off her shoes before she collapsed back onto the makeshift bed, completely spent.

Her eyes were already closing when she mumbled, "You don't have to sit in that chair all night. We can swap?"

St. Michael smirked slightly, sitting down and kicking his feet up on the desk. "Honestly, I've done it before. It's fine."

It wasn't. His back would hate him for this in the morning. But that wasn't the point.

He glanced over at her one last time. She was already out cold.

Shaking his head, he leaned back in his chair and muttered under his breath, "Stubborn thing."

But he wouldn't have it any other way.

CHAPTER 16
A Moment's Peace

Lucy stirred at the sound of rustling paper. As she opened her eyes, it took her a moment to remember where she was—St. Michael's office.

The events of the night before replied in her mind over and over. Nanjing, the Nexus, the fight for Hong Xiuquan's life, and the voice of her mother, distant yet guiding.

She shifted under the weight of the blanket St. Michael must have draped over her at some point. Her limbs were stiff, her muscles aching from battle and exhaustion.

At his desk, St. Michael was already dressed in fresh clothes, flipping through a thick stack of papers with practiced efficiency. The sound of her stirring caught his attention, and he turned, setting the papers aside.

"Ah—sorry, I didn't mean to wake you," he said, his voice low but warm.

Lucy blinked the sleep from her eyes, rubbing at her face with one hand. "You didn't," she mumbled, though the way she stretched and yawned immediately betrayed her.

Her hair was a disaster. Stray strands falling in every direction, a perfect mess of bedhead. She probably looked half-dead.

St. Michael smirked, clearly noting the state she was in but wisely choosing not to comment. Instead, he moved to the small kitchenette, reaching for the coffee pot. "Coffee?"

Lucy exhaled, sinking back into the couch. "That would be lovely," she said, her voice still heavy with sleep. She wrapped the blanket tighter around her shoulders, then added with a sluggish wave of her hand, "just… give me a few minutes to defrost."

St. Michael chuckled. "Take your time. I doubt the Nexus is sending an army before breakfast."

The exhaustion ran deeper than her aching muscles, deeper than the bruises blooming across her arms and face like ink stains on parchment. It was the weight of it all. The sheer, unrelenting tide of time pressing down on her. She had stepped into something far greater than herself, and no matter how much she tried to gain control, it felt like treading water in an endless ocean. She couldn't see the coastline. She didn't even know if one existed.

Her mind replayed the horrors she'd witnessed. The fear in the faces of those fleeing the Great Fire of London. The desperation, the screams swallowed by the crackling inferno. The chaos in Nanjing, the bodies strewn across the streets, the metallic scent of war thick in the air. The way life had simply *left* the eyes of men who had fought and died before her.

She shivered despite the warmth of the blanket still wrapped around her shoulders. Time had always seemed distant to her, something studied in books, discussed in classrooms, reduced to footnotes and historical accounts. But now? Now it was raw. It was violent. It was *real*.

And she was drowning in it.

"We killed people last night."

Lucy's voice was flat, hollow, as if the weight of the thought had just dropped onto her shoulders like a ton of bricks. She hadn't considered it in the chaos of the moment, but now—now it was all she could think about.

St. Michael paused mid-pour, the steady stream of milk swirling into the dark coffee as he turned his head slightly. "Sorry?"

"We killed the Nexians," she repeated, her tone eerily devoid of emotion. "Before you arrived, I set one on fire. They fell from the roof." Her throat tightened. "And then obviously you..." She trailed off, unable to bring herself to say it.

St. Michael stirred the drinks slowly, his silence stretching between them. He took in a measured breath, his expression unreadable, but the way his shoulders tensed told her enough.

"I know," he said finally, his voice carrying a quiet weight.

Lucy studied him, searching for something— guilt, grief, anything. But he seemed... composed. Unshaken as he finished preparing the drinks.

However, when he spoke again, his voice was firmer, more resolute. "They were going to change history. We had no choice." He picked up both cups and walked over, settling beside her on the makeshift sofa bed before offering a mug.

"Thank you," Lucy said as she stared at the swirling surface of the drink.

She wasn't entirely sure what she was thanking him for. The coffee? The justification? The fact that, despite everything, she wasn't facing this alone? Maybe all of it. Maybe none of it.

"We also don't know if the Nexians' plans would have worked," St. Michael said, his voice thoughtful as he leaned back against the worn-out cushions. "Maybe killing Hong wouldn't have ended the war. Maybe it would have. Maybe it would have made it worse." He exhaled, running a hand over his beard. "Like we've been told all along, interference is unpredictable. It could've caused one of those... *time collision thingys*."

Lucy, despite herself, sniggered. "Quantum Time Collisions?" she corrected, arching an eyebrow.

"That's the ticket," St. Michael said, pointing a finger at her with mock confidence before taking a sip of his coffee.

But then, almost to himself, his voice dipped into something lower, something edged with regret. "Not that I can be the one to preach about that."

Lucy caught the shift immediately. "What do you mean?" she asked, concern threading through her tone.

St. Michael hesitated for a moment.

"I interfered," he admitted, his voice quieter now. "Remember I said I was backed into a corner?" He glanced at her, and Lucy nodded.

He sighed. "Just before that, a Taiping soldier was about to kill this woman and her child. They were just trying to escape. I saw them—saw the fear in their eyes, the way the mother shielded her son." He shook his head, his grip on the cup tightening. "I couldn't help it. I just—" His voice grew more animated, more strained. "I just saw Teddy and Michelle. I saw *them*. And before I could even think, I smashed the soldier over the head with a brick or something."

Lucy watched him carefully, then shifted, placing a reassuring hand on his shoulder. "It's okay," she said softly. "You did the right thing."

St. Michael let out a hollow laugh, shaking his head. "But did I?" His voice was raw, uncertain. "It goes against everything we've been told. It's exactly what *they* would do." There was disgust in his voice as he spat the word *they*.

"Michael," Lucy said firmly, "they target historical leaders, as we've seen. They want to reshape entire events, rewrite history in their favour. *All you did* was save two innocent people. Yeah, it might have caused a collision somewhere, but I really don't think it's the end of the world."

He let out a slow breath, nodding, but the doubt still lingered in his expression. "I hope so."

Lucy leaned back, stretching her arms with a dramatic sigh. "Well, we're still here. Everything looks the same." She tilted her head toward the window. "I'll just go check outside to make sure it hasn't caused, I don't know… an apocalypse or something."

St. Michael let out a chuckle, shaking his head as Lucy grinned. The tension broke, if only for a moment, the weight of their actions settling into something they could carry, together.

Lucy pushed herself upright, wincing as the aches and bruises from the previous night made themselves known. She barely had a second to brace before St. Michael set his coffee down with a hurried clink and reached to steady her.

"Easy," he said, his hands hovering, ready to catch her if she wobbled. "Take it slowly."

"I'm alright, I'm alright," Lucy said quickly, waving him off. The last thing she wanted was a fuss.

Still, he didn't move away entirely, watching her carefully as she adjusted her stance. She exhaled, rolling her shoulders, trying to shake the stiffness from her limbs.

A beat passed before she spoke again, her voice quieter this time. "So… you think we did the right thing? With the Nexians?"

She hated how uncertain she sounded, how she still needed reassurance, but the guilt still clung to her like a shadow.

"Absolutely," St. Michael said without hesitation. "I mean, one was literally about to kill you."

Lucy paused, the memory flashing in her mind. The crackle of lightning, the way the Nexian had stood over her, victory within reach. She had thought, for one terrifying moment, that the mask would be the last thing she'd ever see.

But then another memory surfaced. A voice.

"I was under strict instruction not to kill you."

The words sent a chill through her, an unease settling deep in her gut.

"Strict instruction," she muttered, almost to herself.

"Huh?" St. Michael tilted his head, his focus sharpening. "Come again?"

Lucy met his gaze. "The Nexian—he said he wasn't supposed to kill me. He'd been told not to."

St. Michael frowned, his brow furrowing. "By who?"

"He didn't say." She exhaled sharply. "He just referred to me as *the Eleventh*." Then, after a pause, she added, "Though I don't think he was listening to his orders anymore by the end."

"Sounds about right for them," St. Michael said dryly. "But why would he say that?"

Lucy groaned, running a hand through her already messy hair. "Ugh, I don't know, Michael." Frustration creeping in, her patience fraying. "It's like one step forward and about ten back."

St. Michael straightened slightly. "What do you mean?"

Lucy let out a bitter laugh, pacing slightly. "You pull a string, and the whole fucking thing comes undone." She gestured vaguely, as if trying to grab hold of an answer in the air. "Why weren't they supposed to kill me? Why did Mum write like she'd be there, but she *wasn't*? Why can I *hear* her?" Her voice rose with each question, frustration giving way to something raw, something close to breaking.

She stopped, took a breath. When she looked at St. Michael again, her voice was quieter, devoid of hope.

"Every time—I think, maybe I'll find her." She choked up slightly. "But all I ever find is another reminder that she's gone."

Silence.

St. Michael held her gaze, his expression unreadable at first. He didn't have the answers. He couldn't fix this.

"We are getting closer, Lucy," he said gently. "And we *will* figure it out."

Lucy didn't answer.

He studied her for a moment longer before offering something softer, something that carried the warmth of familiarity.

"You know… you are *so* like your mum."

Lucy turned to him, blinking as if caught off guard. "How so?"

St. Michael leaned back slightly, hiding a small smirk. "Well, if there was something that didn't make sense, boy, would she get the hump about it."

The smallest, breathiest laugh escaped Lucy's lips, barely there but real.

"Yeah," she said, shaking her head. "That sounds about right for her."

St. Michael turned away, stretching slightly as he spoke. "So, I was thinking… have you got anything on today?"

Lucy blinked at the sudden shift in conversation. "Michael, I don't even know what day of the week it is anymore," she admitted, rubbing her forehead.

He chuckled. "It's Sunday."

Lucy thought for a second. "Umm, well, I *should* be starting to look for a job."

St. Michael raised an eyebrow. "What do you mean?"

"Oh, since this began I've missed a deadline at work. Can't imagine the conversation about it tomorrow will go too well," she said, waving a dismissive hand.

"Oh." His face softened. "I'm sorry."

"Don't be. It's *shit*." She shrugged. "But I probably need to start looking on LinkedIn. Reckon I can add 'Trainee Time Traveller' to my experience?"

St. Michael let out a genuine laugh at the irony. "I mean, yeah, go for gold."

Lucy smirked, but then her curiosity kicked in. "Why do you ask?"

He turned back to face her, a thoughtful glint in his eye. "Well, I'm not saying you're a *bad* tour guide, but so far, we've been to Nazi Germany and two war zones." He gestured loosely. "Maybe we could go see some of history's *better* side? Only if you're up to it, of course."

Lucy paused. It almost *shocked* her that she hadn't thought of that before. They could go anywhere. See *anything*.

"Abso-bloody-lutely!" she exclaimed, grinning.

St. Michael laughed at her enthusiasm but gave her a measured look. "Only if you're sure you're up for traveling?"

"No, genuinely, I think it's a good idea."

"Amazing." He turned away from her, heading towards a carrier bag in the corner of the room that Lucy hadn't even noticed before.

"What's in there?" she asked, leaning around him as he bent over, rummaging through it.

"Whilst you were asleep, I went to a few charity shops and found us some clothes that could *probably* work for most places over the last hundred years or so," he said, almost guessing at his own estimate.

Lucy raised an eyebrow. "You *really* do think of everything, don't you?"

St. Michael let out a playful scoff, enjoying the flattery. "What can I say? It's—"

His words cut off as his phone vibrated. Immediately, his expression shifted, his attention fully absorbed by the screen.

Lucy, noticing the change, tilted her head. "What is it?"

"I just thought, after last night, I'd check in with Michelle—just to make sure she and Teddy were okay. Y'know, in case the Nexus turned up there."

Lucy nodded and held up her hands, giving him a thumbs-up and thumbs-down. "And…?"

"Oh, nah, they're all good," St. Michael said, still reading the message. "Michelle's still a bit… offish… with me after the last time I saw her, but they're fine."

"Well, that's the main thing," Lucy said.

"Exactly." St. Michael finally put his phone away. "Anyway, get yourself freshened up and get into this—I sort of had to guess," he added, pulling some clothes from the bag and tossing it toward her.

Lucy caught it with mild suspicion. "Oh god, I dread to even look." She sighed. "I'll think about where I wanna go while I get changed."

"You do that," St. Michael said, smirking as he turned back to his coffee.

"Oh," he called just as Lucy was about to leave the room.

She turned, glancing over her shoulder.

"There's some shampoo, toothpaste, and all that kind of stuff in there for you too," he said casually.

Lucy paused, then smiled, the gesture small but genuine. "Thank you, Michael."

He gave her a small nod in return, and for the first time in what felt like forever, she allowed herself to take a deep breath, shake off the weight of the past, and look forward.

* * *

Lucy stepped back into the office, dressed in a simple yet versatile outfit that could easily blend into most of the past century. She wore a crisp white blouse tucked into high-waisted charcoal trousers, the cut timeless enough to pass

321

anywhere from the 1920s to the present. Over it, she'd thrown on a fitted brown leather jacket, worn enough to look lived-in but sturdy enough to withstand the elements. A pair of well-polished oxford shoes completed the look, practical yet stylish. It wasn't perfect, but it was adaptable, and that was all that mattered.

She found St. Michael adjusting his cuffs. He'd gone for a classic button-down shirt in muted blue, layered under a dark waistcoat that added an air of quiet sophistication. A long grey coat draped over his shoulders, paired with trousers and polished black shoes.

Lucy chuckled as she glanced down at herself. "Well, it all fits… more or less."

"Yeah, sorry if anything's not quite right," St. Michael said, brushing his sleeve.

She smirked, tilting her head. "And you, sir, look like a most distinguished gentleman, Mr. Olabode." She exaggerated her accent, adding an air of aristocratic flair.

St. Michael huffed a laugh, shaking his head. "Why thank you, Miss Calder."

She grinned. "So, where are we going first?"

St. Michael thought for a moment before his face lit up. "How about the moon landing? New York. Times Square. Right in the middle of the crowd watching it happen."

Lucy's eyes widened, the thought thrilling her.
That *was* a good one.

"Your wish is my command," she said with a smirk, rolling her shoulders as she prepared to focus.

She closed her eyes, letting her mind zero in on Times Square, July 20th, 1969. The crowd, the grainy black-and-white footage on the towering screens, the sheer electricity in the air.

She extended her hand toward St. Michael. He took it without hesitation. As their hands connected, the air around them seemed to tighten, the familiar pull of time wrapping around them like an invisible current. The office blurred, colours smearing together in a streak of motion before dissolving into darkness—then, just as quickly, light and sound rushed back in, the distant roar of a crowd filling their ears as they landed in the heart of Times Square, 1969.

* * *

The moment they landed, Lucy was struck by the sheer *energy* of Times Square. The place buzzed. Not just with the usual hustle and bustle of city life, but with something electric, something *monumental*.

They had arrived just back from the main crowd, standing at the edge of a swelling mass of people gathered beneath the towering neon lights. The streets were alive. Horns honking, people chattering excitedly, vendors shouting about hot dogs and pretzels. The faint scent of roasting chestnuts mingled with the unmistakable smell of petrol and warm asphalt.

The New York Times building loomed above them, its front adorned with flashing news tickers feeding updates about the Apollo 11 mission. Nearby, department store windows displayed televisions stacked together, each screen flickering with grainy black-and-white images from NASA's live broadcast.

Above it all, the screen—the massive display mounted high above the crowd—held everyone's attention. The footage was grainy, almost ghostly in its transmission, but it was unmistakable: the lunar module, perched on the surface of the moon.

All around them, people stood shoulder to shoulder. Office workers who had spilled out of buildings, families who had brought their children to witness history, young couples huddled together, their eyes glued to the broadcast. Strangers leaned against cars, barely breathing as they watched.

323

Lucy felt a shiver crawl up her spine, not from the summer night but from the significance of it all. She had read about this moment, had seen the footage in documentaries, but being *here*—standing among them—was something else entirely.

Then, Neil Armstrong's voice crackled through the speakers, distorted slightly by the limitations of the transmission but still clear enough.

"That's one small step for man, one giant leap for mankind."

For half a second, the world seemed to pause.

Then roar.

The crowd erupted. Cheers, whistles, applause so loud it drowned out the city itself. People hugged, some openly weeping, others laughing, clapping, high-fiving. It was pure joy, unfiltered and unrestrained.

Lucy found herself grinning, caught up in the swell of emotion. St. Michael, standing beside her, was smiling too, nodding along as a man in a suit slapped his back in celebration.

They weren't from this time, they didn't belong here—but none of that mattered.

As the cheers finally began to settle, St. Michael turned to Lucy, his voice carrying an amused lilt.

"It's your turn. Where are we heading next?"

Lucy barely hesitated before answering. "Well… it's a bit of a rogue shout, but… when England won the World Cup?"

St. Michael raised an eyebrow, surprised. "Didn't have you down as a football hooligan."

"I'm not," Lucy chuckled. "But my dad loved football. He would never shut up about '66." She hesitated, grinning. "Which makes sense now, doesn't it? He probably saw it himself. I dunno… it just reminds me of him."

St. Michael studied her for a second before nodding. "Well then, to Wembley we go."

They slipped away from the crowd, weaving through the lingering celebrations, the city still buzzing with the thrill of history in the making.

Lucy took a steadying breath, closing her eyes, focusing. Wembley. July 30, 1966. The rush of the game, the chanting of the crowd, the heat of the summer day.

She extended her hand to St. Michael.

Times Square faded away—replaced by the deafening roar of another crowd, just as electric, just as legendary.

* * *

Wembley hit them moment they arrived.

Lucy barely had time to process the traversal before the sheer scale of the stadium's energy consumed her. The crowd was alive, a massive sea of red and white.

She had seen Wembley in modern broadcasts, sleek and pristine, but this Wembley—Old Wembley—had a rawness to it. The grand towers loomed over the stands, their pale stone catching the sun as it dipped lower in the sky. The terraces were packed, bodies pressed together in anticipation, an unrelenting wall of noise as the crowd sang, shouted, prayed for victory.

A humid mix of cigarette smoke, beer, and warm summer sweat thickened the air, blending with the scent of trampled grass and stadium food. Men in suits stood alongside factory workers in flat caps, women in floral dresses gripping their handbags tightly as they cheered, voices strained from ninety minutes of tension.

On the pitch, the game was still on a knife's edge.

The scoreboard confirmed it: *England 3 - 2 West Germany.*

Extra time. The final moments.

The players moved with pure exhaustion now, their kits clinging to them with sweat, their legs heavy but their determination unbreakable. Every pass, every tackle, every clearance drew gasps from the crowd, like the whole of England was holding its breath at once.

Lucy and St. Michael had landed at the back of the crowd, blending into the standing section, their arrival unnoticed amidst the sheer frenzy of the game.

Lucy exhaled, trying to take it all in. The colours, the sound, the emotion. It was overwhelming.

And yet…

Something was off.

She wasn't sure what, but a prickle ran down the back of her neck, an unease that didn't match the exhilaration surrounding her. It wasn't something obvious. No men in Nexian masks lurking in the crowd, no eerie anomalies in the timeline.

Just… a feeling.

Maybe it was paranoia. Maybe it was tiredness.

They had just been in Times Square, celebrating one of the greatest achievements in human history. Maybe travelling so quickly from one historic event to another was making her restless. Maybe her mind was still in battle mode, unable to switch off.

Maybe she was just waiting for something to go wrong.

She clenched her jaw, forcing herself to shake it off.

This was a good moment in history. A pure one.

She wanted to experience it, to feel what Edward must have felt when he was here, lost in the crowd, witnessing this exact moment.

So she didn't say anything. Didn't tell St. Michael about the gnawing unease creeping up her spine.

Instead, she focused on the game, on the way the entire stadium seemed to lean forward as one, eyes locked on the ball as England pushed forward again.

The match wasn't over yet.

Then, it happened.

Geoff Hurst surged forward, his movements fuelled by sheer adrenaline, the ball glued to his feet as he powered toward the goal.

The entire stadium held its breath.

Lucy swore she could feel the very earth still beneath them, as if all of Wembley—all of England—had frozen in anticipation.

Hurst struck.

The ball rocketed past the West German keeper, slamming into the net with a force that seemed to shake the stadium itself.

For a split second, there was silence, just a moment of stunned disbelief, the collective brain of the crowd catching up to what had just happened.

And then—

Pandemonium.

The roar that erupted around them was like nothing Lucy had ever heard. It wasn't just cheering; it was a blend of sound, an explosion of pure, unfiltered joy. People screamed, strangers grabbed each other in wild hugs, beer splashed through the air like confetti, and men wept openly, overcome with relief, with *euphoria*, with history being made before their very eyes.

Some fans jumped the barriers, rushing onto the pitch in their sheer elation, their arms flung wide as they sprinted toward the players. Flags waved frantically, hoisted onto shoulders, swung over heads, held aloft as if trying to capture the moment itself.

Lucy had no choice but to be swept up in it.

She jumped, clapped, cheered, her voice lost in the thousands around her, her hands thrown into the air as Wembley *erupted*.

St. Michael, however, remained still, watching with amusement but not joining in.

Lucy, catching her breath, elbowed him lightly. "You not gonna celebrate?" she asked in jest.

He let out a short laugh, shaking his head. "I'm Nigerian, aren't I?"

Lucy smirked. "C'mon, you're living in England now. Just for today, let's call it a win?"

St. Michael chuckled, rolling his eyes before finally raising his arms, giving in. "Fine. It's a win."

Then, with pure sarcasm, he threw his arms up dramatically and bellowed, "come on England! Three lions on the shirt and all that!"

Lucy doubled over, laughing harder than she had in what felt like forever.

It wasn't a chuckle or a quiet smile. It was a proper, belly-shaking, face-hurting, tears-forming at the corners of her eye's kind of laugh. The kind she hadn't realised how much she missed.

St. Michael grinned, clearly pleased with himself.

The two of them stood there, soaking in the atmosphere, the sheer *madness* of history unfolding around them.

After a moment, Lucy nudged him again. "So? Where else do you wanna go?"

St. Michael thought for a second, glancing around the stadium before his face lit up with an idea. "How about the unveiling of the Eiffel Tower?"

Lucy arched an eyebrow. "Ohhh, boujee."

"What? It's a significant moment!" he said, hands raised in defensiveness.

She laughed again, still breathless from the euphoria of Wembley. "Alright, alright, fair play."

They both turned back to the pitch, watching as Bobby Moore lifted the Jules Rimet Trophy high into the air, the golden glint of it catching the sun as the roar somehow grew even louder.

Lucy took one last look at the pure elation of England's victory before reaching out her hand.

St. Michael took it without hesitation.

The air tightened, the sounds of Wembley fading into a blur—

—until suddenly, the warm haze of a Parisian afternoon surrounded them.

* * *

The Eiffel Tower was there, but not as Lucy had always known it. Not rust-red, not yet the beloved cultural icon immortalized in film and postcards. Instead, it was a raw, unpolished skeleton of iron, its framework still gleaming with the freshness of construction. It stood unfinished but undeniably monumental, rising defiantly against the Parisian skyline like some mechanical giant of the industrial age.

They had landed just shy of the main crowd, their presence unnoticed in the throng of well-dressed Parisians, journalists, and sceptics who had gathered for the unveiling. The air was alive with conversation, an excitement rolling through the people as they craned their necks to take in the sheer scale of the structure. Some gazed in awe, others in distaste, the clash of wonder and scepticism thick in the atmosphere.

Lucy and St. Michael mingled effortlessly, blending into the sea of waistcoats, lace collars, and top hats.

But then—it hit her.

The feeling.

It was that primal instinct—that sensation of being watched.

Lucy stiffened, subtly scanning the crowd. She turned her head slightly, her eyes darting from face to face, posture casual but senses heightened. She took in every possible angle, every man in a top hat, every woman in a corseted dress, looking for something, someone.

Nothing.

Nobody was looking at her.

Yet the feeling didn't go away.

She forced herself to breathe, then leaned toward St. Michael. "Hey… do you feel anything weird?"

He turned to her, his expression shifting to curiosity. "Weird how?"

Lucy hesitated. How did she explain it? It wasn't like there was an armed Nexian standing in front of her, mask on, ready to strike. It was subtle. A creeping, gnawing unease sitting deep in her gut.

"I don't know. It's just… something doesn't feel right."

St. Michael scanned the crowd himself, as if he could see what she felt. After a moment, he shook his head. "I don't feel anything off."

She exhaled, nodding as if to shake it off. "Maybe I'm just overthinking."

St. Michael took her in for a moment. "Are you sure you're okay? We can go back home if you want."

His concern was genuine, and she could tell it wasn't just about the feeling. He was watching her closely, as if worried that traversing this often was beginning to wear her down.

She shook her head. "No, it's nothing like that. I feel fine, really." Then, as if to convince herself as much as him, she added, "It's probably nothing."

But still, she took another glance around.

St. Michael, sensing she wanted to drop it, let it go—at least for now. Instead, he turned his attention to a group of men standing nearby, engaged in a heated discussion in rapid French. He leaned in slightly, then nudged Lucy. "What are they saying?"

Lucy listened, her mind automatically translating as she caught their words. "They're debating it," she said. "They think it's an ugly stain on Paris."

St. Michael scoffed, shaking his head. "They've got no idea it's about to become Paris."

They moved closer as the murmurs of the crowd settled, and Gustave Eiffel himself stepped forward to address the gathering. He stood proud, his thick mustache neat, his tailored coat brushing against his boots as he took in the crowd. His voice carried over the murmuring city, firm and confident as he defended his creation.

"This is the world before it knew what the Eiffel Tower would become," she murmured. "Before, like you said, it became Paris."

St. Michael nodded, arms crossed, eyes still fixed on the tower. "And yet, even now, it's breathtaking."

Lucy wanted to soak it in, to appreciate the moment. But she couldn't.

The unease hadn't left.

She found herself looking around again, her body tense, her eyes scanning beyond the gathering, beyond the tower, as if some part of her knew—just knew—that something wasn't right.

St. Michael noticed.

"Hey." His voice was softer this time as he tapped her shoulder. "Are you sure you're okay?"

Lucy hesitated, then forced a nod. "Yeah, I just can't get rid of the feeling that something isn't right."

"Let's go back, then," St. Michael said firmly, no longer offering—insisting.

She exhaled through her nose, shaking her head. "Honestly, I'm all good. I really do think I'm just being paranoid."

St. Michael studied her, his eyes searching for certainty. "Are you sure?"

Lucy straightened, pulling herself together, and nodded firmly. "Genuinely."

She could see that he needed that reassurance. He was worried about her. And while the unease still sat deep in her gut, she wasn't about to let it dictate her actions. Not yet anyway.

She forced a smirk. "So… where next?"

St. Michael's expression lingered on her for a moment longer before he let it drop. He exhaled, then gave her a thoughtful look.

"I'd love to see a Nelson Mandela speech."

Lucy's face lit up. "Oh my god, same." Before asking St. Michael, "Which one, though?"

St. Michael chuckled at her enthusiasm. "The one after he was released from prison? Cape Town?"

Lucy felt a rush of excitement at the idea. "Done."

They stepped away from the crowd, the debates over the tower fading into the background.

She reached for St. Michael's hand.

The moment their fingers connected, the world folded in on itself. The warm Parisian air warped, the scent of iron and bread dissolving—

And then—

Sunlight. Heat. The buzz of a very different crowd.

They landed in *Cape Town*.

* * *

When they arrived, the air was electric.

Not just with sound, but with anticipation that ran through the streets of Cape Town like an undercurrent, uniting the thousands upon thousands of people surging forward, packed shoulder to shoulder, eyes locked onto the balcony of Cape Town City Hall.

The heat was intense, the South African sun bearing down on the sea of faces, but no one seemed to care. This was bigger than discomfort. This was history.

They wove into the crowd, blending seamlessly into the ocean of people waving banners, fists raised, voices thick with emotion. Drums pounded somewhere in the distance, voices chanting, singing, waiting—waiting for him.

Then, the balcony doors opened.

And Nelson Mandela stepped out.

Lucy felt the weight of it instantly, the sheer gravity of his presence, commanding yet calm.

He was an old man, yet he stood tall, strong, wearing a suit. There was no bitterness in his posture, no anger in his face,

only an undeniable strength, a steadiness that had carried him through 27 years in prison.

And when he raised his fist—

The crowd erupted.

A roar of cheers, of weeping, of pure, uncontained joy.

St. Michael exhaled, shaking his head in awe. "God, to actually be here…"

Lucy couldn't speak. She was too caught up in the sound, the sight of it all.

Mandela waited, allowing the people their moment. And then, when the crowd quieted just enough, he spoke.

His voice, steady and rich, rang out over the square, amplified but unwavering.

"I stand before you not as a prophet but as a humble servant of you, the people. Today, the people have spoken. The road to freedom is long, but we have taken the first step. I have walked that long road. I have climbed the hills, and though the journey is not over, I know that we will reach the summit together, hand in hand. Our freedom is not just for one race, but for all races, for all people who have fought for justice. We will build a South

Africa that belongs to every man, every woman, every child who calls this land home."

For Lucy, it was impossible not to feel the weight of the moment.

And yet—

The unease remained.

Like a whisper in her mind. A shadow just beyond the edges of her vision.

She tried to ignore it, to push it aside, but as she scanned the crowd, her eyes caught on something—

A figure.

Toward the back, slipping just beyond the shifting bodies of the people. Not engaged. Not cheering. Just… there.

She wasn't certain. The crowd was dense, shifting constantly, faces appearing and disappearing in a tide of movement. It could be nothing. It could be her mind playing tricks on her.

And yet—

The figure turned. Moved away.

Leaving.

Lucy didn't think.

She stepped away from St. Michael, weaving through the bodies, following.

Lucy pushed her way through the crowd. She fought against the crush of bodies. She barely noticed the protests of those she shoved past, her focus locked on the figure ahead.

Ten rows deep.

Then, finally, an unobstructed view.

The figure had stopped.

Slowly, deliberately, he turned.

A white mask.

A lifeless, expressionless face stared back at her, the eye slits hollow and empty, yet somehow watching her.

Her stomach dropped.

The Nexian raised a single gloved hand and pressed a finger against the mouthpiece of his mask in a calculated, taunting *shh* motion.

She turned instantly, panic taking over.

"Michael!" she screamed.

Her voice was swallowed by the roar. People near her turned in confusion, just as a loud clang rang through the square.

The sky, once bright with the African sun, split open.

A bolt of lightning came crashing down, slamming directly into the balcony where Mandela stood, narrowly missing him.

The crack of the impact reverberated through the city, a deep, violent boom that rattled Lucy's bones.

Another.

And then another.

The heavens unleashed, jagged bolts of energy raining down in precise, unnatural succession.

This wasn't natural. This was Nexian.

The crowd exploded into chaos.

Screams.

Bodies surging in every direction.

Fear took over. People ran, pushing, shoving, stampeding toward safety, their panic swallowing Lucy whole as she fought against the tide.

"Michael!" she called again, her voice frantic, but the name was lost in the hysteria.

She tried to run against the flood of people, dodging and weaving, but the sheer force of the panicked crowd was too much.

Someone slammed into her shoulder.

Another tripped over her legs.

The third hit her with full force.

Lucy hit the ground.

Pain shot through her ribs, the breath knocked from her lungs as people rushed past her. She barely had a second to recover before she forced herself to look up, searching.

And then—

She saw him.

St. Michael.

He was standing just beyond the crowd, turning wildly, his expression torn between trying to find Lucy and trying to comprehend the attack.

Relief hit her in a wave—

Until she saw the figure behind him.

Her heart stopped.

Another Nexian.

He moved quickly, slipping between the fleeing people unnoticed, stepping right behind St. Michael.

Lucy's mouth opened—

Too late.

The Nexian grabbed St. Michael hard, an arm looping around his throat, yanking him backward in a chokehold.

St. Michael gasped, his body tensing in an instant reaction. His hands clawed at the arm around his neck, his feet struggling for purchase as he was pulled to the ground.

"No!" Lucy screamed, scrambling to her feet.

St. Michael fought, his legs kicking wildly as he thrashed, struggling to break free. His hands grasped at the Nexian's grip, his eyes wide with desperation.

Then—

He saw her.

Their eyes met.

Lucy saw fear in his. A fear she had never seen before.

His struggles became more frantic, his body twisting as he tried to throw the Nexian off. But the masked figure held tight, stronger than he had any right to be.

Then, as if to taunt Lucy, the Nexian turned his masked face toward her. He pressed a finger to his mask.

Shh.

"Michael!" Lucy ran, shoving through bodies, desperate to reach him.

The air around them shifted.

The space around St. Michael and the Nexian warped, distorting like ripples in water.

Lucy lunged, her fingers outstretched—

They vanished.

Gone.

Taken.

Lucy's scream tore from her throat, raw and desperate. "No! No!"

She stumbled forward, falling to her knees where they had just been. The ground beneath her was still warm from where they had stood, as if reality itself hadn't quite caught up with what had happened.

But they were gone.

The Order of the Nexus had St. Michael, and she had no idea where they had taken him.

Lucy felt like she was falling, a sickening void opening in her chest.

She had lost him.

She pressed her hands into the dirt, her fingers clawing at the ground, as if trying to ground herself, as if trying to hold on to something real.

St. Michael was gone.

And she was alone.

For a second—just a second—Lucy was paralyzed.

And then—

She moved.

She had to move.

She had to find him.

Her mind locked onto a single thought.

Alaric and Solric.

She needed help. She needed them.

Lucy didn't even care if someone saw. She couldn't afford to care.

Tears burned in her eyes as she clenched her fists, forcing herself to focus.

Kilchurn Castle.

That was all that mattered.

The energy surged around her, the fabric of time bending to her will—

And she vanished.

* * *

Lucy landed inside Kilchurn Castle in a breathless panic. The moment her feet hit the stone, she was already moving.

The castle looked the same. Warm torchlight flickered against the cold stone, casting restless shadows along the corridors. The air carried the faint, familiar scent of old parchment and smouldering embers from the hearth. It felt lived in.

But the silence was wrong, like the entire castle was holding its breath.

"Alaric!" she called, her voice sharp, desperate.

Nothing.

Only her own voice, bouncing back at her, distorted and empty.

She ran, her shoes pounding against the flagstones as she tore through the halls, ignoring the burn in her legs, ignoring the way panic clawed at her ribs.

She reached the window at the end of the corridor and froze.

Down in the courtyard, beyond the arched stone frame, she *saw* it.

The burnt tree.

Its scorched trunk stood as a reminder of her training, of the fire she had conjured, of the control she had learned here with Alaric.

She was in the right place.

And yet, he wasn't.

Lucy whipped around and sprinted up the staircase, two steps at a time, until she reached his study.

She shoved the door open—

Empty.

The chair—*vacant.* The books—undisturbed.

"Alaric!" she screamed again, her voice breaking.

Silence.

Lucy turned frantically, her eyes sweeping the study for anything—any sign of where he had gone.

Then—

Her gaze locked onto something on his desk.

A scroll.

It sat there, unrolled just enough for the ink to glisten in the dim light, the words standing stark against the parchment. It looked fitting for the time period, but wrong. Out of place.

She stepped forward, reaching for it with trembling fingers, the dread pooling in her stomach before she even read it.

The Order of the Nexus awaits The Eleventh.

They had taken him.

"*Fuck!*"

The word ripped from her throat, raw and furious, filling the room with the only sound it had heard in far too long.

The echo mocked her, bouncing off the cold stone walls as if it were laughing back at her.

She slammed the scroll back down, her hands shaking, her mind spinning.

They were taking them.

First St. Michael.

Now Alaric.

A new fear gripped her chest, crushing and relentless.

Solric.

Even with the Archives' defences, even with his knowledge, his power—

They were too aggressive now.

Even he wasn't safe. No one was. Not anymore.

Lucy had wasted enough time.

Forcing herself to steady her breathing, to take control of the panic threatening to swallow her whole.

Her mind locked onto a single destination.

Stonehenge.

The Timebound Altar. She needed to reach The Temporal Sanctuary.

She commanded the traversal.

Time bent to her rage, to her fear, twisting and tearing around her as she seized it with an iron grip.

The castle vanished in a blink—

* * *

Lucy arrived at Stonehenge.

Darkness cloaked the ancient monument, the sky overhead thick with restless clouds. A fine mist of drizzle clung to her skin, cool and weightless, seeping into her clothes. The wind whispered through the standing stones, low and mournful, carrying the scent of damp earth and old secrets.

But beneath it all—beneath the night, beneath the wind—there was the hum.

Lucy stepped forward, her feet pressing into the damp grass. Her breath was steady, measured, but her heart hammered. She studied the towering stones, searching—knowing—that she would be guided to the right one.

The hum shifted, deepening, vibrating in her chest like an unseen force pulling her forward.

Then—

It intensified.

A deep resonance, unmistakable. A pulse in the air, in her bones, in the very fabric of time itself.

Lucy stopped.

A sharp prickle ran down her spine.

This was it.

Slowly, deliberately, she raised her hand, fingers outstretched—

And the Sanctuary responded.

the space in front of her began to bend.

The hum grew louder.

The Timebound Altar had opened.

And Lucy stepped forward.

* * *

The moment Lucy arrived at the now broken Sanctuary, the weight of its devastation crashed down on her once more.

Another reminder of them.

Not like she needed any more reminders.

She didn't stop to take it in.

She ran.

Her shoes pounded against the worn stone as she tore through the ruins, weaving through the crumbling Celestial Bridges, past the remnants of the once-grand Garden of Tranquillity. The ancient pathways stretched toward the ruins of the Assembly Hall. The place she had first met Solric.

"Solric!" she screamed, her voice echoing through the hollow chambers of history.

No answer.

She reached the massive grand doors of the Assembly Hall.

Lucy shoved them open, the doors groaning in protest.

No sign of Solric.

"Please be in the Archives. Please still be here." She muttered to herself between breaths.

She forced herself to focus.

Solric had granted her access to the Archives of Time last time she was here. She didn't know if she could do what he had, but she had to try.

Stepping forward, she raised her hand, mirroring what Solric had done before.

For a moment—nothing.

Then—

A slow tremor beneath her feet.

A deep vibration that pushed through the air, building, growing, until the very foundation of the chamber seemed to shift.

The ground beneath her shuddered.

Lucy stumbled. She had gone too far forward.

She took three quick steps back, making sure she didn't fall into the chamber as it opened.

With a deep rumble, the stone floor parted, ancient mechanisms groaning as a hidden passageway revealed itself. The stairway to the Archives of Time yawned open before her, the descent bathed in flickering golden light as the air crackled with untapped energy.

She had done it.

She took a deep breath, willed her legs to move.

They didn't.

"Come on, Lucy," she muttered to herself, forcing her body into motion.

She stepped forward, descending.

With each step, the ethereal lights lining the walls ignited, responding to her presence, casting long, wavering shadows against the stone.

She moved carefully, but with pace, her breath shallow as she neared the bottom.

Then—

The doors to the Archives began to open.

Lucy stopped.

She hadn't done that.

She hadn't extended her hand.

She hadn't even reached the threshold yet.

The doors—massive, carved from a seamless blend of stone and shimmering energy—groaned as they moved on their own, parting slowly.

Something wasn't right.

She hesitated, watching, waiting.

The doors continued to open.

And she wasn't alone.

The light from within the Archives spilled into the stairwell, purple and ethereal, obscuring the silhouette of the man standing in the doorway.

Lucy's fingers twitched behind her back, ready to summon a raging fireball if necessary. The Nexus—they had to be here already. They had taken St. Michael, they had taken Alaric. If they had come for Solric, she might already be too late.

Then—

"Lucy!"

A familiar voice, deep and commanding, filled the stairwell, carrying with it a weight of concern.

Solric stepped forward, emerging from the shadows. "What are you—"

Lucy grabbed him.

Before he could finish, she threw her arms around him, holding on with a force that surprised even herself. She could feel his body stiffen, completely taken aback by the sudden embrace.

"Oh my god, you're okay," her voice trembling, barely holding back the overwhelming relief crashing over her. "I thought—I thought—"

Her words broke, on the verge of tears.

Solric hesitated for half a second before slowly placing his hands on her shoulders, stepping back enough to study her properly. His expression softened.

"Lucy," he said gently, his voice steady, anchoring. "What's going on?"

Lucy sucked in a breath, trying to steady herself, but the words rushed out before she could think.

"It's The Nexus," she said, her voice unsteady, her emotions barely restrained.

Solric's expression hardened instantly. "What about The Nexus?"

"They've got St. Michael," she gasped, shaking her head as if she still couldn't believe it. "They—they just took him, right in front of me. I don't know where, I don't know if he's okay—"

Solric opened his mouth to speak, but Lucy kept going, unable to stop the flood of panic rising in her throat.

"And Alaric," she pressed on, her voice rising. "I—I went to Scotland, to Kilchurn Castle, to where he was hiding, and they've got him too!"

Solric's jaw tightened, his hands still firm on her shoulders, his eyes dark with thought.

"I was worried they had you too," Lucy finished, her breath shuddering. "So I came straight here."

As the words left her, her body finally gave in to the emotion.

Tears spilled over, running hot down her face, her breath uneven as the sheer helplessness of it all sank into her.

Solric sighed deeply, his grip on her shoulders grounding. "Lucy, I'm okay. No one has been here since you."

The sentence was meant to comfort her. Meant to be a relief.

But instead, it unleashed something else inside her. Guilt.

A deep, suffocating wave of it.

"This is all my fault," she whispered, her voice broken.

Solric's expression shifted as she shook her head violently, more tears falling.

"I got Michael involved in this. He's been taken because of me." She took a shallow breath. "They must have followed me to Scotland. That's how they knew where Alaric was. They knew because of me."

She couldn't breathe.

She couldn't fix this.

She had led them straight to the people she was meant to protect.

Solric, still gripping Lucy's shoulders, wiped a stray tear from her cheek with a thumb. His touch was steady and warm.

"Lucy, this isn't your fault."

His voice was firm, yet gentle. A quiet strength, unshaken by the storm raging inside her.

Lucy swallowed hard and tried to smile. But it was forced, weak, the kind of smile that didn't reach her eyes.

Because she didn't believe him.

Solric studied her for a moment but didn't push. Instead, he asked, "Do you have any idea where they might have taken them?"

Lucy shook her head, frustrated. "No." She exhaled sharply, her arms crossing over her chest as she hated how useless she sounded. "I've got no idea."

Solric nodded, already shifting into action. "Okay, well, let's start by looking at—"

He stopped.

The air shifted as the colours of the room changed.

The steady, deep purple glow from the Fragments of Time lining the towering bookshelves was drowned out, smothered by a pulsating, angry red.

Solric immediately let go of Lucy, turning sharply toward the disturbance. His gaze was sharp, calculating.

"An interference," he muttered, his tone laced with something Lucy didn't quite recognise.

"It's them," Lucy said automatically.

"No." Solric's voice was measured but firm. "This is different."

Lucy blinked, confused, her heart still racing. "What do you mean? Different how?"

Solric's gaze remained fixed on the shifting red light as it flickered across the Archives like a heartbeat. His fingers twitched slightly, as if feeling the pulse of the disturbance in the air itself.

"Normally, when there's an interference, the room turns a steady red," he explained, his voice edged with something close to concern. "The colour comes from the point in time that's being altered. It doesn't pulse like this."

Lucy's stomach knotted. "So what does it mean?"

Solric's expression darkened as he turned toward the disturbance's source.

"We need to find it," he said, urgency creeping into his tone.

Without hesitation, he strode forward, his long robe trailing behind him as he navigated through the maze of towering bookshelves, their usual glow now drenched in flickering red light.

Lucy hurried after him.

Whatever this was, it wasn't just another Nexus interference.

They walked through rows and rows of towering shelves, their steps quickening as the pulsating grew stronger. The red pulse intensified like a warning, a heartbeat reaching its climax.

Then—

They found it.

At the very end of the shelf, nestled among the purple crystalline records, was one that pulsed with unnatural speed, its glow erratic.

"Here," Solric said sharply, reaching out and grabbing the record.

"I don't believe it," he muttered, his voice laced with disbelief.

Lucy stepped closer, peering over his shoulder. "What is it?"

Solric picked up the record, studying its surface with sharp, calculating eyes.

"This doesn't belong here," he paused a moment. "It's not part of the archives."

The words made Lucy's stomach drop, but as she looked closer, she saw what he meant.

The record was foggy.

All the others around it were clear, their surfaces depicting frozen moments in time, each carefully preserved, meticulously crafted by Solric himself.

But this one—

It was empty.

A blank slate. A ghost of something not yet written.

Solric's fingers traced the edge of the record. "See here—there's nothing in it, and yet it's responding to the Universal Timeline."

Lucy's throat felt dry. "Can I have a look?"

Solric hesitated for a fraction of a second before nodding. He carefully placed the ominous record into Lucy's hands.

The moment she touched it—

Everything changed.

The pulsating stopped.

The flickering red snapped into something else. A swirling, shifting vortex of white and black, spiralling within the crystal's foggy depths.

Then—

The fog inside cleared.

Letters began to form.

Lucy felt a cold shiver run down her spine as she read them aloud.

"Beyond the shifting sands of Zerzura, where the sun kneels to the void, the lost shall find their reckoning."

She barely had time to process it before the letters began to shift again, rearranging themselves into a new sentence.

"The hand that writes history has already turned the page."

Another shift.

"As the Codex shatters, our lost city awakes."

"What does that mean?" she asked, her voice tight, her hands gripping the record as if afraid it would disappear.

Solric, still staring at the object, muttered under his breath—"The Oasis of Little Birds."

Lucy blinked. "Sorry?"

Solric turned toward her, his expression unreadable, but his eyes grave.

"In the thirteenth century, Zerzura was described as The Oasis of Little Birds." He paused. "But the city itself was lost. We searched for hundreds of years for it."

Lucy opened her mouth to speak, but—

The letters shifted again.

One final message.

"Step forward, Custodian. You are expected."

The words burned bright, searing into the crystal before fading into nothingness.

As Lucy read the final message, the record in her hands pulsed brighter.

The swirling white light intensified, spreading outward and flooding the Archives of Time with a blinding glow.

Then—

More pulsations began.

A powerful thrum reverberated through the room, pushing outward in rhythmic waves.

Solric stumbled back, bracing himself against a nearby shelf as the vibrations rattled the very foundations of the chamber. Crystalline records began to shake loose, falling from their places.

"Lucy, put it down!" Solric bellowed, pushing forward against the invisible force.

Lucy tried.

She gritted her teeth, willing her hands to release the record, to let go—

"Lucy, drop it—now!" Solric's voice was sharp, his usual composure cracking as the room shook around them.

She couldn't.

The energy reverberated through her fingers, through her arms, through her very being, wrapping around her like unseen chains.

It was pulling her in.

"Solric!" she gasped, eyes wide, panic creeping into her voice.

Solric struggled to his feet, forcing himself forward against the relentless pulses. His hand reached for her—

But then—

One final, massive pulse exploded outward.

A force like a hurricane's blast tore through the chamber, knocking Solric off his feet.

The light swallowed everything.

Solric slammed onto the cold floor, his vision blinded by the outworldly glow. He shielded his eyes with his arm, the deafening hum roaring in his ears.

Silence.

The energy vanished.

The air stilled. The pulsing ceased.

Solric groaned, pushing himself up, blinking away the lingering white-hot streaks in his vision.

Then—he froze.

The records that had been dislodged littered the floor, scattered in fragments of history. But among them—

Lucy was gone.

The record she had held—

Gone.

And somewhere, beyond time's reach, the Nexus was waiting.

CHAPTER 17
Our Journey's End

It wasn't like traversing through time. There was no familiarity, no feeling of The Universal Timeline shifting around her. This was violent. It was wrong.

Lucy felt herself being wrenched from existence. She was being dragged. The pressure clamped around her like invisible hands, twisting, yanking, pulling her deeper into a void that wasn't dark but blinding. An endless, searing white expanse that swallowed her whole.

There was no sound, only the silence pressing against her skull. Her body spasmed, as if rejecting whatever force had taken hold of her, but she couldn't fight it. She was nothing here. Just raw consciousness adrift in an overwhelming nothingness.

The light gave way to a rush of colour—gold, ivory, sapphire. It swirled around her, dizzying and unreal, until her feet hit solid ground. The impact of landing came with a jolt, her vision still blurred from the transition. But as the shapes sharpened, where she was—what she was seeing—became horrifyingly apparent.

She had arrived in *Zerzura*.

It stretched before her like a mirage, only this was no illusion. The city sprawled across the desert in an expanse of pristine white limestone, its buildings adorned with intricate golden ornaments and crowned with sapphire-blue domes that shimmered under an unmoving sun.

Zerzura was untouched by ruin. No crumbling walls, no dust, no decay. Time had not weathered it—it had been held still.

At the city's heart, rising high above the streets like a temple to something beyond mortal comprehension, stood a building—The Grand Hall. Its colossal columns stretched so impossibly high they seemed to scrape the sky itself, each one carved with symbols too ancient for her to recognise. The entrance, a pair of massive bronze doors, gleamed with an unnatural sheen, as if polished daily despite the passage of centuries.

The Nexus hadn't just claimed Zerzura; they had moulded it, reshaped something ancient into their own vision of eternal, unyielding control.

And above it all—the sky.

It was wrong.

The sun hung in limbo, locked at the edge of the horizon, casting the city in an eerie half-light. There was no dusk, no dawn.

She stood at the heart of a wide avenue, its width vast enough to hold an army. On either side of her, towering statues loomed, sculpted with breathtaking precision— each one depicting a figure in a long, flowing robe, its face obscured by a smooth, white mask. They stood silent and watching, mirroring the living silhouettes that now surrounded her.

She was not alone.

Lining the street in perfect formation, at least a hundred living figures stood motionless, their bodies shrouded in black robes. Their faces were hidden behind the same white masks, blank and expressionless, yet each seemed to regard her—waiting.

Nexians.

Lucy's hands snapped up, instinct overriding thought. Sparks crackled to life at her fingertips, surging up her arms in branching tendrils of raw lightning as she braced herself for an attack.

But no one moved.

The Nexians did nothing.

Not a single shift in posture. No rush forward, no raising of hands, no preparation to strike. They simply stood there—watching.

The unnatural stillness sent a ripple of unease through Lucy. They should have reacted. She knew they were relentless, merciless, precise. And yet, here they were, unmoved by the power she wielded in her hands.

She fought the urge to unleash the incantation anyway. Her fingers twitched, the arcs of lightning surging brighter in warning. Still, nothing.

"I'm here!"

Her voice cut through the unnatural stillness, laced with anger, thick with fear. She hadn't meant to say it like that—to let them hear the tremor beneath the fury—but what else could she do? She knew she couldn't win against them. Not like this. Not here.

But yet still, nothing.

The Nexians remained silent, their masked faces unreadable, their bodies as still as the statues that lined the street.

"Where are they?" she demanded, louder this time, her voice carrying down the wide avenue.

No response. Not even a flicker of acknowledgment.

The stillness, the silence—it felt deliberate. A game she wasn't privy to.

She exhaled sharply and began to move, placing one foot cautiously in front of the other. The Nexians didn't move, but their gazes followed her. She could feel it—all of them, their masked faces tracking her every step, their silent attention locked onto her.

It wasn't the simple act of being watched that unsettled Lucy—it was how they watched. Their heads didn't turn all at once, but one by one, in a slow, eerie cascade, each following her movement with precise, unwavering synchronization. As she moved further, she could almost hear the shift—the slight rustle of robes, the near-silent scrape of leather against marble as their positions adjusted ever so slightly.

The lack of reaction, the lack of anything—it was infuriating.

Her frustration boiled over. "I said, where are—"

A sound shattered the silence.

A deep, resonant groan rippled through the air as the massive bronze doors of the Grand Hall began to shift. The noise reverberated down the street, rolling like thunder, shaking the very ground beneath her feet.

Lucy instinctively stepped back. The sheer weight of the doors, the way the sound echoed through the city—it felt like the opening of something ancient, something monumental.

And as one, the heads of every Nexian turned.

Their attention snapped away from her, shifting in perfect unison toward the doors.

Lucy knew that meant something.

She couldn't see past the yawning entrance, couldn't make out what lay in the shadows. But as the doors finished their slow, grinding descent outward, a single figure emerged from the darkness.

A lone Nexian.

He stepped forward with measured grace, his movements fluid, unhurried. His robes were the same as the others—black, flowing, untouched by the desert's dust—but something was different. It wasn't just the way he moved. It was the weight of his presence.

The other Nexians remained motionless, their focus locked onto this figure as though awaiting a command.

Lucy's mind worked fast, piecing together what instinct had already decided.

This was their leader.

Not because they had declared it, but because every Nexian here—a hundred strong—had turned towards him as one.

And now, he was looking at her.

Lucy took a step toward the centre of the street, steadying herself as the lone Nexian began his descent down a grand staircase. His movements were slow, deliberate, each step echoing through the hushed city like a heartbeat in the silence.

And still, the others watched.

Their heads remained fixed, their masked faces turned toward him as though he were the only thing in existence. Not one Nexian shifted, not one made a sound.

Her muscles tensed, her hands still crackling with lightning as she kept her stance firm. She watched the approaching figure.

The Nexian reached the bottom of the stairs, stepping onto the same smooth marble that Lucy occupied. He walked along the avenue until he was directly across from her, close enough that she could see the faint shimmer of the golden etchings along his robes.

For a long moment, neither of them spoke.

Lucy's breath was shallow, her hands still alight. She shifted slightly, keeping her eyes fixed on the Nexian before her while still trying to watch the hundred others that lined the street.

She took a slow breath, forcing herself to speak, her voice firm but edged with barely contained urgency.

"Where is Michael?"

The Nexian stood silent for a second too long, as if measuring the weight of his response. Then, at last, he spoke—his voice carrying that same indistinguishable tone, distorted by the mask.

"He's here. He's safe."

She hadn't expected that answer.

"Where!?" she demanded.

The Nexian tilted his head ever so slightly, and then, slowly—too slowly—extended a hand toward her, palm facing downward, fingers outstretched in a gesture that felt almost… soothing.

"Lucy, lower your incant," he said, voice steady, level. "You're safe."

Safe?

The word didn't belong in a place like this.

She held her ground, her lightning crackling.

The Nexian took another step closer. The crowd remained motionless.

"Honestly, Lucy," he continued, almost patiently, "we mean you no harm. Neither you nor Michael."

She narrowed her eyes, lips pressed into a hard line. But still, something inside her hesitated.

Slowly, reluctantly, she lowered her hand just a fraction—just enough to show she wasn't striking first. But she didn't extinguish the incantation.

"What about Alaric?" she asked, her voice sharp, testing. "Where is he?"

The Nexian let out the faintest chuckle. It was barely a breath, but it sent ice through her veins.

And then, he moved.

His hands rose to his hood, the black fabric shifting as he pulled it back, revealing black hair streaked with silver.

Lucy's stomach turned.

No.

No, it couldn't—

With unhurried precision, the Nexian reached up to the edges of his mask. He hesitated for just a second.

And then, he removed it.

Alaric.

She felt the floor tilt beneath her, as though her body rejected what her eyes were seeing.

His face was unchanged. The same worn lines, the same silver streaks in his dark hair, the same piercing eyes that had once looked upon her with nothing but understanding. Trust.

But here, in this place, he was a stranger.

Lucy's entire body locked into place, her horror and confusion crashing into her at once.

Alaric. The man who had reached out to her. Taught her. Trained her.

Standing here.

Wearing that mask.

One of them.

And then, after what felt like a lifetime, he spoke.

"I'm fine, Lucy."

Her mind was spinning too fast to grasp onto a single thought, a single emotion. It was all crashing together—shock, betrayal, fury, grief.

Her lips parted, but for a moment, nothing came out. Then, her voice broke through the haze, raw, uneven, disbelieving.

"You're a Nexian?" It barely sounded like her own voice.

Her stomach twisted as she stared at him. At Alaric. At the face she had trusted. At the man who taught her to fight against the very thing he now stood for.

Her hands trembled, and without realising, the incant in her palms fizzled out, vanishing into the still air.

Alaric took a slow breath. "Yes, Lucy, however—"

"You fucking lied to me." The words ripped from her like a wound torn painfully open. "About everything."

She wasn't just angry. She was hurt.

A deep, cutting kind of hurt. The kind that made her heart ache, the kind that turned anger into something cold and sharp, something unbearable.

Alaric exhaled, slow and measured. "It's not quite as simple as that."

"It fucking is," she screamed back at him.

Alaric sighed, not with regret, not with guilt, but with patience. Like he had expected this reaction, like he had already run this conversation through his mind a hundred times before she had even set foot in Zerzura.

"Lucy," he said, his tone even, steady. "It's not as simple as you have been led to believe, as I had to lead you to believe. Nor what you understand about the Nexus."

Lucy let out a bitter, breathless laugh. "I understand well enough."

"Trust me, Lucy, you don't."

Her hands curled into fists, fingernails biting into her palms as she took a single, deliberate step toward him. "How so, then?"

She met his gaze, challenging him, daring him to give her an answer that made sense. That made any of this make sense.

Alaric studied her for a long moment. Then, slowly, he turned, taking a step forward, his expression unreadable.

"Well," he said, almost lightly, "as we have done before… walk with me?"

He moved toward her side, closer, until he was standing next to her, his hand reaching up—slowly, carefully—to rest on her shoulder.

Lucy stiffened.

The touch was familiar, but everything about it felt wrong now. Her body coiled with resistance, her instincts screaming at her to pull away. To run. To fight. To do something. *Anything*.

But she didn't.

Not yet.

She forced herself to move, to let her feet follow his lead. One step. Then another.

She wasn't sure if it was the shock still settling over her, the sting of betrayal, or the simple, suffocating wrongness of all of this, but her body refused to relax.

Alaric had always been the one person she trusted without question. Since the day they met, he had been a guide, a mentor and an ally in this chaos. And now, with every step she took through the streets of Zerzura, that trust was unravelling.

"As you can see," Alaric spoke at last, his voice smooth, as if they were simply discussing the weather, "you really are in no danger here. Violence is not in the nature of the Nexus."

Lucy stopped walking.

"Umm… I'm sorry, what about the Schism?" Her voice was sharp with condemning irony. "Or the Nexians in Nanjing and Austerlitz? They tried to kill me, Alaric."

Alaric sighed, a flicker of something deep and tired passing across his face.

"The Schism was deeply regrettable," he said, "The darkest day in both Custodian and Nexian history. But it does not define us, Lucy. We sought a new way of life. A better one. For Custodians, Nexians, and humans alike."

Lucy let out a sharp, bitter laugh. "By interfering."

Alaric gave her a measured look. "But is it?"

"We have evolved as a species since the dawn of the first Custodian and the Codex," he continued. "It has taken centuries, but we understand the Universal Timeline better now. We have an opportunity to become true protectors."

Lucy shook her head. "Protectors," she repeated, challenging the very word.

"I understand your hesitation," Alaric said, his voice as calm as ever.

"The events of Nanjing and Austerlitz were not meant to unfold the way they did," Alaric went on. "The Nexians present disobeyed my orders. They were never meant to harm you."

Lucy's fists tightened.

"Oh, and I'm just supposed to believe that?" She exclaimed. "Let's all just shake hands and go home."

Alaric's face softened, and for the first time, there was something else in his expression. Regret. Real, heavy regret.

"It's evident now," he said, "that their actions have tainted your view of us entirely. And for that, I am sorry."

His voice was low, sincere, but Lucy wasn't sure if she could allow herself to believe him.

"After Nanjing," he continued, "I realised this was escalating out of control. That's why I thought it best we speak now. Here."

Lucy narrowed her eyes. "By kidnapping Michael?"

Alaric exhaled, shaking his head slightly. "Not kidnap," he corrected. "However, I knew that after what had happened, you wouldn't accept an invitation. I knew you would see us as enemies before I ever got the chance to explain. St. Michael is absolutely fine. He's waiting for you here."

Something in Lucy hesitated.

She didn't want to trust him. She shouldn't trust him.

But his words weren't spoken like a lie.

They weren't laced with deception, or at least, not in a way she could see.

Still, she refused to let it show.

"Then why have they been following us outside of any traversal?" she asked, the words sharp but more measured now.

Alaric turned his head slightly, regarding her with something that looked almost like admiration.

"Lucy, we have long been admirers of you," Alaric said softly.

"But the extent of your abilities and power were an unknown," he continued. "However, when I met you, it became clear—you could become the most powerful of us all."

Lucy's mind raced, whirling back to Kilchurn Castle, to when she had first met Alaric. He had been a Custodian then, or at least that's what she had believed. He had spoken to her of the Codex, of duty, of non-interference, all with the quiet reverence of someone who had lived by its rules for a long, long time.

And yet, it had all been a lie.

She hesitated. "So, when we met—why did you—"

"Appear a Custodian?" Alaric finished for her, his voice calm, measured.

Lucy nodded.

Alaric's hands were clasped behind his back as they continued walking, the silent Nexians still lining their path, still watching.

"Lucy," he said carefully, "never before, at least to our knowledge, has a Custodian been left untrained. Never before has their powers come to fruition unguided. Especially not one like you."

Lucy knew what he meant.

Her eyes flickered downward, barely whispering the word. "Finite."

She didn't say she had learned this from Solric. Somehow, she knew better than to reveal that now.

Alaric gave a small, approving nod. "Exactly."

"I knew before I even met you," Alaric continued, "that your views of the Nexus would potentially be one-sided. That you would see us as nothing but the enemy. And I knew you needed to be shown how to use your powers— to control them. That's why I taught you the only way I knew how. The Custodian way, hoping you'd see the cracks in the Codex's teachings for yourself."

Lucy's fingers twitched at her sides. She wanted to argue, to throw his words back at him, but something in them stung with a painful truth.

She had considered the contradictions in the Codex. The flaws in its rigid non-interference stance. But that didn't mean she believed in *this*.

Her parents had believed in the Codex. That was enough.

She turned to Alaric. "But my parents believed it." The words came out quick, defensive.

Alaric didn't hesitate. "And they were brilliant, Lucy. Truly brilliant Custodians of extreme knowledge and power."

His voice was steady, but there was something almost wistful in it.

"Their love for one another brought a new air to the Council. They, as individuals, were extraordinary. But their surroundings? Their surroundings were toxic."

Alaric glanced at Lucy. "The Codex was archaic by nature, Lucy. It was rigid, unmoving. Even they questioned it at times, like we all did."

They questioned it?

She thought back to her mother's notes, to the things Evelyn had never told her. Had there been doubts? Had there been things her parents never wanted her to know?

She turned to Alaric, her gaze sharp. "And so you were the ones that acted." It wasn't a question. It was a quiet accusation.

Alaric's expression didn't change, but the regret in his eyes was real.

"We never intended for things to go the way they did." His voice was softer now. "The Schism—what happened that day—was not our plan."

"Then why do it that way?" Lucy asked. "Why not— "

Alaric's next words hit her like a punch to the throat.

"Because I had to save my family."

Lucy froze. It wasn't what she expected.

Alaric stopped walking, and for the first time since stepping foot into Zerzura, Lucy saw something crack in his carefully controlled demeanour.

His usual poise, his measured patience. It faltered, if only for a second. He turned away slightly, his gaze drawn toward the Grand Hall, looming above them at the top of the wide marble steps. But he wasn't really looking at it. He was looking at something else entirely. Somewhere else.

Lucy didn't know what to say.

There was something different in his voice now. Pain.

And then he spoke again, voice low, distant. "It was thirty years ago."

Lucy watched him carefully as he continued.

"I met Rachel." He let the name hang there for a moment, as if saying it aloud made it real again. "She was… incredible. Strong-willed, quick-witted. She had this way of looking at the world that made you feel like everything—every little detail—mattered."

A small, hollow chuckle left him, but there was no humour in it.

"I loved her," he admitted. "More than I ever thought I could love someone."

He glanced at Lucy then, as if checking if she was listening. If she was truly hearing him.

Lucy said nothing, allowing him to continue.

"I told her what I was," Alaric went on. "A Time Custodian. I took her through history—showed her the very best of it. The moments most people only dream of seeing. And I married her."

Lucy felt something twist in her chest.

"Soon after, we had a daughter. Ella," Alaric said, letting out a shaky breath.

"She was… she was perfect. She had Rachel's eyes. Her laugh." He paused, voice tightening. "She loved the stars. Every night, we'd lay out on the grass, and she'd ask me to tell her stories of different times. Different people. I always told her she could be anything she wanted to be. That she'd have the whole world ahead of her."

Lucy felt the first real crack in her own defences.

Because there was no deception in his voice. No calculated speech.

Just loss.

Alaric inhaled sharply, his jaw tightening before he spoke again. "And then, one day, they were gone."

Lucy swallowed hard.

"A car crash." Alaric's voice was quieter now, but no less pained. "Something so preventable. Something so… small. Not a war. Not a moment of historical significance. Just an accident. A senseless, meaningless accident. I knew I would outlive them, but I didn't think I'd get such little time."

Lucy stared at him, suddenly feeling like the world had shifted under her feet.

This man had lived through history. He had watched empires rise and fall. And yet, with all his knowledge, all his power… he had been helpless to stop it.

"I begged the council," Alaric continued, his tone growing heavier. "I pleaded for an audience. Asked for special permission to interfere. To bring them back."

Lucy could already see how this would go. She had heard enough about the Codex to know what the answer would have been.

But she let him say it.

"The Council debated," he said, "but in the end, it was ruled against. Thaloc Eryndor, The Time Sovereign, made his stance very clear."

Thaloc. The name felt like a shadow in Lucy's mind.

"His influence was too strong," Alaric said bitterly. "And the others followed. They told me the Quantum Collision would be too unpredictable. That the risk was too high. That no matter how small a change seemed, it could turn into disaster."

His voice hardened. "But what I heard was that my family—their lives—weren't worth it."

"We had all this power, all this knowledge, and yet I was expected to stand there and accept that I was powerless. That I was supposed to let them stay dead." He shook his head. "And I couldn't."

Lucy stayed silent. She understood that feeling but in a different way.

That overwhelming, unbearable weight of grief and helplessness. The way it could consume you, make you question everything.

Alaric turned to her then, his eyes searching hers. "I sought others. Custodians who had lost someone, just as I had. Those who had been too afraid to ask to interfere. I found them, one by one, and together… we made a choice."

Lucy didn't know what to feel. "I… I'm so sorry, Alaric."

The words slipped from Lucy's lips before she could think, before she could stop them.

And the worst part? She meant them.

She hated him for what he had done. She hated the lies, the deception, the truth he had kept hidden from her.

But this. This wasn't something she could hate.

Because beneath all of it, beneath the betrayal, the Schism, the war between Custodians and the Nexus, was something so painfully human it made her ache.

A father. A husband. Desperate to save his family.

Alaric nodded, his gaze cast downward for a moment before he looked back at her.

"As am I, Lucy." His voice was heavy, but steady. "Your parents… and the events of the Schism deeply disturb me. And it is something I will regret for the rest of my life."

Her anger didn't vanish. But it softened, just enough for doubt to slip in.

Would she have done the same?

Faced with the loss of someone she loved—her mother, her father, St. Michael in the same circumstances—could she have just accepted it?

Would she have stood before the Council, listened to them tell her that the people she loved were beyond saving, and simply walked away?

Because she didn't know.

And that *terrified her.*

"Come, let me show you the Grand Hall. There is much to see here." Alaric's voice was calm again, composed, like his past had been momentarily set aside.

Lucy hesitated, still feeling the remnants of everything he had just told her pressing against her ribs. But she needed to keep moving, keep talking, keep thinking.

"Where even are we?" she asked, carefully choosing her words.

She already had some idea—Solric had mentioned Zerzura before—but she wasn't about to reveal what she knew. She needed Alaric to tell her his version.

Alaric gave a knowing smile. "This is Zerzura, Lucy."

His gaze flickered over the golden spires, the marble streets, the ever-perfect sky above them. "Some call it paradise."

Lucy glanced around, taking in the pristine beauty of the city once more.

It certainly looked like paradise.

They began their ascent up the wide marble steps, the Grand Hall towering above them. Each step was smooth, polished, untouched by the erosion of time. The entire city felt like something out of myth.

"But I thought Zerzura was lost?" Lucy asked. "Or just… the stuff of legend?"

Alaric chuckled, the sound light, almost nostalgic. "After all you've seen, does the 'stuff of legend' really surprise you, Lucy?"

Lucy scoffed, shaking her head. "I guess not."

Alaric gestured toward the towering entrance ahead. "This place was lost, that much is true. And you, Lucy, have travelled back probably the furthest you've ever gone."

"How far?" Lucy asked curiously.

Alaric exhaled. "We're not entirely sure exactly what year it is. Zerzura seems to exist separate from the Universal Timeline, much like how the Sanctuary existed yet traversal seems stable."

Lucy froze.

'Existed.'

The word sat wrong in her mind. She knew the Temporal Sanctuary was still standing. She had seen it herself, stepped into its halls, spoken to Solric within its ruins.

Had that been a mistake? A slip of the tongue?

Lucy glanced at Alaric, but his face remained unreadable, his eyes focused ahead as they neared the top of the stairs.

She shook off the unease. Maybe it was nothing. Maybe.

Instead, she focused on the sight before her. The gleaming city, the endless sky, the towering Grand Hall that awaited them.

"It's beautiful," she admitted.

And for the first time, she truly meant it.

Lucy kept her posture firm, but inside, something was shifting.

Alaric's words cut through her defences, slipping into the cracks she didn't even realise had formed.

"I'm sure you're wondering why you're here?" Alaric's voice was steady, deliberate. Not forceful, but with purpose.

Lucy exhaled sharply, crossing her arms. "You could say that."

Alaric stopped midway up the stairs, turning to face her fully. His expression was unreadable, but his eyes—those sharp, knowing eyes—were locked onto hers.

"You feel it, don't you? That ache." Alaric's tone was filled with certainty. "That question that lingers in the back of your mind: What if I could have stopped it? What if you didn't have to stand by and let history repeat its mistakes?"

Lucy opened her mouth, ready to push back, to say something—anything—but before she could, Alaric continued.

"But tell me, Lucy—what if protecting the Universal Timeline also means saving the people within it?"

Lucy remained silent.

"The Custodians would have you believe that history is sacred. But how sacred can it be when it is built on suffering?"

"History is—" Lucy paused, searching for the right words, but they didn't come as easily as they should have.

"We don't rewrite history for power, Lucy." Alaric's voice softened slightly, but the intensity never faded. "We do it for them."

Lucy should have thrown his words back at him. She should have stood her ground, argued, called it manipulation.

But something in his words lingered.

For them.

She thought of Nanjing. Of the woman and her child, the ones St. Michael had saved, defying the Codex to do so.

She thought of Austerlitz, of the Nexians who had tried to kill her, yes—the fire incant that had burned away Evelyn's words before she could read them.

Conflicted, but she did feel it. That pull.

But she wasn't ready to let him know that.

Lucy hardened her expression, kept her voice even. "And who decides which suffering is erased? Who gets saved and who doesn't?"

Alaric smiled, as if he had been waiting for her to ask. "We've come so close, Lucy."

He began walking again, slowly, each step up the stairs as deliberate as his words.

"We've studied, we've learned, we've refined our methods until we are almost there. With every step, we've found ways to heal history's wounds without shattering its foundation."

Lucy followed, but her mind spun.

It was dangerous. The way he spoke, the way it made sense even when she wanted it not to.

Alaric reached the top of the stairs, the Grand Hall's doors loomed in front of him. "But there is something— someone—we've always been missing."

Lucy waited for him to continue.

"Someone with the strength to bridge the final gap between what is and what should have been," Alaric said, turning toward Lucy.

"With your power, and our knowledge, we could finally bring it all together." His voice was steady, unwavering. Seemingly all knowing. "We could mend what was broken, save those who were lost, and shape a world where history doesn't repeat its cruelties."

Everything in Lucy screamed not to listen. To call it absurd. And yet, she didn't.

"Together, Lucy," Alaric said, "we could make time right."

She didn't answer.

Because for the first time since this all began—she wasn't sure she could.

"I…" The word barely left Lucy's lips, caught somewhere between resistance and doubt. She hesitated, the certainty she had clung to slipping, unravelling too fast to catch.

She wanted to reject this outright. She wanted to tell Alaric he was wrong. That the Custodians were right, that the Nexus was reckless, dangerous.

But wasn't this what she had wanted?

What she had *really wanted*?

The chance to fix things.

To save people.

To save her parents.

She looked away, her voice quieter now, less sure. "I don't know."

Alaric remained still, his expression unreadable. He was watching her closely. Not with triumph, not with arrogance, but with patience. Like a man who had already anticipated this moment, who had seen her come to this exact crossroads before she had even known it existed.

Lucy forced herself to continue, needing something to hold on to. "You say the Nexus has almost perfected it. That with me, you could finally get it right. But how do you know? How do you know you won't just make things worse?"

For the first time, a flicker of something new passed through Alaric's gaze. Not frustration, not condescension, but something almost… approving. Like he wanted her to ask.

"We don't act blindly," he said smoothly, stepping toward her. "Every change, every correction—it's calculated, studied, refined. The Custodians would have you believe that one shift could send the world into chaos. But we both know that's not true."

He tilted his head slightly, his voice dropping just enough to make the words hit deeper. "You've changed history, haven't you? You and St. Michael," he continued, leaning forward slightly. "You've broken the rules."

She wasn't sure how he knew, but she knew he meant Nanjing. The people who, according to the Codex, should have died.

"And yet," Alaric continued, "here we are. The sky hasn't fallen. The world hasn't ended."

Lucy didn't answer. She didn't know how to.

Alaric studied her for a long moment before giving a small, knowing nod.

But something still didn't make sense.

Lucy steeled herself, shaking off the pressure that had mounted within her.

"Yet, you were the one who told St. Michael and me not to interfere." Her voice was sharper now, as if pushing back would steady her footing.

"Yes," Alaric said simply, as if he had already expected the question. "And rightly so."

Lucy narrowed her eyes. "But then you're contradicting yourself."

"Like I told you… this is something we have been working to perfect." His voice was softer now. "Had you made a correction, it would have been done blindly. At the wrong moment."

Lucy frowned, the contradiction digging into her.

"The right interference, at the right moment, will significantly negate the consequences," Alaric continued. "The Custodians would never acknowledge this—never mind attempt to perfect it. But together…"

His expression was calm, certain.

"Together, we all can."

Lucy took a slow breath, but inside, her thoughts were colliding like a storm.

Her parents had believed in the Codex.

Her parents had followed its laws, dedicated their lives to its teachings. Surely, they couldn't have been wrong.

And yet, standing here, listening to Alaric, she couldn't ignore the truth twisting inside her. For the first time, the Nexus's vision made sense.

She had heard their rhetoric before in Nanjing and dismissed it as dangerous, as reckless. But now, with every word Alaric spoke, with every crack he made in the foundation of everything she had been taught… she knew.

She was going to have to decide.

The massive doors groaned as they swung open before them, revealing the vast expanse of the Grand Hall's entrance chamber.

Lucy stepped inside and immediately felt the air change. Thicker, weightier, as though the very walls held the gravity of history itself.

The halls were lined with tapestries, their deep crimson and midnight blue fabrics illuminated by torches set along the marble walls. Each tapestry depicted a version of history that had never been.

Lucy's eyes darted from one to another.

Wars that had ended before they began.

Kings who had never fallen.

Empires that had never crumbled.

She exhaled slowly, realisation sinking in.

These weren't moments they had altered. These were moments they planned to alter.

Plans. Possibilities.

What could have been.

Lucy turned to Alaric, but he gave no explanation. He didn't need to.

Lucy couldn't shake the creeping sense of familiarity.

The Assembly Hall Lobby at the Sanctuary. This place… it resembled it too much.

The architecture, the layout—were they copying it?

Lucy frowned. The Custodians and the Nexus were supposed to be opposites, divided by their beliefs, by their ideologies. Yet, the deeper she walked into the Grand Hall, the more she felt like she had stepped into a distorted reflection of the Sanctuary.

Her eyes shifted, drawn to something to the left-hand side of the chamber.

A mirror.

No, not just a mirror—something else entirely.

It was massive, spanning from floor to ceiling, its frame sculpted from a material so dark it seemed to absorb light rather than reflect it. The glass itself was impossibly black, rippling with faint distortions, as though the surface wasn't solid.

It looked less like a mirror and more like a void.

Alaric followed her gaze, drawing a knowing smile.

Lucy didn't take her eyes off it. "What is it?"

Alaric moved toward Lucy's side. "We are unsure of its exact origin. But those here have come to name it— The Obsidian Mirror."

Lucy kept her voice even. "It just looks like a mirror to me."

Alaric chuckled softly. "This is not merely a mirror, Lucy."

His tone was almost reverent.

"Mirrors reflect," he continued. "This projects. It reveals."

Lucy finally tore her eyes away to glance at him. "Reveals what?"

Alaric's gaze was steady. "Those who stand before it see who they could become. Paths not yet taken. Power not yet realised."

"Some," Alaric went on, his voice almost distant now, "have had better results than others. Some visions are blurred. Others have burned too bright."

Lucy had seen a lot of impossible things since she first slipped through time. But this? This was something else entirely.

She stepped forward, drawn toward the Obsidian Mirror, her feet moving before her mind could catch up.

The closer she got, the more the surface seemed to ripple—not like glass, but like something alive, something sentient. It didn't just reflect her; it watched her.

A challenge.

A warning.

And perhaps, most dangerously—a *temptation*.

She stopped just a breath away, staring into its depths. At first, nothing. She saw, nothing.

And then, it changed. It showed her—she was somewhere else now.

The Temporal Sanctuary.

But it wasn't the broken, ruined version she had walked through before. This one was whole, its grand halls standing strong, the celestial bridges untouched by decay.

At the centre of the chamber stood a podium.

It wasn't her mother's. It wasn't her father's.

It was hers.

And etched into its surface was something that made her blood turn cold.

Lucy Calder - Time Sovereign.

She was older, standing before the Codex of Time. The Custodian Council gathered before her, watching— waiting.

But she wasn't just a Custodian.

She was leading them.

She was standing where Thaloc Eryndor once stood.

A wave of cold terror and awe crashed over her in equal measure.

No, that wasn't possible. That wasn't her path.

Was it?

Behind her, Alaric approached, his presence barely registering in her mind as she stared, unable to look away.

"What does it show you?" His voice broke through her thoughts, and Lucy tensed.

"Can you not see?" She tried to keep her voice steady, but something in it wavered.

Alaric shook his head. "No. The Mirror's projection is personal. It only reveals itself to the individual."

Her mind still spinning, still trying to process what she had seen.

She couldn't tell him.

She didn't even know what to make of it herself.

"It was a blur," she said quickly, forcing a frown onto her face. "I couldn't make sense of it."

Alaric watched her carefully, searching for something—doubt? Fear? Interest? He couldn't tell.

After a long moment, he gave a small nod. "Understandably."

His tone was almost reassuring. "It's rare for a clear vision straight away."

Lucy forced herself to nod back, but inside, her heart was still pounding.

Because it wasn't a blur.

It was clear as day.

And the mirror supposedly spoke truth…

"What have yours shown?" Lucy asked, her voice quieter now, laced with something she couldn't quite place.

Alaric's gaze remained steady, but there was a flicker of something more in his expression now. Something softer.

"It has varied," he admitted.

Lucy watched as his posture shifted slightly, his usual composed presence tinged with something raw.

"It has shown me my family." His voice was measured, but she could hear the weight behind it. "It has shown Ella, standing next to me—but older. Alive."

Alaric's hesitated for the briefest of moments before he continued. "It has also shown me projections of time—times of peace, a world where suffering is minimized." Then his eyes locked onto hers.

"But it has also shown me you and your parents."

"My… my parents?" Her voice barely made it out.

Alaric gave a slow nod. "Yes, Lucy."

Her parents.

She had been chasing ghosts, piecing together fragments of their lives, following the trail her mother had left behind like a puzzle she couldn't solve. She had wanted answers, not hope. Never hope.

Because hope was dangerous.

Hope could be ripped away.

And yet, here was Alaric, standing before her, speaking in absolute certainty.

"Like I said," he continued, his voice calm but purposeful, "once we have perfected corrections, we can save the ones we love. That includes your parents."

Lucy felt herself swaying—not physically, but in her mind, in her beliefs, in the certainty she had carried for so long.

It had seemingly been drilled it into her: *history must remain untouched.* The timeline is sacred. No interference. No exceptions.

But standing here, hearing Alaric speak of her parents, of her family, how could she ignore it?

Could she really just accept their deaths as a tragedy?

Could she really walk away from the chance to bring them back?

The thought terrified her.

Because for the first time… she wasn't sure what she would do.

"I need to show Michael this." Her voice wavered slightly, but she forced herself to keep going, trying to redirect the conversation. "Can we go to him?"

Alaric's expression remained unreadable for a moment, but there was a slight glint in his eyes. Satisfaction.

"Of course," he said smoothly, "he's through here."

He turned, gesturing toward the arched passageway at the far end of the lobby.

With a small movement of his hand, the massive doors opened, the heavy mechanisms shifting as if they were answering his command.

Lucy exhaled slowly, steadying herself.

She wasn't sure what was behind those doors.

But right now, she wasn't sure of anything at all.

The main hall stretched out before them, vast and imposing, its architecture eerily reminiscent of the Assembly Hall of the Sanctuary. The layout was similar. The grandeur, the height, the sheer weight of history pressing down upon it.

But the differences were what unsettled her most.

Where the Sanctuary had been a place of balance, this hall felt darker, heavier.

The black marble floor stretched endlessly beneath them, polished to such a perfect sheen that Lucy could see her own reflection as she stepped forward.

Her eyes traveling toward the far end of the hall where a throne sat.

But not just any throne.

It was carved from black stone, its surface rough and jagged, as if it had been chiselled. The back stretched high.

Next to it, a small concrete table stood—simple in design but heavy with significance.

Upon it lay the Codex of Time.

But it was wrong.

Bound in thorns, the once-pristine tome looked as though it had been constrained, held captive. The vines wrapped tightly around it, the sharp points digging into the leather cover as if it were alive, resisting.

And then—

To the right of the Codex, standing still, his expression unreadable—

St. Michael.

"Lucy!"

St. Michael's voice cut through the chamber, panicked, urgent. "Alaric's behind it all! You need to get away from him!"

Lucy's heart lurched, but her feet were already moving. "No, no, it's okay! We're okay!"

She ran toward him, desperate to reassure him, to make him understand.

"He's explained and—"

The words died in her throat.

Her eyes finally saw it.

St. Michael wasn't standing freely.

He too was bound.

Thick, twisting thorns coiled around his wrists and legs, tight enough that they dug into his skin. Dark, jagged vines knotted around his ankles, like a prisoner awaiting judgment. The cruel bindings cut deep, their serrated edges biting into his flesh, and Lucy could see the faint glint of blood where they had torn through skin.

His face—his face.

The left side was swollen, an ugly bloom of violet bruising creeping from his temple to his cheekbone. A gash split his lower lip, dried blood crusting along the corner of his mouth.

The room spun around her, her mind snapping between what she had been told and what was right in front of her.

This was not free will.

This was not choice.

The thorns around the Codex, the thorns around St. Michael. They were the same.

Restraint. Control.

Alaric had spoken of a world without suffering, of corrections, of balance, of a perfected timeline.

But here was the truth.

A man beaten and bound because he refused to submit.

Because he was not part of their perfect vision.

Because he was an obstacle, and obstacles had to be controlled.

The Nexus would stop at nothing to get their utopia.

Lucy felt sick.

This was proof of what the Nexus was willing to do.

People didn't matter.

The vision did.

And if someone stood in the way of that vision?

They were cut down like weeds.

She had been so close to believing.

And that realisation made her want to tear the world apart.

"What… what's happened?" She asked St. Michael. Her voice was barely more than a whisper, careful, controlled—but with an air of something breaking beneath it.

His lips parted, but the words came weakly, barely holding form.

"They… they—"

"It was a necessary precaution," Alaric interjected smoothly, his tone regaining its calculated calm.

Lucy's eyes snapped back to him.

A precaution?

A *precaution?*

She wanted to scream. Wanted to tear the words from his mouth.

Before she could speak, St. Michael's voice cut through the moment—hoarse, strained, but still his. "They want… the Archives."

The words lodged themselves deep into her mind, slicing through every conversation, every fragment of knowledge she had gathered.

The Archives.

Solric.

He had warned her. The Nexus had come for the Archives before.

They had failed.

But now… now it all made sense.

It was never about her.

It was never about her power, never about what she could become.

They wanted her for the Archives.

They wanted access.

That was what all of this was. That was why she had been brought here.

A pawn. A key.

"Enough!" Alaric's voice boomed across the hall, shattering the air between them.

Lucy's pulse pounded, her body stiff, locked in place but her mind was already moving faster than it ever had before.

"Is that true?" Lucy's voice cracked slightly, the weight of her realisation pressing against her chest. She had been manipulated.

She had been a means to an end—and she hadn't even seen it until now.

Alaric exhaled, his expression still composed, but there was something different in his eyes now. Less patience, more calculation.

"The Archives is an enigma, Lucy," he said smoothly. "Solric was always coy about its usage and its potential, but we need you to unlock it, to use it to its true potential."

Lucy's fists clenched at her sides.

"And what of Solric?" she asked, her voice sharper now, scepticism lacing every word.

Alaric gave a slow shrug. "I'm sure he will understand and agree," he said, dismissively. "But he has been locked away in there for too long and has lost sight of any real sense of purpose."

Lucy narrowed her eyes. That was a lie.

She knew Solric. She had spoken with him. He was one of the few people who had given her the truth, without expectation, without an agenda.

He wasn't lost. He was protecting something.

And now, she knew exactly what.

"I doubt he'll just hand you the keys," she said, her words deliberate, pushing.

Alaric met her gaze, and his response came without hesitation. "No, but he has to you."

There it was.

Her suspicions, now confirmed, sealed in the very words Alaric had just spoken.

Alaric stepped closer, his voice dropping into something almost persuasive again. "There is no doubt that the Archives will aid us in saving our families. In bringing you to your parents."

Lucy felt a pang of deep longing, the ache of everything she had lost swelling up inside her.

"Isn't that what you want?" Alaric added.

She didn't have to think.

"More than anything in the world." Her voice came soft, almost fragile.

Alaric smiled, the tension in his shoulders easing slightly.

But Lucy wasn't finished. "But not like this."

Alaric's smile faltered, his expression shifting into something colder, unreadable. A look of quiet displeasure, as if Lucy were a flawed equation he had miscalculated.

She had disappointed him.

Lucy took a step back, her voice stronger now, steady with certainty. "You talk about peace. Freedom for all. Yet those who oppose you are chained and beaten. This isn't the way, Alaric."

The words poured out of her now, her anger burning through the last shreds of doubt. "It's not what the Custodians stood for. It's not what my parents stood for. And it's sure as fuck ain't what I'll stand for."

Alaric's expression shifted. Not quite anger, but something deeper. Something colder.

He tilted his head slightly, his voice becoming more enigmatic, his control returning like an iron grip. "Change is the only constant, Lucy—why should the past be any different?"

His eyes gleamed, unreadable. "The Codex was built on fear, but the Nexus? We are built on possibility."

Lucy let out a bitter laugh, shaking her head "Possibility? You mean control."

Her voice cut through the air like a blade. "To change the past, you don't just alter history. You take away the very thing that defines it—choice. You remove free will. The rights of every single person who is affected by your so-called 'corrections.' You decide what stays, who gets saved, who dies."

She took another step back, her breath unsteady but her conviction stronger than it had ever been. "That isn't peace."

The hall fell into a thick silence.

Alaric watched her for a long moment, his expression unreadable—not furious, but something worse.

Disappointed.

His voice came low, sharp. "You're clinging to a dying ideology, Lucy."

The weight of his words settled in the air, thick with finality. "While I'm building a better one."

Lucy stood halfway between Alaric and St. Michael, her body still tense, her heart still racing.

She had been standing in the space between them for too long.

But she had made her choice.

Lucy lifted her chin, her voice steady, unwavering. "Not one I want to be a part of."

And with that, she turned away from Alaric, toward St. Michael.

She reached him in quick, purposeful strides.

Lucy inhaled, lifting her hand over them, fingers spreading.

A gentle flame flickered to life in her palm. Not like the destructive bursts she had used before, but something controlled, delicate, precise.

The fire licked at the thorns, burning them away without touching him, reducing them to smoke and ash that vanished before they hit the ground.

The moment the bindings released, St. Michael collapsed forward, catching himself on his hands.

Lucy touched his shoulder. "Let's go home."

Before St. Michael could answer, Alaric spoke.

And this time, his voice was cold. Dark. Final. "If you will not join us, then stay out of our way, Lucy Calder."

Lucy slowly turned back to face him.

His expression had shifted entirely. The patience was gone, the warmth erased.

This wasn't the mentor she had known.

This was the leader of the Nexus.

Her spine straightened, her shoulders squaring as she met his gaze. "You know I can't do that."

The words were quiet, but they carried the weight of everything.

For a moment, the entire Grand Hall was silent.

Then—

The first spark cracked.

A flicker of blue lightning crackled to life between Lucy's fingers, twisting along her knuckles, coiling around her wrist.

Alaric's eyes narrowed, his hands slowly rising—and with a single movement, fire bloomed from his palms. Its heat pulsing against Lucy's skin even from where she stood.

She looked back at St. Michael over her shoulder. "Get behind the throne."

Despite his injuries, he didn't argue. Without hesitation, he moved.

Lucy strode to the centre of the Grand Hall, her footsteps echoing in the vast chamber. The throne loomed behind her, St. Michael now crouched low behind it, watching.

Alaric hadn't moved.

He stood by the massive doors, his posture unchanged, his expression unreadable, the golden glow of the torches casting flickering shadows across his face. The leader of the Nexus, unwavering, unshaken.

"If you want to rewrite history," Lucy said, her voice steady, "you'll have to go through me first."

For the first time, Alaric tilted his head slightly, his mouth curling into something that wasn't quite a smile, but close enough to be unnerving.

"Then we reach our journey's end."

The hall went silent.

Then—Alaric moved.

He jolted forward, his hands igniting in an instant, a roaring incant of fire bursting from his palm, streaking toward Lucy in a wave of searing heat.

Lucy reacted in a blink, lightning crackling from her fingertips, meeting the blaze in the middle of the chamber with an explosive clash.

The two elements collided, fire and lightning intertwining, twisting into each other like living forces battling for dominance.

For a moment, they were locked in a standstill.

Then Alaric's fire pushed forward.

Hard.

Lucy's feet skidded back slightly as the heat surged closer, her arms trembling under the strain of holding the lightning in place.

Alaric's left hand flicked upward, fingers slicing through the air with precise, practiced control.

At his command, small, jagged rocks materialized from nothingness above Lucy's head, hovering for just a breath.

Another flick.

His right hand shot up—and instantly, each stone ignited into molten fire, their surfaces glowing red-hot like falling meteors.

Lucy's eyes snhot upward as the burning projectiles began their descent, raining down toward her.

She had no time to disengage from the lightning she was still holding.

Thinking fast, she lifted her free left hand, fingers curling as she willed the air above her to shift, to ripple—

A swirling mass of water formed in an instant.

The moment the burning rocks fell, they collided with the water, hissing violently as steam erupted from the impact, extinguishing the molten heat before they could reach her.

Lucy didn't waste a second.

With a sharp twist of her wrist, she commanded the now heated, swirling body of water forward, hurling it toward Alaric with the force of a crashing wave.

It struck him hard, drenching him in the scorching remnants of his own incantation, the impact forcing him a step back.

That fraction of a second was all she needed.

With a surge of energy, Lucy pushed against the fire pressing toward her—

Her lightning snapped forward, tearing through his flames with a violent crackle of raw power.

Alaric stumbled back, his robes still smouldering, his expression shifting ever so slightly. Not with fear, but with something new. Recognition.

Lucy straightened. She hadn't just held her ground. She had struck back.

And Alaric knew it.

From behind Alaric, the great doors of the hall groaned open once more.

Figures emerged from the shadows beyond, their movements silent and precise. One by one, Nexians flooded into the chamber, lining up across the width of the hall behind their leader.

And then, in eerie synchronization, they raised their hands.

"No!" Alaric's voice thundered through the hall, a sound so forceful it shook the very air around them.

The Nexians froze.

Alaric's chest heaved, his eyes ablaze with something dark, possessive, dangerous. "She's mine to dispatch!"

And with one violent motion, he lifted his hand.

A barrier of crackling energy erupted between him and the Nexians, rippling outward, expanding until it formed a dome-like shield, cutting them off.

It was just him and Lucy now.

And Alaric was done holding back.

He lunged, thrusting his arm forward. Alaric's fire swelled, pushing Lucy backward.

Her heels scraped against the floor, sliding as she gritted her teeth, holding firm.

Alaric's left hand shot forward, joining his right, creating a massive surge of power between his palms. His eyes burnt with fury and intent.

Then—

He wrenched his arms downward.

The moment his hands met the air, the entire battlefield reacted.

Their incantations snapped out of existence, fire and lightning vanishing in an instant—

And then Alaric screamed, a guttural, raw sound of exertion, of fury, of absolute command—

A shockwave of pure force erupted outward.

The sheer impact of wind ripped Lucy off her feet, launching her violently backward. The throne behind her shattered into pieces, the massive stone crumbling under the force.

St. Michael was thrown with it, his body slamming against the far wall, the Codex spinning through the air before hitting the ground with a heavy, resounding thud.

The entire chamber trembled, dust and debris falling from the high vaulted ceiling.

Lucy gasped, struggling to orient herself—

But Alaric was already moving.

His feet left the ground, his body rising, hovering above her like an untouchable force of destruction. His robes billowed around him, and for the first time, he looked truly unearthly.

Lightning coiled around his hands, twisting together into two spear-like bolts of pure energy, their tips crackling with lethal intensity.

Lucy's eyes widened.

Before she could react, he hurled them.

She barely had time to throw herself to the side as the first one slammed into the marble where she had just been, sending cracks spiderwebbing through the floor.

The second came fast—too fast.

She rolled, barely avoiding it—

But then a third struck her.

And a fourth.

And a fifth.

Each one felt like it was burning through her core, the searing heat of the energy spreading through her bones, her veins, her entire being.

She crashed to her knees, breath ragged, the residual electricity dancing across her limbs, crackling beneath her skin.

Then—

Alaric slammed into the ground before her, landing with a thunderous force.

Before she could even move, before she could catch her breath, he lifted his hands—

And the barrier around them shifted.

Lightning surged outward, enclosing them both inside a ring of pure energy. The field shrank, trapping her inside, and before she could escape—

The lightning turned against her.

Bolts lashed out from every angle, striking her over and over, each one sending bursts of pain through her body.

Desperation fuelled her next move.

She summoned what little strength she had left, wrenching her arm upward, and in a burst of fire, she sent a gust of flame straight toward Alaric's face.

It didn't hurt him.

It didn't even stun him.

But it distracted him.

For one second.

The lightning ring shattered, dispersing into the air as Alaric pulled back slightly in irritation.

Lucy staggered, her body aching, but still she managed to glance toward the far end of the hall—

St. Michael was moving. He was alive.

She exhaled in relief—

Only to whip around just in time to see Alaric throw out his hands once more.

Air exploded outward—

Lucy was hit with the full force of the wind, her own counter-incantation failing instantly against its power.

The impact threw her like a ragdoll, her body slamming into the far wall with a force that made the entire hall tremble.

The moment she hit the ground, everything spun.

Pain seared through every inch of her body, her muscles screaming, her lungs burning as she tried to move—

But before she could, she saw Alaric, standing at the centre of the destruction.

And he wasn't finished yet.

Lucy turned her head, struggling to focus through the haze of pain.

St. Michael was clutching the Codex, his fingers trembling, his knuckles pale with strain. His eyes were locked onto hers.

And in that single glance, his eyes said everything.

They didn't need words.

This was the end.

The fear in his gaze was not for himself, it was for her.

It was the silent understanding of inevitability, the knowledge that this battle was lost.

Lucy forced herself to move, to fight against the unbearable weight of her battered body.

She turned back toward Alaric, her vision blurring at the edges, struggling to push herself up against the wall.

Alaric didn't stop her.

He watched.

Mockingly.

Like a man indulging a final, pointless act of defiance.

Lucy's legs shook as she rose, barely holding herself upright, her skin burned, her body ruined.

Alaric's head tilted slightly, studying her.

Then, in a voice as smooth as steel, he said, "Mercy is the privilege of the powerless."

His hands shot forward.

A storm of fire and lightning erupted from his palms, colliding with her in an instant.

The force pinned her to the wall, slamming her against the unyielding stone, her limbs convulsing under the unbearable power.

The lightning tore through her, crackling inside her very bones, each jolt searing through her veins, setting her nerves alight with agony.

The fire followed, consuming her clothes, her skin, everything.

The ends of her hair curled and blackened, the scent of burning fabric, burning flesh filling the air.

She let out a choked scream, but the sound was lost in the roaring rage that engulfed her.

Her body refusing to move, her lungs failing under the heat, her vision shrinking into darkness.

The fire stopped.

The lightning vanished.

Alaric lowered his hands, the attack ceasing as suddenly as it had begun.

Lucy collapsed.

She crashed to the floor, her burnt hands barely catching her before she hit the ground fully.

Her hands pressed against the cold marble. The contrast between the freezing stone and the burning agony in her body was unbearable.

She lifted her gaze slowly, every movement a struggle.

Alaric made one step forward.

"Goodbye, Lucy Calder," he said as he lifted his hands once more, summoning his final incant.

A long, sharp rock materialized between his palms, its surface bristling with serrated edges headed by a sharp tip.

It hovered above his head for a moment, glowing with power, before he stretched his arms wide to the side.

The air shifted.

A wind began to stir, subtle at first, like the whisper of inevitability.

Lucy's body sagged, her strength gone, her mind slipping toward a single realisation.

This is it.

This was what the extinction of the Custodians felt like.

The wind rose, faster, stronger, a force of pure power.

Alaric's arms snapped forward.

The jagged spear of stone hurtled toward her.

She closed her eyes.

She braced herself, waiting for the piercing pain, waiting for the moment her body would break apart—

And then, a different impact.

Not her.

Someone else.

The sound of flesh tearing, of a body absorbing the force that was meant for her.

Lucy's eyes flew open.

St. Michael.

He stood before her.

Facing her.

His shoulders shaking.

And then she saw it.

The rock.

It had pierced straight through him.

The blood—the dark, pooling red that spread across him, dripping onto the marble floor beneath him.

Her stomach twisted, nausea flooding her chest.

His breathing was shallow, each breath a struggle, his body trembling under the weight of the wound.

And then, he lowered his head slightly.

His eyes met hers.

And for the first time, they weren't filled with fear.

Only resignation.

Acceptance.

In one final breath, he whispered, "Get… out."

He toppled.

His body fell to the right, crashing against the ground, the rock still embedded within him.

The force of it boomed through the chamber, a final, resounding thud that sent shockwaves through Lucy's chest.

Everything in her screamed.

Her body wouldn't move. She couldn't breathe.

She couldn't process it.

He had jumped in front of the strike meant for her. Now, he lay there, motionless, the jagged spear of rock protruding through his chest.

A horrible, soul-crushing weight of guilt crushed her ribs, hollowed out her lungs, and left her drowning in the knowledge that she had brought him here.

That this was her fault.

Her hands trembled violently as she staggered forward on unsteady legs.

No.

Her mind couldn't process it, couldn't accept it.

This wasn't how it was supposed to go.

They had made it this far. They had fought together, survived together.

He had stood by her side.

Something inside her snapped.

"NO!" The scream ripped from her throat, raw and broken, a sound that shook the very air around her.

It wasn't just grief.

It wasn't just pain.

It was fury.

The kind that burned hotter than fire, hotter than lightning, hotter than anything she had ever felt in her life.

The heat spread through her veins, a raging fury inside her, her very soul igniting with the sheer force of it. Her body seethed with a new, terrifying energy—

Alaric's eyes widened.

For the first time. He looked truly startled.

This wasn't what he had intended.

Lucy's breath steadied, the overwhelming agony twisting itself into unrelenting, merciless rage.

She stepped forward, her hands lifting, and with a violent motion, she unleashed hell.

A torrent of fire erupted from her palms. Not just flames, not just heat, but an unrelenting, furious cascade of destruction.

The flames roared as they surged toward Alaric, the sheer force of the incant slamming into his own fire, meeting it head-on.

The impact exploded outward, sending waves of heat scorching the marble floor.

Alaric gritted his teeth, holding his ground, but the power behind Lucy's fire was unlike anything he had ever faced.

His was pushed backward, inch by inch, the force of her incantation forcing him toward the wall of energy separating them from the Nexians.

In the centre of the inferno, where their flames collided violently, small orbs of fire burst outward, spinning wildly before splintering into the air, setting the hall ablaze.

The heat was unbearable, the energy so volatile that the very air crackled with impending destruction.

Lucy's fury did not wane.

She wanted him to burn.

Alaric's stance shifted.

His right hand pulled away from his incantation, the flames still raging from his left, and with a single motion, he reached toward the barrier behind him—

And lowered it.

"KILL HER!" he roared.

The Nexians surged forward, stepping to his side, their hands rising as incants materialized instantly.

Lightning crackled, arcing between their fingertips.

Water swirled, forming twisting, jagged tendrils.

Stone lifted from the ground, reshaping into sharp-edged projectiles.

They unleashed all of it at once.

The combined power of their incants collided into the growing core of fire at the centre of the hall, amplifying the destructive energy rather than extinguishing it.

The swirling storm of elements became something monstrous, something unstable—a fusion of fire, lightning, water, and stone, twisting together into a pure, chaotic force of devastation.

Lucy felt it pushing back toward her.

She could feel the heat intensify, the sparks of electricity crackling too close to her skin, the sharp sting of water and rock twisting within the mass of destruction.

The force of it was too strong.

She couldn't hold it back.

The energy pushed closer.

Closer.

For all her power, for all her rage, this was too much.

Her feet dug into the ground as she took a single step forward, summoning everything she had left, throwing her hands toward the storm.

And in that moment, she pushed back.

For just an instant, the energy halted, caught in the delicate balance between overwhelming power and unyielding defiance.

A searing blue light ignited behind Lucy, illuminating the chamber in an ethereal, otherworldly radiance.

Lucy turned her head backward.

The Codex of Time sat where St. Michael had dropped it, but it was no longer bound in thorns.

The once-restrictive vines burned away, consumed by blue flames that did not harm the book itself. The pages, once sealed shut, now fluttered as if being turned by an invisible force.

The energy spread.

Lucy whipped back toward Alaric and the Nexians, eyes widening as the same searing blue power ignited from the core of the battlefield.

A ball of radiant energy emerged in the centre of the hall, shifting, writhing, twisting into something more.

It was alive.

It moved like a conscious force, streaking across the room, circling them all like a predator deciding where to strike.

Alaric's composure finally broke.

"What is this!?" he demanded, his voice edged with something Lucy had never heard from him before—

Fear.

Lucy held her incant steady, her fire still locked.

It moved—faster now.

It looped around the Nexians, sending them crashing to the floor, their incants disrupted, shattered.

Then, it twisted in the air and appeared beside Alaric.

The shape shifted, the once formless energy now growing limbs, features—becoming something more than light.

A figure emerged.

Floating beside Alaric, its voice echoed through the chamber, layered and reverberating with power.

"Alaric, you disloyal bastard!"

The words hit like thunder, vibrating through Lucy's chest.

She knew that voice.

It was warm.

It was familiar.

And as the energy began to move toward her, it began to solidify, as the edges of its form became defined, she saw him.

Robes.

Not just any robes—Robes of the Timeless.

And beneath them, a face she'd know anywhere.
Her father.
Edward Calder.
His feet touched the ground, his body still flickering,
translucent, but unmistakably there.
Lucy shuddered, her fire wavering for the first time.
Then, Edward turned, placing his hands over hers.
The moment he touched her, his energy flooded into
her, reinforcing her power, making the fire roar even
hotter, brighter, pushing Alaric back further.
"Lucy," he said, softly.
The way he said her name—gentle, proud, full of
love—broke something inside her.
"Dad." Her voice cracked, emotion swelling up her
throat, her eyes stinging with unshed tears.
She had spent her whole life chasing ghosts.
Now, for the first time, one had finally found her.
Edward's gaze flickered toward Alaric, still holding the
fight, but then back to her. "Lucy, you don't have much
time. I can hold this while you get out."
Lucy was about to speak, to argue, before Edward
interrupted. "Get the Codex and St. Michael and go back
to the Sanctuary. Solric will be there,"
Lucy's body refused to move, her mind rejecting the
reality of what was happening. "What about you?"
Edward's expression softened. "I'm just energy. A,
moment in time. When you go, I'll lock this part of the
timeline, make it lost again. But you must go—otherwise,
you'll be trapped here too."
Lucy's hands trembled. She didn't want to go. She
didn't want to leave him.
She had just found him.
Edward squeezed her hands, a soft smile forming
despite the battle raging around them.
"You're so much like your mother, Lucy." His voice
was thick with emotion, his eyes shining with something

deep and unshakable. "Fierce. Brilliant. Stubborn beyond all reason."

A tear slipped down Lucy's cheek.

He continued. "We love you. And we are so proud of you."

The words shattered her.

Her legs nearly buckled, her body trembling under the weight of love and loss all at once.

But she forced herself to nod. To listen.

Slowly, she stepped away.

Edward took over the incant, his fire pushing harder, stronger, slamming Alaric backward toward the collapsing walls of the Grand Hall.

"No!" Alaric roared, realising what was happening.

He tried to lower his hands, to cancel the incant, to escape—

But he couldn't.

His body locked in place, unable to break free.

His rage twisted into something venomous, furious, helpless.

"Even in death, you defy me!" Alaric roared.

Edward held firm.

His expression did not waver, did not crack.

"You took everything from me!" Edward roared.

His eyes flickered back one last time—

And met Lucy's.

She crouched, the Codex clutched in one arm, St. Michael barely conscious but held tightly in the other.

The energy around them shifted, the weight of time itself bending, twisting, preparing to send her back.

She felt it pulling her, wrapping around her.

She felt the inevitable loss creeping in, the finality of this moment.

Her heart ached.

She looked at her father, memorizing his face, his voice, everything about him.

"I love you." She said it with everything she had, everything she had never been able to say before.

Edward smiled.

And just before the world vanished around her, before she was pulled through time itself, before she lost him again—

She heard him say it back.

Edward stepped forward, the energy between him and Alaric surging, burning through the air with intensity.

Each step he took pushed the fire closer, forcing Alaric back, inch by inch, until there was nowhere left to retreat.

Edward's gaze remained locked onto Alaric, unwavering, determined.

Alaric snarled, his face contorted in fury, in defiance, in disbelief.

With a final step, Edward closed the distance between them.

"Time… is… relentless, Alaric." Edward lifted his hands—Alaric's hands met his. "But now, so am I."

The moment their palms connected, a blinding shockwave of blue fire erupted outward, engulfing everything, consuming the space around them.

And then—

It all began to disappear.

Zerzura—the lost city, the stronghold of the Nexus, the place that had stood outside of time itself—

vanished.

Gone.

The energy surged, swallowing everything.

Zerzura would become what it was always meant to be.

A legend. A myth. A place erased from time.

The world around them shifted into nothingness, a swirling mass of white light, of empty time—of absence.

Edward held firm, his grip unyielding, as the last traces of Zerzura vanished into the void.

Locked away.

Lost to time forever.

* * *

They landed with a thump, the weight of their escape crashing into them as their bodies hit the stone floor.

Lucy lifted her eyes, her vision blurred with exhaustion, pain, and everything she had just lost.

The purple glow of the Archives was the first thing she saw.

They were back.

"Solric!" she shouted, her voice breaking, raw with desperation.

No answer.

"Solric!" she called again, more frantic this time.

She heard it—footsteps.

Racing, urgent, coming from beyond the towering shelves, rounding the corner like a force pulled by gravity itself.

"Lucy!"

Solric's voice was soft but panicked, relief and alarm mixing as he reached them. His gaze flickered over her, taking in her burns, the remnants of the battle clinging to her skin, the raw devastation in her expression.

Then his eyes fell to St. Michael.

The rock was still embedded in his back, its jagged edges dark with blood.

Solric stilled, his face paling.

Lucy couldn't breathe.

She couldn't do anything but press down harder on St. Michael's chest, as if the weight of her hands alone could keep him here, tether him to her.

"Alaric," she gasped, tears finally spilling over as the words tore from her throat.

"Alaric was behind it all. The Nexus. The Schism. Everything."

The admission felt like an open wound, a revelation that had cost too much.

Solric didn't respond.

He only knelt beside them, his palm coming to rest against St. Michael's forehead.

St. Michael's eyelids fluttered, just barely.

A flicker of awareness.

"Michael," she whispered, forcing a shaking smile through her tears.

His gaze drifted, unfocused, before finally landing on her.

"We're back," he murmured.

His voice was weak. Too weak.

Lucy swallowed back the rising terror in her chest, forcing herself to hold on, to keep him with her.

"Yeah, we're back," she said, nodding fiercely, as if saying it would make it true. "And you're gonna be okay. I promise."

But St. Michael gave her a look—one that made her stomach drop.

A look of understanding. Of finality. "I think we both know that's not the case, Lucy."

No, she wasn't accepting that.

She shook her head, voice turning frantic. "No. We're going to get back home, and I'm going to get you help. We just need to get back, okay? Just stay with me, Michael. Please."

Her own pulse pounded in her ears, drowning out the rational part of her that was screaming at her, telling her this was slipping away.

"Just one thing," St. Michael said, his breath coming in ragged gasps, each one weaker than the last.

Lucy swallowed hard.

"Anything."

His eyes searched hers. "Just look out for Teddy," he whispered. "Keep an eye on him."

Lucy's vision blurred completely.

"Michael, you're going to be okay," she insisted, shaking her head, refusing to hear it, refusing to let this be the end.

"You're going to be fine. We just need to—"

He didn't answer.

His gaze lingered on her, soft, steady.

Then—it was gone.

The rise and fall of his chest stopped.

His body stilled.

The weight of absence settled over him, over her.

The moment hit like a physical blow, something deep inside her fracturing, breaking apart in a way that would never be whole again.

"Oh my God—Michael." Her hands shook violently as she pressed against his chest, as if she could force him to keep breathing, as if she could demand his heart to beat again.

"Stay with me. Please, don't leave me here. Don't—"

She rocked forward, her forehead pressing against his chest. She clung to him as though she could pull him back.

But he was already gone.

"Lucy." Solric's voice was so soft, so gentle it was barely a whisper.

She didn't move.

She couldn't.

Her body was wracked with silent sobs, her throat too raw, too broken for sound.

Solric's hand rested on her shoulder, his other against St. Michael's head. "He's gone."

The words split her apart.

A sound—low, pained, torn from the deepest part of her soul—escaped her lips as she collapsed fully against St. Michael, her tears falling freely.

She had spent her whole life losing people.

But this?

This was unbearable.

Her fingers gripping the fabric harder, as if letting go would mean losing him completely.

"No," she choked, her voice raw, desperate. "There has to be something you can do."

Lucy looked up sharply, tears streaking down her face, locking onto Solric like he held the only answer she could accept.

"You know more about time than anyone. You—you can fix this. Just—just tell me what to do. I'll do anything." Her voice broke. "Please."

Solric's own eyes were wet, his face etched with grief.

But his voice was steady, gentle, but unwavering. "Take him home, Lucy."

She shook her head again, refusing to hear it.

"Take him home."

Her body folded beneath it all, her forehead dropping against St. Michael's chest once more, her sobs breaking fully.

The Archives had never felt so empty.

So cold.

CHAPTER 18
In Name and Nature

Two weeks later.

A bitter chill swept through *Highgate Cemetery*, curling through bare branches and weaving between rows of lichen-stained gravestones. The sky above was an unbroken sheet of grey, heavy and low, as though the clouds themselves had forgotten how to lift. Rain didn't fall so much as it lingered—misty and persistent, soaking the earth with the kind of damp that seeped into bones and stayed there.

The air carried that sharp scent of cold stone and wet leaves, familiar to anyone who had lived through enough English winters to know that this—this muted mourning in the sky—wasn't unusual. The wind whistled low through the iron gates and the twisted trees, not quite howling, not quite still.

It wasn't what Lucy had imagined.

In the days leading up to the funeral, she had pictured something cinematic. Skies cracked open with thunder, mourners cloaked in black beneath a sea of umbrellas, each raindrop striking the earth with purpose. She had imagined the kind of storm that made people speak in hushed tones. Something dramatic, symbolic. Something that mirrored the weight of his loss.

But this—this quiet drizzle and overcast calm—felt wrong in a way she couldn't name. Not because it lacked sadness, but because it lacked ceremony. The day had no grandeur, no performance. Just the grey stillness of a

London winter afternoon. And somehow, that made it harder. It was just an ordinary, normal day.

Lucy watched from afar, half-sheltered beneath the gnarled limbs of an old oak tree. The branches bare and skeletal above her, reaching out like silent witnesses to the day. From her vantage point, she could see the gathering begin to shift—the slow, reverent procession unfolding like a quiet tide—and yet, she couldn't bring herself to move any closer.

The guilt sat heavy in her chest, unshakable and coiled like wire.

Why did she email St. Michael?

Why did she drag him into this?

Why did he follow her through fire and history—only to die for it?

Every step he had taken toward her had led him here.

She slipped her hands, still stiff and aching from burns that hadn't fully healed, into the pockets of her long black coat. It matched the rest of her outfit. Black sweater, black trousers. A muted uniform of mourning. Not quite funeral attire, not quite wrong either. But she didn't feel like she belonged here. Not among the mourners. She and her bruises—visible and not—stood back as the casket began its slow descent through the grey.

The procession moved slowly, steady as the rain.

Among the sea of black coats and bowed heads, Lucy caught glimpses of vibrant blue. Sashes draped across shoulders, headwraps knotted with care. A quiet tribute. No one spoke of it, but it pulsed through the gathering like a heartbeat, a nod to his Nigerian roots that didn't need explanation. It was remembrance without words, culture woven into mourning like thread through fabric. Woven into the moment like memory.

As the casket was lowered into the waiting earth, an older woman stepped forward. Her attire was traditional, regal in its simplicity. She leaned in, whispering something Lucy couldn't quite make out, soft syllables lost to the rain and the hush. A prayer, perhaps. A farewell. One not meant for the living, but for the soul moving on.

Lucy watched in silence as, one by one, people stepped forward to pay their respects. Friends, relatives—immediate family, perhaps. She didn't know. She hadn't known these people, and they hadn't known her. She had only known St. Michael for a handful of days—barely enough time to learn how he took his tea or even when his birthday was. And yet, in that short time, they had lived more than most do in a lifetime.

They had shared joy and fear, laughter and loss. They had stood together beneath the firelit skies of civil war, amidst the roar of Wembley Stadium, under moonlight broadcast to the world. They had seen a dictator rise and a nation's leader set free. And through it all, St. Michael had saved her. Again and again.

Not just from Nexians or Incants, but from something deeper. He had saved her from the crushing loneliness that had wrapped itself around her life. From the quiet ache of having no one. From the dark came St. Michael. Not as a hero, but as a companion. A light she hadn't known she needed until it was gone.

Lucy's thoughts drifted back to the first time they met and how awkward she'd felt asking about his name, how he'd smiled with that mix of pride and self-awareness when he answered. *St. Michael.* A name that had sounded almost too big for one person to carry.

"You certainly did live up to it," she murmured, barely a whisper in the wind.

As she watched the crowd, Lucy's gaze caught on someone she did recognise.

She didn't need an introduction, she'd seen the photos. A little boy stood near the front, dressed smartly in a black suit a size too big, the sleeves brushing his wrists. His tie was crooked, his shoes slightly scuffed. He wasn't crying. He wasn't speaking. He simply stood there, still and small, as if the world had suddenly become too large for him to exist in.

Teddy.

Even from a distance, Lucy could see into his eyes. And it cut her. Not with sharpness, but with a slow, cold ache that settled in her chest and refused to leave. Because she recognised that look. She had worn it herself.

The silent scream of a child who's lost something irreplaceable. The quiet confusion of knowing something terrible has happened but not understanding why. Teddy hadn't been told to be brave, but he was. Because sometimes the world doesn't ask—it assumes. It puts grief on children like ill-fitting jackets and tells them to carry on.

She had been that child once. Standing beside Evelyn in her best clothes. Questions blooming in her mind like weeds: *Where did he go? Why him? Will he come back?* And the silence that followed.

They had both lost their fathers to a war they never chose, a war no one told them existed. A war fought in the margins of time and history, invisible to everyone but those caught within it. No medals. No headlines. Just absence. Just the hollowness of knowing someone is gone and not knowing why.

She wanted to reach out to Teddy, to tell him she understood. But how could she? What comfort could she offer, when the truth was buried in a war he may never be allowed to see?

As Lucy looked back at Teddy, her thoughts spiralling through memory, a sudden voice cracked through the quiet like a misplaced trumpet.

"Two thousand and twenty-five years, and *this* is a delicacy?!"

She blinked, startled, then couldn't help the smile. Turning, she found Solric standing behind her, holding a prawn sandwich with the disgusted reverence of a man who had just discovered it was made of shoe leather and regret.

"What's wrong with it?" she asked, unable to keep the amusement out of her voice.

He gestured with the sandwich like it had personally offended him. "You take some sea-dwelling crustaceans, slap them into a tasteless paste, wedge it between two slices of…what is this? Softened wall insulation? And call it *lunch*?"

"It's a prawn sandwich," Lucy said, laughing now.

"Well, I've had better from the thirteenth century. And that was sold from a wooden cart next to a pigsty. And I suppose it's also normal to have this many buttons?"

He stepped up beside her, still clutching the offending sandwich, and Lucy took in the full sight of him. He was wearing the suit she'd found in a Brixton charity shop. A black, slightly shiny number that didn't quite fit in the shoulders, with a tie knotted a little too tightly. His expression screamed discomfort.

"You asked what people wear to funerals," Lucy reminded him, smirking. "You said, and I quote, 'Ensure it is traditional.' So I did."

"Yes, well, no one said tradition involved *all these buttons*," he grumbled, tugging at his collar like it was strangling him. "Or this pointless strip of fabric around the neck. Honestly, what's the function? Is it ceremonial? A sign of status? A noose for the grieving?"

"It's a tie," Lucy said, biting her lip to keep from laughing.

"I've seen time cults wear fewer layers," he muttered, eyeing the suit like it was trying to devour him. "And don't even get me started on these shoes. Who designed them? A sadist?"

"You said you wanted to blend in," Lucy said, folding her arms.

"I didn't mean *suffer*," Solric shot back.

They both laughed quietly, gently. It wasn't loud enough to disrupt the stillness of the cemetery, but it was enough to feel like a small rebellion. A crack in the grief. A breath of air after too long underwater.

Solric looked down at the sandwich once more, then gave an exaggerated sigh and took another bite.

"Still dreadful," he muttered through a full mouth. "But slightly less dreadful now that I'm emotionally numb."

Lucy snorted. "You're welcome."

Lucy's smile faded, just slightly, as she glanced toward him. "Thank you for coming today," she said quietly.

She didn't say more, didn't need to. The fact that he had left the Sanctuary, stepped into the present day with all its noise and nuance, that said enough.

"It was the least I could do," Solric replied, his voice softer now, the edge of humour gone. He looked out toward the grave, the drizzle clinging to his brow like mist. "I've lived in fear of the Nexus since the Schism. Always watching. Always waiting. And then you two came bumbling along, rewriting what we thought was fixed. You gave our kind a future, and a hopeful one at that."

He paused, eyes narrowed as though searching for something far beyond the horizon.

"It's cruel, in a way," he added. "That we can see what has gone before with such clarity… but not what's still to come."

Lucy said nothing. She didn't have to. The silence between them held the weight of every sacrifice, every loss wrapped in that so-called hopeful future. She had seen the cost and paid it.

Lucy let the silence linger between them as they stood beneath the skeletal branches of the oak, watching the final moments of the funeral unfold. Someone sobbed quietly near the front. Another placed a single white lily on the casket, its petals already collecting droplets.

Finally, Lucy spoke.

"Back in Zerzura," she said, her voice almost lost in the wind, "there was this mirror. Alaric called it Obsidian, or something like that."

Solric nodded, eyes fixed on the crowd. "Obsidian glass. Yes."

She hesitated, her thoughts still half in that lost city, half in this rainy graveyard. "When I looked into it, it showed me… as the Time Sovereign. But Alaric said that when *he* looked into it, he saw my parents. Alive. Standing beside him." Her voice cracked slightly. "Do you think that's possible—"

"Lucy," Solric interrupted gently, turning to face her. "Did *you* see your parents in the mirror? Or is that just what Alaric told you?"

She swallowed. "He said he saw them."

Solric exhaled through his nose, quiet but firm. "Obsidian glass is one of the purest materials in all creation. It reflects essence, not illusion. It doesn't fabricate hope. It has no agenda, no desire. Which means if you didn't see them… then Alaric was manipulating you. Just as he always intended to."

"But do you think it's possible?" she pressed, voice laced with something between desperation and defiance. "Was there *any* truth in what he said?"

Solric looked at her then, really looked, and his expression softened. "The mirror wouldn't lie, Lucy—but people would. And Alaric lied often, and well."

Lucy's voice dropped to a whisper. "But my dad came."

Solric paused, the rain beading across his forehead as he considered how to answer.

"From what you described, it was an Echoform. Residual, raw energy, and incredibly rare. But the Codex—" he stopped, adjusting his tone, more certain now. "The Codex *recognised* you. Not just as Evelyn and Edward's daughter, but as its protector. As a Custodian. When that happens, it doesn't always bring answers… but it brings what its chosen needs. Not always a person. Sometimes strength. Sometimes clarity. Sometimes… comfort. In that moment, you needed him."

"It *recognised* me?" she asked, her brow furrowed. "The Codex?"

"Yes," Solric said. "You have to understand, Lucy— it's not just a book, or a record, or some sacred relic. It's alive. It breathes in harmony with the Universal Timeline. It reflects the state of history, of memory, of possibility. It's a consciousness, as ancient as time itself. You don't simply read the Codex. It reads you."

She was quiet for a moment, then asked, gently but pointedly, "Then why didn't it respond during the Great Schism? Why didn't it stop the Nexus from tearing everything apart?"

Solric's gaze darkened, his shoulders tensing slightly beneath the ill-fitting suit. "I don't know," he said, voice low. "I've spent many nights asking the same question. And every time, I'm left with silence."

He looked away.

"Maybe it mourned with us," he added softly. "Or maybe… it was waiting."

Lucy turned back to the procession just as Teddy reached out and gently clung to the hand of another figure she recognised. Michelle stood upright, composed, but there was a tightness. She didn't cry, at least not in the way people expected. Her grief was quieter, heavier, buried deep in her chest where no one could reach it. It lived behind her eyes and in the tension of her shoulders.

When the final prayer faded into silence, Lucy watched Michelle whisper a single word to herself.

As the mourners began to drift away, someone handed Michelle a blue envelope. She glanced at the unfamiliar handwriting and slowly opened it. Inside was a simple condolences card. Nothing elaborate. No ornate verses or poetic flourishes. Just a brief, awkwardly scribbled message:

St. Michael was a true friend and fiercely loved you both. May the enclosed bring good fortune and a bright future.

She stared at the words for a long time. Then, tucked inside the fold of the card, she found it.

A lottery ticket.

Her expression shifted instantly. Confusion flaring into something sharper. She held it in her hand like it might disintegrate, as if it couldn't possibly be what it appeared to be. Her lips parted in disbelief. Then her fingers clenched around it, her posture stiffening.

It felt wrong. Crass, even. As if someone had mistaken tragedy for an occasion. As if this loss could be soothed with numbers and an unlikely payout. She looked down at Teddy, then back at the ticket, eyes narrowing. The colour drained slightly from her face. Not from sadness, but from a flicker of anger. Or maybe the insult of absurdity. A lottery ticket? On *this* day?

Her thumb ran across the barcode like she was trying to erase it.

She said nothing. But the look on her face said enough.

Lucy watched Michelle's expression twist through confusion and disbelief, and a faint, knowing smile formed. It wasn't smug, exactly, but there was a satisfaction in seeing something *work*. Something small. Something that mattered.

Beside her, Solric turned slowly, catching the look on her face.

"Lucy…" he said, half warning, half exasperation. "You didn't."

His tone was scathing, but it was threaded with warmth, like a tired uncle scolding a favourite niece for stealing the last biscuit.

"I couldn't bring him back," Lucy said, her voice low but sure. "I can't undo my mother working with him. I can't take back the email that pulled him into all of this. I can't change the fact that his son has to grow up without a father."

She paused, watching as Michelle knelt to whisper something to Teddy, who still clutched her hand.

"But I *could* protect their future."

Solric blinked, lips parting slightly. "You did that?"

"I mean," she said, brushing a strand of wet hair behind her ear, "I checked this morning. No one had won yesterday's draw. So I wrote down the numbers, slipped back to the yesterday and picked one up from the newsagent down the road from me. I dropped it into the envelope before the service."

She shrugged, almost sheepishly. "It's a Quantum Time Collision I can live with."

Solric stared at her, brow creased as though he were trying to summon the proper rebuke. But none came. Instead, he exhaled through his nose with a dry huff, and a small smile cracked through.

There was something deeply human about her in that moment. This woman who had faced The Nexus and elemental storms, who had danced through centuries and watched history burn. And yet here she was, bending time not to win battles or change fate, but to give a grieving family a little light.

It wasn't protocol. It wasn't clean.

But it was *kind*.

Solric nodded slowly, eyes softening. "Well… I suppose there are worse things you could have done."

Lucy grinned. "I'll save those for next time."

As the final handful of mourners stepped away from the casket, the earth beginning to settle into its silence again, Lucy turned to Solric.

"Where's the Codex now?" she asked.

"I've returned it to the Archives for now, at least," he replied, adjusting his tie. Again. "I don't really plan on making many more trips beyond the Sanctuary, so I figured… best to keep it close. Easier to monitor, safer that way."

"Yeah," Lucy said absently, her eyes flicking back to the thinning crowd. "That makes sense."

Solric went on, his tone thoughtful, something about fixing parts of the Assembly Hall. But Lucy wasn't really listening.

His voice began to drift. Still present, but increasingly distant, like a radio losing its signal in a tunnel. Words stretched out, then curled into nothingness.

Because on the far side of the cemetery, just beyond the wrought-iron gate partially hidden by bramble and stone, a figure was standing very still.

Watching.

Everything else faded. Solric's voice, the rain, even the soft chatter of the dispersing mourners. The world narrowed into a single, frozen moment, sharp and impossibly quiet.

Lucy blinked. The figure remained.

The figure wasn't dressed in black like the others. There was no veil, no mask, no signs of mourning.

Instead, Lucy saw the unmistakable outline of a woman—just the side of her frame.

She wore blue jeans and trainers, the kind worn from comfort rather than fashion. A red jumper peeked out beneath the unzipped front of a black padded puffer jacket, its hood draped down her back.

She stood still, hands by her sides, posture unreadable.

Lucy couldn't see her face.

But she didn't need to.

Lucy took a sudden step forward, leaving Solric mid-sentence. His voice faltered as he turned toward her, confused by her abrupt shift, but Lucy didn't look back. She didn't explain. She didn't need to. Her eyes were fixed on the figure at the edge of the cemetery.

"Mum!" Lucy called out, her voice cracking through the gentle hush of the rain.

A few heads turned. People glanced back—some startled, some confused—as she broke away from the solemn cluster and stepped out into the open, shoes crunching wet gravel. But she barely noticed them. Her eyes didn't leave the figure, her breath catching in her throat as she picked up speed.

Her walk turned into a jog, then a run, cutting through the graves with the desperate urgency of someone chasing a memory. She ducked under low-hanging branches and skirted tilted headstones slick with moss. Her coat flared out behind her as she ran, the damp earth soft beneath her, sucking slightly at each step. Twigs snapped underfoot.

The figure hadn't moved.

Lucy pushed forward, legs burning now, hair sticking to her face, rain blurring the edges of her vision. She weaved between timeworn tombs, barely noticing the names etched in their surfaces. Her heart hammered. Not from the run, but from something deeper. Fear. Longing. That dangerous spark of belief.

She slipped on a patch of wet leaves, caught herself against the edge of a crumbling angel statue, and kept going, faster now. The trees at the edge of the cemetery loomed ahead, black-limbed and heavy with rain. The path narrowed, framed by tall yews that seemed to close in the closer she came. She hurdled a broken slab, her breath ragged.

The spot was just ahead.

The place where the woman had stood.

Lucy skidded to a stop. When she reached the far side of the graveyard, there was no one.

No blue jeans. No red jumper. No black puffer jacket. No trainers. No familiar face.

Nothing but a hum.

It lingered low in the air, like the aftertaste of a dream. Faint, but unmistakable. A ripple in reality. A residue of something having just been *here*. Lucy knew it immediately—*Time Traversal*. She'd felt it enough times to recognise the feeling it left behind.

The air here was heavy. She glanced around, her eyes scanning the shadows for any trace of her, but there was nothing. Not even a footprint in the thin layer of mud and grass.

The stillness clung to her like damp fabric. Not quiet, exactly—more like everything was holding its breath.

She stood frozen, her heartbeat loud in her chest, listening for anything. A footstep. A voice. A breath.

But the cemetery had returned to its silence.

Whoever the figure was—if she had even been real— was already gone.

"Mum!" Lucy called out again, her voice echoing sharply across the headstones.

Still nothing.

Nothing but the hum. That faint, familiar vibration in the air—softer now, already beginning to fade. A vanishing trace.

Behind her came the awkward slap of shoes unsuited to mud and uneven ground. Solric stumbled through the grass, breathless, tugging at the lapels of his ill-fitting charity shop suit.

"Lucy," he wheezed, catching up beside her, "what is it?"

"She was here," Lucy said, eyes still sweeping the tree line, still scanning every stone, every shadow. Her voice was taut, filled with something between disbelief and certainty.

"Who was?" Solric asked, his breath still ragged, his tone breaking into concern.

"My mum," Lucy said, turning to him. Her face was pale, soaked from rain and sweat and something deeper. "My mum was here. She was watching."

"I—" Solric started, but Lucy cut him off.

"Why can she be here but not *talk* to me?" she demanded, the words tumbling out before she could stop them. "Why does she keep slipping through the cracks? Why does she keep *leaving*?"

Her voice cracked on the last word.

"Why has she gone again?"

Solric stepped closer, his expression shifting from confusion to sorrow. His voice lowered, calm and measured, but not cold.

"Lucy—"

"She's dead. I know that," Lucy said quickly, sharply, as if saying it aloud might anchor her. "But she was definitely here. I saw her."

Solric reached out and placed a hand gently on her shoulder. His grip was steady. Present. Human.

"Why can't she just tell me something?" Lucy asked, her voice trembling now. "Anything. One word. One message. I don't need her to fix everything—I just need to *know*."

For a moment, Solric said nothing.

Then, quietly, he replied, "Time takes what it must, Lucy. But it also leaves gifts… for those who know where to look."

The words fell into the silence like stones dropped in deep water.

Lucy looked up at him, her eyes glassy with emotion, and met his ancient gaze. There was something in it—compassion, wisdom, weariness. But also… hope.

"Then I'll keep looking," she whispered.

Solric nodded once, firmly. Not as an answer, but as an affirmation. A pact.

The wind stirred the trees again, brushing the red leaves along the path like drifting echoes.

Behind them, the last of the mourners had gone. Only the casket remained, half-lowered, the earth still unsettled. A few petals clung to the wet grass like memories too heavy to lift.

"Come on," Solric said softly, his hand still resting on her shoulder. "Let's get back. You can show me more of these 'delicacies' you call sandwiches."

Lucy let out a quiet breath, somewhere between a sigh and a laugh. It barely rose above the hum that had now faded entirely.

She cast one last look at the spot where the woman had stood. Empty. Silent. Still.

Then she turned and walked away beside Solric. Her coat heavy with rain, her heart heavier still. The mist curled around them as they made their way through the stones, two figures swallowed by the grey, pressing forward toward a future neither of them could yet see.

And the graveyard returned to stillness once more.

EPILOGUE
The Time Custodian

The flat was silent when Lucy returned. Not the silence of absence, but the kind that settles in after something has ended. Thick, knowing, and impossible to ignore. The kind that didn't wait for permission to enter but had been there, quietly settling in while she was away.

She closed the door with a soft click and leaned against it for a breath too long, her coat still damp from the lingering drizzle outside. The same grey rain that had hung over the cemetery now tapped gently at her windows, as if the world outside hadn't moved on either.

Lucy crossed the room slowly, the heels of her shoes echoing faintly against the worn wooden floor. She placed her keys on the desk with a clink that felt too sharp, too sudden for a space that demanded softness. The same space where she'd spent sleepless nights pouring over her mother's work and learning how to survive.

Now it felt smaller. Dimmer. As though even time itself had lowered its voice out of respect.

The air was heavy with the scent of old paper. She took off her coat, throwing it over the arm of her sofa. She turned on the lights. And then stood still, letting the quiet drape itself around her like a second skin.

She hadn't expected the gravity of the day to follow her home. But it had. Even here, surrounded by the familiarity of her own walls, her own things, she could still feel the rain. Not just on her skin, but inside her, soaking through the layers she'd tried to hold together.

St. Michael was gone.

And for the first time since this all began, Lucy felt it—truly felt it—not just in her mind, but in her bones: She was alone.

Her eyes drifted toward a few boxes stacked by the far wall. Evelyn's handwriting stared back at her. Familiar, looping and measured. And yet, in all the thousands of words her mother had left behind, there were still too many that hadn't been said. Too many silences that felt deliberate.

Why had she appeared only in fragments, in whispers and shadows?

Why hadn't she spoken to Lucy directly, not once—not really?

And then there was that other question. The old one. The one that had burned a hole through every page Lucy had read, every timeline she'd visited, every impossible truth she had learned:

How did she die?

If she even did.

Lucy had seen too much now to take anything at face value. She'd watched history unfold, seen wars from rooftops and revolutions in the dirt. She had stood in cities that no longer existed and escaped from moments that were never supposed to be witnessed. She'd watched men pull fire from thin air and had done it herself. She knew now that time was not a line, but a living, breathing thing. Unpredictable. Merciless. Alive.

And yet, that one truth remained elusive.

How could someone like Evelyn Calder—a powerful Finite Custodian—simply disappear without a trace? Why was there no record, no witness, no moment? Not even the Nexus had offered a definitive answer, and they seemed to know everything else.

The thought twisted in her mind. Was Evelyn still alive? Had she ever truly died?

Lucy wanted to believe the funeral had closed a door. That this grief had shape and certainty. But it didn't. Not yet.

Because even now, with the storm behind her and silence all around her… she could still feel her mother's presence.

Not a ghost. Not memory. Something else. Something real.

Lucy looked back at her mother's work—stacked and ordered, yet still dense with mystery—and her thoughts drifted to the storage unit.

It had become a strange kind of sanctuary over the past few weeks. In the wake of St. Michael's death, when the world had narrowed to grief and survival, she'd returned there. Quietly, methodically, she'd moved everything from his office—every book, every file back into that cold, familiar space.

This time, though, it was different.

The chaos that once defined the unit was gone. There were no haphazard towers of paper threatening to collapse, no frantic scribbles or overturned boxes. Now, everything had its place. Grouped, catalogued, as precise as she could manage. It was still overwhelming, but now it felt *possible*.

She hadn't begun to scratch the surface. Not really. The sheer volume of Evelyn's research, her real research. It was like staring at the bones of a forgotten world, waiting to be reconstructed.

It had become a pattern, when tragedy struck, she ended up there. Packing it up. And yet, this time was different. She wasn't running from it. She wasn't avoiding the weight of what remained. She was preparing. Preparing to read it all. To *understand*.

Lucy moved to the pile of works she'd brought back from the unit which piqued her interest.

Lucy was interrupted.
Three knocks.
Her front door.
Sharp. Evenly spaced. Purposeful.
Lucy froze.
She glanced toward the door, the notepad still in her hand, heart rising fast in her throat. The knocks hadn't been hurried or casual. There was intention behind them. An authority in their rhythm that made her skin prickle.

She set the notepad down gently, quietly, as if afraid to startle the silence now pressing in. Moving toward the door, she peered through the spyglass.

No one.

She exhaled through her nose, more annoyed than afraid. Her block had a reputation. It wouldn't be the first time the kids from the floor below had played Knock and Run, of which she'd been a victim to. They loved a good chase, especially when it ended with confused adults peering into nothing.

Still, something felt off.

Lucy unlocked the door and opened it, stepping just beyond the threshold.

The wind curled around her legs, damp with the scent of rain and concrete. She looked out across the exposed balcony that wrapped around the block, giving a clear view of Brixton's rooftops below. Neon signs flickered faintly in shop windows. Streetlights buzzed overhead. She turned her head slowly—first left, then right.

No footsteps.

No echoes.

No slamming door in the distance.

There hadn't been enough time for someone to get away. Not without a sound. Not without being seen. Whoever knocked… they hadn't walked off.

She frowned.

Then, as if the air itself shifted, she looked down.

At her feet was a box.

Not the kind stamped with logos or barcodes. Not a delivery left behind by a courier. This was something else entirely.

The box was wooden. Dark, polished, and clearly handcrafted. Intricate carvings adorned its surface, delicate swirls that wove into sharp, deliberate lines. The patterns shifted subtly in the low corridor light, catching her eye like a puzzle half-solved. It looked… expensive. *Really* expensive.

Lucy crouched, running her fingers along the grooves. The wood was cool to the touch, the carvings so precise they felt etched by time itself.

"Handmade," she murmured under her breath.

At the front of the box were two steel catches, brushed silver and curved into sleek clasps that held the lid tight. They weren't locked, but they *felt* secure, like opening them should come with a whisper of ceremony.

She lifted the box, surprised at how light it was—far lighter than it looked. It didn't strain her arms. It felt… important.

Balancing it against her hip, she stepped back inside, her heel catching the door behind her and nudging it shut with a soft click.

The flat welcomed her back with silence.

Box in arms, questions in her, Lucy moved deeper into her hallway and then onto the living room.

She carried the box into the living room, setting it down gently on the coffee table. It sat there like a question, silent and immovable, casting long shadows beneath the dim light. Lucy lowered herself onto the sofa opposite, eyes fixed on it as though it might move on its own.

She didn't want to open it.

She didn't know why.

It wasn't fear, exactly. More like hesitation born from something deeper. Instinct, maybe. A feeling she couldn't name. The kind of pause you take before stepping into water you can't see the bottom of.

She had no idea what the box contained.

Was it a trap?

Would opening it pull her into another moment, another place in time?

Or, more absurdly, was this all some bizarrely elaborate marketing ploy from the kebab shop down the road trying to reinvent takeaway loyalty?

Her lips curled at the thought, but the humour didn't settle.

Lucy leaned forward, hands brushing over the carved surface. The wood was smooth, but the patterns were raised just enough to trace. Swirls giving way to straight lines, lines curving into sharper angles. The carvings felt intentional, almost ceremonial. A language written in texture.

Her fingers drifted to the steel catches.

Left first.

It clicked open with a soft, satisfying snap.

Then the right.

Both clasps released and the lid waited.

She flicked it open.

No blinding light. No sudden shift in air pressure. No temporal time-bending nonsense sucking her into another century.

Just silence—and something far stranger.

Inside, resting atop some white fabric, was a single sheet of parchment. Cream-coloured, thick.

Lucy reached for it slowly, feeling the texture of the paper before lifting it free.

She knew the handwriting instantly.

That meticulous, looping script. Elegant, purposeful. The kind of handwriting you didn't see much anymore.

Evelyn Calder's handwriting.

Her mother's.

The ink read:

Lucy Calder

Flat 56, Buxton House

4, St Matthew's Road

Brixton. SW2 1NE

There was something almost ceremonial about the address being written out in full. Her eyes dropped to the bottom of the page.

To be delivered on Monday, January 27th, 2025 at 16:43.

She glanced at her watch.

Monday. January 27th. 16:45.

Two minutes. The knock had come exactly two minutes ago.

Whoever had delivered this had done so with precise timing. Not a second too early. Not a second too late.

Lucy opened the letter, the first line leaving her heart in her throat.

"My darling daughter Lucy,"

She didn't need to read it aloud. She could hear it—her mother's voice—gentle, but commanding, steady in her head as though Evelyn were sitting across from her.

"You've made it further than I ever could. And though I wish more than anything that I could be there with you, standing at your side, I think we both know that's not possible.

I know how many times you searched for me. How often you reached into the past, hoping to find me waiting. But I was never where you looked. I couldn't be. Not anymore.

Of all the regrets I carry, none are heavier than the truth I kept from you. I told myself it was to protect you, to keep you from being drawn into a war I knew would take everything from you, just as it took everything from me. But in the

Lucy thought back to Nanjing—lightning splitting the sky, striking St. Michael's attackers. The note left behind in Austerlitz. The voice of guidance, the pieces falling into place. It had all been deliberate.

*would make the same choice again, even
now."*

St. Michael's name caught Lucy more off guard than
she'd expected. Her throat tightened. She wasn't ready to
let go… not yet.

---

*"I tried to help you in the ways I could,
leaving what traces of myself I could
manage, guiding you to the Timebound
Altar, to Solric, even to Alaric. I know
the truth about him is difficult to accept,
it was for me too. But you were always
meant to see through him. His illusions.
His delusions. His lies. And in the end,
even he helped you find your path.*

*You remind me so much of your father.
Edward would have been so proud of
you, just as I am. You have his fire, his
determination, that unshakable sense of
right and wrong. Except for your
control of Incants, that's all from me!*

*But you never needed me to find the
answers. You never needed me to show
you who you are. I see now that you
were always meant to step into this role,*

*not because I led you here, but because
it is yours.*

*You are a Time Custodian, Lucy.
Perhaps the greatest of us.*

*And that is why the contents of this box
now belong to you."*

Lucy looked down, lifting the edge of the white fabric in the box.

What she pulled free made her stomach turn.

It was a robe. Long, flowing, unmistakably familiar. The fabric shimmered faintly in the low light, heavy with significance. It smelled of lavender.

Her mother.

---

*"The Timeless Robes are not just a
symbol of what we are, they are a
promise. A commitment to time, to
history, to the truth. To wear them is to
accept the weight of all that has come
before and all that is still to come. They
are yours now, as they were once mine.*

*I spent so many years trying to keep you
safe. But you do not need my protection,
you never did.*

But this is not the end, Lucy. Not for you.

There are still Custodians out there. Some in hiding, some keeping to the old ways, and others who have found new paths in the wake of the war. They are watching, waiting, unsure if our kind has a future. Show them that we do. When the time comes, seek them out. Unite them. The Custodians are not gone, and neither is our purpose.

And do not let yourself believe the Nexus has been defeated. Your father bought you more time. They are wounded, but they are not broken. They will rebuild. And when they rise again, they will be stronger, more calculated, more dangerous than before. I fear now, more than ever, that other forces, long dormant, may also come for everything we hold dear.

You must be ready for what comes next. This fight is not over. Not yet. Because you are not just a Time Custodian. You are its protector. And time does not stand still. Neither can you.

*But no matter where you go, no matter
how far through time you travel, know
this, my love,*

You will never be alone.

Always,

—Your Mum"

Tears slipped down Lucy's cheeks. Silent, unannounced, and warm against her skin.

But it wasn't grief. Not exactly. It was something heavier and lighter all at once. Something closer to *peace*, threaded with sorrow. A quiet ache that didn't scream like the grief she'd known, but lingered softly in her chest, like the final notes of a song she wasn't ready to stop playing.

Reading her mother's words wrapped around her like a memory made solid. Each word had landed with weight. The pride, the regret, the love. Evelyn's love had always been fierce, measured in absences and half-answers. But now it was here, carved into every looping letter.

And in that same breath, Lucy felt it, that sickening confirmation.

She really was gone.

Maybe not entirely. Maybe never fully. But *gone*, all the same.

The letter didn't give her closure, not completely. It didn't solve the riddle of Evelyn's disappearance, didn't explain the years of silence, or where she'd gone when time had bent and broken and carried her away. The questions still burned at the edges of Lucy's thoughts. *Why didn't she speak to me sooner? Was she watching the whole time? Could she have done more?*

She read the letter again. And again. Searching. Hoping.

Maybe there was something tucked in the curves of the ink, some hidden message. Maybe some Custodian code Evelyn had embedded for her to find. A cipher, a date, a name. Something. Anything.

But there wasn't.

All she found was her mother, saying goodbye the only way she could.

Lucy inhaled slowly, her throat raw, her hands trembling. She blinked hard, refusing to let the tears smear the page. She angled the parchment carefully away, made sure none of her grief would stain it. Not this. Not something so final.

With the reverence of someone placing a relic on an altar, she set the letter down beside her.

Then she sat there in silence, the emptiness of the room swelling around her like a tide.

Lucy turned her gaze back to the box.

The robes were slightly unfolded and draped over the side of the box. Unfolded and disturbed in Lucy's haste. The white fabric that had concealed them now felt like a veil, lifted only when the moment was right.

She reached out, slowly, almost afraid to disturb them. Her fingers brushed the fabric first. Smooth, cool, and impossibly soft beneath her skin.

She drew the robes from the box, unfolding them with careful hands. They spilled across her lap in gentle waves, and she caught her breath.

They were beautiful. Striking.

Like Edward's, just as she had described in her Schism notes, regal in their structure, unmistakably Custodian. But where his had been midnight blue, deep and solemn like the ocean at night, hers leaned into a richer hue.

Closer to purple. Like bruised dusk or the space between stars. Something, noble, and quietly powerful.

The trim shimmered gold. refined. It caught the light from her flat's ceiling light, dull as it was, and reflected it. There was purpose in that gold. Symbolic, maybe.

Lucy turned the robes gently, letting the fabric fall into her hands, and found herself looking at the neckline. The stitching there was finer, smaller.

Two letters. Delicate. Threaded in gold just above the inner seam.

E.C.

Evelyn Calder, Lucy thought.

But there was something else in that moment too. And its meaning was clear.

This was more than an inheritance.

It was a mantle. A legacy. A truth made tangible.

And now, it belonged to her.

Lucy, slowly… gently, unfolded the robes and drew them around her shoulders.

The fabric slipped over her like a second skin, smooth and soft, whispering against her arms as she slid her left arm into its sleeve, then her right. Each movement was deliberate. A ritual. A claiming.

The robes were almost weightless. And yet, with every second they clung to her body, they grew heavier. Not in fabric, but in meaning.

She felt it pressing down on her chest, blooming behind her ribs.

Legacy.

Cost.

Responsibility.

This was no longer just Evelyn's war. No longer just a history she'd stumbled into. It was *hers* now. Every inch of this robe was stitched with what came before. Sacrifice, failure, resilience, truth. And now she wore it. Now she *carried* it.

Her mother had mentioned the Order of the Nexus in the letter. A warning. Unmistakable. That they would rise again. That they weren't the only threat. That something *else*—distant, darker—was watching from the edges of time.

Lucy didn't know what. Or who.

Didn't know how or when.

But she knew this:

She wasn't the same girl who went hurtling into the Great Fire of London, confused and frightened, desperate for answers.

That Lucy was gone.

She had a responsibility now.

She had purpose.

She had *direction*.

Lucy stepped toward the mirror.

The face staring back was familiar but transformed. Steady. Certain. The grief, the aching questions, they hadn't vanished. But they no longer defined her.

Of all the unknowns that lay ahead, she was certain of this:

Time moves.

Time heals.

Time remembers.

And now…

So will the Time Custodian.

The End.

Acknowledgements

This book exists because of a great many people, whether they realise it or not. There was a time when reaching this final page felt impossible, which makes writing it now all the more meaningful.

To you, the reader. Thank you for choosing this story and for giving it your time. As a debut author, knowing that someone was willing to take a chance on these pages means more than I can properly express. Time is the most valuable thing we have, and I am genuinely grateful that you chose to spend some of yours here.

To my friends and family, thank you for your patience, your support, and your belief. Thank you for listening to me talk endlessly about this story, even when the ideas were half-formed, contradictory, or made very little sense out loud. You never made me feel like it was a burden, and that mattered more than you know.

I would also like to thank my mum, dad, my brother Ryan, and my Aunt Christine for reading early drafts of this book. They challenged ideas that didn't yet work, asked difficult questions, and offered thoughtful suggestions that helped refine the story. Their feedback shaped the novel in ways that may not always be visible on the page but are felt throughout it.

To the school teachers who helped me learn to read and write. I am autistic and dyslexic, and for a long time words felt out of reach. Reading took effort. Writing took longer. Spelling single words often meant flash cards, repetition, and starting again when frustration set in. There were moments when it would have been easier to assume I simply couldn't do it. You didn't. You stayed patient when I was discouraged, and you kept believing when I struggled to believe in myself. This book exists because you refused to give up on me, and that is something I will carry with me always.

The cover design and formatting for this book were undertaken by me. Taking on that work meant learning an unfamiliar and often technical side of publishing, one that demanded as much patience and problem-solving as the writing itself. The result is the product of that learning process, shaped carefully and deliberately, with the hope that it serves the story as faithfully as possible.

This book began with a throwaway conversation with my brother about time slips. It became something real because of the people who encouraged it, supported it, and believed it could exist. For that, I am truly grateful.

C.R. Stalley
January 2026